My Constant Lady

Jane Fenwick

CIP catalogue record for this title is available from the British Library.
ISBN 978-1-916195-72-1

Cover design by Charlotte Mouncey
Cover illustrations iStockphoto.com
Giuseppe Milo (pixael.com) - Sunset in Bude from https://www.flickr.
com/photos/giuseppemilo/ Creative Commons Attribution 2.0 Generic

Printed in Great Britain by
TJ International Ltd UK

www.janefenwick.co.uk

the master shipwright a perfect view of the comings and goings of the fleet. Kemp was in overall charge of shipbuilding; the man had thirty years experience and had impressed the young man at their first meeting. Today Gabriel was in Whitby to finalise the plans and pay over the first instalment by bank draft.

'There is a growing need for transporting coal from the great coal fields of the North East down along the Yorkshire coast south to places like Whitby and Hull and I am determined to expand further and transport down as far as London. My new idea is to move grain to Holland and iron ore to anywhere that has a need of it. There is also trade to be had with the Baltics shipping timber. A new ship will help make my plans a reality.'

William Kemp handed Gabriel a brandy and invited him to take a seat.

'I am excited by the plans.' Gabriel continued, 'and at the same time a little apprehensive at such a large undertaking. This is the first big decision I have taken since my father's death.'

The Shipwright sought to reassure him: 'The cost of the ship will be great but it will quickly pay for itself I am sure. It is a large undertaking, have you considered getting investors, perhaps three or four to share the cost and as insurance?'

Gabriel shook his head: 'There are plenty who would be keen to take a share in the ownership of such a vessel, the Reynolds name holds sway on the East coast but I intend to fund the full cost myself; it is a risk but not a great one I hope. With shareholders I would have to consult – this way I can be my own man.'

'You have chosen a good time to expand sir, as you say there is a growing need. How many ships do you have in your fleet?

'There are two ships in our, or should I say, my fleet already but a third vessel is fundamental if my expansion plans are to materialise.'

'You are welcome to view the building of your ship whenever you are in Whitby. Are you a frequent visitor to the town?'

'Since my father's death I am afraid I seem chained to my desk, it will be a good excuse to come to Whitby to see how she grows.'

The meeting concluded Gabriel felt his insides groan; it had been a long time since he broke his fast. He set off in search of an inn. He had heard The Freelove's crew were ashore, they were known to get rowdy – he was keen to avoid them. The Fleece was busy with others also eager to steer clear of the newly arrived crew.

Alone he sat in the corner of the harbourside tavern. He had just eaten a mutton stew swimming in grease and was now regretting it. He downed the ale from his tankard in an effort to rid himself of the taste.

He began to read a broadsheet but the small windows let in little of the bright evening sun and he had to narrow his eyes to read. As he put aside the paper having decided his eyes could strain no longer, he thought of his earlier meeting at John Barker's yard. Gabriel hoped he had made the right decision; he wondered if his father would have approved.

He looked about the inn. A redheaded girl caught his eye, she stood out in this drab little tavern. She sat with a rabble of sailors who looked to be drinking hard but were not loud or troublesome. Another dark haired woman, who seemed a little worse for wear and shabbier than her friend was in the group. Both young girls were attractive but the redhead had a bloom about her which made her striking rather than beautiful. Her burnished hair shone in the candlelight and reached to her trim waist. In an effort to tame its abundant waves a bright green scarf was tied around her head. Her hair was her crowning glory and was by far her best asset. She also had slightly more reserve than her talkative friend who, at that moment had decided to sit on the knee of one of the sailors.

Gabriel signalled to the landlord for more ale. The serving maid, carrying a brimming tankard, began to squeeze her way through the crowded bar when the redhead quickly stepped in front of her. Gabriel had at that moment looked down to fold his newspaper and missed the intervention

The redhead slipped the maid a coin, took the ale and headed over to Gabriel's table. She placed the drink before him.

'Your drink sir.' Had he been aware who brought his drink he may have looked up; as it was he continued to think of his expansion plans. 'Can I get you anything else?'

'No, thank you.' He glanced up absentmindedly and was surprised to find the attractive girl he had noticed earlier had appeared in front of him. She was smiling at him beguilingly.

Gabriel sat up straighter pulled his long legs in and suddenly felt more awake, his interest aroused. The pressure of the earlier meeting was still uppermost in his mind, a little distraction would be welcome perhaps; he had had little time for company recently. An attractive serving wench might be diverting.

'Won't you sit awhile or will the landlord have something to say about that?'

'No sir I'm a free agent and can bide awhile if you would like company.' Gabriel emptied his tankard in one draught. He signed for more drinks and when they both had brandy in front of them Gabriel looked her straight in the eye. He was surprised to notice her face flush.

'You are not from these parts sir?' She sipped the brandy.

'From Alnmouth – I am here in Whitby on business.' He guessed she would be totally uninterested in his business affairs. 'You are Whitby born and bred I take it?' he asked.

'Well yes, although I now reside in Sandsend – it is only three miles down the beach from here, it's a little village in a valley.' She was very becoming he thought; blue eyes.

He ran his fingers through his thick, dark curls and rubbed his chin, which this late in the day had a dark stubble shadow. His fingers felt the rasp as he rubbed his knuckles down his cheek. It was a habit he had when he was trying to make up his mind. He liked the look of her, the decision was made.

'You don't seem the usual type of girl one sees in The Fleece or any other tavern in Whitby for that matter – you must be very popular.'

'I don't know about that.' She flushed again.

'You blush! How quaint, it's very fetching,' Gabriel leaned further over the table and as he took her small hand in his he caught a hint of a flowery scent – rose water?

'This hand certainly does not look like it has seen hard labour – what is your name?'

'Charity sir.' Gabriel threw his head back and laughed.

'And are you?'

'Am I what sir?'

'Charitable of course, do you offer your company to the visitors of Whitby for free?' he teased.

'You don't look like you're in need of charity sir.'

It was true; although soberly dressed the cut of his clothes showed them to be expensive. The white linen of his shirt contrasted with his tanned face. He continued to hold her hand.

She turned his hand over in hers and said, 'I could tell your fortune, I know how to read palms.'

Gabriel smiled and arched an eyebrow, he suspected it was going to cost him but if it meant keeping the girl close for a while longer he did not mind. He was in need of company, female company. Since his father's death he had led a solitary life.

'See my hands are calloused, they show I am not afraid of hard work – there that is a clue for you.' He noticed how soft her hand felt in comparison to his. 'Very well, tell me what you see, I pay only for good news I warn you now,' he smiled as the girl looked intently at his hand. Her head down he saw long lashes smudge shadows on her cheeks.

'You have to cross my palm with silver first.' She

7

giggled as he took a coin from his pocket. It was as he expected. He watched her closely as she began. Her pale skin had a sprinkling of freckles across her nose which had a tiny bump beneath the bridge.

'You will marry a dark haired beauty and have many children – all of them boys.'

Gabriel laughed: 'How do you know I am not married already and have a family of girls?'

'You do not look married and if you were a married man I should hope you would not be engaging in conversation with a strange woman in a tavern.'

'You do not seem strange to me, quite the contrary in fact.' He was amused by her. 'You are right – I am not married but the marriage state does not stop most men from a little flirtation with a pretty girl when they are away from home.' He saw her purse her lips and narrow her eyes before continuing.

'You have recently felt a personal loss and there will be another though not so grievous as the first.' Gabriel had only been half attending as he was appreciating her charms but now she had his full attention. He knew it was all nonsense but she had hit a raw nerve.

'Your business will grow and prosper with the help of your wife; you must make sure to value and respect her opinion if the marriage is to be enduring.' He saw her look up and smile impishly. She bit her bottom lip in concentration. She had perfectly kissable lips he thought.

'You will remove from your home town as your wife will want to remain in Whitby near to her own family but you will enjoy life here, you will build boats, a family and a good reputation.'

'Ah, so my wife will also be a Whitby wench,' he laughed. He saw her face redden but this time he saw a flicker of something in her look – annoyance, a flash of irritation perhaps? He was a little surprised.

'A new venture you are about to embark on will lead to more than just wealth, it will be the beginning of an enterprise which will change the course of your life. You will grow rich and die in your bed at an advanced age.' She dropped his hand: 'That is all I can see, will you please excuse me for a moment.' She stood to leave.

Gabriel narrowed his eyes in confusion. It seemed an abrupt end – she appeared to want to leave? 'Are you running away, I thought we might talk a while – perhaps come to some arrangement?' She assured him she would return.

Gabriel watched the golden haired girl return to her friends with a touch of regret. She had a pleasing figure, not too tall with a slender waist and a straight back, her long hair spilling over her pale shoulders, the tight bodice of her dress accentuating her curves. Her blue eyes, burnished hair and ivory skin gave her a Celtic look; he guessed she was probably of gypsy descent.

As he watched he saw one of the sailors grab her hand; she pulled it free dismissively without looking at the man. The thought of tumbling amongst that hair galvanised him and he rose to his feet, the thought of spending another night alone spurred him on.

♥

Eleanor, for that was her real name, looked about her – she was suddenly anxious someone would see her, recognise her; she had stood up too quickly and felt a little dizzy. The heat of the tavern and the gin and brandy she was unaccustomed to drinking, made the room swim for a second.

Eleanor pushed her way through the throng on her way back to her friend Eva Drage who lifted a glass in tribute and laughing said:

'Need some Dutch courage,' then laughed at her own jest, 'Are yer on then? 'Spect 'e be staying 'ere so if you go wi' 'im I'll be waiting fer yer to come back down.' Eleanor looked at her friend she could see Eva was merry with drink now; the Dutch sailors were being generous.

'Yer 'aving second thoughts about our bet are yer? Want me to tek over?' 'A bet's a bet but yer done well, shall yer call yerself the winner? I should say so.'

Eleanor watched as Eva pushed one of the sailor's hands from her leg. ''E's right handsome – if yer passing 'im up I'll gladly tek 'im off yer 'ands. If yer change yer mind it don't matter, it were just a jape; this life in't fer the likes of you Eleanor.'

Eleanor was wavering; the heat and noise of the inn were crowding in on her. 'I am not used to strong spirits, my head is spinning. Perhaps you are right I should go before any real harm is done.' She looked across the inn to where he sat; he was watching her. She could feel his mesmerising eyes on her – up close she had noticed they were a bluish-grey. She felt her stomach lurch in a way she had never experienced before. Was it fear or excitement, perhaps a little of both?

'The bet's a daft idea Eleanor; yer never could resist a challenge, I thought all along nothing but a laugh would come of it. 'E looks well enough but save yerself fer some sweetheart who no doubt will be kind and gentle, that's what I'd do if I 'ad a choice. E looks summat kind but yer can never tell, tek my word fer it, I've had some turn nasty.' Eva glowered then kissed one of the sailors on his ruddy cheek.

Eleanor took a deep breath and turned a little unsteadily on her feet; indecision was not something she usually suffered from. Her impetuous nature often got her into bother, as it was about to do now, but her actions could lead to more than a little trouble if she continued down this path.

Eleanor realised she was at a crossroads. When the bet was taken it felt thrilling, somewhat liberating, but now it suddenly felt like madness. Selling herself to a stranger in some sordid inn was reckless. Did she really want to do this? Then she saw his expectant face, his twinkling eyes. She could still change her mind.

He stood before her; he held out his hand. 'It has been a long day and I have an early tide to catch tomorrow, will you join me.' She hesitated then raised her eyes to his, took his hand and allowed him to lead her up the stairs.

2

When Gabriel Reynolds' father died unexpectedly, his only son became a rich man. Gabriel at four and twenty, inherited his father's shipping freight business, stakes in a number of ships and a rope making business. There were also stocks and shares, ownership of some local houses which were tenanted and also land above the estuary which was currently let to a farmer. Jack Reynolds had also left substantial monies at the bank.

Gabriel had been well trained by his father to take over the business but had been grieved to do so as he had not foreseen having to take on so much responsibility so soon. As an only child he felt his aloneness. He was forever grateful for having one good friend in the world.

That friend was Bendor Percy whom he had met at school. One supposed Bendor was a cut above Gabriel, him being an aristocrat, but there was an instant liking on both sides. Bendor was as fair as Gabriel was dark. His was the sunnier character, while Gabriel had learnt to be melancholic from his father at an early age. Both were scholarly young men but red blooded nonetheless – they were also keen to continue their education outside the classroom.

'Emma is a sweet girl, she is an orphan,' Gabriel announced while walking back to school late one night. They had discovered they could buy sex like every other commodity; it was a revelation to them. 'Most of the girls have no family, who knows what would happen to them if they did not support themselves in this way although I should not want a sister of mine to have to sell herself to survive, yet we take our pleasure, toss them a coin and leave satisfied. I sometimes think it wrong.' The two friends already realised their extracurricular activities involved real women with real feelings and felt an uncommon respect for them. An older boy from school had led them to an area of town where a certain type of woman could be bought for the price of a brandy or a couple of gins.

'Of course it would be preferable to be with women who did so of their own free will and not because they were being paid,' Both had soon come to the conclusion all young men of their position had come to; that ladies of their rank were constantly chaperoned and so not available at any price before marriage.

Bendor sighed. 'I know such handsome bucks like us should not have to pay,' he laughed, 'but even when we managed to bed those two lovelies at Whitby fair, you have to agree, it was the same transaction as we had with the brothel: we paid for their pies and their ribbons, we showed them the freak show, we won them trinkets at the shooting gallery and then they let us tumble with them behind the tent. We still had an exchange but there was no actual money passing between us yet we still paid for our delights.'

After their first fumblings with the opposite sex they had grown more discerning and graduated from tavern wenches to the more high class establishments where a better class of woman could be procured. As they had the means at their disposal they did not have to resort to sordid encounters in dark alleys but could experiment in the relative comfort of a high class brothel. Gabriel the more fastidious of the two was happy to pay more for a cleaner, sweeter smelling girl.

'When I fall in love I will give up paying for my pleasure once and for all.' Bendor said, 'Well, when I marry at any rate!'"I agree, why marry at all if not for love, we are both fortunate in that neither of us have to marry an heiress.'

'Though should a beautiful one present herself I might be tempted!' Bendor winked.

Sir Bendor, as he was now did not fall in love with an heiress but became acquainted with a young lady named Grace; she had a noble name but a mean dowry. Gabriel had been thrown together with Caroline Hodgeson, the daughter of his father's best friend. As it happened she would eventually inherit her father's fortune and the joining of the two families was considered an advantageous match.

Both young men had been attracted to these women but knew until the wedding night they would be lucky to steal a chaste kiss; chaperones were notoriously hard to lose. So their weekly lessons in love continued until they left school and became engaged to their respective mates. At University, Bendor was often to be found in the pleasure gardens of London while Gabriel was to find his needs met when a chance meeting literally threw a woman in his path.

By the Christmas holiday the term before Gabriel was to leave school he was a strapping young man, well muscled as a result of rowing and assisting at his father's business. He was back in Alnmouth for the festivities and had just concluded a business transaction on behalf of his father. The north westerly wind was an idle one that cut a path through a body rather than around it. The thin layer of snow had frozen overnight and the cobbles around the bay were slippery and treacherous under foot.

Gabriel turned up his collar to head for home when a woman carrying a basket slipped and fell right there in front of him, her purchases spilling out and rolling away. 'Let me lend a hand – are you hurt?' Gabriel helped the young woman to her feet but could see even in the darkening December gloom the arm was swelling. He rescued her shopping from the ground. 'Here take my arm, you look a little unsteady, do you have much pain?'

'It is only my arm sir I think, little else hurts.' She looked at her arm which she cradled carefully as if it were made of glass. Her face showed the pain she felt.

'Let me escort you home, it is so slippery you should not risk another fall. I can carry your shopping. Do you live hereabouts?'

'Just around the corner sir, thank you that would be most kind but I should hate to cause you trouble.' They introduced themselves to each other. Her name was Libby Lawson.

They arrived at a small house not in the worst part of town but not far from it. He followed the woman into a room which although small was clean but sparsely furnished. It had no fire in the grate – the room was icy cold.

'Is there something I could use to make a support for your arm to make you more comfortable Miss Lawson?' She directed him to a thin shawl and he attempted to make a sling with it.

'Let me make you a dish of tea, perhaps you could take something stronger for the pain and the shock. Do you have brandy?

'I am afraid not,' she said. He set about making the tea. 'If you will permit I will send a doctor I think your arm may be broken. I saw a similar sight on board my father's ship once and the doctor used splints to keep it still and in time it was as good as new.'

Libby looked concerned. 'Oh dear I need to work and without use of my arm I will be hard pressed as I live alone as you can see. I am sorry sir you have been most kind but I cannot afford to pay the doctor. I will do as you say and attempt to keep it still and hope that the swelling goes down by morning.'

In spite of her protests, Gabriel went off to summon a doctor nonetheless. He also went on board his father's ship, the Jack and Alice and threw a bag of coal over his shoulder – if there was one thing that they had much of it was coal.

On his return he saw she was gratified he had not only brought coal but set about making a glorious fire. 'You are most attentive sir – without your assistance today I do not know how I would have managed.'

She was older than Gabriel by perhaps six or seven

years and was handsome in a dark particular way. He had also thought to bring brandy and gave her a tot hoping it would ease the pain.

The next day he called to see how she did. 'I am glad to see the doctor has been, the strapping and splints will help I think.' Gabriel had also brought her food from home. 'Our cook always makes too much food for my father and I.' He placed a cheese pie and a fruit tart on the small table. 'This should keep you fed for today I hope. I have called and paid the doctor this morning so you need not worry about that.'

She smiled and thanked him. 'You said yesterday you had to earn your own living – do you not have friends or family who can help you?'

'I have neither friends nor family I am the only daughter of a merchant from Alnwick. When father died my brother, who was my only relative, lost all our property and money.' She looked ashamed. 'First he speculated and bought shares in a ship that sank and then got us into further debt. Finally he drank himself to death leaving me destitute.' She sat by the fire that Gabriel had built up. 'I never had to earn my own money when father was alive, I kept house for him and had a good standard of living. now am brought low, I am reduced to taking in sewing as I have training for little else.'

'It is a sorry position you find yourself in and not of your making.'

'I would like to try to be a governess or perhaps a companion to a lady and move back to my home town of Alnwick.'

Gabriel listened and being a practical sort was all the

time thinking how he could help her until she could again help herself. He said, 'If it would help I could arrange for a girl to come in each day to assist you? Please do not worry about the cost I am able to pay. I have also arranged for Dr Chaffer to check on how your arm is mending, he will call again in a week or so.'

For the next few weeks Gabriel sent over food and coal and called to see Libby himself whenever he was able. The weeks passed and her arm began to mend. Gabriel returned to finish school.

One evening a year or so later as Bendor passed the port to his friend, they discussed Gabriel's liaison. 'On the surface I am aware the transaction with Libby may be seen as disreputable, it happened unintentionally that Libby became, well my mistress I suppose you would call her, for I see that is what she is.'

Bendor laughed, his fair skin was becoming flushed the more he drank. 'You inadvertently found yourself calling on a pretty lady who was willing to -'

'Ben! I helped her when she was in distress, she was in need. The other thing came about slowly: I share her bed, I leave money discreetly. Neither of us ever mention the fact – it is not like that at all! I know the money keeps her from further ills and I admire the way she has coped with the hand she has been dealt; she does not pity herself and is determined to pull herself out of the hole she is in.'

Bendor smiled his crooked eye tooth showing. 'It cannot be easy for her yet I bet she blesses the day she fell at your feet.' He looked about for the cigars and not finding them pulled the bell.

'When I left school and was back in Alnmouth I began to call upon her – I only meant to be friendly, keep an eye out for her, she had had rotten luck with that brother of hers. I bought her trinkets and ribbons thinking to cheer her – I had no ulterior motive'

'I believe you thousands wouldn't!' Bendor refilled their glasses. Both were a little worse for wear – Bendor loosened his neck cloth.

'I have been in the habit of calling most weeks when I am not away on business, now I am in Alnmouth full time; it is convenient I suppose but recently—.'

'I'll bet it's convenient you lucky dog!'

'You make it sound sordid, it is not. It was innocent at first as I said; I had not meant it turn out this way. She is older than me but it is I who have the experience not her; she is not a common prostitute. I truly like Libby; we are friends but I do not love her of course, I love Caroline.'

'Then where is the harm? You are not keeping her prisoner she is free to act as she chooses, you are doing her a favour.' Bendor winked suggestively.

'I have considered trying to find her some other sort of employment but she says she would prefer to sort her own life.' Gabriel shrugged. 'I have helped her remove to a better neighbourhood where I think it safer for her at any rate.'

'So long as the arrangement suits you both I cannot see a problem though I expect Caroline would not see it in those terms, but so long as you are discreet – you are a young man what else are you to do?'

'It has suited us both but now – we have little in common apart from the obvious of course.' Gabriel shuffled uncomfortably in his seat then laughed. 'She gets a handsome, virile, undemanding lover and I have the attentions of an attractive, older woman while I wait to marry, then bed my fiancée.

'You are a lucky beggar Gabe, I am still playing fast and loose with the kitchen maid; if mother catches me I shall be in for the high jump.

'Truth be told since father died the relationship with Libby, if you can call it that, has run its course I think. I have had much to do, father left everything in good order but well...my priorities have changed I suppose.'

'There you go – Mr Moody has reared his head!' Bendor cuffed his friend jovially, 'Do not start becoming maudlin, you are young have some fun for goodness sake, Lord knows you have had a hard time of it recently. You are always pessimistic but you are over the worst now.' He squeezed his friend's arm affectionately. 'I know you feel the burden of your father's businesses upon your strong shoulders,' He slapped him on the back, 'but do not get down hearted.' They raised a glass and Bendor proposed a toast. 'To women, bless them all.'

3

Throughout her early life Eleanor Barker had grumbled to her twin Tomas that she was a girl and not a boy. Now they were growing up he had freedoms she could only dream of.

'I wish I were a boy! You get to have all the fun, it is so unfair you will have all the freedom and I shall be so restrained.'

'I do not see how that is; you do all the things I do Eleanor, you ride and fish and swim -'

'But for how much longer will I be able to rough house with you? You will be sent away to school and I too possibly. Even if I do not go away I will not be able to run around as I do now I shall be expected to act like a lady and wear ladylike clothes.'

Eleanor sulked. 'As a consequence of you being born a boy and I a girl our lives will follow such different paths from here on in,' Eleanor told her sympathetic but uncomprehending twin. 'You will be prepared as son and heir to follow in father's footsteps, you will have responsibility, wealth and power while I, as a mere woman will be trained for what? To be a wife and an ornament on my husband's arm.' She was petulant, downcast. 'I shall make my own money so I do not have to depend on any man, I shall invest in my own future by investing in whaling; there is money to be made in this new enterprise I hear. If I can become rich in my own right I shall not need a man although if I am to have children I shall have to have a husband of some sort I suppose.'

'It will do you no good to seek your fortune for when you marry all your worldly goods will go to your husband along with a dowry. Why look so shocked – you know how the world works.' She glared at him when he laughed. 'It is as you say, unfair but there it is. I could marry an heiress and never do a day's work after that; her wealth could keep me idle for the rest of my days. Along with father's fortune I shall be rich, but fear not I will always take care of you so you have no need to worry.'

'I would be bored being idle and so should you after a while I am sure.' She was irritated by his lack of understanding. 'Were you not listening Tomas? I do not want to depend on any man, not even you. What if you decided to become a gambler and lost our fortune I should be dragged down with you. There must be a way to keep the money I make if only I can think of it; if the worst happens and I get rich and I marry which I see is inevitable, then I shall have to put the monies in your name to keep them safe for me and pray you do not make reckless investments. Not ideal but as yet I can think of no other solution. It is so frustrating.'

'Are you expecting to marry a pauper, why the need to make your own fortune? You will make a good marriage and your standard of living will be at least the same as it is now.'

'Money is power, I want to do things with my life not sit and drink tea and breed. Although I shall want lots of children and a handsome, kind husband who will adore me, we shall build our own empire, together.'

Tomas laughed, 'It will be as you say and I for one will be glad when you stop stealing my breeches.'

Being a twin, Eleanor and her brother were of a similar height, build and colouring so up until the age of twelve she had been used to borrowing his clothes to go with him, to ride and to explore in the woods and on the beach. The beach was her special place; her sanctuary. With her hair tucked up in one of his caps it was hard to tell them apart and Eleanor regularly fooled the servants, their governess and even their parents on occasions.

'If Mama catches you escaping through the kitchens to go to the beach after dark you will be in for a roasting.' Eleanor was fond of taking the rough, winding path down from the cliffs overlooking Sandsend beach, splashing through the beck where the stream met the sea. 'I know but you will not tell her for if you do I will tell of your late night escapades to Lythe.'

'I am sure our parents know already, I am a man; they know what young men get up to I am sure.' Eleanor threw a cushion at him in frustration.

Her twin said, 'Perhaps you should take a leaf out of our sister's book; Atalana is the perfect daughter, sober, quiet, compliant. Their older sister was married to an unyielding Quaker, Obed Coffin, who in Eleanor's opinion was a dour excuse for a man. The two sisters could not have been more different in temperament and character. 'No thank you, she does not live life she simply exists.' Eleanor shuddered. 'And her husband I would not accept wrapped in gold and tied with a ribbon if he were the last man on earth.'

Tomas pinched his sister playfully. 'If, as I suspect you have been wandering further afield at night to Whitby – unchaperoned – and you get caught you will be locked up and the key thrown away.' The Barkers' lived on the family estate, Mulgrave House at Sandsend north of Whitby. 'Three miles is quite a way to go alone and at night, it is unsafe you must see that?'

'Do not fear for me, I can take care of myself.' Eleanor was becoming irritable, she hated being lectured.

As they had risen in the world the Barker family had moved away from the blubber houses and the attendant sail yards, ropers and chandlers to a new, impressive mansion house more in keeping with their status. Eleanor missed the hustle and bustle of the town.

'Anyway who says I have been into Whitby?

'I saw you, do not deny it,' Eleanor was just about to protest,

'You were arm in arm with a slovenly looking chit – if you are found out—'he mimed slitting his throat and moved quickly out of his sister's reach as she aimed a blow at him.

Their family history showed they had been Quakers in the past and had always been associated with shipping. Although their forebears had been devout, the Barker children's upbringing had been somewhat less strict. John and Anne Barker had seen to that, but now Eleanor was becoming ever more wayward

Her father, John Barker, had enjoyed a Quaker

education shielded from the depravities of the world but his own children, although educated at a Quaker school, had also had a non Quaker governess to equip them to live in the modern world. As a result of the break with The Friends, Eleanor and her sibling were no longer expected to wear the plain sober garb which made Quakers so distinctive, nor did they have to abstain from some of the luxuries their station provided. The fact her sister still chose the Quaker way was bewildering to Eleanor.

Eleanor enjoyed dances, attended balls and drank alcohol in moderation like any young lady of her position; her sister did none of these things. Now Eleanor was taking advantage of her parents' lax attitude and exploring the world in a far more free way than they would have agreed to had they known.

'Like Mama, I still agree with some of the founding Quaker principles of equality and egalitarianism but I am relieved we no longer have to sit in quiet contemplation at the Meeting House.' Eleanor pulled a face, 'Yet still I get bored stuck out here.'

'You have been allowed to follow your own path, have your own views, some of which seem unconventional. Our sister would have a fit if she knew half of what you get up to! Have a care Eleanor, you stray further than our parents would ever imagine; you are sailing very close to the wind. Sometimes I think you forget you are engaged to be married. What would William say?

Eleanor shrugged. 'I take your point brother but fear not, I can handle William.'

♥

Captain William Seamer, tall, dark and imposing, was shown into the library where his fiancé was writing at a small desk by the window. He walked purposefully to stand before her and noted with irritation she did not immediately look up but continued to finish what she was doing. It made him feel like a small boy standing before his headmaster; his lips tightened, he breathed deeply.

Eleanor looked up and half smiled: 'William, good morning; this is a surprise.' William registered it did not appear to be a particularly pleasant one. 'Good morning Eleanor, I came to invite you to ride out,' he tapped his crop against his highly polished riding boot, 'We seem to have spent so little time together whilst I have been ashore this leave, other than dances and dinners that is. Possibly I will be off again by Monday week and I thought it might be enjoyable to spend some time together – alone; perhaps I could buy my fiancée a trinket?' He noted the ink stains on her long fingers.

He smiled, knowing many a lady was impressed by his elegant good looks and confident manner. It was a confidence borne from knowing he was handsome and from the fact his father's ship building business, which he would one day inherit, had made him one of the most eligible bachelors in Whitby until, that is, his betrothal to Eleanor Barker. Sometimes, like now when she was so obviously distracted he wished he had matched himself with Sabrina Scoresby, or even Emma Whitbread; at least they might have shown gratitude.

'Trinkets?' She said absent mindedly. He watched as she looked over her shoulder where grey clouds were building, 'It looks like rain; perhaps we could have tea instead.'

Without waiting for his assent she pulled the bell and ordered tea. William, tricorn in hand, watched her walk to the fireside trying to control his irritation.

'As you wish my dear,' he lifted an eyebrow, 'many a lady would jump at the chance to be offered a ride into Whitby with the possibility of a gift at the end of it.' He felt the urge to upset the neat piles of papers on her desk. 'I had not realised you were made of salt! Should you dissolve in a little light rain – I thought you enjoyed riding in all weathers?'

'I prefer the dry although as you say I am not averse to riding in rain but I rode out early, before breakfast when it was sunny.' She smiled amiably enough but William could sense she was still preoccupied. This encounter, he noticed was similar to many he had endured before, he felt his good mood dissipate as battle lines were drawn.

When Eleanor had dismissed the maid and tea was poured William said: 'Just averse to my company then perhaps?' He glared at Eleanor who offered a plate of biscuits which he declined.

'I seem to remember you remarking recently about my "unseemly behaviour" when I rode alone? Would it not be improper to ride with my fiancé without a chaperone?'

'Of course your maid could accompany us; I had not thought to put your reputation at risk.' He smiled hoping for a thaw.

'These biscuits are lemon, they are favourites of mine. Have you ever put your tongue on a whole lemon, tasted its sourness? Yet the bitterness is gone when baked with sugar there is still the tartness but no sharp unpleasantness.'

William knew she was toying with him like a cat plays with a mouse. She enjoyed leading him on he suspected. He moved in his seat and re crossed his sturdy legs. He would enjoy their wedding night; he imagined she would be responsive, receptive he thought to an experienced man's attentions. He certainly hoped so after what he had endured of late. Eleanor Barker could be most provoking; he meant to tame her in every way except the bedroom.

'My maid is from home on an errand – there is no one else available I should think.' She smiled triumphantly.

'Not even a second footman or a groom? William did not bother to hide his displeasure now and frowned at his red haired fiancée as she sat opposite him. The door opened and Eleanor's mother entered the fray.

'Ah good morning William, I did not know you were here, I should have been along sooner had I realised.' She nodded and smiled as her future son-in-law brushed his cold lips on her hand. She sat beside him and Eleanor passed her a dish of tea.

'Megsy Moran is at death's door Eleanor! I have come to ask you to walk up the valley with me and see what is to be done. Cook is preparing a basket for us to take; I thought you could accompany me?' She turned a bright smile on William. 'Megsy is a tenant of ours she's a grand old age. We try to do what we can for our tenants, you do not mind William?'

Like her daughter she did not wait to find out. Anne Barker was a paler version of her daughter. Her once red hair was now more gold than red. She headed for the door saying: 'I will need to change my shoes but then I shall be ready Eleanor.' William was exasperated. He could see where Eleanor got her strange ways from, the entire family were unconventional but the women were the limit. Even the quiet sister was odd.

He thought to detain Eleanor a little longer; she would not have it all her own way. 'Last night I was supping with Charles,' he mentioned a friend of his whom he knew Eleanor thought little of,

'After we had supped we went for a walk by the harbour to take the air.' He thought he detected a slight tightening of Eleanor's fingers on her teacup. 'As we went over the drawbridge, it was just as it was coming dark, I saw a young girl sitting on the harbour wall at Tin Gaut, for all the world, apart from her clothes that is, she was the spitting image of you!' He waited for her to squirm. 'Her red hair was in a loose plait as yours is today, she was with a rough looking wanton, not the sort of woman you would fraternise with of course.' He looked hard at his fiancée's face hoping to see discomfiture; he saw nothing but a feigned interest.

'Have you ever heard it said we all have a double?' he continued, 'It would be most strange if yours were living in the same town would it not my dear? She was very like you in all respects. Did you sup at home last night?'

'We did, we were en famille.' She smiled sweetly. 'I have heard of this phenomenon, it is odd as you say that there is another William Seamer somewhere in the world, perhaps you will meet him on your travels one day.'

William pressed on. 'While I am ashore I will watch

out for this young woman, had we ridden into Whitby this morning we may have come across her, who knows? I would have liked to see what you thought of her, whether you could see the resemblance. Now I come to think about it her dress was a similar colour to the one you are wearing now.'

'I thought it was almost dark, what an imagination you have William!' He thought he saw a chink in her armour.

'You will be at the Whitbreads' this evening? He knew she was trying to change the subject.

'Of course, make sure to reserve the first three dances for me my dear as recompense for my wasted journey here this morning.'

'Was it wasted William?' she looked up at him through long lashes 'Did we not take tea? In future perhaps send a note so I might let you know my arrangements, then you will not be affronted.'

'I am not slighted,' he said archly. 'However my dear, when we are married I hope you will behave with a little more thought for your poor husband, a neglected spouse can be a cantankerous thing I expect. A little more consideration from you would not come amiss; I shall look forward to your undivided attention this evening.' He stood to leave.

William glared at Eleanor with unguarded antagonism. He continued. 'In marriage I understand there must be compromise, give and take if you will; if the marriage is to be satisfactory that is. Perhaps you could use the rest of our engagement to consider how you will accommodate my needs as I consider yours.' He gripped his tricorn tightly. 'Your unusual habits may be misconstrued for wilfulness my dear.' William could see Eleanor bristle, then struggle to hold herself in check. He was pleased he was piercing her reserve; he felt he was regaining the upper hand.

William smoothed the fabric of his uniform jacket as Eleanor moved towards him. She reached up and placed a soft kiss on his lips, then smiled demurely. He was temporarily taken aback. He had been waiting for her to bite back with some withering taunt as she had done many times before.

'Forgive me William. You are right, I am sometimes too distracted with my own affairs, I shall look forward to this evening – perhaps we might try to slip away to the garden – alone if my sister turns her back.' She kissed him again. 'See your visit has accomplished what you intended; are we not alone now?' He put his arms around her slender waist just as a footman entered and said Mrs Barker was waiting for her daughter.

Anne Barker watched William take his leave from the hall then returned to the library and sat down; earlier she had been listening at the door like an errant scullery maid.

'Are you ready?' Eleanor asked not resuming her seat.

'For what – oh my little ruse! I just saw Megsy at the kitchen door making a nuisance of herself. Cook has placated her with something I dare say. '

'So at the kitchen door then not death's door!'Eleanor laughed.

'My love, will you not reconsider your engagement to William, no one will think the less of you for calling the wedding off, there is still some time. I was relieved with the postponements but why not call the whole thing off.' She patted the seat beside her and Eleanor sat down.

'Why should I do that, who else would I find who suits me better? I think the postponement has just made him keener.'

'Yet he does not suit you! You do not love him, you said as much when this idea was first mooted. Neither I nor your father ever thought you would agree to the proposal – as I say it is not too late for a change of mind the wedding is still a way off.'

'William is good looking, charming and quite dashing; some of my friends are envious of my engagement. He can even be quite amiable when he isn't being pompous and, as I am finding out, he can be quite easy to stage-manage – most of the time.'

Anne found Eleanor's pragmatism unnerving. 'Marriage is a lifelong commitment and you need to understand this Eleanor! He may be handsome but good looks fade in time.'

'I have to marry someone if I am to have children, and I dearly want lots of children,' Eleanor laughed, 'Who else could I get that would be a better fit? William is at sea so much, another great advantage I think. His absences will leave me free for my own projects and any children when they come along. Also my marriage to William will cement a relationship with another important ship builder in Whitby therefore it is the best solution all round, Papa should be pleased.'

'Papa would be happier if you loved your betrothed, yet you do not love him Eleanor, I doubt if you even respect him – we certainly do not! He does not take after his kindly father at all.' Anne wrinkled her nose.

'Mama, no one I know will marry for love; all my friends and I can hope for is someone young and passably handsome which also makes William "a catch". Who else could I have: someone like Walter Edwards?' She named a middle aged, bent over widower with three daughters who her friend Hester engaged to. 'At least any children we have will be tolerable to look at.' Anne knew Eleanor was referring to Walter's mousy, plain daughters.

'Yet still I hate to think of you married to William, I sense a cruel streak if he is riled, be careful my love I am sure he has a temper. With your red hair and his short fuse I see troubled waters ahead.'

Eleanor was unfazed. 'Yet when I am in the mood can I not pour oil on those tempestuous waves, as I said I am sure I can manage him, do not fret Mama all will be well.

♥

When she was younger Eleanor had been content to go to the beach alone at night but now, as her twin suspected, she had begun to explore further afield. She found Whitby was an exciting place, especially when she went alone and unchaperoned. It was a different world after dark, full of character and intrigue, the port was always busy and there was much to see. On one such excursion she had met a girl of a similar age who was sitting on the sea wall, her name was Eva Drage. Eleanor took a liking to this simple young woman, they may have been of a similar age but how different their lives were. Eleanor knew the girl had to work for a living.

They walked into Henrietta Street and passed the milliners where they stopped to admire the hats and ribbons. Eva told Eleanor she was a sail maker and Eleanor told a fib saying she was a governess. She liked to play act.

'I can sew well enough but not the sort er sewing that could mek summat as fine an' beautiful as the 'ats in the window. The kind er sewing I do meks me fingers bleed. Sewing 'ats would be fine work an' easier on me fingers. 'Spect it'd pay more an' all. I 'ave to try to mek "a bit extra" on account of 'avin' a sister who 'as three kiddies an' a dead 'usband,'

Eva was smaller and slimmer than Eleanor, it was a thinness brought about through want she suspected. Eleanor saw that Eva was pretty and that she tried to make the best of herself. Her work dress though patched was clean and modest, her shoes polished. Although her dark hair was thick it was not lustrous. Eleanor thought that with the right clothes and with her hair washed and styled Eva could even be a beauty.

Eva said. 'Do yer fancy a bit er summat to get warmed up? The Fleece is just away round the corner, I fancy a drop er gin.' Eleanor realised her new acquaintance thought she might have money; she suspected Eva was used to tapping friends for favours. She wondered what it was like in a tavern and her curiosity could be satisfied with the help of this girl she realised but she declined the offer, she had already been out longer than she had intended.

'Perhaps another time I need to get back in case I am missed.'

Since that first night the two had met up whenever Eleanor could slip away. After their first meeting she saw the benefit of befriending Eva; she could hardly go into a tavern alone but with Eva's help she might blend in a little.

Besides, she had grown to like Eva, they got along, they chatted like old friends. Eleanor often gossiped with her maid, so she did not feel any particular constraint or reservation talking to the young woman. She just had to remember she was supposed to be a governess and act accordingly, she did not know why she carried on the subterfuge but it was fun pretending to be someone else, it all added to the fun.

Eleanor could not imagine the drudgery of Eva's life but she was keen to help her in any small way she could. Each time they met, Eleanor brought something for Eva or her sister's children; she hoped to try to save Eva from degrading herself but knew there was only so much she could do.

'Come and wait while I change,' Eva said the next time the two women met, 'I live but a step away.' They set off up a winding path – Eleanor would never have ventured to this part of town.

The cottage clung to the east cliff and was packed in tightly to its neighbours in front and to either side; there was an open sewer by the door that smelled excessively. It was tiny, cramped and insanitary. Eleanor could barely breathe and suppressed a gag; the rancid stench almost overpowered her.

The villagers on her father's land in Sandsend lived poorly but nothing compared to this. Their tenants had fresh sea air at least and a small garden to grow vegetables. They were spaced out more giving a little privacy to the inhabitants. Her father's Quaker beliefs hung about him still which meant roofs were repaired making them at least dry.

They ducked their heads as Eleanor followed her friend into the dark, rank room. There was no natural light, the room being at the back of the house and built into the cliff side, the walls gleamed with damp and the floor was bare earth

Eleanor shocked, was keen to escape from the squalor but did not want to appear rude. Eva self consciously changed her work clothes for a dress which had belonged to Eleanor's maid; she had brought it for Eva the week before. Eleanor noted the girls shift was thin and much patched but clean. Eleanor could not imagine how she kept herself as well as she did under these conditions.

'See the frock fits well enough now 'ave altered it. I never 'ad a spare 'en afore.' She smoothed the skirt proudly. I had to chop off some from the bottom but look it's med a belt and a matching scarf.' She beamed as she wound the scarf around her head.

'It is well you are good with a needle, I can barely sew a button on.'

'How do you manage being a governess? Surely you must 'ave to sew for the kiddies?' Eleanor had spoken without thinking and tried to rectify her mistake by muttering something about the maids taking care of the children's clothes.

As they left the hovel Eleanor was determined to do something more for Eva but she did not know what, she would think about it on the way home.

♥

One evening a few weeks later, they were passing the Dolphin Inn when Eleanor was stopped in her tracks; heading down Grape Lane, with what was clearly a very low sort of woman on his arm, was William Seamer – her fiancé! She didn't even know he was back ashore; she purposely only came to Whitby when she knew he was at sea. Momentarily she was stunned, then outraged. She stepped back into the shadows even though he was walking in the opposite direction.

'What's up love seen a ghost?' Eva laughed.

'Just someone I know who comes to my employer's house,' Eleanor lied. 'I don't want him to see me, he may tell the mistress.'

'The sea captain there, 'E allus makes a bee line for Saucy Susie when 'e's ashore knows she'll be down "Grope" Lane. Eva explained: 'Round 'ere everyone knows Grape Lane is where men go to find a woman of a certain type.'

'You mean you know him?'

'Well know 'im by sight, not in that way,' she laughed. 'I think 'e prefers Susie, she got a reputation for pleasing men in particular ways I 'eard!' Eleanor was furious but at the same time curious; she did not dare ask what Eva meant. Eleanor had little experience of the opposite sex but how dare he walk out blatantly with this—this harlot.

Eva laughed and nudged Eleanor in the ribs, 'Men'll

be men.'

Eleanor vowed this was the last time she would take the risk of coming out alone at night: What if she had met him face to face – she did not dare to think what might have happened. Yet it was he who should be ashamed not her, she may have been unchaperoned, at night in town but he was her intended! He was the one who should be embarrassed; he was the one cavorting with a common street walker! Eva tugged on her arm and they moved on, Eleanor's temper still hot.

As the two women walked through Arguments Yard to sit on the wall looking out to sea, Eleanor thought about what she had just seen; she would love to confront William but knew it impossible. She was still furious. She wondered if Tomas knew about his escapades and realised he probably did. She would have words with him too. Eleanor was only half listening to Eva who was gossiping about a man her sister knew.

'My education has grown since meeting you. We may be the same age but you are worldly wise compared to me.' When Eva talked about men it astonished Eleanor. 'Yer grow up quick when yer dad abandons yer when yer only ten, I had to learn me lessons the hard way.' Eleanor realised she had led a sheltered life until now.

She also knew Eva went with men for money for "little extras". The "extras" were actually necessities such as food and clothes for her sister's children.

In a lull in the conversation Eleanor screwed up her courage and asked a question she had been thinking to ask for a while now. If she did not ask now she told herself she never would.

'What's it like… to be with a man. You understand my meaning?' Eleanor could feel her cheeks burning.

'I aren't ever bin wi' a man other than fer money an' that's not fer me pleasure. 'Spect if yer be in love wi' the man it's meant to be different cause then 'e might care about yer. Of the ones I've known some are rough an' coarse, some are right enough on a dark night but if I'm lucky they be quick an' get it over wi'. I 'ad a sweetheart once but I din't let 'im touch me an am glad cause 'e went off wi' me sister's best friend; she did let 'im touch 'er!'

Eleanor, despite her jaunts had a more romantic idea gleaned from a novel she had read that a girl at school had smuggled in. This earthy description was at odds with what she hoped it would be like. Her notion was some strong handsome man would carry her aloft and they would seek pleasure in each other's company after he had pledged his undying love for her. Even though over the last few weeks she had seen a different side to Whitby, rougher, coarser, she still naively held to a romanticised view of the life, possibly because in between her excursions she went home to good food, servants and a comfortable bed!

Seeing her fiancé arm in arm with a common prostitute was shocking; she had given little thought to what William did when not with her, she did not love him but she imagined he had some regard for her; he clearly did not.

The two girls headed for The Fleece, Eleanor reasoned if this was to be her last jaunt to Whitby at night she would sample the delights of a tavern at least. They entered the dimly lit room, the rowdy, rollicking men watched as they were jostled and bustled along like flotsam. Voices were pitched higher, stale ale and sweat mingled with the fug of smoke and made Eleanor's eyes water. Eva was very free and easy with the men, some of whom she knew.

'Come on,' Eva shouted over her shoulder. ''Ere's a crew that look like they would buy a girl a drink.' Eva plonked herself at a table and set about flirting. Eleanor soon realised "the bit extra" Eva had talked of would come from the pockets of these men tonight.

Drinks appeared in front of them and Eva introduced her friend to the table of men most of whom were quite inebriated. Eva and Eleanor were very popular with the Dutch sailors in particular. 'These lads'll see us right,' Eva nudged Eleanor. 'Sit yer down and enjoy yerself.'

The sailors had been ashore for a few hours and were in high spirits. Eleanor, unused to strong liquor was at first careful not to drink too much too fast but soon found her inhibitions loosening even though the gin was rough tasting. She could speak a little Dutch and began to relax; most of the sailors were young boys out to spend their few coins on trying to act older and impress the two women; there was much laughter and flirting.

After an hour or so Eleanor thought of leaving; she had accomplished her goal of experiencing a tavern in all its glories and was beginning to tire of the spectacle. Then she noticed a different type of man eating his lonely supper in the corner away from all the commotion.

When the bet was first taken it had felt exciting. Why should she not behave like a man? They could please themselves and so could she. Eva added a warning to the bet but Eleanor was feeling wayward now. If she had exercised a little more caution and had not allowed herself to be challenged, she would not have found herself in Gabriel Reynolds' room.

The room above the bar was small and dark. A meagre fire gave off scant light. He found three candles and lit them. 'That's better,' he said. The room could now be seen more clearly; a blue and white pitcher and ewer on a chest, his kit bag on the floor by a saggy chair; and a bed. He took her hand and pulled her towards him and began to kiss her. She felt small in his arms. 'You smell sweet, like flowers.'

At the last moment Eleanor turned her head, he caught her cheek with his lips instead. 'You don't have to play hard to get with me.' He laughed and pulled her closer. Her face stung where his unshaven chin had caught her face; her thoughts flew to William's face which was clean shaven at all times – she tossed the thought aside. Before he could kiss her again she thought to stall for time.

'You have to pay first sir.' When the bet had been discussed Eva had laid down the rules of being 'on the game' as she called it; rule one according to Eva was to get the money first, they had not discussed how much.

'So Charity by name but not by nature eh,' he smiled amiably.

'My name is Gabriel, Gabriel Reynolds; you need not call me sir under the circumstances.' He smiled again.

'How much?' He thrust his hand in his waistcoat pocket.

'A half crown if you please.'

'A half crown!' he looked incredulous. 'The union

rates have increased have they not!' He put a coin on the chest of drawers and removed his jacket and moved towards her. Eleanor swallowed hard. He seemed to tower over her yet she did not feel afraid, the drink was making her brave. He began to stroke her hair gently then placed his arms around her waist and began to kiss her long, hard and urgently.

Eleanor felt the room begin to spin crazily; it was not only the drink making her knees shake. She had never been kissed like this before. His mouth, hard but sensuous explored her neck, her cheeks her lips. His hands began to explore her face, neck, and body. She felt herself begin to respond and melt into him. She shivered as he stroked her cheek; when he cupped her face in his hands she kissed him back. She felt his breath warm on her neck, he sighed as he began to unlace her dress.

Eleanor suddenly woke up to the situation and tried to cover her modesty before more harm could be done. She leaned away from him and pushed her hands against his hard chest.

'O mercy! 'No I cannot! This is not a game to get more money from you; I do not tease' She continued to struggle trying to free herself from his strong arms.

At first he laughed at her but then must have seen the look of terror on her face, for he loosened his grip. She continued to push him away; he let her go, took a step back then raised his hands in the air as if in surrender.

'If you are an actress you are a good one for you look scared for your life.' She saw the confusion on his face. 'Come I will not hurt you, surely you know the score?'

Once free Eleanor backed away feeling with her

hands for the door knob not taking her eyes from him. 'I am sorry,' she said, 'I made a mistake I am not what you think I am.' She turned her back to him fumbling for the key; turning it frantically she almost fell out of the room. She ran off stumbling down the tavern stairs.

Eleanor, holding on to the banister and breathing hard looked about for Eva, true to her word Eleanor saw her friend had been looking out for her. She grabbed Eleanor by the arm and dragged her outside and down the dark ginnel that ran to the side of the tavern.

'What… That were quick! Were 'e bad …did 'e not want to pay? Did 'e 'urt yer?'

Eleanor leaning against the damp, mossy wall trying to get her breath back laughed with relief; she was shaking.

'No, no I just couldn't do it. You win, I lost my courage but found my sense.'

'Yer lucky to get out! Were 'e angry? Most men wouldn't 'ave let yer go. Did yer get paid like I telled yer?' Ever the pragmatist Eva looked hopeful.

Eleanor told her what had transpired, the story gushing from her like a spring tide. Now the encounter was over she suddenly saw the funny side. 'What a fool I am!' she laughed. She realised what Eva said was true, most men would not have let her go so easily. If he had wanted to he could have stopped her from leaving and taken her by force if necessary. They walked back over the bridge arm in arm, her knees still weak.

'Well, that's the last time I gives up a 'andsome trick to you me girl, yer should've grabbed the key in one 'and and and the 'alf crown in the other. That would've bin a dear kiss fer 'im if that's all 'e got. Two and six! Yer put a 'igh price on yerself girl!' She laughed and nudged Eleanor with her elbow. Eleanor too laughed but sent up a silent prayer of gratitude for escaping intact.

At the top of the jetty which led to Sandsend beach the two parted, Eleanor began to run the three miles home. The wind in her hair, the salt spray and the thought of his kiss made her feel alive! Her stomach fluttered just thinking of the surprising softness of his lips and the strength of his arms about her. His eyes when he looked at her were an intense grey-blue, the colour of a spring sky. His dark curls had felt soft against her cheek. She had a strange sensation in the pit of her belly.

Eleanor exhilarated, allowed herself a whoop of joy as she splashed through the surf. It had been a lark but not one she would care to chance again. Back home and safely in her warm bed her thoughts returned to the handsome Mr Gabriel Reynolds and his exceptionally handsome face.

♥

Meanwhile the object of her desire kicked off his boots and lay back on the bed pulling off his neck cloth. Dear God, he thought to himself, I cannot even bed a bar wench now, that's a first! When he and his old school friend Bendor used to go whoring in the later years of their school days they never had such trouble.

His thoughts returned to this evening, was he suddenly grown repulsive? He was not a vain man but knew he was not a toad! Then he remembered the look on the girl's face, if she was play acting she should be on the stage for she had looked scared to death. Pure terror had been etched on her face as she had pushed him away.

She had come upstairs willingly enough, brazenly even, she had seemed eager. It was a riddle and would no doubt make for a self deprecating tale next time he and Bendor were in their cups; his best friend would no doubt find it comical. He told himself in the future he may find the incident amusing himself but right now he failed to see the funny side.

Yet Charity, if indeed that was her name, had made an impression on him – she was captivating, fascinating; intriguing. Holding her close he had felt alive for the first time in months, not alone not so melancholic.

The empty, gloomy room was not helping his mood. He undressed and lay on the bed. She was different from any other young woman he had ever encountered; she certainly was not like Caroline – or Libby for that matter. She was not his usual type at all. It was years since he had propositioned a serving wench – why would he? But he had been drawn to this woman – perhaps it was just the need for company, a need to feel close to another human being.

He let the air from his lungs slowly and stretched out on the bed, it was too short, his feet stuck out over the bottom.. The woman was not willowy like Caroline or dark like Libby; she had something about her he admired, her hair for certain attracted him but there was also a rare quality that was indefinable, a sort of wildness, an animal magnetism. It was not solely the way she looked, he could not explain it, it was a feeling of longing and belonging. He lay on his back with his hands behind his head and sighed; he was becoming poetic in his old age, it was not the drink – he had drunk relatively little, yet he felt intoxicated.

He could have sworn she had at first returned his kisses, pressed against him – until she had suddenly turned, changed her mind, pushed him away. It was baffling. He blew out the candles and watched as the wick glowed, he was again reminded of her hair and what hair it was; waist length waves restrained by a piece of soft green silk. He fell asleep frustrated in more ways than one.

4

Gabriel landed at his home port and headed straight for Westshore the house he had shared with his father until his death last year; he missed him still. The large, imposing house now felt empty without him.

Westshore was built in the modern style and sat in a slightly elevated position and in isolation along the beach from Alnmouth Bay. It looked out over a private beach and the cold North Sea.

Gabriel strode along the shore enjoying the exercise after being confined onboard. He entered the garden through a gate in the dry stone wall, kit bag over his shoulder, tricorn pulled down hard to stop it blowing off in the wind that seldom dropped on this North East coast. He was sweating by the time he reached the door which opened before he reached it. Abner Boatwright, his manservant and his father's before him, stood in the doorway.

'A saw yer comin' along the bay through me spyglass.' Abner never went far without his precious lens. Gabriel dropped his kit bag on the hall floor, peeling off his heavy coat.

'The weather is hot for the time of year is it not? Bring

me something to slake my thirst I am as dry as the beach.'

He went to his study with its glorious views of the sea, Abner followed him. 'Small ale do yer?' Gabriel nodded. The sun, blazing in a cloudless sky, streamed through the windows, the sea sparkled. The air was still and dust motes danced in the golden light as he stowed papers in a desk drawer. Abner returned and handed his master a tankard.

'Any news I need be aware of?' Gabriel asked as he gulped the refreshing drink. He sat in the high backed chair in front of the desk and wiped the sweat from his brow.

'Nowt of concern, but there be a letter come yesterday, that's it there.' Abner nodded in the general direction of the desk then turned and limped towards the door.

'Bring another bottle I'm going to bathe now. I'll possibly be glad of the drink afterwards.'

Gabriel recognised the handwriting as that of his friend Bendor Percy. It was a short note inviting him to a house party at his estate in Dunstanburgh. It was to be the following week. Gabriel knew he would go for he loved to spend time with Bendor and his family but first he had other, less pleasant, business to attend to.

He needed to see his fiancée Caroline as soon as possible. He wrote a short note then rang the bell, he knew he was not going to have any peace until the task was off his mind.

Get Jax to take this to Miss Caroline and tell him to wait for a reply.' Abner took the letter and went to find the stable hand. Jax was a fairly new addition to the household. Realising Abner was getting on in years

Gabriel had taken on a young boy as stable lad and general helper. He was a good lad and had been working in the coal mines in Newcastle before coming to work in Alnmouth. He was an orphan and Lisbet Cotter, Gabriel's cook cum housekeeper doted on the boy.

Gabriel left the room by the open French doors removing his boots on the terrace and discarding other garments as he marched on well muscled legs down the beach toward the sea. Without hesitation he slammed into the sparkling sea, catching his breath as a wave carried him under. He plunged beneath the surface until he could hold his breath no longer, the freezing water rinsing from his dark curls and into his eyes. He shook as a dog shakes its coat to rid itself of the excess. The roar of the waves washed over his powerful body, he swam out further with long, powerful strokes. He couldn't remember a time when he couldn't swim, as he had learnt to walk he had learnt to swim and he sea bathed summer and winter alike.

Walking back to the house dripping rivulets of salt water as he went, he picked up the discarded garments till he reached the terrace where he picked up the huckerback towel Abner had left for him on the housekeeper's instructions; she did not want seawater dripped over her polished parquet floors. He ran up the stairs to change feeling better for the exercise as he always did but his mind was still preoccupied with Caroline and the meeting he was going to have with her.

After his solitary dinner he took his brandy outside to the terrace and sat in the late afternoon sun looking out to sea.

Abner brought a note from Caroline saying she was engaged to play cards with the Fitzherberts and so would not be at home to receive him. He screwed it into a ball and aimed it at a plant pot. He did not expect her to be at his beck and call but he was frustrated he would not now get off his chest what was bothering him. He paced about the terrace.

He had thought to take a ride on the beach when he heard a familiar voice halloing from just beyond the gate. He had been so caught up in his thoughts he had not seen Caroline's father approach.

In usual circumstances Gabriel would be pleased to see Thomas Hodgeson, his late father's oldest friend and prospective father-in-law. He was like family to Gabriel, especially since the death of his father; he had known Thomas all his life. But on this spring evening with the thoughts of ending his engagement to his beloved only daughter, Gabriel met Thomas with a note of caution which felt awkward and insincere.

'Saw your ship had come in ma boy and I thought to call on you this warm evening, what weather we are having!' He laughed heartily as he sat down without being asked. Abner had seen the guest arrive and brought a tray of canary wine and rum. Gabriel handed the rum to Thomas and picked up his own drink to toast.

They sat together talking of business, the price of coal and Gabriel's trip. The light stayed long in May and the heat of the day had dissipated into a pleasant coolness. After a spell of companionable silence Gabriel broached the subject uppermost in his mind.

'I'm not sure whether to talk to you of something

unpleasant which has been on my mind for some time now. It's a matter that is regrettable to me and I know will be regrettable to you too.'

'Why don't you know if you can talk to me? Have I not known you since you were a boy, does it concern business or Caroline?' Thomas always went straight to the point.

'If it was business I would not hesitate to discuss any matter with you for you know I trust and respect your judgement – it is regarding the latter, Caroline.'

'Had a tiff have yer? No I can see by your expression it's more serious than that.' An awkward silence fell as Gabriel tried to weigh the words he was going to use to convey that he wanted to jilt the daughter her father loved more than life itself. Damn it! Gabriel thought, if Caroline had been able to see him tonight he would have been having this conversation with her now. He had come this far so he had to continue as the worried look on Thomas' face grew more concerned.

'Before I left for Whitby I needed to talk to Caro about our engagement, it was always said we should marry when she was one and twenty and that is in December as you know obviously.'

'That's right a Christmas wedding just as her dear departed mother and I had.' Gabriel saw Thomas looked wary. 'I think I can guess where this conversation is leading and I am not sure I like the sound of it.' He lit his pipe.

'Caroline and I have known each other all our lives, except for when I was at school we have never been apart. We have no surprises left for each other. Each of us knows the other inside and out.' Thomas interrupted:

'And that is not a good thing? Many have to marry with little or no acquaintance.'

Gabriel scraped his chin with his fingers. 'This past year since father died I have done a lot of thinking and have begun to see her as a friend, a good friend, rather than a wife; I saw her last week and said as much to her.'

Thomas frowned. 'What did she say?'

'Almost the same as you at first,' Gabriel stood and looked out to sea with blind eyes; all he could see was the hurt on Thomas' face.

'After we talked more she said she understood a little for she felt the same but was disturbed if the engagement were to be called off then she would be humiliated in front of her friends. I had not wanted to hurt her but then I came to see perhaps she didn't love me either.' There was another awkward silence.

Thomas was a good man and Gabriel knew he would be reluctant to say something he would later come to regret. Caroline was his only daughter and since her mother died her father was fiercely protective of her, sometimes spoiling her more than he ought. After a while Thomas rose to stand a little behind Gabriel.

'Well I never expected to hear those words from your lips.' Gabriel saw the dejected look on the older man's face. 'I cannot understand this turn of events, you two are good together! You are well matched in class and temperament. Is your mind made up then, for I know you and know when you have reached a decision, for right or wrong there is no one on this earth that will make you think again.'

'If I could change how I feel I would for I cannot bear to hurt Caroline or you, the both of you are like family, even more since father passed, I know this will be some shock to you.'

'It is – I had no clue for Caroline has not told me of this perhaps she was thinking it would not come to pass.' He puffed hard on his pipe.

'Do you want me to intercede with her on your behalf, perhaps hint we have talked of this matter? It might help if she is further prepared somewhat before you two meet again?'

'What sort of coward would that make me? I need to see her myself.'

'I just meant to let her know she has my support; try to help her as best I can to face this; I would not say ought that should not come from your lips but how can I sit at supper with her and not say we have spoken? It would make it deceitful when it comes out.'

Gabriel paced up and down the terrace putting distance between the two men.

'I hope it does not come to it Gabriel but if she feels her humiliation less by suing you for Breach of Promise then I'll support her even though it would grieve me to do it I always thought you would love and care and protect her like I have always done. Will other men even look at her now she's been jilted?' Gabriel was pained to see Thomas frown at him.

'Of course they will, she is a handsome woman. Never think I will not love and care for her in your stead, she will always be dear to me. Whether she will want me interfering in her life after this is another matter, but there now Thomas, you will be among us a good while yet,'

'A new troubling thought has entered my head; I hope there's no deceit in this on your part Gabriel there is not a woman in another port waiting for you eh?' Thomas sat down heavily as if the weight of information was suddenly too much for him to bear.

'No. No!' Gabriel almost shouted the words. 'There is no one else I swear.' It was true despite his encounter the night before his mind had been made up for some time now. Gabriel felt the hurt he was causing and sat down heavily opposite Thomas his shoulders slumped.

'I believe you, for I have always known you to be honest just as your father was.' He shook his head in disbelief at all he was hearing.

'I know this is a bitter blow to you but in time you will come to see it is for the best, Caro will meet someone who she will truly love, a mature love not like our childish love.'

The setting sun sent streaks of yellow, orange, red and purple across the darkening sky. 'What of you, shall you be easy in our company after this? For we have always been in each other's lives. It will be damned awkward in a town as small as ours where everyone knows everybody's business; I agree with Caroline in thinking the gossips will be busy.'

'That they will I am sure but I cannot marry Caroline just because there will be talk, it is going to set tongues wagging but it will be over and gone on the next tide.'

Thomas looked downcast; he picked up his crop and made ready to leave.

'If I had known what awaited me here this evening I would have done well to stay away. I see your mind is made up, I cannot say I am happy Gabriel, what your father would make of it heaven only knows but,' he sighed deeply, 'who knows, in time I might be able to see the sense in it. You've always been like a son to me and I know you to be a good man, I'll take my leave and bid you goodnight. I'll deliver your message to Caroline and hope she sees you sooner rather than later.'

'I wish you would not Thomas, it is I who need to talk with her but you must do as you see fit; I shall ride over in the morning.' Thomas headed down the path to find his mount waiting and was gone.

Gabriel wished he felt differently about ending the long standing engagement but knew deep down, and despite all the hurt he was causing, he was doing the right thing. He looked out to sea and thought: This is best for everyone not just myself; Caro deserves to be happy and she would not be if she were married to a man who might grow to resent her.

Glowering clouds began to advance upon the shore. There was going to be a storm. Quarrelsome waves clamoured and heaved and the sky began to boil and darken.

'Damn.' He cursed to the sea and sky, the melancholia was upon him and he hated himself for giving in to it.

♥

The swell the next morning was choppy; the northerly wind blowing cold; the change in the weather from yesterday was remarkable. He took a deep lungful of fresh, sea air as he strode purposefully down the beach. The waves were high, the backwash could be dangerous to a novice swimmer but Gabriel enjoyed the challenge.

After a restorative swim his body at least felt better but his mind was still troubled thinking of the meeting he was to have with Caroline. He just wanted to satisfy himself all could be amicably resolved. He did not care if she chose to sue him although it was something which had not occurred to him until her father had mentioned it last evening.

After dressing he picked at his breakfast. Lisbet Cotter his housekeeper, a garrulous Geordie who prided herself on her cooking and housekeeping skills had known Gabriel all his life. She came to clear the table.

'You sickenin' for somethin' yer've hardly touched them kippers?' She glared at him.

'I am well – thank you Lisbet.' He wiped his mouth with his napkin.

'Well yer don't look it, yer look like yer bin on a bender!'

Lisbet Cotter was often over familiar but was always forgiven as she was irreplaceable in the kitchen. She was well trained but like all good cooks she was instinctive not needing to weigh ingredients nor look at a receipt.

The cook saw the scowl on her master's face and knew she had overstepped the mark. She found it hard not to trade on the relationship that had grown between them; it had never been a strict household where the servants didn't speak unless spoken to.

Abner and Lisbet had served the family as it prospered in wealth if not in size. Even Lisbet had not been able to get 'caught' though she and Abner had lived as a married couple the whole term of their employment. The household seemed fated to be a small one.

'No doubt you will find out soon enough the reason for my long face when you are about your marketing in the next few days if I know the good folk of Alnmouth, and when you do I dare say you will have an opinion on that too.' He scraped back his chair and with a frown slammed the door behind him.

Lisbet had dished up breakfast for herself, Jax and Abner and rested her heavy body on the settle alongside the scrubbed kitchen table. 'Well, he be in a bad-tempered flunk this mornin'! Nearly bit ma head off and hardly touched his snap.' Abner rubbed his knife on his trouser leg.

'Mr Hodgeson went off scowlin' last night an' all, him just rode off, he do usually stop and pass the time of day. Preoccupied he were.'

'Well master said no doubt A'll be hearing about it when A be about ma shoppin'? Mebbe he's had words with Miss Caroline?'

Just then Gabriel entered the kitchen, he had meant to tell Lisbet to get Abner to bring his horse but she had so irritated him he had forgotten; he saw Abner was still eating. The two servants looked at each other no doubt hoping Gabriel had not overheard their conversation.

'Oh you are still at table, no matter I'll fend for myself with Jax, is he about?'

'Aye master he's in the stable mucking out, A can come right away.' He half rose from his seat.

'No, I'll get Jax to saddle Copper – I will not want

57

dinner Lisbet.' Still frowning he headed out to the stable.

'See, telled yer there's somethin' up.'

'Aye well old woman, we shall find out in the fullness of time if it concerns us an' you should be happy as you got less work to do now he don't want dinner.'

'How you work that one out? I still got to look after the rest of us yer great lummox.'

The gallop across the bay was bracing. Gabriel could be cured of most ills by a swim or a ride but not today. He left his mare with the Hodgeson's groom, the door was opened by a footman Gabriel knew by sight but had for the moment forgotten his name. The footman had not forgotten the visitor's name for as soon as he saw who was at the door he said, 'Ah Mr Reynolds sir, I have a letter for you, please step inside while I get it for you,'

A letter! This was too much!

'Is Miss Caroline at home? I had hoped to see her today.'

'I'm afraid not sir, here you are.' He passed a sealed envelope on a silver platter towards Gabriel who was looking positively sullen now. Gabriel took the letter thanked the footman whose name he suddenly remembered was Ribble and headed for the beach leaving Copper in the stable to pick up later. Once alone amongst the dunes Gabriel broke the seal and read the letter. It began:

Dear Gabriel,

I am sorry you find me absent from home this morning but I have gone to be with my Aunt Kitty in Scarborough for the near future.

Having spoken with father last night I see all has been settled without the need to bother me. My views are not needed! I see the last statement does sound somewhat churlish, but I do not mean it so. I simply mean that your mind is obviously made up and me seeing you this morning will not change it. While you were at Whitby, I too had time to reflect on our future and came to the conclusion you are right! We do not have a shared future together; it is as you say we have grown apart and have become as brother and sister. It is a shame we should part, as we are well matched in station, yet we have grown to be quite different in temperament and aspirations.

Having said that I still have feelings for you and my father assures me you feel the same. If perchance I should end my days as a spinster of this parish I should be glad if you were to be a friend should I have the need.

Gabriel had to smile at this part for he knew Caroline well enough to recognise her irony!

The letter continued:

I have not left today to hide a broken heart. As you suspected at our last meeting, I am not in love with you Gabriel. I do love and esteem you as a true friend and always will. I know and trust you know the difference for you feel the same, I am sure of it. However I have left like a thief in the night for I am sufficiently vain as to bother what my friends and neighbours think of my being jilted. No doubt the shame will pass when I meet a Duke or at least a Sir.

Again Gabriel had to smile; trust Caroline to take it so well. At that moment he felt a deep affection for this lady who he had so callously abandoned but even now he knew he had done the right thing. She had admitted she was no longer in love with him, if ever she was in the first place.

The letter finished with:

I shall of course return anything of value you feel you would rather maintain for any future wife. I will not be suing for Breach of Promise even if it would delight the populace of Alnmouth and the environs enormously. I have asked father to announce the break between us as mutual and hope that meets with your approval.

Until we meet again dearest Gabriel,
Yours with affection
Caroline

Gabriel staring out at the grey sea did not notice the light drizzle that began to fall; slate grey clouds threatened a downpour. His feelings were mixed; he was pleased to be released from his promise with so much ease but at the same time he still felt he had somehow betrayed Caroline or at least let her down. He felt it should have caused him more trouble. He was fundamentally a man of principle and liked to think when he made a decision he stuck to it, but the decision to marry Caroline was one that was made when he was so young and he had been much guided by his father who had wanted the two families to be joined together, as had Caroline's father. He did not want to blame others, ultimately it had been his choice, but he knew he had asked her in some part to please his poor departed parent. He was only glad, as Thomas had intimated that he was not here to see his wish would not now be fulfilled.

At The Hope and Anchor Gabriel ordered ale. He realised he was suddenly starving and could not think why until he remembered he had left most of his breakfast. He ordered food and found, surprisingly, he had an appetite; he felt a little guilty. He hoped Caroline would feel she did not have to stay away too long. As for himself the great and the good of Alnmouth could say and think what they liked.

5

Sir Percy's invitation to a house party at his country seat could not have come at a better time; Gabriel needed a distraction. The news of his broken engagement had been told around Alnmouth and the gossips were having the time of their lives. Caroline was still at Scarborough waiting for the whisperings to stop while Gabriel had become very popular with mothers who had daughters of a marriageable age. Lisbet, at first sympathetic, was now having her patience sorely tried.

'Is every mother with an unmarried daughter "just passin"? Someone it seems is calling every day – I got enough to do without forever baking and brewing tea!' she complained. 'I'd like to see yer wed but A don't see A have to broker the deal maself with my cooking and cleaning.

'They are not here by my invitation; learn to turn them away – say I am not at home then both of us will be happy,' he turned his attention back to his broadsheet.

Mrs Dobson and her particularly plain daughter had just left leaving both himself and Lisbet ill-tempered. The invitation to Dunstanburgh gave him the excuse he needed to escape from the bothersome mothers and their unmarried offspring. When he wanted a wife he would find one for himself without the need of introductions.

Ordinarily, Gabriel would have looked forward to the cliff top ride but his mood was spoiling the day, to add to this it was threatening rain. The wind was whipping up, the fret obscuring the sea views and the magnificent ruined castle which stood proudly overlooking Craster and the North Sea; he would be lucky to arrive without a drenching. The weather brought his mood lower still as he trudged along, mulling over the situation now his engagement to Caroline was broken. Bendor he knew was happy with his marriage and Gabriel wanted the same for himself. Mothers and their daughters were not the only thing driving him from home; loneliness was.

♥

Sir Bendor Percy was a very distant cousin of the Earl of Northumberland, so far distant they had nothing to do with each other but the name was an old one and opened doors. This was useful when he inherited the family seat of Dunstanburgh at just eighteen. He had been guided in running the estate initially by an older cousin while he finished his time at Cambridge.

Bendor, fair haired and slim of build, had recently married into a family which had breeding and connections but were the kind of nobility whose forebears had squandered their money on gambling and unwise investments so when Grace came to the marriage she had very little in the way of dowry. As Bendor's large estate was prospering this was of no matter to him as he was marrying primarily for love; a rare thing in these times.

Grace had two, as yet unwed, sisters both of marriageable age. Cora at twenty three was the eldest and Jane the youngest. Their mother, Lady Beadnell, was keen to engage her daughters to the likes of Bendor as soon as possible, especially Cora, after all a woman had a shelf life and Cora at the advanced age of three and twenty, was about to "go off".

So it was that unbeknown to Gabriel, before he had set foot in the door, he was a target for one or other of the sister's hands. When Grace had heard the news of Gabriel's broken engagement she was delighted. She was not, it has to be said hard hearted, far from it, but she had never cared much for Caroline. She knew as the two men were such friends she would have been thrown into company with Caroline all too often and now it would not be the case.

This turn of events provided an opportunity whereby one of her sisters could be joined with a handsome, well off man of whom she thoroughly approved; if only Cora or Jane could catch him they would be as happy with their lot as she was with hers.

By the time Gabriel arrived there was an almighty storm raging; he was soaked. Bendor, having just changed, was about to come down the sweeping staircase when he met his oldest friend dripping wet on the landing.

'Dear God, did you swim here for if you tell me otherwise I shan't believe it.' They both laughed as they shook hands and Bendor, ever the more demonstrative of the two, pulled Gabriel towards him to hug him and slap him on the back.

'Have a care Ben you'll be as damp as me! Watch out for your fine velvet or you'll have to change again.' Bendor followed Gabriel to his usual rooms; he stayed so often he always had the same suite. As they talked, Gabriel peeled off his sodden clothes, since school they had always shared this easy intimacy and camaraderie. Bendor poured brandy for them both and after a brief but sobering talk of the break up with Caroline, Bendor sought to change the melancholic mood.

'Well my friend I warn you now you are not to remain a single man for very long if my scheming wife and mother-in-law have anything to do with it. They have lined up not one, but two ladies for you to choose from.'

Gabriel groaned and told of the stream of unwed daughters he had left behind. 'Please no! I'm of a mind to stay a bachelor all my life or until I get old and infirm and need a wife as a companion to look after me in my dotage.' He frowned at Bendor who threw his head back laughing.

'Man alive, as if the weather weren't bad enough you have brought more gloom with you.'

Gabriel, now changed from his wet things, peered into the looking glass to tie his still wet hair into a queue; he had the good grace to laugh at himself.

'Well lead the lamb to the slaughter my friend though I promise you love affairs are the furthest thing from my thoughts right now, but wine from your excellent cellar, along with your company and I will soon be cheered.' Bendor landed Gabriel a hearty punch on the shoulder as the two men went down to dinner.

The house party consisted of twenty five of the

best of society from around the East coast, there was a hum of chatter as the guests mingled. As they entered the drawing room Gabriel remembered the first time he had ever seen this room with its fine furniture and large ancestral paintings; he had been overawed with the size and splendour. He had not felt out of place for long. Bendor's family were warm and welcoming and made him feel comfortable from the outset. He had been twelve at the time and the two boys had just begun their long friendship.

'Come and see Mama, she keeps well and has been looking forward to the party,' said Bendor.

His mother sat on a sofa of pale gold velvet, and was flanked on one side by Bendor's mother-in-law and on the other by Jane, Grace's younger sister.

'Ah there you are my boy,' Bendor's mother smiled warmly at Gabriel and offered up her hand to be kissed. 'What a terrible journey you must have endured I should hate to ride in the thunder and lightning! You remember Lady Beadnell and her pretty daughter Jane?' Bendor's mother smiled up at Gabriel in all innocence. No one would have guessed she was aware of her daughter-in-law's plans. Just as a conversation was about to start up, a set of four people came bustling in the room laughing and apologising for their late arrival and making a distinct show and clamour.

It appeared a tree had come down in the storm and barred their carriage by Embleton and they had had to make a detour. Gabriel looked on; he did not know the party which was unusual as he knew most of the local gentry. One of the men was dressed in a sea captain's uniform. With him were two other men and a striking woman of about five and thirty whom he did not know either. Gabriel saw Bendor's mother look down her nose and make an aside to Lady Beadnell.

'Now Gabriel shall you be shooting tomorrow or like Bendor, do you still avoid it at all costs?' She already knew the answer to this question.

'I am sure Bendor and I will find some other pastime to amuse us while the others go tramping the moorland in search of some poor, dumb creatures to blast out of the sky.'

Bendor's mother laughed and looking to Jane said, 'Have you ever heard such sensibilities in young men today? And his father's fortune built on harpooning larger, poor dumb creatures out of the sea.' Gabriel knew she enjoyed teasing both of them and did so without malice knowing they would prefer to row on the lake, or if the weather was poor, head for the library and their books. Just then the dinner gong sounded. Gabriel offered his hand to take Jane in to dinner as he knew he was expected to do.

Gabriel was seated next to old Squire Sadler to his right and Cora, Grace's older sister to his left. Jane was across from him, he was hemmed in. When they were served the first course, Cora turned to Gabriel, 'So do you favour a spring wedding or do you prefer the autumn?' Gabriel, taken aback, looked puzzled. Perhaps she had forgotten his marriage to Caroline was off? He raised his eyebrows but before he could reply she continued. 'Well I should think my family are planning for autumn so you do not have time to change your mind again, your last engagement gave you far too much time to reconsider. We obviously are not to be consulted in the matter, we just need to turn up and say our vows then everyone will be happy!' She delivered this last statement with a sarcastic smile. Gabriel had met Cora several times since Bendor's wedding and remembered her ready wit and sense of fun – he played along.

'Why not truly scandalise them and elope tonight in this storm. How romantic would that be?'

'Not at all! We would most probably drown before the honeymoon,' she said ironically. Gabriel, amused, rolled his eyes.

Cora was easy company; Gabriel had simply to nod and agree occasionally as she filled him in on all the local gossip and made critiques of all the dresses the ladies were wearing. She could be brutal in her judgements but Gabriel couldn't help but smile as so often her comments about "that neckline" or "that dress colour" were often very near the mark in his opinion too.

As the soup plates were cleared the sound of laughter was heard coming from further down the table. It was the late arrivals who now seemed to be enjoying themselves excessively, the captain and the lady looked a little flushed and heads turned to them.

'Ah I have saved the best until last,' Cora said tilting her head towards the couple, 'the scandalous Lady Isabelle.'

'I am afraid I don't know either of them,' Gabriel said looking at the sea captain more closely.

'You don't mix in the same circles my dear,' she answered. 'She is a widow, very rich now her husband has met his end in some accident on their estate, a shooting accident I think. She is also a Percy; the Duke of Northumberland is a cousin's cousin or some such, nearer related than Bendor anyhow. Since she shed her widow's weeds, or some might say before, she has been out and about with the Captain in a very forthright way. They are the talk of the county!' Cora arched her eyebrows, but it was clear she was thrilled with the scandal. She loved to gossip, 'He is engaged to be married to some ship owner's daughter from Scarborough I think, or is it Whitby? I think he has hooked a bigger fish now; they are not exactly being discreet as you can see, one wonders by being so obvious whether perhaps he wants to be found out?'

'Not very gentlemanly behaviour by any means, his fiancée will be well rid of him in that case.'

'Gabriel you are so chivalrous, if he trifled with me would you fight him in a duel?' He knew she enjoyed teasing him; she hid a grin behind her fan.

'As I am quite sure you can fight your own battles and as we are not yet betrothed, I think not.'

The ladies made to leave the gentlemen to their port. As she stood, Cora said in an aside 'I shall tell Mama we have decided on spring for our nuptials then shall I? I always look my best in spring sunshine.' She smiled leaving Gabriel to ponder his fate.

The gentlemen regrouped to gather at the head of the table as they began to light cigars and pass the port. The notorious Captain Seamer was now seated across from Gabriel; he introduced himself. He found the Captain was from Whitby and so for some moments the talk turned to their respective connections there. 'You are in shipping eh, a precarious business these days. My family are ship builders, I captain one of my father's whalers – we arm our ships nowadays.'

'I have recently commissioned a new ship to be built in Whitby; I am expanding my fleet.'

'Good choice, which yard are you using?'

Before Gabriel could reply they were interrupted by Bendor who came to sit next to Gabriel with a decanter of crusted port in his hand. Captain Seamer regaled them with the story of the broken axle on his carriage which had made him late in arriving. He apologised to Bendor for their lateness.

The man had a certain charm about him but Gabriel could not help but think the man's eyes were too close together. He seemed watchful as though he was sizing up the company; Gabriel thought him full of himself and not a little arrogant.

'We should have set off earlier if truth be told but you know what women are like. Bella takes an age to pack, always does. You would think we were coming for a month,' the captain said.

Gabriel, now that Cora had enlightened him to the relationship thought he talked in a very familiar fashion about the lady who was not even his betrothed. The conversation petered out as one of the captain's friends joined them.

Gabriel turned to Bendor. 'Your sister-in-law is certainly good company, forthright, but amusing if you are not the one on the sharp end of her tongue. I now know everything that has happened to every person of note in the county over the last six months! I also know what is in fashion and who should never be seen in green!'

Bendor laughed and leaned in conspiratorially, 'There is one thing dear Cora, bless her, isn't aware of yet… Grace is with child again.' Gabriel was genuinely pleased; he knew they had suffered a miscarriage last year which had rocked them both.

'Congratulations Ben that is news worth celebrating.' They raised their glasses.

'It is not common knowledge yet but I wanted you to know. I am supposed to want a son and heir I know, but I would be surely pleased with a miniature model of Grace,' he said suddenly looking bashful.

'Whatever you have I am sure it will be very welcome; is Grace well?'

She is and following doctor's orders I'm pleased to say – after what happened last time – Bendor broke off and collected himself.

'She is enjoying herself now she can eat for two, you know Grace's appetite!' Grace, small and pleasantly plump was renowned for her liking of all things sweet.

'I am sure all will be well this time, you are a lucky man.'

The men rejoined the ladies and Bendor led Gabriel towards Cora and Grace who were seated by an open window, the evening breeze wafting in making it pleasantly cool now the storm had blown itself out. For a while the four chatted amiably with Grace promoting her sister's virtues shamelessly until Bendor and his wife moved off to make a set at cards leaving Cora and

Gabriel alone.

'My sister is not subtle as you can bear witness!' she tilted her head and her bright eyes danced with mischief, 'She would sing my praises to any man who is not feeble and drooling, please excuse her she is shameless in her promotion of me but she means well.'

'She has much to preen about; you are an attractive woman Cora, any man would be proud to get you. I sometimes wish I had siblings to look out for me but alas it was not to be, Bendor is the nearest I have to a brother.'

'Ah thank you kind sir but don't think he doesn't have your best intentions at heart, that is why he warned you earlier that you were to be a target for Jane or myself. At least you get a choice; pretty petite Jane with her blond hair and blue eyes or tawny eyed, tow haired rather too tall me!' Gabriel smiled and refused to be drawn.

'How do you know he warned me?'

'I'm a witch of course or you could call me perceptive!'

Cora was amusing, clever and eye-catching in her own way and Gabriel wished he could oblige everyone by joining with her but he could not. He did not feel an attraction to her, or her prettier sister Jane, for that matter.

Cora was a perfectly good woman and he knew there would not be a dull moment for any man who chose her for his bride, but whatever the spark of attraction that made someone fall in love with another, was not there for him. He knew he would be happier with a wife who depended upon him, someone of whom he could take care. Cora was far too strident; he would never have a minute's piece.

He did not fool himself Cora was in love with him either. Once when they had been in earnest conversation about a year ago, Cora had hinted to being in love with someone who was out of her reach as he was a happily married man. She would not say who the man was but Gabriel, in a rare moment of perception, thought the man she spoke of was Bendor. He had felt pity for her in any case, regardless of who the man was, and knew then Cora would not be content with, or without, a husband for she could never have her heart's desire.

'Now the lady in blue who has just come in the room is a new addition to the county,' she interrupted his musings. Gabriel saw a tall shapely lady dressed in the very latest style. She was strong featured and attractive and had a presence about her that turned heads as she entered even though she was not the most beautiful woman at the party.

'Her husband is possibly double her age and does not get about as much as she: I hear she gets about a lot,' she arched an eyebrow, 'with a different escort each time,' she added. Cora attempted to look outraged but could not quite pass it off. 'She has a son I believe, so she's fulfilled her end of the bargain. They have removed from Scotland and are living at Rothbury.'

'She is striking – is most of the county in entanglements with the other half?' Before Cora could answer the lady approached them and Gabriel was introduced.

'Is your husband not attending the party Lady Berwick?' Cora asked innocently.

'He had intended to but he has the gout, he suffers greatly with the condition. It is in his leg and so has to miss this gathering I am afraid,' she said looking candidly at Gabriel. 'Your name seems familiar to me sir, I have heard it spoken of recently have I not? Yet I cannot remember in what context.'

Gabriel had no doubt it was in relation to his recent broken engagement but was not about to avail Lady Berwick of this.

'Should you be so kind as to take a turn in the garden with me Mr Reynolds? It is monstrous hot in here I think.' Cora gave Gabriel a look they both understood and taking Lady Berwick's arm he led her out into the cool of the evening.

'It is nice to meet new people, I have been enchanted with the company hereabouts since my husband and I moved to England. There are some very handsome men in these parts,' she looked at Gabriel unashamedly. Her dress had been chosen to draw attention to her best feature. Gabriel liked his women curvy, her gown was very revealing.

'You have been living in Scotland?' Gabriel asked as he looked about him.

'Yes but besides the hunting, the society is very dour, as is the weather. I understand you are very friendly with Sir Percy; we are distant relatives though I have never met him and his charming wife until now. Do you visit often being so close by?' Lady Berwick seemed to know more about him, than he did of her.

'Yes I have been coming here since Bendor and I were children we were at school together and have remained friends ever since.'

'So are you staying in the house, I understand the

74

shooting is good here?'

'I always stay when I can; neither Bendor nor I shoot or hunt. We have never taken to it.'

'That is a shame for I imagine you look well on a horse. What sport do you favour if not hunting and shooting? I only know one other pastime that could entertain you.' She fluttered her fan. Gabriel was not to be drawn, he deliberately misunderstood her meaning. 'I do not favour cards either but Bendor does, he seems to lose more than he wins from what I can see. We both rowed at school and often take a boat out when we can.'

She tapped his arm playfully with her fan. 'Yes rowing is good for building up the muscles I'll wager.'

Gabriel tried to steer the lady back towards the house as they were approaching a quieter part of the garden where the torch lights did not quite reach. He had no interest in this woman and would prefer to return to the party, he was no prude but she was too obvious in her intentions. He enjoyed a flirtation as well as any other man but she held no appeal for him.

Lady Berwick stopped and looked up at Gabriel in what she imagined to be a beguiling way.

'I think I remember where I heard your name. You have recently jilted your fiancée have you not; perhaps you need comforting?' She did not wait for a response. 'You know the house very well if you have been coming here since boyhood, which cannot be so long ago.' She fluttered her eyelashes. 'You will no doubt know the east wing? I am in the room which is the third door on the left. So there can be no mistake I shall tie a red ribbon to my door handle.' She smiled and without further conversation swept up the steps into the house leaving Gabriel strangely irritated. She had taken it for granted he was going to accept her blatant invitation and she had not even waited for a reply.

The band was tuning up, the sound drifting out onto the terrace, soon the dancing would begin. He went in and attached himself to Bendor's party.

Mrs Plait and her three unmarried daughters were of the group. He turned his brooding gaze from one to the other. The eldest was pretty in a simpering sort of way but the other two, though they had good complexions, were mousy and dull.

Gabriel wished himself away from them and looked about for Cora, at least she was entertaining. He hated to dance but felt the obligation to choose one or other of the three Plait girls. He felt duty bound with so few men and so many young ladies. He turned to the youngest, Julia, thinking she looked a little overwhelmed by the society. He told himself to buck up and to forget the odious Lady Berwick's presumption. He did not intend to be a notch on her bedpost so why let her sour his mood?

'May I have the pleasure of the next dance?' If he had to dance he thought to choose the one who might appreciate it most. Julia blushed crimson. 'Thank you sir, if mama will allow it.'

'I shall look forward to it.' He bowed and moved off to where Cora was talking with Captain Seamer. 'You have escaped Lady Berwick's clutches?' she whispered. 'Perhaps you shall accompany her on the dance floor and we shall admire you both?'

'I am promised to Miss Julia Plait for the next two,'

he said.

'The youngest mouse; how thoughtful of you.'

'Her mother looks daggers at me for not engaging the eldest.'

'Ah yes, the trials of the unmarried eldest daughter I know only too well the burden we are to our nearest and dearest.'

Gabriel who had not thought to inflict pain on Cora was sorry for his tactless remark. He had spoken thoughtlessly and was embarrassed. 'Or perhaps you are not so considerate after all and are simply putting the cat amongst the pigeons for sport?' Cora laughed, clearly no offence had been taken.

She turned to speak to Lady Isabella, Captain Seamer looked to Gabriel. 'There are some very pretty ladies in these parts, you are a lucky man – are you married Reynolds? Not that marriage precludes a little side bet eh? I noticed the lady you escorted just now – I would wager she stays the course if you get my meaning.' He smirked at Gabriel.

'I am not married and if you will excuse me I am engaged to dance.'

Gabriel moved away to lead Julia out to the dance floor. He noticed Captain Seamer saunter over to Lady Berwick and they too joined the set. Gabriel seeing Miss Plait was a little timid at first, tried to put her at her ease. He found the mouse, as Cora had called her, had hidden qualities.

'You dance well Miss Plait,'

'Thank you sir, it is one of my favourite pastimes, but alas I seldom get the chance to practice.'

'In that case I am glad we shall dance the Gavotte together too if it will give you pleasure.'

When he took her into supper later he found her to be intelligent and more confident than he had first imagined. She also smelt pleasant, which to him was always welcome. Looks, he thought, can often be deceiving. The mother continued to simper to his face, he could see where the eldest had learnt the trait, but he was certain she was annoyed with him for passing over the older daughters.

After supper Lady Berwick joined their party and the contrast between the plain Plait girls and the flamboyant lady was striking. Gabriel made ready to dance the Gavotte with Julia. As Lady Berwick moved to approach him; he nodded and smiled as he passed her by leading Julia onto the floor ready to begin.

The snub had been noted by Julia's mother. She suspected her daughter was being used as a decoy to put the rest of the party off the scent; 'I have heard the rumours about the Lady's affairs; she is notorious,' Mrs Plait said to her eldest, a look of disdain on her face, 'and he's broken his engagement with Miss Hodgeson! You should be glad he has passed you over.' The eldest daughter was not of the same opinion. 'I hope Julia will not be too upset to find the eligible gentleman has no interest in her.'

♥

The next morning the breakfast room was mainly filled with those who were to hunt. Grace, as hostess, was in evidence as was her sister Cora. Gabriel sat opposite them, Cora had a look on her face which meant Gabriel was in for a grilling.

'What happened to you last night Gabriel? It appeared you had been hooked by a very determined looking lady.'

Gabriel helped himself to eggs. 'Looks can be deceptive,' he threw back distractedly. He knew she was just having sport with him. He saw the two sisters exchange a glance; Cora was not to be deterred.

'I suspect the little mouse was used to put us off course, the real object made herself very clear. So tell me, for I know this sort of thing goes on all the time, how does one know which room to go to for a liaison? The rooms are not numbered and the corridors dark. Or do you have an assignation and are taken to the lady's room directly?'

Gabriel looked at Cora and was about to shoot her down when she winked at him and smiled. 'I only ask in case I get an offer and the man gets lost and ends up with my maid in error.' Gabriel sighed but relented. He liked to banter with Cora even though he would have preferred to eat his breakfast in peace.

'I was not late to bed as it happens, I went alone. After accompanying Julia Plait I had done enough dancing, as you know I am not a fan. On your second point I understand some ladies tie a coloured ribbon onto their door handle and wait for their nocturnal visitor that is the protocol I think.'

Grace looked indignant. 'My house is used as a brothel! Am I not a Madam then?' Bendor, looking like he needed reviving, appeared just in time to hear this last comment from his wife. 'Are you in need of an income my dear, I was unaware you were short of funds. What on earth are you talking about?'

Grace explained. Bendor said, 'Before I was a happily married man I favoured the assignation approach myself, for one coloured ribbon looks much the same to me as another in the dark. I remember once –'

'Thank you husband I think we have heard quite enough.' Grace was the kind of wife who was tolerant of her husband's past indiscretions but did not wish to have her nose rubbed in them over breakfast.

'So are you to marry the mouse or do you favour a liaison with the more experienced lady?' Cora said.

'Cora why are you so concerned for my well being may I ask?'

Bendor reached for the beef. 'A man cannot be happy all his life, it is his duty to put an end to his frivolous ways and get married and be miserable like the rest of us.' Bendor directed this statement to his wife with a cheeky grin.

'I just wish everyone would allow me to sort my own affairs as I see fit,' Gabriel was in danger of becoming tetchy.

'Ha yes! "Affairs" being the operative word,' Gabriel watched as the guests including Cora rose to ready themselves to hunt. Bendor went to make sure the arrangements ran smoothly.

Gabriel and Grace were left alone. 'Congratulations Grace, Ben has told me your good news.'

Grace smiled, her dimples making an appearance. 'We are so happy, Ben is all for wrapping me in cotton wool – you can imagine!'

'I can. After what happened last time you both must

be a little anxious but as Ben always says worrying will not change anything.'

'I feel well, last time I did not, I am sure all will go according to plan.' She sipped her coffee then changed the subject. 'Do you need my commiserations; your engagement is definitely off?'

'It is – I am afraid we have drifted apart, not just that if I am honest we have different ideas about things, different values I suppose. We have grown up and apart.'

'Oh, different in what respect?'

'Family matters mainly; I always thought all women wanted children but it seems Caro does not.'

'They are hard to avoid if one marries.' Grace puckered her brows.

'She said she realised I would require a son and heir but that once she had done her "duty" then she hoped the wet nurse would be better acquainted with the child than her. She is not maternal it seems.'

Oh dear. I can see how you are incompatible; I know you have always wanted children.'

'I have and the thought of an only child goes against the grain. I am an only child, I was happy but I think the more the merrier – as I said I always thought most women wanted children.'

'Do most men? I think you are the exception to the rule, most men like the "idea" of a son and heir but once the "getting" is done they prefer gaming, killing things and drinking do they not?' Grace helped herself to another slice of ham.

'Bendor will be a good father; he even fancies a baby version of you he told me.' Grace laughed. 'I bet he will love the playing but none of the chastising, he will leave the rearing to me as most men do.'

'My father did the rearing after my mother died, sadly he had no choice. Actually he did, I could have had a nanny but he did as much as he could, with Lisbet's help, when he wasn't building his empire. He was a kind father, a good man.'

'You are a chip off the old block as they say.' Grace squeezed his arm.

'I just want a happy wife and a houseful of noisy brats about the place.'

'There is still plenty of time,' she smiled wickedly at him, 'my sister Jane has child bearing hips and loves children, you could do worse.'

'I would be flattered-'

'I am in jest Gabriel! Seriously I hope you meet someone to be happy with as Ben and I are happy. You deserve a good woman's love, I am sure they will be queuing up now you are unencumbered.'

'Oh believe me they are, or at least their mothers are, I could be bent and crochety...'

'They are not solely after your money, had I not married Bendor you would have made a very respectable second choice, you are an attractive man.'

'Is that supposed to be a compliment?'

Grace giggled. 'It was meant to be; what I was meaning to say is that you are bound to be the top of every guest list now, better dust off those dancing shoes.' Gabriel groaned.

'Tell me what you want in a lady and I will invite a selection to our next soiree for you to meet.'

Gabriel sighed. 'My expectations are the same as most men's I suppose. Children we have already discussed but just someone who feels they can depend on me, someone I can cherish, take care of.' Gabriel suddenly felt embarrassed. He had always been able to talk to Grace – if Bendor was like his brother Grace was like a sister but he had not spoken of his feelings to anyone much before. Grace stood to leave 'I shall make arrangements, I feel it my mission to put you on the road to matrimony again.'

Gabriel laughed: 'I had better look to my liberty then, ladies today seem very capable – could you perhaps find me a compliant wife do you think?'

'I have made a note: biddable and likes babies! What could be simpler?

Bendor found Gabriel in the library; he had a new book he wanted to show his friend.

'Grace is on good form, she looks well.'

'She is – she would be even happier if you married Jane or Cora.' Bendor laughed and handed Gabriel a leather-bound volume.

'She knows my requirements; she has assigned herself the role of matchmaker.'

'Man alive, your days are numbered. Speaking of determined ladies I heard Lady Berwick made a play for you last night – did you take her up on her offer, were you just being discreet at breakfast?'

'I did not – I can see how some might be attracted, experienced woman and all that, but not I – she is very insistent, is that the right word, determined to get what she wants it seemed – she presented me with a fait accompli.' Gabriel lounged on the sofa and crossed his legs. He told Bendor of her tactics in the garden.

Gabriel browsed a book from the shelf nearest to him. 'She has had several conquests I believe since moving to these parts, so her wiles are appreciated more by others than by you, my man. Her husband is very old and not at all pleased as you might expect to have such an agreeable looking wife.'

'Agreeable looking perhaps, but not agreeable by nature I think – she has very little of interest to hold my attention.'

'Gabe so serious! Why not enjoy the sport and know she will have a new amour on the morrow. You are young, free and, the ladies tell me, handsome, not that I can see it myself, but I think I know the reason for your reluctance,' he smiled. 'Does the name Caroline mean anything to you?' Gabriel rubbed his chin and traced the outline of his jaw with his thumb.

'I suppose having just ended one relationship I feel it would be disrespectful to her to start a scandal, you know how gossip travels but in this instance I was not even tempted. However, I have a story of a flame haired Whitby wench you will like to hear I am sure.'

'Tell me, I see your face has brightened up, you have made a conquest?'

'Quite the reverse.' He told his friend about the night at The Fleece. Bendor roared with laughter.

'Do not spare my feelings my good friend!'Gabriel affected to look hurt.

'I am sorry but the thought of you run out on by a gypsy is all together funny, did she not predict this in her palm reading. I take it she slipped away with your coin?'

'That is the strange thing – she did not. She looked scared for her life! It was as if she had seen a ghost or something.'

Bendor chuckled to himself. 'When next you are in Whitby I think you should look out for her, you seem oddly smitten or otherwise why would you mention her? You might have known I would laugh at your misfortune, you know me well enough.'

'Look her up and do what, ask her why she had changed her mind, I have some pride!' Gabriel laughed too; he could now see the funny side.

'You say she was not a beauty yet she seems to have made a lasting impression on you.'

'She was as I say, an attractive woman, not a classic beauty like Caro but very eye catching with the most tremendous titian red hair.'

'She has left her mark, you are waxing lyrical, I never heard the like from you before.'

'For all the good it will do me.'

'My advice is to play the field, have some fun.'

'Perhaps but I do not feel so inclined. I want more than that, I want a companion, a loving relationship with some sweet natured girl who will depend on me as my mother relied on father.'

Bendor smiled: 'Perhaps my scheming wife will come up trumps.' Gabriel thought about what Grace had said about Jane, then quickly dismissed the idea.

'Come on, do not get disheartened, try this brandy and tell me if you can taste whether the duty has been paid on it! Cheer up, who knows you may run into this wench again – you know which inn she frequents if you want to find her.' Bendor let out a bellow of laughter.

'That would get the tongues wagging if you gave up an heiress for a serving wench.' Gabriel was not so amused.

6

Back at Westshore, Gabriel sat at his desk and stared at the sea, it was quiet and glinted grey-blue in the mid afternoon sun. He was trying to understand an agreement and finding it impenetrable; his mind kept wandering to the girl from The Fleece Inn; she held his interest far more than Lady Berwick or this confounded contract. Perhaps it was injured pride which made him remember her? Or could it be that he wanted what Bendor had; a loving wife and children to fill this big empty house, he felt his isolation on his return to Westshore.

Some wench in a tavern was hardly likely to fulfil his needs in that direction he chastised himself. Still she would have been a pleasant distraction; he remembered how it felt to hold her and sighed. He shook himself, he could feel the gloom descending ashe began to sort through other documents which needed his attention. The documents were equally dry and dull; he found himself reading the same part over again.

His stomach began to growl. He looked at the clock; it was past five of the clock, no wonder he was hungry. Why had not Lisbet fetched him his dinner? He rang the bell and began to tidy the papers into piles and stuffed them in a drawer. Time passed and no one came. He then remembered Abner was in the smoke house. Earlier in the day he had been looking for Abner, Lisbet had said he had spotted a shoal of herrings through his spy glass. 'He's gone out to fetch the silver darlings, afore you know it they'll be smoked and on yer plate,' she had told him.

Lisbet would usually answer the bell if Abner was out or busy elsewhere. The kitchen was empty so he went to the stable yard just as a dishevelled Lisbet appeared rubbing her hands on her apron. Before Gabriel could ask about his dinner, she called brusquely across the yard, her Geordie accent in evidence.

'A only have one pair of hands and they've not been doing yer dinner – Abner Boatwright wouldn't sort the lad out! Him too keen to get smokin' them herrings.' Jax appeared by the stable door.

'Man alive! What has happened to you, where is your hair gone?' Jax looked sullen.

'He had lugs! That be where the worst of the varmints be, in his hair, so no hair no crawlies! He's had a close shave but it'll grow back soon enough. You said as he could move into the house soon when he has proven himself trustworthy, A think he's passed the mark but am not having him in the house with a head full of lugs!'

'Well,' laughed Gabriel 'how do you feel about that?'

'Me 'ead's cold but I reckon it's first time A've not itched in years.' He stared at Lisbet as if worried for another attack.

'I meant about moving into the house.'

'I dunno A'm alright sleeping in the hay loft, it's warm

enough.'

'It will not be so in the winter, I will leave the decision to you Lisbet but I will not have a frozen child on my conscience.'

Gabriel remembered a few months ago when the boy had come to work for him. He had asked him if he could read or write. The boy said he could not read but he could write his name.

'Show me,' Gabriel had ordered. The boy had spelled out laboriously "J A X." He stood looking at his handy work. 'Jax!' he had announced proudly. Gabriel did not have the heart to rectify the spelling error so he had been known as Jax ever since.

'Well get to the smoke house and help Abner.'

The boy scurried off holding the rolled up trousers Lisbet said he would grow into. Gabriel followed his cook into the kitchen where she bent over the fire basting the meat, her large bottom almost as wide as the fireplace.

'It'll be ready soon if yer can manage to wait – I'll bring in the brandy to keep yer spirits up.' Gabriel saved her the trouble and picked up the decanter and headed to the dining room; he poured himself a glass. Soon enough Lisbet brought his dinner, a stream of talk entering the room before she did. 'The attic room will be best fer him are yer thinking? A know he says he's happy in the stable but the lads a good un and he would be better inside, A'll sort it.'

Gabriel knew better than to disagree with her and was happy enough to let her order things as she saw fit. Lisbet hurried back into the kitchen where she set three places at the kitchen table for their own dinner. She muttered under her breath as she put fruit, cheese and a tart on a platter to take to Gabriel later.

'He'll be right as rain in that bedroom when A've made it nice fer him, bless him,' she said to herself as she wiped a plate with a clean cloth.

7

Now Gabriel had a new ship on order he was eager to watch its development; he thought to take Walter Kemp up on his offer to view the progress of his ship so when John Barker, the enterprising ship builder and owner of the yard invited Gabriel to a dinner at his home he accepted. Gabriel was keen to call at the shipyard and see how his pride and joy was coming along but it would also be a chance to do some business.

Gabriel was shown into a large elegant drawing room, Mulgrave House did not sport the ancestral portraits and large ancient pieces of heirloom furniture as Bendor's house did, it was more like Westshore, being newly built in a modern style. The other guests were dressed in their finery and were standing in small clusters drinking canary wine.

'Here you are then Mr Reynolds,' his host laughed jovially putting Gabriel at once at ease. His clothes were well cut and if not of the latest style, were far from old fashioned. He was a tall man with a tendency to stoop as many men who had spent a lifetime on cramped ships were prone to do. He was middle aged but still handsome, his sandy hair showed no signs of thinning.

'Did you call at the yard to have a look at her?'

'I did, very impressive. She reminded me of a whale skeleton, she appears huge.'

'My men are the best in Whitby, they are craftsmen with an eye for detail but they are not building ships to sit in bottles to be admired. They are building strength and she, with her flat floor, will be able to carry her cargo with ease. I expect she will be in excess of three hundred tons when finished. Whitby built ships are renowned for their strength and solid construction; at ninety seven feet long and twenty seven feet wide she will be impressive.'

'She certainly looks the part she will put my other two ships to shame.'

John Barker nodded, 'Her round stern and double hull will protect her from ice should you expand into the Baltics like you think to do.'

'I can't wait to see her finished and launched; it will be a special day.' Gabriel looked as excited as a boy on Christmas morning.

'You must have a Boat Blessing for her, just the ticket; she obviously will not be ready for this year's ceremony but quite possibly next year if all goes to plan.' Gabriel looked questioningly at his host.

'Here in Whitby we have a ceremony every year in July where all the new boats and ships are blessed by the church. From cobles to schooners to colliers like yours. It is a carnival atmosphere and all enjoy the spectacle, it is a chance to show off what we do best; build boats! Come let me introduce you to my wife, where is she? Ah there she is by the piano.'

Gabriel followed Mr Barker across the room and was

introduced to a handsome woman in her middle years. Gabriel thought she must have been a stunning woman in her youth; indeed she still was with her coppery hair, pale skin and sparkling blue eyes.

'My husband tells me you are expanding your fleet sir.'

'Yes it is an exciting time for me I intend to extend my horizons and transport further afield.'

'You have chosen the right town to order a ship; Whitby has the best shipbuilders in England and the best reputation for building strong reliable vessels.' John Barker took his wife's arm. There was protectiveness, but no claim of ownership, in the gesture.

'My dear, Mr Reynolds' ship is already under construction there is no need to convince him.' He smiled at her with affection.

They were a handsome couple and Gabriel thought, with a touch of sadness, of his own parents whose married life had been cut short. From the corner of his eye he could see a striking redhead dressed in a fashionable green silk dress. The colour suited her; the shade of green reminded him of something he had seen recently.

She was speaking animatedly to a man in uniform, she was frowning, her jutting jaw showed she was in disagreement with her companion. Her colour was high.

'I see you have spotted my youngest daughter sir, come, let me introduce you, her fiancé looks like he needs rescuing!'

Gabriel followed his host across the drawing room with a growing feeling of unease. Surely he recognised the lady? Daylight began to dawn in his mind.

'My dear, let me introduce you to Mr Reynolds from

Alnmouth.' Gabriel saw the shock sweep across the lady's face; she had been in earnest debate with her fiancée and had not noticed them approach. Her colour, already high, grew more so when she saw him.

'May I present my daughter, Eleanor.' The one curtsied, the other bowed. Gabriel took the outstretched hand and kissed it lightly, keeping his eyes down.

'And this is her fiancé, Captain William Seamer.' For the first time Gabriel looked at the man and recognised him as the late arrival at Bendor's house party.

Gabriel said, 'Sir, we have met before I believe; at Sir Percy's in Dunstanburgh?'

'Ah yes, I remember my carriage was caught in a storm,' he looked Gabriel in the eye then quickly looked to Eleanor as if passing the buck, clearly signalling she should continue the conversation. Gabriel saw her swallow hard, she recovered herself. Her voice was perfectly modulated and calm.

'How does the fine weather suit you sir. Is it not a glorious day for so early in the year?'

'It suits me very well indeed, if I had not been to your father's shipyard this morning I would have sea bathed.' He searched her face for signs of recognition.

A young, good looking man approached. 'Here is my son Tomas come to join us!' As they were introduced Gabriel noticed Eleanor twist the stem of her wine glass.

'We met this morning father at the yard – we had a very interesting talk about the fittings, Mr Reynolds has some innovating ideas of his own he is keen for us to implement. I think they will be improvements on the original plans but simple to implement.' For a while they discussed the ideas and Gabriel avoided looking in Eleanor's direction. Then there was lull in the conversation.

'It is a little warm in here I think I shall go out to the terrace to see if I can catch a breeze if you will all excuse me?' The captain took her hand and led her away from the group which continued to talk of Gabriel's ship and his new venture.

Gabriel watched her being led away. How could this be? He was certain she was the one he had met at The Fleece, how could he forget her but he could not organise his thoughts to be coherent about the matter. At the unexpected sight of this woman, not now Charity, but Miss Eleanor Reynolds, he was bewildered! How could such a deceit have been practised? She was the daughter of a renowned shipbuilder and a woman of rank and society, it was hard to believe yet he was certain now it was his "Whitby wench" as her flustered countenance had shown.

Since the encounter he had chided himself on the occasions he had thought about her; he was not a school boy but had to admit he felt smitten. It had been a flirtation, an attraction undoubtedly on his part, but nothing that could ever be acted upon again. The way the meeting had played out had somehow added an extra frisson to the encounter. He would have liked to meet her again if only to find out why she had run out on him; now he had and he possibly knew why.

Here she was and engaged to Captain Seamer. He remembered the conversation with Cora about how Seamer was betrothed to a lady from Whitby or Scarborough. Either way she was unavailable to him. It was just as well he thought, what sort of lady carried on as she had done that night at the inn; she and her future husband were well matched it seemed.

In the refreshment room Gabriel was introduced to Obed Coffin, he was the husband of the eldest daughter and clearly from his clothes and manner, a Quaker. He was also in shipping. He was obviously a Friend, yet lax enough to join a family party, although he was drinking lemonade. They talked for some time about the whaling industry that continued to grow but Gabriel felt restive and tried to divert the conversation to the Barker family, he was curious about the younger daughter in particular. He thought to quiz Obed Coffin.

'Your wife is not here today sir.'

'We do not go to parties per se – I view today's event as business, my wife would not enjoy such an event.'

'Do you have children?'

'We have twins, a boy and a girl, they are four years old, we are very blessed. Twins as you see run in the Barker side of the family.' He could see by Gabriel's face he did not understand. 'My brother and sister-in-law are twins. Temperamentally they are very similar, as are our children, although Atalana and I are hoping our two are a little more conservative than their Aunt and Uncle. We intend to lead by example and they will be raised Quakers.'

'I see, are your father and mother-in-law not Quakers?' Gabriel knew little or nothing about Quakers or Methodists, he seldom went to church himself.

'They were Birthright Friends yes, but have been disowned. This is not the Quaker way, this free living.'

He spat the words out contemptuously. 'Abstinence, sobriety and pacifism are Quaker traits that have gone by the wayside here. He no longer attends the Meeting House.' Coffin was as much a zealot as some Methodists Gabriel knew and he disliked those too.

'I see. What of his wife and children?'

'Eleanor and Tomas have, in my opinion, been given far too much latitude in their upbringing. Tomas in particular has some extraordinary ideas about how to conduct business. John is blinded to his faults I fear. Eleanor, too, has a tendency to impulsiveness.'

Gabriel thought this an arrogant speech, after all Gabriel was a stranger; it showed a lack of class in Gabriel's opinion. To criticise one's hosts in such a way led him to think the man's religious beliefs were superficial at the least. Gabriel was still keen to discuss Eleanor and fought the urge to move off. 'Miss Barker is engaged to be married I understand.'

'She is and when she marries she too will be disowned as her choice is an Anglican. So you see the Barkers will no longer be one of the leading Quaker families of Whitby, they shall set no example to our children.' Gabriel was tiring of the man and could see he was to find little else of value about Eleanor from this quarter.

Just then John Barker came to rescue him. 'Let me introduce you to someone who may be a useful contact for you Mr Reynolds.' Before he led him away he said quietly, 'My son-in-law is a devout man, I fear we disappoint him but we must each follow our own path I believe.'

'I agree sir. It cannot have been easy for you in a town

like Whitby where there is a big Quaker community.'

'It was not sir but I saw the need to be able to frequent private parties, dances and even taverns if I were to continue to grow my business. Previous generations of Barkers, being devout, would not have ventured into such places but times have changed I think. The decision to arm one of my ships in total opposition to the Quaker beliefs, after losing a shipment to privateers, was the last straw for The Friends of Whitby.'

'It is a growing nuisance all ship owners face I am afraid.' Gabriel shook his head.

'Although a birthright Friend I was disowned; most Quaker Friends disapproved of my actions but others joined me. Let those who are so devout follow on to America and seek their puritanical life there, I cannot stand by and watch as others profit from my loss,'

'I too sir, have armed my ships for the same reasons, it is out and out piracy, the seas are becoming ever more dangerous.'

Anne Barker, who took an interest in her husband's affairs joined them and agreed. 'We have a family to support but the need for safe passage does not just affect us; the wives, sisters and daughters of our crews need our protection also. If their men are lost what will become of them?'

'I agree entirely, Mrs Barker, it is for the self same reason I took the decision to arm my ships. We would feel the losses naturally but for the crews and their families it would be the poor house or worse.'

'Whitby has grown rich with money from Quaker investments, in times past before whaling, there was little to invest in save a herring fleet, building cobles to supply the fishing industry. The Scoresbys continue to prosper as the predominant Quaker family yet resist arming their whalers against privateers. Each has to act according to his own conscience; mine says I should hate to lose a shipment but would be loathe also to lose my crew, as my wife says they have families that rely upon them.' Seeing he held similar views Gabriel's respect for the shipbuilder and owner grew.

They began to discuss lighter matters at John's insistence, as he rightly reminded himself it was a party after all. Gabriel looked around, his eyes scanning the room for sight of Eleanor.

He saw nothing more of her until dinner when she was seated some way off from him. The food and wine were all of the best quality and ordinarily Gabriel would have savoured the fare more. Yet his mind was still on the daughter of the house. Gabriel happened to be seated next to Eleanor's brother, Tomas, who made a pleasant dinner companion. Like his father he was easy and amiable, and was freely topping up both their wine glasses whenever he saw that they needed replenishing.

'I was speaking with your brother-in-law earlier he tells me he has twins and that you are also a twin. Tell me, is it true what people say that there is a special bond, a sort of thought transference between you and your sister because of your twinship? I have never met twins before.'

'Hells bells!' Tomas laughed loudly. His face was rosy from the alcohol. 'Who knows what Eleanor thinks sometimes? My sister and I are very close and I feel more attached to her I think, than Atalana my older, more sober sister. But then since her marriage Atalana has become much more a Quaker and less a Barker.' He took a sip of his wine. 'We do think along the same lines on most things, Eleanor and I, but how much of that is upbringing and how much psychical communication I have no idea. She once said she knew I was in danger! As she was trying to stop me from having something that she wanted I am not sure that I believed her.'

'She is a very attractive lady, elegant, refined.'

Tomas laughed again and helped himself to more goose. 'She has always said she wished she had been the boy and I the girl! Anyone who knows her could probably guess that, she appears ladylike but she has always liked to rough house. When we were children we were very similar in looks the servants and our governess could not tell us apart as Eleanor used to insist on stealing my clothes; she said they were more comfortable to play in. We would go to the beach or the woods where we would make sandcastles or dens. She envies my freedoms now that she cannot get up a disguise, she says I can go anywhere and do as I please without remark, while she now has limitations set upon her by "society". Yet by any other standards, her being brought up a Quaker, she has had more freedoms than other ladies of her position.'

Gabriel wondered what her brother and father would think of her disguise that night at The Fleece, let alone her intended, what on earth would he think?

'Your father tells me you are learning the business from him as I did from my father.'

'I am, when I am not distracted.' All the Barkers,

Gabriel noticed, had good teeth.

'There is much to distract you in Whitby?'

'There is if you look hard enough,' he said and winked at Gabriel conspiratorially. 'Shipbuilding has provided Whitby with more wealth and prominence than ship owning and our family have risen from being seamen to prominent shipbuilders in two generations; we are still on the rise thanks to father's forward thinking but I am young,' he nudged Gabriel, 'I like to work hard and play hard if you understand my meaning?' His hair was a deeper red than his sister's Gabriel noticed.

'I have met Captain Seamer before, recently he was at a friend's house party, he seems a sociable sort?'

'Very sociable I should say he and Eleanor have been betrothed a long time; she has postponed the date of the wedding twice. Ladies these days! The wedding must be later this year I think.' Gabriel unexpectedly felt his spirits plummet, felt a stab in his chest.

'Will they reside in Whitby?' Why was he asking these questions – the answers were unsettling.

'The captain has had a grand new house built along the cliffs from here, closer to Whitby you understand, so Eleanor shall not have to give up her precious beach. She is inordinately fond of the beach.'

After dinner and the port the men returned to the withdrawing room. Gabriel looked about him but saw no sign of Eleanor. He attached himself to his host's party but made sure to stay at arm's length from Obed Coffin, he was not keen to be preached at again. He heard John Barker enquire of his wife the whereabouts of his younger daughter and was told she had a headache and had asked to be excused.

The afternoon wore on pleasantly and Gabriel was introduced to several gentlemen who could be useful business contacts in the future. He was grateful to Mr Barker for the introductions.

Captain Seamer, who had been in conversation with an attractive dark haired lady, made his way over to Gabriel. 'It is a small world is it not? We meet again.' Gabriel looked at the captain who was a head shorter than himself. 'It is as you say captain.'

'We are both men of the world I daresay,' he looked candidly at Gabriel. 'My future father- in- law is the ship builder you have engaged to build your ship?'

'He is and you are engaged to his daughter I see.'

'I am and have been for an eternity it seems. Young ladies these days are as changeable as the weather, I have been "on a promise" for the longest time. We should be married now if it were not for Eleanor's procrastination. First she postponed our nuptials when she slipped and had a fall – granted a bride does not want to wear bruises on her wedding day but the second delay was pure folly. I never did understand her reasoning.'

'Did you try?'

'Evidently not as I cannot for the life of me remember what the grounds were. All I know is I was forced to entertain myself elsewhere in the meantime.' He raised an eyebrow knowing Gabriel understood his meaning. 'The wedding is now set for September, if the capricious Eleanor does not change her stubborn mind again.'

'She has reason to put off the wedding again?'

'Reason is not in Eleanor's vocabulary.'

'I wonder then that you are still keen to marry the lady.' Gabriel could feel himself becoming riled and wondered why he felt the need to stand up for this wayward woman. They seemed a good match on the surface and would no doubt make each other thoroughly miserable in the fullness of time.

'You know how it is, partly it is a business transaction, a marriage of convenience but Eleanor does have her charms, she will be as sweet as a nut I hope when we eventually tie the knot. She is a good looking filly and judging by her mother she will age like a fine wine.' He laughed as he emptied his glass. 'Seem to remember you are a single man – I can lead you in the direction of some sport if you have a mind, there is a very entertaining Molly House by the harbour?'

'Thank you but as Mr Barker's house guest I think it would be bad manners.'

'Suit yourself.' The captain sauntered off to entertain a group of young ladies.

After supper the card tables were set up and Gabriel played a few hands but his mind was strayed and he lost money. After a suitable interval he retired to the room which had been thoughtfully provided for him by his hosts. He wanted time to think.

He lay on the bed and pondered the situation. His thoughts, he realised, were a little befuddled with the drink he had taken during the evening but still concluded it was an extraordinary state of affairs nonetheless; he was intrigued by the shipbuilder's daughter. He wondered how her family would react to her behaviour if they knew and what of her fiancé? He remembered the fresh faced young girl from The Fleece and contrasted her with the sophisticated young lady he had met earlier. He was aware he was attracted to her from the first but to meet her again like this was extraordinary. Then to find she was soon to be married was almost a cruel twist of fate.

He dozed for a while, the effects of the drink relaxing his body if not his mind, until he realised he was still dressed. He began to undress but then suddenly became wide awake, he stepped over to the window where he could see a bright full moon reflected in the stillness of the sea. He decided on some fresh air to clear his head. He had been inactive all day and his body now felt restless; he headed for the gardens.

He could see his way clearly in the moonlight and headed towards the cliff edge which was bounded by a small copse. This took him to the side of the house where he followed a gravel path. The landscaped gardens were extensive and as he turned the corner he could see a cloaked figure silhouetted against the moon looking out to sea. He did not want to alarm the lady and was about to move off when he saw the figure turn as if she sensed she was being watched. As the lady walked towards him he saw the long, red hair blowing freely in the breeze. At the same moment they recognised each other.

♥

In her room, after her alarming encounter with Gabriel Reynolds, Eleanor paced up and down. Her maid Charity knocked on the door slipped into the room.

'Oh thank goodness it's you! Lock the door. If Mama comes tell her I have taken a draught and am sleeping –

no on second thoughts tell her I have run away to sea. Lord I'm in trouble now!'

Charity had been Eleanor's personal maid for five years and more, the pair were more like friends than mistress and maid; they both knew each other's secrets. Charity's family had been her father's tenants for years. Eleanor knew Charity's family were involved in smuggling, but would never tell. Just as Charity knew of Eleanor's night time escapades to the beach but would keep the secret. If Eleanor's parents knew about either, they turned a blind eye.

Charity looked confused. 'You're not ill, what's the matter, what have you done now?'

'I am in hiding – for all the good it will do me; I am about to be undone.' She told Charity about her predicament.

'Flipping heck! It was only a matter of time before you slipped up, how could you get yourself into this mess? This is bad even by your standards, didn't I tell you about going into Whitby!'

'Thank you for those words of wisdom.' She continued to pace. 'Should I run away now or wait to be sent to a nunnery do you think; Mama will flay the skin off me.'

'Your parents have never laid a finger on you, I doubt they would start now but if this man gives you away I expect you will be locked up until September! Oh lore what if he tells William!'

Eleanor flung herself on the sofa and uttered a bad word she had heard Tomas use. 'What shall I do? I think he knows William, what if he tells him? She answered her own question: 'I will just have to lay low and pray this man keeps quiet, there is nothing else I can do. If he spills the beans I am done for.'

♥

Eleanor recognised Gabriel, even in the moonlight. 'Wait please Mr Reynolds, I need to thank you for not exposing me to my parents, unless of course you have done so since I made my excuses and left the party?'She was fairly certain he had not given her away as she had received no summons from either parent.

'I have not and would not betray you Miss Barker. You have my word I will not speak to your father or your fiancé, it is no business of mine how you choose to behave.' She wondered had he meant to sound so arrogant? Eleanor was relieved but slightly irritated.

'Thank you sir, I am indebted to you, what you must think is—'

'None of my business as I say,' Gabriel interrupted.

'Yes it is true sir I took a very grave risk and miscalculated for sure. I do not need to explain myself to you or anyone, save my parents perhaps, yet I feel you deserve an explanation for your kindness in not exposing me – I could scarce believe it when I saw you.' She pulled her cloak around her to stop it billowing in the breeze.

'I admit certainly I am intrigued to know what the circumstances were which led you to put yourself at risk in such a reckless way. Why someone so fortunate and of your standing, a ship builder's daughter, would put herself in such a position but if it causes you distress to explain, then please be assured I will remain silent on the matter; I will question you no more.' He turned to walk away.

'I am a person in my own right sir, not merely an appendage to a ship builder!' How patronising she thought yet despite herself, Eleanor smiled; she noticed again how handsome he was. He had removed his neck cloth but not his waistcoat – his black breeches were moulded to his thighs; now he looked as he had done the last time she had seen him at the inn. He was a very attractive man.

She told herself she owed him some explanation; Eva was right he did not have to let her go that night, she was grateful to him. How would she have felt had she not escaped? If he had forced her against her will? She knew in the cold light of day she had done the right thing in running out on him but here tonight in the moonlight was a different matter; something deep inside her stirred.

Had she succumbed that night, meeting him now would have left her in a vulnerable position she realised, especially so if he had betrayed her to her parents or her fiancé. She felt doubly beholden to him.

She took a deep breath and told Gabriel about her night time visits to the beach and how she had come to meet Eva Drage in Whitby.

'So you have been absconding into Whitby without a chaperone.' It was a statement she could not deny.

'Men do not understand how frustrating it is to be so restricted in one's movements. If you, or my brother Tomas, wish to go somewhere you go without a second thought, you do not have to think of your reputations and whether it is seemly; can you imagine having to be chaperoned everywhere like a child?'

'I have to admit I cannot, but I think your reasoning flawed. A port such as Whitby is a very rough sort of place at night for a lady. If I, or Tomas, came across a group of drunken sailors we could handle the situation, you could not perhaps.' They began to walk on side by side.

'I get so very bored sometimes, I want to see what is happening beyond these gates, it is a risk worth taking I think.'

She did like the look of this man, he had a twinkle in his eye and she wanted to keep him talking to find out more about his character. He was a good looking man. She recalled the softness of his lips so she decided to open up to him.

'I have a history of reckless behaviour; I started young!'

She saw the puzzled look on his face. 'When I was sixteen I absconded to Holland. I wanted an adventure after Tomas had been allowed to go to France with father. It was deemed "inappropriate" for a mere girl to go so I took matters into my own hands.'

'You absconded to Holland?'

'Amsterdam in fact. I borrowed my brother's clothes from the laundry room to disguise myself as a boy. I even cut off some of my hair in order to push it under a cap to appear more convincing.'

She saw the flash of white teeth as he laughed. 'You should never cut your beautiful hair; it is your best asset.' Was he flirting?

'Thank you for the compliment sir.' She wanted him to like her.

She continued: 'I watched and waited for the right

opportunity and it came when The Swiftsure, a collier, came into port one September. I escaped through the kitchens and headed for Whitby Harbour where I stowed away on the ship which was heading for Amsterdam.'

'I am relieved it was not one of my ships on which you stowed – the conditions on board a collier are not very comfortable and my crew not very gentlemanly.'

'Neither were they on board The Swiftsure but I did not have to suffer them long as it turned out. The ship was part owned by Ingram Eskdale and was captained by a huge, blonde haired Dutch man named Bartel Visser, I had seen him in conversation with my father many times. A day into the journey I was discovered and brought before the Captain, as you may imagine he was not pleased and I was angry my adventure was to come to a premature end.

He recognised me despite my feeble, immature attempt at disguise. But still, he was persuaded to let me stay on board rather than be sent back on a passing fishing boat. He threw the second mate out of his cabin and I enjoyed a slightly more comfortable journey from then on.'

Gabriel and Eleanor began to walk down towards the cliff edge and looked out at the huge moon suspended brilliantly in front of them. Eleanor noted Gabriel listened without comment as she carried on telling him about her adventure

'Once in Amsterdam my parents were informed of my whereabouts; again I persuaded the captain to let me stay in Holland, Captain Visser, a typical liberal minded Dutchman, agreed to let me stay on. I think he secretly admired my enterprise, and assured my father I would be safe and chaperoned during my sojourn by his wife, Abalone.

'An unusual name Abalone, like the shell?'

'Yes, she is an unusual woman, we quickly became friends.'

'So you got your wish and enjoyed your trip.'

'I did. It was agreed I would stay with the Vissers until The Swiftsure returned to Whitby. Abalone became my heroine; she was as blonde as her husband, with fair lashes and ocean blue eyes. But it was her character I admired the most. She was intelligent, educated and, most appealing to me, independent. Abalone was keen to show me her native city and showed me a different, more progressive way of life. The Dutch are to be very much admired for their free thinking and liberal attitudes don't you agree?'

'It is true the Dutch have a different temperament to us, possibly we appear "buttoned up" to them, reserved perhaps. Perhaps it is only in the cities where these attitudes are to be found.' Gabriel said.

'Perhaps you are right I never ventured beyond Amsterdam.'

Eleanor continued: 'Despite being married, Abalone had business concerns of her own as well as a passion for portrait painting. She had some of her work exhibited in a small gallery in Amsterdam and sold some of her work. I was very impressed and even tried my hand at painting, which was a dismal failure for I cannot paint!'

'A lady artist – unusual.'

'She is; we became firm friends during those few weeks. To me, she was very sophisticated and worldly wise, the age difference was just five years but to a young, unworldly girl like me she was very much to be looked up to.'

'She certainly seems to have made an impression on you. I have travelled to Amsterdam – by a more conventional route.' He gave her a sidelong look and smiled. He smiled readily she thought. She was warming to him.

'The Vissers lived in a tall narrow house overlooking a bustling canal. From the front the house appeared to have no land but behind the house, not visible from the canal, was a glorious private garden which gave shade from the late summer sun.' She stopped and laughed. 'I am sorry; I digress. I was just remembering how lovely it was.'

'I agree Amsterdam is a fascinating place. When I first visited there I was sixteen too, I went in the school holidays with an old school friend. I remember the canals, the architecture and the galleries, it is an unusual city.' Sorry I interrupted you were saying?'

'Just that we vowed to stay in touch when the time came for me to return home and we have; we write regularly. She and Bartel are to come to my wedding.'

She thought she saw him frown. 'I would not expect your homecoming was a happy one, how did your parents react? Were they very angry?'

'My homecoming was not, of course, a happy one. When I arrived back in Whitby my parents were keen to have the affair hushed up lest Captain Seamer, who was beginning to show an interest in me, decided the match was not a good one after all. Ingram Eskdale was privy to the adventure as Captain Visser's log had showed me as a stowaway, I was quite proud when I found out! He is a family friend and agreed to protect me for my family's sake. Mama insisted my wings should be clipped before I got into more trouble; secretly I think she admired my daring and enjoyed my trip vicariously!' Eleanor laughed and swept her hair away from her face.

'And you very nearly did get yourself into more trouble only recently; it seems you have a knack of meeting people who somehow manage to help you out of scrapes which otherwise might end with dire consequences.' Gabriel smiled. 'I can scarce believe your tale; do you always speak so freely Miss Barker?'

'Mama says so! She realised by telling all to this man she was leaving herself open to his ridicule or worse. Yet there was something trustworthy about him she felt, she knew very little about him, but the little she did know led her to believe he was honourable, he was also very eye-catching. 'I am sorry, I shall not detain you any longer, I hope you will forgive me for chattering on.'

'Not at all, I find your story – enlightening. He raised an eyebrow ironically. 'Your fiancé knows nothing of your escapades of course.'

She told him about seeing Captain Seamer with a "companion".

'So as a direct result of you seeing your captain in a compromising position, I became a bet, a wager, revenge on your unfaithful fiancé?' She saw the half smile; he looked unsure how to react to all he was hearing.

'Yes if you put it like that but then as you know I could not go through with it, sauce for the goose was not for the gander, well, whatever the saying is!'

'I do not have much experience of young ladies, I am an only child but I feel sure Miss Barker, you are somewhat unusual for a young lady of your station.'

'For a ship builder's daughter! She mocked. 'So my fiancé says! I was not jealous but I was surprised to see him at all, thinking he was still at sea so to see him with a woman of ill repute was very... vexing.'

'Vexing! Not jealous? You are a rare lady indeed!' Eleanor turned towards Gabriel the better to see his face; she wanted to see if he was being sarcastic. She saw that he was and sought to defend herself.

'You have to understand Mr Reynolds the captain and I have been promised to each other since I was seventeen; it is a good match which will bring two prominent families together. My parents did not force me to be engaged, they would never do that yet I did feel obligated somewhat after the Amsterdam trip. I think they hope after I marry I will settle down and be more content.'

'You don't love him? I'm sorry; I overstep the mark that is none of my business.'

Eleanor sighed. 'It is not what one could call a love match but we do get along, he is quite dashing – and a woman of my standing has to marry someone, if she wants children that is – and I most assuredly do. How am I to get them without a husband? William is at sea for half the year so I reason I can be as a single woman for some of the time making my life as I want it, running my business affairs, being independent to some degree.'

'And will you be more content do you think – after you are married?'

'Is anyone? My sister married her husband on slim acquaintance, she sought a Quaker to marry thinking he would provide security. She adores her children but I doubt she is happy; she never appears happy to me, and certainly is not in love.'

Eleanor played with a strand of her hair: 'At this moment I am thinking my betrothal is in jeopardy, I do not want to begin a marriage based on lies, nor can I confess to my behaviour... or tell him I know about his, his... strumpet! I do not know why I am telling you all this? You must be very bored by the travails of a silly, misguided girl?' She stopped and turned back the way they had come.

'I do not think you are silly but perhaps you are a little misguided. You are obviously unhappy, I am glad you feel you can talk to me – possibly it is because I am unknown to you – not family, that you unburden yourself so freely.'

'My mother would certainly agree with you about my free speech – she is forever telling me to think before I speak.'

'I do feel for your predicament, I must admit I have never given it a minute's thought, perhaps if I had sisters it would be different. Your sister married for security you say, are you not doing the same?

'Perhaps, but a different kind of security I think. My sister is the odd one out in our family; she is quiet, reserved and a Quaker through and through. She married a man with the same beliefs and opinions as herself but I doubt she loves him as I said; she certainly did not on her wedding day. Since her marriage we do not share intimacies, all our conversations are about the twins now I come to think of it. She needed to feel she could depend on Obed I think, I only need a husband to make any children legitimate.'

'That sounds very cold and calculating to me. You say your marriage contract is in jeopardy but what has changed if you do not love him? You both have black marks against your names from what you say so why does it matter he takes his pleasure elsewhere; you say you are not the jealous type? As it will be a marriage of convenience so as long as he provides for any children you might have I don't see how anything has altered. I am sorry to poke my nose into your affairs but marriage is a big commitment and perhaps should not be entered into lightly. Do you not deserve to love and be loved in return?'

'You sound like Mama; we have this conversation on a monthly basis it seems. I am a realist Mr Reynolds but you are wrong saying nothing has changed, I may not love William but at least I respected him. Now I see how he uses women for his own ends and goes behind my back; it makes me think I cannot admire him after all.'

Gabriel stifled a haughty laugh: 'Yet you yourself were about to take advantage of me and charge me a high price into the bargain!'

'That was different as I said, I was-'

Gabriel let out a cry: 'Ah! What were you saying about geese and ganders!' They began to walk back through the trees; they walked on in silence for a while. Eleanor could not decide whether to be upset by his remark or angry at his condescending tone, perhaps he was just the same as all men only better looking. She thought to make some pert remark but she kept silent, after all she was extremely grateful to him for not telling her parents about her behaviour but perhaps on reflection she had spoken too freely – again.

While they had been walking the sky had begun to lighten but it was darker under the branches of the elms. Before they left the copse she stopped and turned to face him though neither could see the other's expression clearly she thought.

'You have given me food for thought. Thank you Mr Reynolds for being a gentleman and for listening, I expect you think me a spoilt brat with nothing to complain of, I know there are many with worse problems than I have.'

'Can I just ask one more thing which has been bothering me all through your speech, though of course if you would rather not say—?'

'Tell me what you wish to know.'

'Thinking of the night at The Fleece, did you not see the danger of going to a private room with a stranger? Some men would not have let you leave as easily as I did, you could have been taken against your will or...'

'I know. I realised once we were in your room but I am by nature strong willed and impulsive, hot headed sometimes. Thankfully I chose you as my seducer and you proved to be my saviour. I have not been into Whitby alone at night since, nor will I ever do so again, I have learnt my lesson. Still, I cannot promise I might not be tempted to some other escapade!' Gabriel threw his head back and laughed.

'So gentlemen visitors to Whitby are not completely safe yet then! Shall you get out a crystal ball in the market square and predict fortunes; will you perhaps see your own fate?'

'I have already told you what to expect when I read your palm, my own palm does not feature you I think.' She flounced away back the way they had come. She was a little annoyed now, no doubt he was enjoying holding all the cards.

'You must have felt some regard for me – after all you were about to—' he threw the remark at her retreating back as she stalked off.

Over her shoulder she said; 'I must go in Mr Reynolds or I really will be indisposed if I stay out in this chilly night air much longer.' She saw him hurry to catch her up.

'I will return by the kitchen again; it is still dark enough that no one will see me.'

'Let me walk you back.' He stepped to her side and took her arm; it felt good to be close to him though she was still a little irritated by his last comment. When they could see the light from the kitchen they stood in the shadows. Eleanor reached to touch Gabriel's arm and standing on her toes kissed him lightly on the cheek, 'Thank you Mr Reynolds, I am obliged to you.' Before he could respond she disappeared into the light of the kitchen leaving him alone in the dark.

♥

After breaking her fast Eleanor set off to take her dog, Slate for a morning walk. The dog had been a gift from her father for her eighteenth birthday. She was a grey whippet, fine boned and elegant. When Eleanor had first seen Slate she was a little disappointed, she would have preferred a terrier of some sort but she had come to love the dog dearly. As the puppy had grown, Eleanor saw in her a tenacity and strength she had not expected from a dog that looked so delicate. Slate could keep up the chase when Eleanor rode out; she was hardy and was as fast as a bolt. At full speed she had a grace and elegance glorious to behold. She was also quite a character. She could be loveable but also could curl her lip and snarl if she felt like it; Eleanor and her dog had a lot in common.

After walking along the beach from Sandsend to Whitby, they followed the path that led to the harbour. It was a warm, sunlit morning and Eleanor felt the pleasant breeze as they reached the quay. The fish wives were busy sorting and gutting the herring that had been brought ashore earlier, the fish made Slate's nose twitch.

They wandered around the harbour looking at which ships were in port. As they approached a collier docked by one of her father's ships, Eleanor saw a rough coated black terrier worrying a piece of tethering rope. As it bowed its head, the dog caught sight of Slate, left off its game and ran snarling and with hackles raised lunging towards the whippet. Slate sprang forward to see off the cur and a small skirmish ensued before a deep, resonant voice from behind Eleanor called: 'Leave it.' The terrier left off and hurried towards the voice, its stumpy tail wagging furiously. Eleanor turned to see Gabriel Reynolds being accosted by a very excited, writhing, bundle of fur which then began to jump four feet into the air like a jack in a box!

'Calm down boy, down,' Gabriel said laughing at the

antics and roughly rubbed the dog's head to try and keep him still.

'My goodness what a welcome, you know this beast?'

'I do this is Scrabble resident ratter on board my ship here,' he said as he nodded his head in the direction of the ship.

'The Jack and Alice?'

'Yes my father named her after himself and my mother,'

'Does your father still take an active role in the business Mr Reynolds?'

'He did until his death last year.'

'Oh, my condolences sir, I am sad to hear that. Does your mother live?'

'She died when I was seven, in childbirth trying to deliver my brother.'

'Dear me, I'm doubly sorry. I remember you said last night you do not have siblings.'

'At my father's death I became the last in the Reynolds' line.'

'You will no doubt feel the pressure to populate Alnmouth with your prodigy then I expect!' Eleanor had the decency to blush. She had realised as soon as the words left her lips that this outspoken outburst was inappropriate; she was glad her Mama was not here.

'I am fast realising Miss Reynolds, that what other young ladies think you have no problem saying. You are unguarded in your speech; I wonder your fiancé lets you out of his sight.'

Eleanor huffed: 'I suppose you would have me thrashed, when all I do is say what others think. I am sorry but I have an inquisitive nature, if you do not ask

119

you will never find out is my motto.'

To her surprise Gabriel laughed. 'For the record I would not dream of thrashing a lady; I find there are better ways of securing a lady's regard.' Against her better judgement Eleanor smiled; she wondered what those ways might be. She would like to find out how this good looking man got his own way.

'Working on your principles Miss Barker please will you answer me a question if you will – are you at the harbour scouting for another poor soul to tell his fortune? I seem to remember you were intent on me marrying a lady who resides in Whitby.' She knew he was teasing her.

'What has that to do with anything? I am not sir, for I see that despite what you said about not being married my father tells me you are as good as; are you not engaged to a lady from your home town? Do all men lie? It is fast becoming clear to me that they do; my fiancé, my brother – you.'

'I did not lie, I am unmarried and besides I would hardly tell a serving wench my life history.'

'Yet you did not mention it in our conversation last night.'

'As I remember it Miss barker, we were discussing you were we not?'

Eleanor made a face. Slate began to prance from one foot to the other; the whippet was impatient to be off. Scrabble took this as a sign to walk in a circle on his hind legs in a very comical way. They both watched the trick laughing at his attention seeking behaviour; it helped to disperse the tension which had started to mount.

'Away with you, show off!' His owner laughed. 'Get on board you fleabag.' Scrabble ran up the gang plank and dropped to the floor, head on paws, waiting patiently for his master to follow.

'Do you not think it strange we met again yesterday and in such different circumstances? I never thought to see you again, perhaps it is fate?' Eleanor blurted out the question realising once again she could be accused of being forward.

'Indeed, I thought the same thing, not fate exactly but an extraordinary coincidence, I was somewhat surprised to see you looking so different and in such elevated surroundings.'

'On a more serious note please know your secret is safe, I give you my word. As I said last night it is your business what you do but now I know you a little better I would be sorry if you were to find yourself compromised in any way; take care of yourself Miss Barker, society is quick to judge, especially where ladies are concerned.'

Eleanor was deciding whether Mr Reynolds was being patronising or thoughtful when saw her father striding towards them.

'I thought I spied you my dear,' he said drawing near and smiling at them both.

'My father likes to keep a close eye on me Mr Reynolds in case I get pressed into action,' she said smiled affectionately at her parent.

'If you knew what scrapes my darling daughter can get herself into,' he shook his head indulgently, 'you would lock her in her room until her wedding day if you were in my shoes. Soon I can pass on the responsibility to

Captain Seamer.'

Eleanor was just about to give vent when her father winked at her and her temper subsided.

'You are on this tide I know Mr Reynolds, so my dear, let us leave Gabriel to his preparations and make haste.' Leave takings said and done, Eleanor and her father headed for home with Slate happy to be on the move once more.

'Gabriel Reynolds is a handsome young man is he not, and rich by all accounts? More than a few of the ladies were all of a flutter last evening I noticed.' Eleanor smiled: 'I think him very intriguing.'

'Good looking, rich and intriguing – I am surprised you can resist him! It is well you are spoken for already.' She glanced at her father.

'It is indeed,' Eleanor said thoughtfully.

8

As his ship pulled out of the twin piers of Whitby harbour, Gabriel stood on deck watching St Hilda's Abbey high on the cliff. It looked dark and formidable against the sky.

They reached the open sea tacking north back to Alnmouth. Soon they would be passing Mulgrave House Eleanor's home, standing tall above Sandsend. From the deck Gabriel watched the silvered clouds shield the sun, the waves hitting the beach were unfurling their frills pushing from him to her, reaching out to embrace the shoreline.

The ship sailed on and drew level with the house. The sun burst upon it before plunging it once more into cloud shadow. Gulls and gannets called and quarrelled, swooped and soared. To net one, he thought, and attach a message and have him deliver it to her door! But what would the missive say?

Sail away with me.

Gabriel shook himself. He was as infatuated as a schoolboy with this siren! He sighed. She had burst upon him like a ripple heading inland that suddenly hits the shore and then smashes and shocks.

This well bred lady, with her air of confidence and status, was in stark contrast to the wench he had met at The Fleece. Whatever had possessed her to want to risk her reputation to spend the night with a complete stranger he could only imagine. She had tried to explain to him but a lady of her class would have been ruined if she were to be found out. Gabriel realised he was fascinated by her, yet oddly disturbed.

She was hard to fathom; attractive, educated and engaged to be married. Yet by night acting the serving wench, or worse! Gabriel was captivated, yet troubled by her. The juxtaposition of class and elegance and a feral, impulsive nature was a combination he had never encountered in a woman before.

Gabriel felt uneasy. He always liked to be heading home but as they sailed past Runswick Bay, his heart felt heavy. He went down to his cabin threw his cocked hat on the desk, loosened his neck cloth and poured himself a brandy. He lay back on his bunk and closed his eyes; not for the first time did Gabriel miss his father.

In the past when they had journeyed together they had talked endlessly, about business about life about their hopes and dreams. His father was a good businessman, a man of principle and a good judge of character. What would he think of Miss Barker's antics? His father had been a man of the world before his marriage but he had also been a faithful and devoted husband. He thought perhaps his father's advice would have been to give this precocious young lady a wide berth!

Why was he thinking in these terms anyway? She was soon to marry. He recalled her face in the moonlight, her russet hair blowing in the breeze; the scent of her, the very essence of her was all lodged in his memory.

Not that he had any thought of replacing Caroline with Eleanor. There could be no alliance between Miss Barker and himself, he knew even if she were free she was far too mercurial, too self reliant too forthright for him; he preferred a woman who would need him for protection, a lady who would be content to support him as his mother had supported his father. He would one day marry – for love he hoped not just to legitimise a lady's children.

Yet he also knew there was a spark between them, a connection if you like, it unsettled him; she stirred him like no woman had ever done before. It was not just her captivating looks it was something else, that sense of coming together on another level. He heard about people saying they had found their soul mate but had never understood it; until now.

Last night he had assured her he would keep her secret and she had confidently met his gaze and returned a look which left him in little doubt the attraction went both ways. On the quayside she had flirted, played up to him, despite having a fiancé.

'Damn her!' he said to the elements. She had picked him to bed her! He refilled his glass and took a healthy swig; his nerves were on edge.

He ruminated on the different ways men and women behaved in society. Most men he knew made use of the services of women. He knew women had desires too, but until now he hadn't given it much thought. Yet what Eleanor had attempted to do was risky, were she to have waited a little while she would be married, she would have had her needs met then. Why not wait?

The same thought could have been levelled at himself he realised, only then he remembered his marriage was not to be. He was listless, confused. He paced about the cabin, not easy for a tall man in the small space. He took papers from his satchel and threw himself into work to stop his mind from dwelling.

9

Eleanor woke to the sound of water being poured from a pitcher. She moved to stretch and at once felt pain shoot up her calf. Last night, on one of her excursions, she had injured her ankle. Pulling the covers back she saw it was swollen and an angry looking red. It throbbed and ached.

'What yer bin up to now? That looks right sore.' Charity came close to the bed and began to inspect the injured limb.

'I tripped last night going down the cliff, and it has grown worse overnight. I sat with it in the stream but it was a struggle to get back.' Sandsend was a close knit community where everyone was related and most had some connection with the free trading that went on in every coastal village up and down the land. Eleanor had seen Ginny, Charity's sister, on the beach walking out with a young man. He looked remarkably like Tomas, but it had been dark and she could not be certain. Tomas was a young man with passions. Eleanor envied him his freedom yet thought him a wastrel where women were concerned.

'T'will need a cold compress and resting up for some

days.' Eleanor knew she was right and sighed with the thought of enforced rest.

When the ankle had been attended to and Charity was dressing her hair Eleanor said, 'Does your family still live at the first cottage by The Hart Inn?' Eleanor watched her maid's face change colour, a faint blush covering her cheeks. 'Aye, though some would say father lives more at The Hart than at home.' She plaited Eleanor's hair.

Last night Eleanor had noticed a light in their candle window a sure sign a load was being brought ashore.

'What does Ginny do for work now?' she asked. She knew her sister had just finished school. Her mother had paid for both the sisters to receive some education.

'She helps mother and my other sister with the bairns, does some sewing and sometimes helps with packing herrings when it is the season. She's good with babies. She helps out at the school a day a week; she's hoping to get a position as a nursemaid.'

'Does she have a young man?'

'I don't think so, why do you ask?'

'Just idle curiosity. How does your young man?' She thought to change the subject. 'Is James still thinking of joining the Navy?'

'He is but I told him it's me or the sea, I shan't sit by waiting while he has a girl in every port.'

'Quite right too,' Eleanor agreed.

At breakfast Eleanor concocted some story about tripping over her dog to account for her injury. '

So you won't be able to ride into Whitby with me my dear that is vexing!' Anne Barker said. 'Mrs Tattishall is closing her shop I have heard, she is to go to Thirsk to look after her brother who has lost his wife. There are bargains to be had I think if she is to be rid of her stock.' Her mother loved hats, she had quite a collection; she also liked a bargain. 'I thought we might go and see what there is before all the stock gets picked over.'

Eleanor chewed on some bread. 'What a pity, I wonder if I could manage to ride Jet, but then when I get there I shall have to stand and I do not feel it would be a good idea until the swelling goes down. You will just have to go without me and if you see anything you think might suit me bring it home on approval.'

Tomas, looking tired, came into the breakfast room and sat opposite his sister. 'What has happened to your ankle?

'I tripped over Slate.'

'So you slipped over Slate; very funny.' Eleanor rolled her eyes in mock disgust.

After greeting her son, Anne rose from the table and left to ready herself for her shopping trip.

'So what did you really do? Not out with the smugglers last night were you?'

'How do you know there were smugglers out last night and why should I be there?'

'Why should you be there? Well because you are often where you shouldn't be little sister. I know there was goings on because I saw the 'all clear' light in the Jenkins' candle window as I was riding back up the valley. I brought Tolly back to the stable then went to look at what was going on. It was a big load last night, should keep bellies full for some time.' Eleanor still marvelled that smuggling went on so close to home.

'So where had you been so late last night? Which poor woman are you in pursuit of now?'

'She is the most beautiful creature and very willing, I really think she is the loveliest girl I've ever seen.'

'Since the last one, who as I recall, was very similarly described. You are a rogue and a heartbreaker, shall you ever settle down?'

'Settle down! I hope not while ever there are maids a-willing in Stiddy Lane. I like to enjoy myself while I'm young and free and -'

'Spare me the details!' Eleanor stood up carefully so as not to put undue weight on the injury.

'I hope you are not leading Ginny Jenkins astray Tomas; her father will be after you with his shotgun.'

'How do you know about Ginny? I expect she has told Charity of my prowess?' He laughed knowing his sister would take the bait.

'Ginny is a lovely girl and you will spoil her chances if you are playing with her – what is a dalliance to you will not be for her. It is cruel to pretend affection to get your way with her, or any other young girl. It is all well and good acting the rake but you are a man of position and you abuse the privilege.' Eleanor felt the heat rise in her face.

'Eleanor, cannot a man eat his breakfast in peace without a morality lecture. Where else am I going to go for some fun? I am not going to pay for what I can get for free.'

Eleanor had hobbled to the door and leaned against the jamb. In all other respects Eleanor loved her brother, they were twins and closer than most siblings she imagined. They looked alike and thought alike but on this matter she was at odds with him.

'You are wealthy and can afford to pay; at least if you visit the brothel no one will get their feelings hurt.' Eleanor did not approve of brothels either but in this instance saw it as the lesser of two evils.

'Imagine if it was me being wronged Tomas. How should you feel towards the man who was just after what he could get then cast me aside? Should you be happy?'

Tomas, who had suffered similar tirades from his sister before thought it expedient to give in.

'Very well Eleanor I know you to be right as always. I will mend my ways.' Eleanor left her brother to finish his breakfast; they both knew he was lying.

♥

After three days of enforced idleness the swelling on her ankle began to go down and Eleanor could at least ride and get out of the house. Her time, however, had not been entirely wasted as she had had an idea given to her by her mother at breakfast the morning after the accident.

She sent off a letter to her bankers, The Widows Hobbs and Clover in Henrietta Street, asking for an appointment. She had ridden into Whitby, against her mother's wishes, but with a groom in attendance in case she needed assistance. She left him in charge of Jet and proceeded to her meeting.

She explained her plan, admitting she was unsure how to put it into practice. 'As I understand it you want to purchase Mrs Tattishall's Milliner's Shop and then let this young lady, Miss Drage, take over the lease and run the establishment. Is that correct?' Mr Price was meeting Eleanor this morning as he dealt with the day to day running of the bank. The widows were always in the background overseeing yet not actually "serving" their customers.

'I wish to buy the establishment as an investment. The business does well I think, if my mother's hat collection is anything to go by but I am keen Miss Drage does not know who has offered her this opportunity.'

'How do you know Miss Drage will accept your offer if, indeed it could be arranged?'

'Because, Mr Price, it is the best offer that she will have ever received, she will scarce believe her good fortune. I know she will need some assistance initially to learn the trade, I am hoping Mrs Tattishall's current staff will be keen to stay on in their posts. All I am asking at the moment is whether my plan is feasible, I know no one else who could assist me in this matter sir.'

'Leave it with me Miss Barker and I will put the matter to the Ladies. It seems quite an undertaking if you don't mind my saying so. How do you intend to fund this enterprise?'

'I thought to sell some shares on advice and I have monies laid down in this bank.'

'I am not sure raising this Miss Drage up out of her current station is a wise one.' His face showed concern. 'How will she live when her circumstances will be so changed? Would the ladies of Whitby purchase their hats from someone who only has experience of sewing sails?'

'I understand what you are saying and I have thought

of this. She would not perhaps be the one serving the ladies, although I think she would learn to do it very well, but her dream is to make hats not sell them! I also thought if the shop could be bought there is living space above it, presently occupied by the owner herself. Eva could reside there and live in much better surroundings than she has at the moment. Her better circumstances would put her in a different class and she would then mix in those circles I expect.'

'You have thought of everything Miss Barker. I will do my best to convince the Ladies of your seriousness.'

Eleanor left feeling the meeting had gone as well as could be expected. Now she had talked openly of the proposition she was not as confident as she had first thought, it was a serious undertaking and not one to be brokered lightly. If she could do this for Eva it would make such a difference to her life. She would dearly love to give her this chance.

Eleanor was not so naive to think the plan was not without drawbacks but she was prepared to take the risk. She knew she could not play 'Lady Bountiful' and change the world but if she could change Eva's world that would do for now. She was mindful of the responsibility that would be thrust upon the girl; was she the type of person who could deal with it? She would wait and see what the Ladies made of her suggestion and be guided perhaps by them.

10

On his return from Whitby, Gabriel received an invitation to the annual Boat Blessing event he had heard John Barker speak of. At first he had thought not to go as he was unable to spare the time, but then he had some business in Newcastle and decided to combine the two. The thought of seeing Miss Barker, was an incentive; though to what end he was unsure. After an overnight stay in Newcastle he took a ship down the coast, then hired a post horse to ride to Whitby for the Boat Blessing.

He was rounding the cliff over Runswick Bay looking down towards Sandsend and enjoying the view. The Boat Blessing he knew was an excuse; he knew if it had not been for the chance to see Eleanor Barker he would not have made the effort. Why he was chasing around the country after a woman who was engaged to another he was unsure. Her fiancé, Captain Seamer, would quite possibly be in attendance if he was ashore. There was a chance the captain might be at sea and then who knows, Gabriel thought, he might get the opportunity to talk to this beguiling woman again. If only to quieten the feelings he had been having, he needed to at least see her again. The horse stumbled on a loose stone and roused Gabriel from his musings. He muttered a rebuff to himself for his foolishness.

As he entered Sandsend Gabriel thought about a conversation he'd had with Bendor the night before. He had told him of his surprise at seeing his "Whitby wench" again. Bendor had been aghast when he had told him who she really was and how they had talked in the garden.

'She's your ship builder's daughter!'

'Apparently so but do not let her hear you say that. She is a lady in her own right, not an "accessory".'

Bendor pulled a face. 'I will never understand women.'

'Nor I. Religion does not interest me as you know; I do not think in terms of sin or sinners but live my life according to how I was brought up.'

'You follow your own moral compass, as do I. Sometimes the needle goes awry but generally we are upstanding.' Bendor smirked. Gabriel continued to use his friend as a sounding board. 'Do I think her immoral for how she behaved? Spoilt? Because if so I suppose I am a hypocrite because I would have behaved immorally, or would have done if she had not put a stop to it.' He grinned. 'I would have bedded her and not given it a second thought.'

'And enjoyed it no doubt!' Bendor laughed.

'No doubt but the point is—'

'The point is you think too much. If you see her at this ceremony, you might get another shot at her – at least you will be in better surroundings and she won't charge you for the privilege.' Gabriel scowled. 'I do not want "another shot at her" as you so eloquently put it, besides

I told you she is spoken for.'

'She did not seem to let that stop her at the tavern.'

Gabriel wished he'd not told Bendor now, he saw what a bad light it showed Eleanor in. 'All I am saying is that as she pointed out, the way women are judged is different to men and perhaps it is unfair. I had not thought of it before; I am glad I am a man.'

'Albeit a confused one.' Gabriel now wished he had kept his own counsel.

Gabriel came back to the present and after stabling his horse he was shown into the summer parlour. A slight breeze was cooling the room which contained seven or eight other guests. There was no sign of Eleanor he noted.

'Good day to you Mr Reynolds you've had a fine morning for your ride I trust?' The jovial John Barker greeted him, the two men shook hands. 'Come and meet a fellow shipbuilder, I believe you have just called at Marske to do a little business, the man I am going to introduce you to is from there originally.'

John Barker led Gabriel towards a middle aged, grey wigged man, who was leaning heavily on an ivory topped cane.

'Here is Ingram Eskdale.' The two men exchanged pleasantries while Mr Barker moved on as a good host should, to greet more guests. Mr Eskdale was talking pleasantly about his business when Gabriel saw Eleanor enter the room with her mother. Eleanor, wearing a blue riding habit which suited her colouring moved to join her father who was talking to a man in uniform; Gabriel was relieved to see it was not Captain Seamer.

Eleanor glanced about the room and he caught her

eye, they exchanged a smile. The guests started to make their way to the awaiting carriages and horses which had assembled ready to take them the three miles to Whitby. By chance as Gabriel mounted his hired horse, Eleanor was being assisted onto her own sleek black gelding. She looked at home in the saddle. They were side by side and having nodded to each other moved off. They began the descent down the cliff path, there being just enough room for the pair to ride side by side in comfort.

'Good day Mr Reynolds, I trust you are well?'

'Good day Miss Barker, I am.' It seemed formal considering the last time they had met she had told him her secrets.

They rode on. 'I must confess I have never attended a Boat Blessing before, I had never even heard of one until your father mentioned the custom, what should I expect?'

'Mr Eskdale has a new built ship to be blessed and I believe there will be two or three others joining in. Eskdales is a rival shipyard – Father is piqued he has no ship ready to be blessed this year. The blessing of the ship it is believed will protect her from misadventure.' She smiled mischievously. 'We shall all gather at the harbour and ships, boats, cobles, large and small, will all crowd in. There will be the singing of hymns and saying of prayers, then the clergyman will board the new ships and bless them in the eyes of God so that they will never sink, break up in rough seas or be boarded by privateers.' Gabriel smiled at her whimsy.

'Then all will be merry on the quayside, for most of the shipyards give their workers a half day paid holiday. Drink will be taken by one and all. If we are able to remount we shall troop back to Mulgrave ravenously hungry and enjoy a good dinner.' She delivered the speech jubilantly.

'Perhaps when my ship is built I shall have her blessed, it sounds like a good excuse for a party, I am willing to take freely of wines and spirits in a good cause.' He looked at her and grinned.

'I know Father is hoping you will, it is good for both businesses to be seen to prosper. Have you thought of a name for her yet?'

'I have not given it much thought.'

'Well I seem to recall one of your other ships is named after your mother and father. Perhaps she should be named after yourself and your future wife; is she a lady from your home port?'

Gabriel shifted uncomfortably in the saddle. He hesitated before replying. 'That might prove a little difficult Miss Barker, as my marriage is ...,' he hesitated being surprised the conversation had turned personal, 'that is to say the engagement is broken.' He stumbled over the words. He had not spoken of the matter to many people yet and the words still sounded strange to him. Gabriel stared purposefully ahead as if there was something of great interest on the horizon.

'Goodness there I go again, another blunder! I am so sorry to hear that, please forgive me I had no idea.'

'You were not to know, it is but a recent occurrence.'

They had reached the straight part of the road that began to funnel down towards the harbour and they joined with others on horseback and on foot who were all heading to the ceremony. Conversation was halted as they merged with the crowds and they paid attention to where they were going. They dismounted and gave their horses to the grooms who were waiting to lead them away from the crowds.

The Boat Blessing happened just as Eleanor had described except the clergyman, clearly not a sailor, almost tripped and fell into the sea before he had time to board Eskdale's ship which amused everyone but himself. The journey back to Mulgrave found Gabriel in the company of Eleanor's mother and father, having got separated from Eleanor in the crush to retrieve their horses. She was ahead with her sister. He admired her from behind.

Once back at the house dinner was served; they were ravenous just as Eleanor had predicted. Once again Gabriel was separated from Eleanor as he was placed between Ingram Eskdale and Eleanor's sister Atalana; he wished, ungraciously, she could have changed places.

'I was speaking with your sister on my last visit and she tells me she has an interest in shipping herself, do you have business dealings Mrs Coffin.' The name sounded gloom laden to his ears.

'My husband has sir; I have never been so inclined.' Her hair was more auburn than red and where her sister had a pale translucent skin her sister's was as clear but rosier. She was attractive in her own way but she would not have caught his eye he realised; she lacked vitality.

'You will forgive me for asking, I know you are a Quaker yet I know very little about the philosophy. What exactly happens at the meeting house; is the service similar to an Anglican or Methodist one?' He had no real interest but was at a loss to know what to talk about with this black clad woman; he could scarce believe she was a Barker.

'We do not have a minister, all are considered equal. Usually we sit in quiet contemplation, unless someone wants to debate an issue or raise a point. We do not pray as such, in the traditional sense, or sing.'

Gabriel could think of no suitable response and was relieved when the next course created a diversion and he sought to change the topic.

'Your sister still attends the meeting house?'

'Sadly not since father was disowned, she has given up, she always found it difficult to sit quietly especially when we were children.'

Gabriel thought pulling teeth might be easier. He did not usually falter in social situations, especially with ladies but he found Eleanor's sister hard to engage.

'I understand you have twins?'

'Yes a boy and a girl, they are very fond of their aunt, she is so good with them. Sometimes I think they would prefer to live with their Aunt Eleanor than with me, she has a natural affinity with children.'

'I am sure that is not true; it is perhaps because a mother has to reprimand her children whereas an Aunt can have all the fun and indulge them.'

'You are possibly right although they are well behaved children; I seldom have cause to reprimand them.' She smiled for the first time and Gabriel could at last see some family resemblance.

At that juncture Ingram Eskdale asked Gabriel a question and he turned to speak with him; like Gabriel's family he had made his fortune through whaling, so they had much in common to discuss. The man was keen to hear about putting his money into coal as a less risky investment. Gabriel was giving him the benefit of his advice when the ladies rose to leave the men and John Barker came down the table with the port and sat opposite.

'I was sorry to hear of Eleanor's travails John, a bad business I must say. At least the scoundrel was found out before the event'. Gabriel, a puzzled look on his face, looked at the father and waited for his response.

John Barker shook his head; anger clouded his usual sunny countenance. 'It is as you say Ingram – her mother and I are only glad we have found out before the marriage! Pardon me Mr Reynolds, you may not have heard; my daughter's fiancé has been found to be false to her and has been, openly it seems, carrying on a relationship with another. It is not certain but we think he made the affair plain for all to see so it would get reported back to us and then we would be forced to call off the engagement. Perhaps he thought to avoid a Breach of Promise suit, well I can tell you straight he is wrong there!'

Gabriel thought it strange he had never in his life heard this term before and now in a matter of weeks he had heard it twice!

'Who knows? Perhaps the snake wanted to slither out of the marriage and was too cowardly to face her; I had thought more of him than that – always found him straight forward enough.' John Barker poured more port for Ingram and Gabriel but did not refill his own which was still almost full.

'Poor Eleanor she didn't deserve to be treated badly,

shabby behaviour on his part; and cruel. It has other consequences as well of course; our two families have been close for years. Indeed we do business together and William is shareholder in various ventures and concerns I am involved in. It's awkward, I don't mind telling you.'

Eskdale said: 'I noticed his father absent today, he must feel it too no doubt?'

John Barker nodded. 'He at least, has acted the gentleman in all this. He came to see me on Monday; he is at a loss. He feels the trouble his son has caused, but when all is said and done he is his son.' John Barker continued. 'In typical Eleanor style she refuses to be cowed by this, her mother and I had expected her to lie low while the talk dies down, but Eleanor is not for skulking in her room wringing her hands. She has done nothing wrong she says, quite rightly, so why should she hide away. We never expected her to come today but here she is fine and dandy and looking splendid! She's always had spirit, as you know Ingram, too much sometimes, but in this case I'm glad she's got backbone.'

Gabriel felt strange emotions. She had not said anything about her troubles earlier but then why would she? It was no one's business but her own, yet she had the opportunity to tell him when he had told her of his own broken engagement.

Gabriel pondered the change of circumstances; when they had first met they were both betrothed to other people. Now they were both free, it certainly put a different slant on things. Gabriel was struck by the similarity in both their situations; both had broken not just with fiancées, but with close family ties too.

The chairs began to be scraped back as the men rose to leave the dining room. In the drawing room Gabriel once again found himself talking business with Ingram Eskdale.

Eleanor, sitting with Atalana appeared jolly enough, perhaps she was playing a part knowing others were watching her; or perhaps she was relieved to be free? He dearly wanted to speak with her but in such a small party could not see how this was to be achieved. He was only half attending to what Eskdale was saying as he watched the turn of her head, her golden hair shining in the candlelight, the bloom on her cheek, her twinkling eyes. She was truly lovely.

♥

Later in the evening, supper was taken and the more local guests made to leave soon after. Gabriel was one of only three house guests staying the night at Mulgrave House but yet again he was sat away from Eleanor; he did not get the chance to speak with her alone again.

He was in the same room he had occupied on his last visit. He opened the curtains and looked out to sea; there was a sliver of moon highlighting the edge of a cloud. He heard a faint knock and turned to see a note pushed under the door. It read:

Mr Reynolds, would you do me the honour of meeting me? If you wish to do so be at the kitchen door in fifteen minutes. If you turn left at the end of your corridor instead of right, you will find the servants' stairs lead to the kitchen and you won't be seen; if you have no wish to see me please destroy this and think of it no more. EB

143

Gabriel smiled to himself, trust her to find a way, she was very inventive. He had no idea why she wanted to see him but he didn't care, he realised he was grinning inanely, he was glad she had found a way. Then he checked himself; 'This woman is not for you, she would never fit the criteria!' He re-tied his neck cloth as he looked at his reflection in the mirror and saw he was still smiling. 'Watch your step; you could end up in a world of trouble with this young lady.' He laughed at himself as he headed to the door.

Eleanor was lighting a small lantern and was checking to see the candle had caught; she turned when she heard footsteps behind her. He saw her smile as the light illuminated her face, she wore a cloak over her gown, it had grown cool.

'I was unsure whether you would come.' Her voice was soft. The sound of the sea gently rolling upon the shore could be heard below.

'I was glad to get your message – I had been eager to speak with you all evening.' They walked side by side following the same route they had taken last time. As they neared the copse Eleanor said, 'Not that way, it will be too dark as there is not the moonlight we enjoyed last time, there is a small summer house close by.'

He followed her and saw it at the edge of the cliff. They entered and sat side by side. A tawny owl called from somewhere behind them.

'I think you should know Eleanor I am aware of your broken engagement. I am sorry.'

'I expected you would find out this evening but just in case I wanted to tell you myself, I could have said something earlier when you told me about your situation but I thought it not the right time.'

She pulled back the hood from her head and smiled. 'I am the latest topic for scandal no doubt; perhaps the good people of Alnmouth should get together with the gossips of Whitby and have a good chinwag about us both! After all we are in the same boat.'

Gabriel frowned remembering his earlier resolve. 'Well not exactly; I was not running around with a rich widow for everyone to see – I'm sorry that was rude. You did not deserve to be treated so badly by him.'

'I did not but were you not very nearly "running around" with a young woman named Charity? Is it not the same thing except you thought her poor – why are men so fickle? Is it beyond them to show self-restraint, some degree of faithfulness?' The atmosphere changed; he saw she was irked.

'What of your conduct? Were you not going to show signs of unfaithfulness that night? You cannot have it both ways Miss Barker; it is a double standard surely? Perhaps both of us behaved badly.'

He saw the flash of temper in her eyes. 'Men are allowed to get away with indiscretions because it is expected they will sow their wild oats,' he continued, adding fuel to the fire.

'Firstly, I was provoked!' she spat back, 'Seeing William with that woman! Men are free to sow their wild oats but women must just sit and sew, it is unfair – are men and women so different? Do we not all share the same dreams, desires and ambitions?'

'When you say "we", you obviously mean people of our

rank for I am not sure the lower classes have the time, or leisure, to have dreams let alone desires and ambition.' Gabriel wanted to change the tone of the conversation; he had not expected to meet her to bicker like children.

The tawny owl's mate called back breaking the silence which had fallen between them.

'Yes it is easy to lose sight of how lucky we are despite our current trials but sometimes I feel so restricted by what I can and cannot do or say; just riding unchaperoned is frowned upon, going into a coffee shop is unthinkable! Is it not absurd? I have told you how I feel before.'

It is ridiculous in some instances I agree, I have never thought of it before talking with you; that is because I enjoy the freedoms of being a man I suppose. The poor do not have the time to debate the inequalities of the sexes I think. I give thanks daily for the good fortune of my birth for I should make a miserable peasant.' He smiled again trying to lighten the mood. Even with her furrowed brow she was still charming.

'That is what I learned from my night time adventures in Whitby, I had food, shelter and leisure unimaginable to people like my friend Eva – the conditions she endures daily are terrible, my family has always tried to help our tenants but it is never enough I am sure, we are indeed privileged.'

They left the summer house and walked along a path that led around a shrubbery, the sound of the waves below accompanied them.

'What of Captain Seamer? How do his ambitions fair I wonder?'

'I care not; his dreams and desires are no longer my

concern!' She suddenly giggled and looked up at Gabriel, a wicked glint in her eye; she clearly was not heartbroken. 'He possibly has achieved his ambition by unloading his troublesome fiancée!' She laughed again self mockingly.

Gabriel was unsure how to respond but he need not have worried as Eleanor asked: 'What of your intended, Mr Reynolds is she very distressed for if she is I am sorrier for her than I am for myself as I was never in love.'

Gabriel told Eleanor the story of his break up with Caroline in the most gentlemanly way he could, careful not to be disloyal to the woman he had possibly once loved.

'Our stories are similar in that we will both be thrown into each other's company through our close proximity; at least William is at sea for quite a lot of the time.'

She turned a radiant smile upon him: 'How gloomy we have become, when I asked you to meet me I had not expected it to be so.'

'Why did you ask to meet? Was it only to tell me of your broken engagement or did you want to confess to some other misdemeanour you have got up to in my absence?' He joked hoping to make her smile.

'Another one of my impulses I suppose, Mama is always telling me to think of the consequences of my actions but I'm afraid I am deeply stupid for I never seem to learn that lesson.'

'I like you just the way you are; your impetuous nature is refreshing. So many women calculate their behaviour in order to show themselves to the best advantage, every move and turn of the head is calculated to show them in a good light.' He thought of the artful Lady Berwick.

'Thank you for the compliment for myself but you are harsh regarding the rest of the female population, you sound like you have a vast experience of women!'

'Perhaps that came out a little judgemental, I seem to have condemned all womankind but in truth I have little experience of women. I have no female relatives, save an ancient Aunt and I became engaged at eighteen. One tends to mix only with the people of a certain rank who act in accordance with the rules set down in polite society.' They reached the furthest part of the garden where the cliff dropped away sharply.

Gabriel sighed deeply. 'I am glad we have had this time alone together.' He turned to face her but could not see her expression in the darkness. He hesitated to speak but wanted Eleanor to know how he felt. While they had been talking it was if she had cast a spell over him; he was strangely attracted to this contrary creature; he felt her impulsiveness must be catching; before he could stop himself he said:

'We have known each other only a short time but we enjoy each other's company, do we not?'

She looked up at him, they were standing very close. 'Then do you not think this is the foundation on which tenderness could be built?'

He knew there was certainly a physical attraction for them both; for his part he had relived the night in the room above The Fleece on more than one occasion. He remembered how she had felt in his arms, how she had kissed him back, but then she was playing a part he told himself. He wondered how she felt now.

He found he admired her; her conversation was

stimulating, she made him question his beliefs. She had a strong character and he liked that about her too. She was also forthright and entertaining, argumentative even. Suddenly he wanted to know more about this complicated lady; he could imagine a life with her even though he thought she may not always be easy to understand. However, he was unsure if she felt anything other than a physical attraction for him.

'Tenderness; that I already feel I believe,' Eleanor said. 'By keeping my indiscretion a secret you have endeared yourself to me.' She smiled at him cheekily. 'Yet as impulsive as I usually am, I hesitate for both our sakes – you have just broken with Caroline and I with William can we, do you suppose, move slowly and see if the tenderness grows?'

'Of course; as we live at some distance from one another it means that of necessity we are not thrown into each other's company all the time. I suppose that in itself will put a natural brake upon any relationship that may develop. It is as you say, very soon after our respective break ups and I would not want to rush you and thereby risk any future we could have together.' He took both her hands in his as he continued.

'Yet that vital energy, the spark which can turn liking to loving has already begun for me I realise. After the last time we were here in the garden I have thought of you often but as I knew you to be engaged to another I tried to put you from my mind; now I have a chance and intend to pursue it. Do I speak too free for you?'

'It is not that,' she smiled up at him. 'I like what you have to say but let us try to be patient and enjoy what we have, here and now, without rushing headlong into the future. If you knew me better you would not believe I am erring on the side of caution! I am usually the one leaping ahead without a thought; this is out of character for me to hold back. It is only that I see the importance of our situation. I think perhaps we could have a future together, that is why I pull back a little.'

'Given the encouragement then I feel my future journeys to Whitby will be worthwhile – I will give you time Eleanor if that is what you want but I will be waiting. Just say the word and I will tell you what is in my heart.'

'Perhaps we could write to one another, as we will not see each other often? That would allow us to get to know each other better.' she suggested.

'I should look forward to receiving letters from you, but I warn you, I am no poet, I have no experience in writing love letters.' He reached out and pulled Eleanor into his arms and kissed her passionately.'

'Is that why you asked me to meet you?' he asked.

'It had not been at the forefront of my mind but it is now.' She kissed him back with equal passion.

♥

When he was dressing the next morning Gabriel heard children's voices outside in the garden. He moved to the window and looked down. There were two children, a boy and a girl being chased by Eleanor. These must be her sister's twins he thought.

Squeals of delight carried up to his room until the boy tripped and fell; without hesitation Eleanor scooped up the child and held him high in the air. The boy looked as if he was about to bellow when he looked down at his Aunt but grinned instead.

He watched them playing roughly, all three looked excited and carefree. Her face, flushed from running and with her hair coming loose from its pins, Eleanor looked younger than her years.

He went over in his mind the conversation they had had in the garden the night before. He had hardly expected Eleanor would be free when he had started this trip; he had no expectations other than to see her again yet suddenly there he was making declarations!

Events had turned quickly; what he had been calling an infatuation had quickly changed once he knew her to be released from her engagement. He had acted instinctively but he did not regret it he found. As he watched, his heart swelled, his imagination leapt forward and saw this woman at Westshore playing with their own children. He allowed himself to hope, to dream. Then he laughed: he had asked Grace to find him a compliant wife. Eleanor could never be described as biddable, far from it; it seemed he did not know his own mind.

After Gabriel had broke his fast he was to leave Sandsend; he would ride part of the journey then return his post horse before sailing back to Alnmouth. He was glad he had made the journey; had he not he would still be in ignorance that Eleanor was free from her engagement. He looked about hoping to speak with her before he left but she was nowhere to be seen. As Gabriel reached the top of the stairs Eleanor came through the door which led from the servant's stairs. The sight of her brought a smile to his face.

'Good morning, I was hoping to see you,' he said.

'Good morning, you slept well I hope?'

'Yes thank you but sadly I am about to leave, have you eaten?'

'Yes earlier with the twins who woke me *very* early.' She smiled warmly.' They felt a little tongue tied.

'I need to get my kit bag and I will be on my way.'

'I was just about to go for a ride myself – would you care for some company for part of the way?'

'That would be very agreeable, are you to wait for a chaperone?' He teased thinking of their previous conversation.

'I will go before anyone notices,' she said as she moved to the door.

'When can you be ready?' he asked.

'I'm ready now.'

Once mounted they left the stable yard turning north along the cliff tops. The day was shaping towards grey, the air felt damp but as yet it wasn't firm enough to be called drizzle; a watery sun made an appearance. They talked easily and without artifice, their earlier clumsiness gone.

'Those were your sister's children I saw you playing with on the lawn this morning?'

'Yes, they are adorable and can twist me around their little fingers. The girl is named Harriet but everyone calls her Harry as her given name is much too ladylike for her. I fear she is much like I was at her age! The boy is Edward and he has the sweetest nature.'

'They are boisterous are they not and have good lungs on them,' he said.

'Yes! In particular, Harry has an ear piercing scream when she forgets herself; my mother says I had the same annoying habit when I was her age.'

They were approaching a path that went near to the edge of the cliffs. 'Those trees there,' she said pointing to three or four windblown stumps, 'mark the top of the cove, I go there sometimes to swim when the weather is hot; I have never encountered anyone else down there as it is quite inaccessible for most people. We could tether the horses and go for a walk on the beach – unchaperoned.' She raised an eyebrow and smiled, 'unless of course you are eager to get back to Northumberland?'

Gabriel knew he should be setting off; he hated to neglect his business, but knew he would stay. He told himself he should take advantage of the situation for who knew when they would be able to meet again.

After tethering the horses they began the descent sliding, slithering and skidding on the loose shale of the cliff side. Some of the way was easier and they could walk down the less steep parts. Gabriel went ahead on another tricky bit of terrain and turned and offered his hand to steady Eleanor, who he could see was picking up speed. He held her hand until they reached the bottom safely. He enjoyed having the excuse to touch her again.

Despite the clouds it had been warm work and they both took off their jackets and threw them over a boulder. They sat on a rock and removed their boots; he caught a glimpse of a slim ankle.

'My favourite thing is to be on a beach,' Eleanor said dreamily.

'It is my favourite thing now, being here with you, I

never expected it.' He watched her unselfconsciously paddling in the surf.

'Do you fish?' he asked.

'For compliments!' She giggled and skipped ahead of him. He caught her and pinned her arms behind her back. 'I am not good with pretty words but I can tell you I think you the most attractive Whitby wench I have ever seen.'

'Attractive! Wench!' I think I need different bait sir.' She wriggled half heartedly to get free, remembering the last time he had held her like this.

'You will have to teach me, show me how to reel you in.' He kissed her white throat as her head went back as she laughed. 'Do you think you could learn to like me despite my wanton ways?' She teased.

'Perhaps, I might learn to tolerate you, in time.'

'And I you,' she said kissing the fingers of his hand and looking up at him.

'I have never met anyone quite like you,' he said stroking her hair.

'You must have led a very sheltered life sir.'

'That was my attempt at a compliment; I thought you were still fishing.'

'Oh I see, thank you in that case.'

She smiled as they edged along the shore line walking in the shallow surf watching the gannets dive for fish. Puffins nested in the cliffs and occasional flashes of colour popped out against the dull, grey sky.

The beach began to incline a little near the headland making the waves behave erratically. Eleanor, holding her skirts up from the foaming sea, was absentmindedly looking up at the cliffs hoping to spy more puffins when Gabriel noticed a much bigger wave rolling onto the beach; he saw immediately this one would wet Eleanor's skirts completely. Without a word he grabbed her by the waist, just as he had seen her do with her nephew earlier, and picked her up. The power of the wave crashing down and the steepness of the beach overbalanced him and he lost his footing. He managed to push Eleanor away from him as they both tumbled onto the wet sand. She rolled away as he threatened to land on top of her; they fell laughing as Eleanor realised what he had been trying to do. They both lay, her on her back, he on his belly, damp and covered in sand.

'I'm sorry! Are you hurt? I was trying to save your skirts from a drenching.' They grinned at each other.

'So gallant, a bit of warning might have helped!' Eleanor hitched herself up so that her elbows disappeared into the soft sand. They were side by side. So close.

Gabriel reached out and pushed a curl of red hair behind her ear.

'I love the way you have no airs, most women I know would not be happy to be wet and covered in sand, yet – you seem to glow.' He leaned towards her and kissed her softly on the lips, they tasted salty.

'What do you know of love sir?'

'Not much I realise until now, but I am a quick learner.'

'Practise makes perfect.' She leaned closer and kissed him tenderly. 'You said earlier you were no good at pretty speeches but you are right – you do learn quickly.'

'Are you on the line?'

Eleanor smiled: 'There is every chance you may have

caught me Gabriel Reynolds.' She stood up and dusted the sand from her skirt. 'I am not sure being likened to a fish is at all flattering now I come to think of it.' She puffed out her cheeks and made a face like a fish out of water.' Gabriel laughed and took hold of her hand.

'We are very visible from here are we not?' They looked up at the cliffs where there was a path. Eleanor led him by the hand to the mouth of a small cave; there was a huge boulder at the entrance that made a perfect seat. A strong tang of seaweed hung in the air.

Now they were completely hidden from view from all angles save the sea. Eleanor sprang up onto the rock and Gabriel sat beside her while she knocked the sand from his shirt. They kissed again drawing closer still as they sat together heads and hands touching looking out to sea and at each other.

'Perhaps I will kidnap you, run away with you to Alnmouth, 'he said cheerily.

'More scandal! Imagine you trying to explain me to your friends and neighbours, tongues would wag.'

'I should not have to as I plan to lock you up.'

'Does your house have a tower or a turret like in fairy stories?'

'Sadly not – I could have one built for you if you want. I find at this moment I would do anything for you.'

'Anything at all Gabriel?'

'Anything.'

She grinned mischievously. 'In that case would you kiss me again?'

'Gladly, but I warn you we should stop soon as I fear I shall take advantage of you.'

'It is I who take advantage of you surely,' she laughed.

It was still a gloomy day but a pale yellow light was trying to push away the grey. Gabriel knew he may not get another chance for them to be alone together for a while and he savoured the moments, yet there was more he wanted to say.

Suddenly Eleanor put her hands on Gabriel's shoulders and pushed him away gently. 'What time is it?' He took out his pocket watch. 'Just past one.'

'Oh no!' Eleanor jumped down from the seat. 'I promised the twins I would let them ride the donkeys round the paddock before dinner – I'm going to be late. My time keeping leaves a lot to be desired.'

Before he could ask her to wait, he wanted to tell her what was on his mind, she had started to run back along the beach leaving him in her wake. He ran to catch her up; they put on their jackets with half the sand from the beach seemingly inside their clothes. Gabriel caught her by the shoulders and breathing hard said. 'Wait Eleanor, I have something I need to say to you my love.'

'I am not sure I am ready to hear any declarations just yet. I know I have feelings for you Gabriel but want to be sure of myself first. I do want to hear what is on your mind, but now is not the right time; it is too soon.' She pulled away from him. 'I am unsure whether any man can truly be trusted; if you really care for me surely you will wait? I feel torn.' He watched as she walked away. 'I know the twins will be so disappointed if they miss their ride, I should hate to let them down.' Gabriel caught her up and together they began to walk and climb their way back up to the top of the cove, the last part was slippery and Gabriel again took her hand to steady her. He thought about what she had just said; he felt his heart sink.

As they both scrambled back up the cliff, sometimes almost on hands and knees, they saw a horse and rider just passing by where their two mounts were happily munching grass.

'Good afternoon Miss Barker, you look a trifle windblown.'

Eleanor flicked a glance at Gabriel before replying.

'That is possibly on account of it being a trifle windy!' Her reply was curt, bordering on rude. Her face showed distaste. Gabriel was looking at the man riding a dapple grey mare then realised who it was; he had never seen him out of uniform before. The man smirked and edged his horse towards them.

'Good afternoon sir, Mr Reynolds is it not?' Captain Seamer looked amused as if he had caught them out. Gabriel looked quickly at Eleanor whose face was thunderous. 'Good afternoon sir,' Gabriel said.

'Are you heading back to Northumberland?' Seamer glanced at the kit bag on his saddle. The captain didn't wait for an answer but turned his gaze back to Eleanor. His smile did not reach his eyes.

'My dear Miss Barker, you are returning to Mulgrave? I can relieve Mr Reynolds of the duty of escorting you – I am going on to Whitby myself; I cannot allow you to go unchaperoned.'

'That will not be necessary thank you, I am quite able to find my own way home,' she bit back as she strode purposefully over to Jet and untied him.

Before Gabriel could help her she was mounted and gathering in the reins. She looked at Gabriel. It was a look of resignation which had a hint of apology in it too.

'Goodbye Mr Reynolds safe journey to you.' She gave the captain a cursory nod, kicked Jet lightly and was off galloping across the cliff tops as fast as Jet could race.

Captain Seamer looked down at Gabriel. 'Young ladies today sir, they are not easily understood!' The captain had a smug look on his face.

Gabriel did not trust himself to reply civilly and went to untie his own horse and mount, the mare half reared as the grey got closer. Gabriel knew he did not like the man; he was boorish and had deprived him of saying goodbye to Eleanor. He could have knocked the man from his horse. He did not like him before today, now he disliked him even more.

'I expect you have heard our betrothal is at an end? Can you see why I wonder? Eleanor is lovely to look at but very wilful. Her parents have indulged her antics.' He shook his head. Both horses were keen to move off feeling the tension in the air. 'Any man taking her on will have to break her first; I had neither the patience nor the will.'

'Then I am sure you feel yourself relieved to be free of the attachment sir, it will save you the trouble of trying to do the impossible. No doubt you have other ladies you can master more easily, good day to you.'

Gabriel felt angry on Eleanor's behalf. He was glad she was shot of this odious man. If this was the true character of Captain Seamer she was well rid of him.

Without a backward glance he turned north and

galloped off. What a detestable man. How infuriating he had appeared when he did. Until William Seamer had spoilt their morning it had been a happy one then Eleanor had raced off. There had been no declarations or fond farewells and who knew when they would meet again? He thought of turning back to Mulgrave but the thought of passing the captain deterred him. In any case what excuse could he give for his return? He turned his mind back to the time on the beach and smiled, at least he had that memory to console him.

11

Gabriel had visited his tailor on Northumberland Street when he bumped into Libby Lawson. He was surprised for he could not ever remember meeting her out of her house excepting the first time when they had met after her fall.

'Libby how are you?' He bowed over her hand. Her simple dove grey dress seemed to mirror the weather. She clutched a basket in front of her as she had the first time that they had met.

'Mr Reynolds, what a surprise you have become a stranger.' She smiled sweetly.

'I have been very tied up with business; my new ship and a new venture I am hoping to start with a friend is occupying a lot of my time. We are hoping to start a stud farm would you believe?'

'How interesting; you look well on the hard work.'

'And you too, Libby.' He noticed she looked a little plumper; it suited her.

Even though they were in a public place, Gabriel could not help but use her first name, it was a habit. It suddenly came to him he had not seen her for some time; it had not been a conscious decision not to see Libby, who he had known for so long, but since the Boat Blessing all his thoughts were for Eleanor. This liaison had long since run its course he realised.

Gabriel felt awkward suddenly. 'My ship is due out on the next tide and she is being provisioned just now,' he said pointing to the Alnmouth Boy with his riding crop.

'I often think of you if I take a stroll along the dock and I see one of your ships is in port,' she said looking towards the sea.

Gabriel felt the guilt fall upon his shoulders as he realised he had left her to her own devices. To his knowledge she had no other friend than he. How lonely this proud woman must be. There was a sadness behind her eyes and an expectancy in her smile. She demanded nothing of him yet he wondered if now she was before him she would expect him to call?

'I am sorry I have not visited, if only to see how you do, it is remiss of me. Can I walk you back home or perhaps you would take tea with me here at Blimps?' He pointed to the tea shop further down the hill.

'I do not think it would be seemly; a single lady alone, besides I am not for home yet, I have other errands to run and I am sure you have much to do yourself.' Again she smiled. He had not thought of her reputation but she clearly still did.

'It was lovely to see you again Gabriel I am glad you do well. I would not presume but if you are passing ever...'

'Thank you, I will call soon, I am ashamed I have been neglectful. As a friend I should have had more thought for you.' He touched her arm lightly and he noticed she turned her head anxious someone would see them. 'Take care Libby.'

He bowed and strode off down to the bay; as he walked he mulled over the meeting. He had known this woman for years now and in a particular kind of way. She was perhaps in her mid-thirties but still attractive, he noticed. He thought it strange they never met before outside her house, they never even took an evening walk together such was their relationship. It had been a furtive connection, stealing in and out of her house and robbing her of her dignity, of her confidence, of her heart? He felt shame. He should have found her a position as a true friend would have done. He knew now he would never seek her out in an intimate way again but he would call soon to tell her and try to help her to find a better life for herself.

12

Social events in the summer months were plentiful to come by as it was much easier to travel any distance on the poor, country roads. Plan an event for the winter and it was likely half your guests would be unable to attend as their carriages or horses would be defeated by the bad state of the highways.

In early September, when the sun was still pleasant and the rain was a relative stranger, Gabriel was invited to a wedding in Warkworth, a small place along the coast road from Alnmouth. It had a ruined castle worth seeing and the River Coquet was a pretty feature with the Hermitage which singled it out from other small towns in the North East.

One of the couple to be married, Christopher Smelt, was known to him from his schooldays and was also a friend of Bendor. Soon, he thought, he would be the only bachelor from their group of friends; he seemed to be forever at one wedding or another these days.

The bride he had never met, but knew her to be the daughter of a man called Brown who had made his fortune in iron ore. Gabriel had met him once along with his late father, when they had shipped some ore to France for him.

On the morning of the wedding Bendor and Grace called for Gabriel at Westshore in their carriage; Grace now being five months into her pregnancy had given up riding. They set off in fine weather for the four mile drive.

On arrival at the Browns' home, which was an impressive newly built mansion house overlooking Warkworth Castle, they were shown into the drawing room where the guests, and there were many of them, were assembling prior to going to the service at St Lawrence's Church.

Gabriel looked about the room and nodded to several acquaintances he knew mainly through business. Grace's sister Cora was a good friend of the bride and was there with a cousin Gabriel had not met before.

'You next Gabriel, for soon you shall be the last man standing!' Cora held out her hand to be kissed; she had a glint in her eye.

'Baiting me is your favourite pastime is it not?

She introduced her cousin, a shy young woman who flushed alarmingly when he took her hand. 'Do you never miss a chance to wound me? You know my heart belongs to you and you alone but you refused me when last we met so what am I to do?' The cousin looked flustered at such openness.

'Refused you! When? Are you mad? I could refuse you nothing Gabriel.' Cora looked to Cousin Mary and said. 'Do not listen to him we are in jest or at least I am.'

'You two should marry for you act like an old married couple sparring and trying to score points off one another,' Grace said laughing. 'Though how compliant my sister is

I am unsure.' She smiled knowingly at Gabriel.

'You have a very cynical view of marriage my dear.' Bendor was amused.

Gabriel saw Mr Brown, the father of the bride, talking in earnest to a man whose profile he recognised, it was John Barker. Gabriel seemed to remember from the depths of his mind John Barker had relatives in these parts. He remembered him mentioning it when he had told him he lived at Alnmouth.

Just then Eleanor's mother joined her husband followed by Eleanor herself along with her brother Tomas. He could scarcely believe it, what luck. She looked elegant in a golden gown of the latest style which suited her colouring. Her hair was stylishly curled and piled high on her head making her appear taller. How different she looked from the last time he had seen her all sandy, salty and windblown.

Before Gabriel could attract her attention a footman announced it was time to leave for the church. 'Gabe who is the lady talking to Mr Brown?' Bendor asked.

Gabriel explained. 'Ah your Whitby wench?' Gabriel nodded self-consciously; he had told Bendor all about their newly emerging relationship.

'It is, well I should hardly call her that now! What a surprise to find her here, I think she is related to the Browns but I am unsure what the connection is.'

Cora was all agog. 'What is this you have been keeping from me? Is it the lady in gold you speak of? What a pity she is so plain! Did she intend to upstage the bride I wonder?'

'Cora! Leave the poor man be! Do not torment Gabriel

you know he has a tender heart.' Bendor admonished her.

'I am sorry Gabriel, I did not mean to sound so venomous but you never did have taste in women otherwise you would have married me long ago.' She continued taunting him. Gabriel was not paying her any heed.

'I can see why you are so entranced by her Gabe; she is uncommonly attractive. Her hair is as you described it, stunning.'

'Bendor can you remember your wife is by your side, is it right you praise another in my hearing?'

'Sorry my love, we are talking of Gabriel's new-'

'Ben, do you think you could be a little more discreet?' Gabriel stroked his cheek which for once was clean shaven.

'I have noticed her, I feel shabby in comparison.' Grace, dressed in a gown of pale blue and wearing some of the Percy family jewels, could never have been described thus.

'We all do, even the bride will I suspect,' Cora said haughtily.

Most of the guests were walking to church as the weather was clement and the walk short. Gabriel and Bendor fell into step, the ladies behind them. 'I do like Miss Barker but she is hard to fathom; attractive, educated and engaged to be married at the time of our "encounter". Yet by night she acted the serving wench – or worse!' She is amusing, eye-catching yet unconventional, I do not know what to make of her.'

'You still seem intrigued by her.'

'Beguiled yet disturbed by her. The juxtaposition of class and elegance and a feral, impulsive nature is a combination I have never encountered in a woman before, I am most certainly drawn to her.' Gabriel was about to say more when Bendor said: 'Yet I wonder would her contrariness become somewhat trying on a daily basis?'

'Only time will tell.' Gabriel snapped back.

'Have a care my friend, she does not appear compliant and that is a character trait you said you favoured. Enjoy a flirtation by all means but my advice would be to steer well clear.'

'Too late for that I fear, I have almost declared my intentions.' He smiled confidently at his best friend.

'Then you are lost my friend, welcome to martyrdom!'

Gabriel's party were seated on the groom's side of the church near the centre while Eleanor was on the bride's side closer to the altar. Although Gabriel was not normally one for weddings he admitted to himself that this was going to be better than he had anticipated now Eleanor was here. He thought over what Bendor had said and realised he was in too deep to revert to a flirtation.

After the wedding ceremony the pews emptied out into the September sunshine and as always there was a certain amount of milling and mingling in the churchyard as greetings were exchanged.

'Gabriel,' a voice from behind him called, 'Good to see you I suspect you are friend to the groom are you not?' Eleanor's father slapped him on the back. This brought a smile to Gabriel's face. 'Yes, I was at school with Christopher, good day to you Mrs Barker.' He kissed her hand. She was a handsome woman but suffered by comparison by being close to her daughter who was just joining the group.

'You are related to the bride Ma'am?' He addressed Mrs Barker while acknowledging Eleanor with a smile and a nod. 'She is my niece; Mr Brown is my older brother.'

John Barker laughed. 'My wife's little joke Gabriel; they are twins, Anne was born twenty minutes before her brother and never lets him forget it.'

'More twins! Gabriel said 'They do not so much run in your family as gallop.' He looked at Eleanor as he said this. He would like twins with this intriguing woman he thought shamelessly; if they were girls and had her red hair they would be adorable.

There was a quaint custom at the church: when there was a wedding the children of the parish fastened up the church gates so the newly married couple had to pay to be released. Coins were thrown to the waiting urchins and the churchyard began to empty. Led by the bride and groom in a carriage the guests began to process back up the hill admiring the view of the ruined castle as they went. They made a colourful spectacle. The locals came out to cheer almost as if nobility were passing by. Eleanor, in conversation with her brother, always seemed just too far away for him to engage her attention.

The wedding breakfast was a long, but grand affair with many rich and varied courses. The wine flowed; champagne, claret, canary and other sweet desert wines were served alongside the delicious food; belts and tongues were loosened. Yet Gabriel hardly noticed whether he ate beef or goose or drank canary wine or claret, as from his position at the table he could see Eleanor but again, was too far distant to speak with her. He seemed destined forever to be seated so near, yet so far from her.

The meal over, the men had drunk their port and the ladies had retired to drink tea and now the musicians struck up and the dancing began. Gabriel was at last able to approach the woman who had captivated him all day long.

'Have you come to mark my dance card Mr Reynolds?' He knew she was teasing him as he had told her he would do almost anything to avoid dancing. 'Why did you not mention in your last letter you would be at this wedding? he asked.

'I hoped to surprise you – when you said you were coming I had hoped we would be able to spend some time together.'

'Had I have known you were to be here today I would have looked forward to it all the more.' He bowed and kissed her hand.

'How far distant are you from here Gabriel?' Since they had been corresponding there was more informality now he noticed.

'Just four miles, it is a coincidence that my father once did business with your uncle.' He explained the connection. 'Will you be in the neighbourhood long?'

'We shall be here about a week, but father and Tomas will leave before for business reasons. My mother has not seen her brother of late and they have much to talk about.'

Gabriel thought he had much to talk about with Eleanor but must content himself with the social niceties for the time being.

'Perhaps you and your family would do me the honour of riding over if you can spare the time? I would be very glad to show you my home town and I could give you dinner.'

'I would like that very much.' Her parents joined them and it was arranged they would dine at Westshore in two days time and that Mr and Mrs Brown should also be in the party. He thought to ask Bendor and Grace so Grace could act as hostess.

Card tables had been set up in the library and people were drifting either there or towards the dance floor as the quartet had begun to play. Gabriel and his party had joined with Eleanor and Tomas; her parents had moved away to sit and talk with relatives. Eleanor was dancing, first with Tomas then with a man Gabriel did not know. Gabriel admired how gracefully she moved.

♥

For her part, Eleanor knew Gabriel watched her while she danced and wished he would ask her but she was not hopeful. She knew she would have enjoyed the intimacy and the chance to talk further. He was talking with his friends; the lady who was with child must be his friend Bendor's wife. He had told her his best friend's wife was expecting their first child. From his letters she was beginning to know people he talked of if not by sight, then by repute.

She wondered who the other lady in their party might

be; she felt a stab of jealousy. She looked handsome and self assured and well acquainted enough with Gabriel to be touching his arm casually. She noticed Gabriel stood out being so tall, handsome and distinguished. Her tummy flipped as she remembered their time on the beach.

Her feelings for him were changing; through their correspondence she thought she saw the real man although she realised they were both showing themselves to the best advantage in their letters, she hoped he was as good as he seemed.

The dance ended and before Eleanor was handed off the floor, Gabriel approached her and led her back into position.

'I am honoured sir!' She laughed.

'Not as much as I – I will try not to crush your slippers but I cannot promise.'

They danced and he enjoyed the chance to touch and hold her, they snatched at conversation as they came together and parted. After it was over they rejoined the group.

They all began to talk and enjoy themselves; the conversation had turned to the young Turk who had danced with Eleanor earlier. Cora, of course, knew all the gossip concerning him. 'He is called Lester Ives and at twenty was married to an heiress who was not of his choosing. After one year of marriage he had taken a mistress, after two years another and it is rumoured,' she paused for effect, that now he has been married three years he had taken a third!'

There was much discussing as to whether it was true

or not as Bendor for one, could not imagine where the man got his energy from to keep three mistresses. Also, and this mainly from the ladies, was a concern for his lack of morals and discretion. No one could quite see the need for three mistresses and some heated debate had begun when Tomas said 'Men have different needs to women.' Eleanor was incensed. Tomas concluded 'Ives possibly keeps three ladies because a change is as good as a rest.'

The men had started to laugh light heartedly but Grace and Eleanor in particular were not so amused.

Supper was being set up and some of the guests were drifting off to eat. Grace, who would have normally liked to continue the debate, said she was hungry again, her appetite since her pregnancy was ferocious. She was keen they move into supper and so started to lead the group away.

♥

Eleanor and Gabriel decided to get some air on the terrace. 'This Ives fellow has the sort of good looks women admire I expect? He dresses like a peacock.'

Eleanor smiled 'I can see how some might admire him.'

'I am reminded of a saying my father used when he saw a certain type of man: "He appears too pleased with himself for his own good." Gabriel laughed.

'Are you jealous?'

'A little perhaps, the man was holding your hand and pressing nearer to you than was seemly I thought. Whatever criticisms I level at him the man is a very good dancer that is also something to hold against him.'

Eleanor smiled 'He is, but then so are you considering you do not practise.' Gabriel thought she was joking.

'I cannot ever remember feeling jealousy before – it is an uncomfortable feeling. I know it is beneath me yet I cannot help it.'

'I am flattered to arouse such passion but I would not be Mistress Number four I assure you, the man has the morals of a tom cat.'

'Ah his wicked ways with the ladies you mean?'Gabriel echoed a point Tomas had made earlier. Men and women are different in their natures, they have different needs, different appetites.'

'You sound just like Tomas! Some men and women are different and some are the same, surely you cannot generalise.'

'Yes but in terms that you speak of -' he did not want to say the word "sex", 'women do not have the same appetites as men.'

'You are a man, how do you know how women feel?' Eleanor was indignant.

'Well society says so I suppose.'

'And who makes these rules that society follow?'

'I know your point Eleanor, you want me to admit it is men who make the rules and it is true generally men do but has it not been for ever thus? Men have always acted on their impulses.'

Eleanor burst in. 'Well why is it women cannot act on their impulses too? The world turns and changes, we are no longer in the dark ages.'

'Do you really believe women want to behave like

men? As I understand it you were just castigating a man for his lack of morals, you have to make your mind up which side of the fence you are on. Some men, married men even, treat whoring as a sport, like cards or baiting. It is an entertainment, a pastime, to distract; women would not behave that way.' As the words left his mouth he remembered the night at The Fleece.

'Do not women want to be entertained and distracted or should they just have their music and their children to alleviate the boredom?' Eleanor had flung the question down like a gauntlet. Gabriel found he needed to pick it up; the conversation was irritating him.

He had thought to have a pleasant stroll in the cool of the evening with a lovely lady by his side. He had not bargained for this war of words. 'All I am trying to say is that women do not have the sort of nature to be duplicitous. They want stability, loyalty and romance.'

'You are very fond of telling my sex what they want Gabriel.' She spat the words out, her colour rising. 'From what you have just said women do not enjoy those three things! If married men take mistresses and treat whoring as something to do when they are bored then most marriages are false!'

Gabriel was beginning to feel cornered; the talk of mistresses was a little close to home and he thought to change the line of thinking.

'We possibly both know of couples who have married for reasons other than love, arranged marriages are not usually ideal. Yet when the couple have produced an heir both the wife and the husband have liaisons, when their obligations have been discharged.'

'I concede this point, it is true even the king goes down this path but what of couples who have married for love, love is sacred between a man and a woman, "till death us do part."'

'You change the subject now surely, we were talking of men being different to women what has married love to do with it?'

'Men and women who enter the married state are not different if they both want to spend the rest of their lives together sharing, "in sickness and in health".'

'For a woman with a Quaker education you seem to know the marriage ceremony inordinately well!' He smiled hoping she would too. She did not. He thought of Bendor's earlier warning. Several other couples were out on the terrace but the others seemed to be having a less troubled conversation.

'All I am saying is that some men, married or not, have greater or lesser appetites and some women equally so. If you understand my meaning,' she said to clarify the point. 'Just as some men like for instance, brandy, some like it so much they over indulge, whereas others are content with a single glass at supper.' Gabriel almost smiled at her ingenious analogy, but did not as he could see she was in earnest.

Gabriel was ready to concede the point, if only to change the subject. He would sooner have spent this precious time they had together in talking about less ardent matters. He did, however, acknowledge he had never really given it much thought, thinking possibly women wanted children and sex was a means to an end. Eleanor broke into his thoughts.

'So if you married and your wife produced an heir, would you then take a mistress to "pass the time" as you put it, or "for a change" as Tomas so elegantly observed?'

'I have no reason to marry for any other reason than for love as I have money enough without marrying an heiress, so I should abide by my wedding vows "till death do us part" as you say, unless of course my wife became fat and argumentative.'

She allowed herself a smile he noticed. 'If I married for love,' he said, 'I should want no other and would expect the same of my wife or otherwise what would be the point, on this we are in accord.' He looked her in the eye and they understood each other.

However, it appeared Eleanor was not so easy to head off. 'I am relieved to hear it but as a single man you are of the opinion, like Tomas, that using women and paying for the pleasure is acceptable?' Gabriel felt cornered. She was like a dog with a bone.

'Most men do not go to the marriage bed inexperienced Eleanor.' He was aware his tone was less than polite. 'Men in my position cannot generally bed the woman to whom they pay court so other ways have to be sought and yes, this does often mean paying, unless one keeps a handy kitchen maid.' Eleanor tutted; he suspected she was provoking him into this frank disclosure on purpose so decided to provoke her in return with this last comment.

'Yes women of my rank are usually chaperoned and therein lies the crux of the matter. Women are patronised, men make the rules to keep women in their place. Men come to marriage experienced; ladies come to marriage in a state of innocence – for men's pleasure! I do not blame you in particular Gabriel, yet men like you and my brother perpetuate the unfairness, the patriarchy.'

Eleanor shifted the discussion back to Lester Ives and Gabriel was relieved to be out of the firing line.

'Is his wife here today?' Gabriel asked. They had made their way back into the drawing room.

'That is the lady, talking with my relations.' Gabriel saw a large lady of middle years and of very plain appearance.

'Man alive she must be...'

'A very nice woman with exceeding patience!' Eleanor glared at Gabriel for his insensitivity.

'Yes, I am sure. She is so much older than him is what I was going to say.'

'I believe she is near to forty, an older lady but one who has met her end of the bargain and she has given him not one, but three sons.'

'I am sure she is perfectly nice but I am glad I am in a position to choose a wife myself for love and not for what she can bring to the marriage in terms of money. After all, one chooses with one's eyes first before anything else is considered and before you can criticise me on that view, allow me to point out I have also known some beautiful women whom I should not dream of pursuing, for although lovely to look at, were dull companions.' Eleanor's brother came to join them.

'Mama has sent me as I am sure she thinks it unseemly you two talk together so closely; that of course is not what she said but it is undoubtedly what she meant when she sent me on this errand!'

The pair looked at each other and Gabriel laughed at the irony whilst Eleanor glared at Tomas who in turn grinned at his sister affectionately. 'Do I get the impression Eleanor is in a debating mood?' I know my twin well.' He asked the question of Gabriel putting his arm around his sister's waist and squeezing her close. 'She does like an argument; she likes nothing better than to play devil's advocate just to provoke a response. Mama is driven to distraction and rues the day money was spent on her education for her debating skills are sharper now than ever. Come sir, let me fortify you with brandy and supper and I will provide you with tips on how to deflect her.' The three went into supper.

13

When Gabriel returned to Westshore he put Lisbet in charge of the preparations for his visitors. She was exceedingly happy as she liked nothing better than a large dinner party and fourteen was large compared to what she was used to these days.

Gabriel had invited Eleanor's parents, her brother Tomas and her aunt and Uncle Brown. In addition Bendor, Grace and her sister Cora could come. He liked Dr Wilson Chaffer, the local doctor, and as he too was a single man it would balance out the numbers. He also thought to ask his lawyer since he had served him well since his father's death yet seldom saw him socially. They were Mr and Mrs Saul Coates and their daughter Felicity, or Fliss, as she was known. Fliss was twenty and unmarried and therefore could be a companion for Cora. The lawyer was an amiable man so would be a welcome addition to the party.

'Grace will check on the morning that all is in order.'

'A think you can trust me to organise things proper like, A bin doing this since afore you were born!' Lisbet was indignant, her happy mood gone. She was always quick to take offence but Gabriel had known her so long he seldom noticed her stubborn ways.

'Ask Abner to come in, I need to talk to him about the wines and spirits. I hope there is enough of the run French brandy left, it is good stuff.'

'There's eight bottles left so there'll be plenty and there's a dozen of the canary that came in on the same ship.' He might have known she would know just as well as Abner what was in his cellar. It was just as well he could trust them as he had no idea what he had plenty of and what needed replenishing.

To appease her he said: 'You decide on the menu, I can trust you to serve whatever is best but send Abner to me anyway. You will need help from two or three of the village girls also, sort it out how you see fit.' Lisbet was mollified and left to start planning.

♥

The day of the party dawned fair, the weather had forgotten it was autumn and thought it spring again; it was mild and still. The sun flitted behind high white clouds and it looked as if it was set to stay dry for the guests' journeys at least. Bendor and Grace had come late in the morning and much to Lisbet's delight, Grace approved of all the arrangements.

The rest of the party arrived and Gabriel was happy his home should be shown to its best advantage. He was proud of it in all weathers but Westshore looked its best when the sun lit up the lofty rooms through the enormous windows, as it did today. He felt a thrill of anticipation. Drinks had been set out on the terrace and as they were assembling Gabriel found himself standing next to Eleanor

'What a splendid house and what a view! I had always thought Mulgrave had the best situation in England with its magnificent sea views, but I am envious of your house's proximity to the sea. The architect who designed Westshore was clever to make all the rooms take advantage of the sea, I am full of admiration.'

'I have my father to thank; he was the one who had the foresight to build in this style; he told the architect exactly what to do and that is why the house sits so well in its position. The light, the huge skies and the sea are captured just as he wished.'

'How clever of him!'

Gabriel was happy she liked his home she looked well here he thought; he could easily imagine her living here – with him.

'The original house on the plot was built by my grandfather; it was demolished when it became rotted and battered by the salt winds. My father built Westshore when the family fortunes increased due to whaling and coal and when he hoped my mother would produce lots of children to fill the numerous rooms he had built, it is three times the size of the previous house. All the rooms are well proportioned light, airy with high ceilings, which I like. I think the French windows frame the glorious sea views letting in as much light as possible.' Gabriel laughed realising he was running on,' 'I sound arrogant do I not?'

'Rightly so, it is magnificent, you are a very lucky man to live in such a house and in such a location.'

'I am; Westshore stands as testament to the rise of the

Reynolds name who are now firmly established as gentry in Alnmouth, all this has grown from two generations, like your own family.'

Gabriel's countenance suddenly changed: 'It is a fine house yet it has failed to live up to expectations, so far it had never housed the large family my father longed for.' He quickly realised this was not the occasion for gloomy thoughts and said: 'The garden is in need of a woman's touch I think. The house is slightly elevated and the garden therefore slopes down to the beach and sea. Father said my mother had wanted to improve the sandy soil and grow a beautiful garden but she died before she had really got started; now the garden looks more like an extension of the dunes.'

On this bright day in September it was a colourful mix of sea campions, thrift and sea holly. Marram grass and seed heads were invading the boundaries threatening to take over and reclaim it.

'Much could be made of it I am sure; our gardens get blown about by strong winds as I expect do yours, it is a question of finding the right plant for the right location.' He watched her closely as she talked 'I adore flowers. Our gardener produces blooms all year round in a hot house, the same could be managed here I am sure.' Gabriel could feel this enterprising, creative woman was growing on him.

The dinner was a great success; the food and the company were excellent with everyone present being jolly and sociable. The extra staff had worked well so the food arrived at the table hot.

After three or more hours the men sat with their port

while the ladies went back out onto the terrace to enjoy the warmth from the sun and admire the view again. As the men rejoined the ladies they began to stroll down the garden towards the beach. Gabriel had been thanking Lisbet for the meal and so was the last man out onto the terrace. John Barker had waited for him.

'I should like a private word Gabriel if you would hold back a while?' Gabriel could see the party moving off and hearing their laughing chatter awould have liked to join them but knew he could not.

'I hope I do not talk out of turn but it is of Eleanor that I wish to speak.' John Barker looked serious. 'Both her mother and I have noticed the looks that pass between you when you are in the same company and we perhaps have seen a growing fondness between the two of you? I do not want to seem presumptuous but would like to hear what your intentions are in that direction? Forgive me if I am mistaken and for my plain speaking.'

'Not at all Mr Barker, it is as you suspect, on my part at any rate. I do have a growing fondness for your daughter, however, although I hope she has growing feelings for me too, I have not as yet discussed a future with her. I had thought it early yet for declarations of the kind that may lead to any commitment. I do not know if you are aware but I have recently become free from a long standing engagement to a local lady. It was as it turns out, mutually agreeable to both of us to end the relationship and the ties were severed amicably I am pleased to say. I know Eleanor has also recently separated from Captain Seamer.'

'She has and that is one of the reasons I wished to

speak with you today. Eleanor's pride has been dented I imagine, as would any young lady who finds herself deceived in such a blatant way. Although since news of the rift we have had a steady stream of young men at our door; that has boosted her confidence I hope!' He laughed and re-lit his cigar which had gone out.

'My daughter can be very spontaneous, for want of a better word, and I should not want to see her become involved in another serious relationship on the rebound as it were. Eleanor knows her own mind I am sure but still she is young and can be a tad reckless sometimes.'

'It is as you say sir; both of us need to be certain of our feelings. I admire and respect her and am aware of her impulsive nature, I find it refreshing. I should have expected she would attract all the eligible young men of Whitby and although I do not want to rush her I shall have to keep my eye on the situation.' He tried to make light of the comment but again felt a pang of jealousy.

'Eleanor is quite independent both in mind and deed! Any man wanting to commit to her should be aware she would not be content to sit at home with her embroidery. She is of an altogether different temperament to my other daughter. Eleanor has a good business head on her shoulders and handles all her own affairs, she has built up quite a portfolio from small beginnings; I have a certain pride in her and she would be an asset to your business, she has an astute business sense.'

Gabriel looked out across the sands where the party had stopped by the rowing boat that was pulled up on the beach. 'I am sorry to interfere Gabriel; I only have her best interests at heart you understand. I do not come to you as an overbearing parent forbidding you to carry on your suit, if that is what you intend, but I would just like you to have a care. I should hate to see her hurt again; I hope I do not offend you.'

'Not at all for I see we are of the same mind Mr Barker. I hope I can put your mind at rest when I say there is no rush on my part to push Eleanor into any relationship in which she is not comfortable.'

'Affairs of the heart can be very trying, when I first met Eleanor's mother I started at the back of the queue, I can tell you. She was a stunning looking woman, still is to my eyes.' He smiled at the memory. 'It was not until she was assured she would not have to give up her lifestyle and become a Quaker puritan wife that I made any headway at all. We were married at The Friends but as you see today we have strayed far from the path. Eleanor has benefited by the doctrine of equality preached by Quakers and has been given some scope, but she has not been stifled by the puritanical aspects of Quakerism. She learnt to debate at the Meeting House and has her own mind and opinions; an opinionated woman is not every man's first choice for a wife, she does not always take well to direction. She has taken after her mother in that respect.'

'I used to think I wanted an obedient wife but Eleanor has changed my mind; any wife I take I should want to have opinions and be able to debate, but I take your warning!'

'I am pleased we have had this chance to talk and for my part I would be happy to welcome you into our family should things progress in that direction and I know her mother approves of the match.'

'Thank you for the compliment sir.'

'Come let us join your guests, I have kept you too long away from them already.' Gabriel was glad to have had this talk with her father for he knew now, despite warnings from Bendor and her father, he was in love with Eleanor Barker.

The rest of the day passed in a leisurely way but Gabriel had little opportunity to be alone with Eleanor until it was time for his guests to depart. When the horses were brought to the front of the house and everyone was preparing to leave, Gabriel moved to help Eleanor to mount.

'So did father threaten you with the shotgun earlier?'

'Not exactly. He just wanted to let me know he has your best interests at heart that is all.'

'I see, I am his daughter I understand, but it is demeaning to be spoken of as if I am a chattel to be passed from one man to another.' Gabriel was surprised to see irritation on her face.

'It was not like that at all, in fact he more or less warned me that if I had any intentions then I should move a little quicker if I was to secure you as other gentlemen were lining up all the way from Whitby to gain your attentions.' He looked up at her and saw her shoulders relax as she gathered her reins.

'And do you?'

'Do I what?' he teased.

'Have any intentions?'

'I have lots of intentions but whether any of them concern a lady fishing for compliments I am not sure.'

'Then I shall no doubt be forced to seek approval from any number of suitors that are, as we speak, camping on my doorstep!' Gabriel smiled up at her and wished she could stay.

'Do you think we could meet tomorrow? I could ride over to Warkworth in the morning.'

'Better if I came to you; I could bring my maid as chaperone.' He noted the pointed comment. 'Father and Tomas are leaving for Whitby in the morning; we are staying on an extra day or two so I will not be missed.'

'I would like that very much, I am unsure when I shall be in Whitby again – not for some weeks I think so another chance for us to get to know each other better would be pleasant.'

'Thank you for today, I have had a lovely visit, it will be nice to picture you in your own home with all your things about you when I return to Sandsend. Now I have seen how you live I will feel closer to you, picturing you walking on this beautiful beach. When I look at the stars I shall imagine you looking through your window seeing them too.'

'Should it not be me uttering these poetic words? Gabriel said. 'You put me to shame, but I agree, that is how I feel too, I often wonder if you have gone out into the garden when all are abed and wish I could be walking there with you.'

'Until tomorrow,' he said. The party began to move off, he watched her out of sight; Eleanor looked back and waved as the dunes began to swallow her up.

Gabriel passed through the kitchen where Lisbet and her helpers were still hard at work clearing up the mountain of dinner plates, platters, bowls and cutlery.

'At last A see which way the wind blows,' Lisbet said nodding her head towards the direction of the departing guests. 'A like the look of her, yer could do a lot worse.'

'Mrs Cotter,' Gabriel tried to keep his face straight, 'have I ever sought your opinion in any matter other than the cooking of my meals? Kindly scrub your dishes and leave well alone.'

One of the young kitchen girls brought in to help looked anxious and waited for a storm to hit. Lisbet grinned, knowing herself to be on firm ground after such a fine dinner. 'I should be pleased to serve her as mistress of Westshore, yer need to hurry up afore someone else gets there first – a young lady such as she will not be waiting long an' yer not a spring chicken yerself now are yer?'

'I shall require you to cook something special for dinner tomorrow; I expect a visitor.'

Lisbet nodded and smiled knowingly.

♥

The next day Eleanor saw him as she rode towards Westshore. He was looking out for her and her heart missed a beat. Charity rode by her side on this blustery day.

'I am glad I shall catch a look at this man that has you all a flutter,' she smiled at her mistress, 'is he very handsome?'

'He is, like a hero from a romantic novel, tall, dark and handsome with the most beautiful eyes which are the colour of the sea.'

'I might run off with him myself in that case, that happens in novels. A girl can dream.' Eleanor laughed. 'Not in this story.'

At Westshore Gabriel came forward to meet them; he helped Eleanor dismount and a stable lad appeared to help Charity.

'This is my maid – Charity.' She raised an eyebrow as she saw him register the name.

'I feel we have met before,' he said confusing the young woman.

'I see what you mean, very good-looking!' Charity whispered to her mistress as she was sent away to drink tea with the cook.

'Come through to the drawing room, it is a little draughty to sit on the terrace today I think.' Eleanor took a seat by the fire and they took tea themselves.

'I am surprised Alnmouth Bay is so small – compared to Whitby I mean, you do well here?' She had seen the port as she rode past, she had expected it to be a similar size to Whitby.

'I do but a lot of my business is conducted from Newcastle which in turn is larger than Whitby.'

They talked about the area until they had finished their tea. She said: 'Might we walk on the beach; where would we come to if we went in the other direction from the bay?'

'Boulmer is the next hamlet but we would have to go around the headland to reach it, it is perhaps three or four miles away.'

They set off without Charity who remained at Westshore and headed north walking close to the dunes which offered some protection from the wind.

'Should your maid not be in attendance?' he raised an eyebrow.

'She would prefer to sit by the fire I expect rather than play gooseberry. Do you not trust me Gabriel; do you think I will compromise you?' She saw Gabriel laugh although he also looked a little taken aback. She thought him quite conservative; she knew it would be easy to shock him.

'Your cousin has left for her honeymoon?' he said.

'Yes I am quite envious; three months travelling in Europe, I have only ever seen Holland. Have you travelled abroad much?'

'I think I told you I too have been to Holland both for business and pleasure. I have also sojourned in France and Italy; twice I have been to the Baltics on business; Denmark was freezing, everyone wrapped up in furs and the snow deeper than any I have ever seen. We took a sleigh ride to our hotel which was quite romantic except I was with my father and not a lady of course.' She caught him watching her and she smiled encouragement. 'We had gone there to set up a regular shipment of timber that is why I need a new stronger ship, it will be solely for these longer trips in the icy, often frozen Baltic seas.

'I should like to see more of the world, I prefer heat to cold but I would welcome the sight of so much snow and riding in a sleigh with a handsome man by my side.' She glanced at him sideways and saw him smile. 'You would not need furs – I should keep you warm.' She had her arm through his and he squeezed her hand. She raised her eyes to his and noticed he was still smiling; her heart beat faster.

'Lisbet will be waiting to serve dinner, are you hungry?' They returned to Westshore and sat down to dine; Charity was absent from the room.

'Your cook is very capable,' Eleanor said as they finished the last course. They had dined on eggs and salad followed by roast pheasant, capon and cutlets. After the fish there had been tarts and syllabub with fresh raspberries and early blackberries.

'She has been with us forever it seems, besides cooking she is also my housekeeper and when I was a boy she was my nursemaid too, after mother died that is.'

'Goodness! A force to be reckoned with, I am surprised she has a minute left in the day to call her own.'

'There is a girl who comes in daily to help too, but Lisbet is not young it has to be said.'

'This is a large house for you alone; you must rattle around in it.'

'It is rather and I do "rattle about" as you put it but I am often at the bay from early in the morning until late in the evening.'

'All work and no play makes Jack a dull boy, or should that be a dull Gabriel.' She tipped her head and smiled. 'As you are an only child I would have thought you would be named after your father?'

'I am; I am Jack Gabriel Reynolds but have always gone by my second name, it was easier. I am named Gabriel after my mother's uncle who used to live with us when I was small. He was killed at sea when he was twenty two. None of my mother's side of the family survive, they were not blessed with long lives; mother was twenty seven when she died.'

Eleanor covered his hand with hers and held it for a moment; she saw what she thought was a vulnerability in his eyes.

'How awful it must have been for a small boy to lose his mother so young, you must miss her still.'

'Father said she struggled to give life to me and the effort weakened what was already a delicate constitution, it took seven more years for her to conceive again and this time the labours of the child bed were too much for her, first she died and three days after my new born brother died too. Father never got over it, we were both heartbroken. My father consoled himself with hard work and by doting on me, his sole surviving son.' She watched as Gabriel ran his fingers down his cheek unconsciously. She wanted to console him.

'How tragic for you and your father; he never married again?'

'His heart was broken; when we Reynolds men give our hearts we give them forever it seems.' Eleanor saw a look on Gabriel's face but did not fully recognise it; sadness mixed with pride?

'He was a good father, when he was not working we were often together. In the evenings we would build model ships together and plan for when I joined the family business but I remember feeling the responsibility of being the most important person in my father's life. I realise now he could have had his pick of the ladies but he would entertain none.'

'That is a lot to put on a young boy's shoulders, was your childhood all sadness?'

'Not at all; it was solitary but like many children who live on the coast I spent much time on the beach and in boats, especially in the summer. After long days at Reynolds' Shipping father and I would take out the rowing boat and cast a line for herring. Most days I would wait in the dunes watching for him to come home along the beach. My father taught me to swim, ride and to read, it was from him I inherited my love of books; pirate stories were always my favourite.'

'How did you come to meet Sir Bendor; are you not friends from childhood?'

'I met him at school. When I was eleven – father sent me away to be schooled at Alnwick, five or so miles from here. He wanted me to have a better education than he had had, he saw the world was changing fast and saw I would need to be equipped with learning if I was to help build the business. For the first time we were to be apart. It must have been a difficult decision for him but he was determined I would not become involved in the whaling industry; that was far too dangerous a pursuit for his only son.' She watched him closely as he stroked his chin which was beginning to darken with stubble.

'I was keen to go to school; I had spent many hours alone or with just the company of my tutor, yet I felt guilt at leaving my father. I knew he would be lonely without me. I am sorry, I am boring you with my life story.'

'Not at all have I wanted to know all about you, I want to know what makes you tick, please continue.'

'You are easy to talk to; I have rarely spoken of my childhood to anyone but Bendor.' She smiled encouraging him to continue. 'He was an aristocrat from a prominent

Northumberland family, distant relatives of the Duke of Northumberland who built Alnwick Castle. They built Warkworth Castle too come to think of it – but it did not seem to make a difference that we came from different backgrounds, we got on well from the start. He was always the more outgoing, he drew me out of my shell as it were; he helped me lose some of my introspection I think.'

They moved to sit by the fire and Gabriel moved a book so he could sit down, 'We both enjoyed reading and sailing; we rowed for the school. School holidays were spent in rowing boats or on Reynolds' ships plying the coast between Alnmouth and Whitby, when we weren't sailing we were in the library.'

'An unusual pastime for young men, I doubt Tomas has ever picked up a book since he left school. I love to read too, my father is always bemoaning the fact I have my head in my accounts or a book.'

'I have a good library here you should have a look if we have the time. Where was I?

'You were getting to the interesting part, 'she raised her eyebrows, when you were becoming young men.'

'I just wanted to say we grew up but not apart; Ben is the brother I never had and a great friend.'

'I would wager you were pleased to have a friend, you would have felt less lonely? I cannot imagine being an only child.'

'I was glad, his family were good to me; his mother tried to guide the both of us – we are still close but Bendor's father died when he was just off to Cambridge; he inherited the title at eighteen – it was a huge responsibility for him ' Eleanor poured more tea.

'Enough about me, tell me about you: I already know some of the more licentious bits!' He gave her a look that made her glad she was sitting down. 'Did you go away to school?'

'We were Quakers then, I went to the Friends school on Church Street.' She pulled a face. 'We also had a governess as father wanted us to know about the "real world", I fear he now rues the day as he thinks I am too worldly wise. She taught us Dutch, not French, which came in useful when I found myself in Holland.'

He smiled easily she noticed; she liked making him smile, his eyes lit up his face. It was a lovely smile she thought; he took her breath away when he looked at her intently like he was looking at her now.

'Mama was keen for her daughters to receive the same rights and expectations as her son, it was one of the Quaker doctrines she held on to and I am pleased she did, any daughters I have shall be just as educated as any sons.' She thought Gabriel looked shocked by her last comment, she enjoyed stirring him up, she suspected he had never thought of such things before.

'You are close with Tomas?'

'Very close; we are alike in all ways but one. As children we did everything together, reading, writing, riding, swimming; Tomas and I learnt to swim supporting each other with driftwood floats. I once stopped my brother from sinking and pumped brine from his lungs to save him; he owes me his life as I remind him often!'

'You are not so close to your sister?'

'I love my sister of course but,' she wrinkled her

nose, 'she has grown very staid, she has always been reserved but since her marriage, she has become more so. I expect she always felt on the outside; Tomas and I were inseparable. I think she was not wishful of our adventures, but envious of the intimacy that was borne from us being twins, it must have been hard for her.'

Gabriel led her through to the library where they perused the books idly for a while.

'While my sister continued to be a Friend and eventually married a Quaker, Tomas has strayed even further from the path than I; he is learning the shipbuilding trade from father and the ways of the world from the inns and taverns of Whitby; this is the one thing we fall out about; his louche ways.'

Gabriel took down a book from the shelf and they discussed it for a while before Gabriel asked: 'You mentioned you are more than a little interested in the shipping industry, you have many business interests?'

'It is common practice for women raised in the Quaker faith to hold shares and investments in their own right. As soon as I was able, when not at the beach or out riding, I could be found poring over my accounts.' She looked at his smiling face. 'Why is that so funny?'

'Most young ladies I know pore over magazines and fabric samples, not profit and loss columns.'

'I take a keen interest in my investments I have been handling my own affairs with advice given to me from my father's accountant, for some time now.'

'You will be quite a catch then.' She knew he was mocking her, she could see just by looking around he was not in need of her money.

'Some of the women of Whitby, whose husbands are often absent for long periods of time and who take high risks of early widowhood when they marry seafarers, are used to doing business, making decisions and handling money; it is commonplace also that widows take over the running of their husbands' ships if there are no sons to continue the line. Have you not come across this in Alnmouth?'

'I cannot say I have, I would have noticed if someone like you had appeared at an investors meeting.' His eyes were mesmerising; she took a book from the shelf and gazed at it inattentively.

'These women were generous enough to advise me on investments when I sought their opinions, so when a bank on Baxtergate founded by two widows opened, I was keen to repay the favour and support these enterprising women by moving some of my banking to them. My father warned me to be careful against moving all my funds and not to put all my eggs in one basket. I heeded his advice; I may sometimes be at odds with him regarding other matters but I respect his financial and business acumen.'

'Your father looks over your investments?'

'Not at all. I started out with small ventures. As you know ships are rarely owned outright, the sharing of risk being the major reason for the practice of having multiple shareholders; five pounds can buy a small stake in a large enterprise, especially in the smaller vessels such as sloops and schooners. Now I have shares in bigger vessels, The Freelove a whaler, and two other Whitby built ships do well for me, she was built and is part owned by the leading Quaker shipbuilders in Whitby. She is a successful whaler and by far my best investment yet. Are you looking for investors for your new ship?'

'I thought of it but I am to fund it myself and that way take all the profit.'

'And all the risk.'

'I think it will be a small one.'

'A pity, I should have liked the chance to invest.' Eleanor had always resented that her money from these investments would go to William on her marriage; she thought perhaps she may not mind so much if she were to marry someone like Gabriel.

When it was time to leave, Gabriel said he would ride back with her to Warkworth. 'I do not want to keep you from your work Gabriel, I can manage with Charity.'

'I would like to see you safe back to your uncle's and besides who knows when we shall see each other again.'

They rode with Charity at a discreet distance behind. 'I was pleased to be out of the way today', Eleanor said. 'Lester Ives of all people is paying a visit to see my Aunt and Uncle.' She arched a perfectly shaped brow. 'I would have been tempted to engage him in conversation about his morals yet I know it not proper and would lead to discord but I should like to know what motivates a man to behave as he does.'

Gabriel half laughed. 'I do not think you would like the answer to that particular question; it is obvious what motivates him is it not. By "asking" do you not mean preaching to him about his disreputable ways?'

'Preaching! It is typical a man would take the man's side.' She hoped Gabriel felt the full force of the look as she glared at him. She reined in her horse.

'It is not a question of sides, for all we know his wife may be happy with the relationship; it was an arranged marriage so she may dislike him, or at least not care if he takes his pleasure elsewhere.' Eleanor could hardly believe what she was hearing.

'Men! You are all of the same mind and not to be trusted it seems! What woman would want her husband being talked of as he is gossiped about; it is humiliating for her surely. As I said before he is not even discreet, he shows no respect for his wife, but then you possibly think she deserves none. She has no rights, she should simply keep quiet and look after her children.'

'You will never get it Eleanor,' he said stiffly.

'Get what?'

'A world where men and women are treated equally.'

'So women should simply be out of sight and out of mind; keep silent and let men carry on being "men",' she bit back.

'Eleanor, please be reasonable – not all men treat women badly. Look to your parents; I notice your father is very considerate of your mother, from the little I remember my parents also were happy in each other's company, they were a partnership. A marriage built on love, trust and respect should be strived for I think. Lester Ives has a different agenda because his is a marriage in name only.'

'I suppose so, it still vexes me however.'

They rode on, the sun hazing over as they came to the River Coquet. 'I can manage from here Gabriel; it is but a short distance. If you come to the house you will feel pressure to come in and your work day will be entirely lost.' They were shielded by a clump of alders and Gabriel dismounted and helped Eleanor down from her horse. She noticed he kept his hands on her waist.

'Thank you for the company and dinner, I am sorry if I appear argumentative, once I get a bee in my bonnet I do not know when to be quiet Mama always says.'

She looked into his eyes which today seemed more blue than grey. He was close enough for her to notice he smelled faintly of sandalwood, she could feel his breath on her cheek as she gazed up at him expectantly.

'I have just thought of a way to quieten you,' he said brushing her lips lightly with his own before closing his eyes and kissing her hard.

Charity had ridden ahead; her horse began cropping the sweet grass of the riverbank. 'This is what you do instead of thrashing a lady is it?' She reached up and put the palms of her hands on his chest.

Gabriel said: 'I wish we could freeze this moment and stay here forever – I will miss you my love, letters are all well and good but-' She kissed him softly, searchingly, she felt herself aroused at his touch. He pulled her into him so they were as one, their bodies moulded together perfectly.

'I had better be on my way,' she sighed. 'Until we meet again.'

Reluctantly he helped her to mount, she moved off wondering how this man had managed to capture her heart so quickly and so completely. Even when she was annoyed with him she liked him. She knew she was leaving Warkworth the next day but longed to stay, she hoped he would find a way to see her again soon.

Charity smiled at her mistress. 'You appear to have it bad.'

'I hope I have it good,' she said smiling back.

14

The autumn continued mild, just the occasional fret spoiling the shortening days. Occasionally the sea cut up rough and the tides were as high as the new moon. Gabriel's breakfast was brought to table by Lisbet, a worried look on her face. She fussed about unloading the tray and frowned. Gabriel waited for the words to begin to tumble, as he knew they would; he had known her so long he could tell she was unhappy about something and sure enough sooner or later, he would know about it. She headed back towards the kitchen but stopped and turned gripping the tray in her plump fingers.

'Can A have a word sir 'bout Jax.' Her tone was more conciliatory than he had expected. It was not often she called him "sir" these days.

'Jax, why what has he done?'

'That's just it; nothing. Well, he's gone sir, he had no dinner or supper an' he's not slept in the stable these last two nights. A waited up for him long into the night; A'm right worried, it's not like him to miss his grub.' Lisbet's Geordie accent was at its strongest when she was upset.

'Has he made friends since he came here? He could have gone to see them do you think?'

'Not that A know about, he's a canny lad, does his errands and A've not known him to go off afore. What if he's had an accident or mebbe he's bin pressed?' Lisbet was close to tears, Gabriel knew the boy was the son she never had.

'Well we can rule out pressing I should think as I have heard nothing of the press gangs hereabouts so far this year. He is such a scrawny thing no one in their right mind would take him; he would blow over in a strong wind but I suppose an accident could befall him if, as you say, he does not wander off generally.'

'He keeps regular hours here Master Gabriel, he likes his snap and he's never missed a meal ever, til now.'

'Have you asked about Alnmouth when you are out doing your marketing?'

'Most folk know him and know where he belongs. He's such a good lad and is allus polite when me or Abner do send him on a job. We allus tells him to be good cause he is representing the Reynolds' family and don't bring no disgrace to the name. A never heard nowt but good said of him.'

'Strange then I agree, send Abner in will you?'

To himself, Gabriel thought no doubt the boy would turn up when he was hungry he was a young lad; perhaps he had found a girl.

Abner limped into the dining room, tray in hand, and began to clear the table. 'Well, what is your view on the lad's disappearance? Has the family silver gone with him?' Gabriel was half in jest.

'Nay I reckon the lad's honest A can't understand it maself. The old woman's convinced he's bin pressed, press gangs are always a threat, thinks he's bin rounded up an' she'll never seen him again.

'So before he went you had no idea he was planning to leave, was he behaving differently? Did he say anything to make you think he was about to flee the nest?' Gabriel liked the lad and thought it would be troublesome to have to find a new stable hand if he had gone for good.

Abner swept the crumbs from the table. 'There were one thing... somethin' out of ordinary like.'

'Go on.'

'A noticed at snap time the lad would eat his fill right enough then A see'd he had a hanky on his knee and was putting bits of his meat in it. He was doin' it sly like and thought a'd not seen him. When he left the table he'd sneak it in his pocket. A watched him after the first time and he were at it every day last week. The lad knows Lisbet denies him nowt; A can't understand what he were up to. A watched him through the kitchen window a few times through ma eye glass as A thought he might be nicking food from the pantry, A never saw him pinching nowt else. A thought he might be giving it to that pesky dog but he knows he gets all the scraps he wants an all.'

'Well I will ask about. Does he go to the inns?'

'Only when A send him to Hope an Anchor for me porter, he allus comes straight back as far as I know.'

When Gabriel's horse was saddled Abner stood by as Gabriel adjusted his girth. 'He got a cushy number here has Jax an' he knows it, A can't think he'd run off like, why would he?

'I'll see what can be done.'

Gabriel set off with Scrabble in close attendance going

down to the beach at a canter, searching the dunes from his high vantage point but he saw nothing of the boy. Scrabble conducted his own search running in and out of the dunes; Gabriel knew if the dog got the scent of Jax he would have gone crazy barking a warning. If the boy was in the dunes injured Scrabble would flush him out, Gabriel knew Jax and Scrabble had become good pals.

Gabriel headed towards The Alnmouth Boy, named after him by his father. She was setting sail on the next tide; he needed to give Nathan Pearson the documents he would need to deliver up the next shipment of coal. Scrabble kept close to the heels of his master.

The mist was clearing and a thin drizzle was blustering about the dock. As he approached his ship, he saw what looked like a pile of old rags. Scrabble ran on ahead and tail wagging greeted the heap of flea ridden detritus, which turned out to be a straggly haired girl. Scrabble was licking her face and appeared to be showing the sort of excitement he reserved for when food was being offered. He could not imagine this half starved waif had food to spare for a dog so why was he so excited? As Gabriel's shadow crossed over her she looked up with sunken eyes.

'How do you come to be friends with my dog?' Scrabble was a fickle character and usually befriended only those who fed him.

'He come every day A see'd him a lot lately. I din't know he were yer dog mister.'

'Was the dog with someone?'

'Aye, wi' a lad.'

'What lad, did he have a name?'

'Aye he were called Jax but A not seen him since

yesterday.'

'How come you know the boy?'

'A don't want to get him in bother but he were kind to me, like.' Her Geordie accent was strong and against the wind that had whipped up Gabriel found it hard to understand her. He squatted down to her level thankful the wind blew the stench of her away from him.

'How was he kind? You won't be getting him into trouble; I need to know where he's gone, he is my stable lad.'

'He's been bringing me snap. Telled me to wait here every mornin' and fer about a week he's come, but not yesterday and not today Am fair famished mister.' She cupped her hands together and looked at him with a practised doleful expression.

He held out a coin in front of her. 'If you see him I want to know, the building over there,' he pointed to his offices. 'Come to me there if you see him today or I will come here again in the morning and if you've seen him or heard anything about his whereabouts there will be another coin for you, do you understand?'

'A'll be sure to keep ma eyes open mister, he's a good lad.'

Gabriel watched her hurry off; the thought of a full belly quickening her step. At least he knew now where the food from the lad's plate was going.

It bothered Gabriel that children as young as six or seven were living rough on the docks and wharves begging for food, apparently alone in the world. Most ports, Newcastle, Sunderland, Whitby and Alnmouth, had this problem nowadays. He suspected some were sent to beg by their parents and did at least have roofs over their heads, even if they were overcrowded hovels. Parents knew that coppers were more likely to be spared to a child than an adult who could often find work, even if it was seasonal and low paid. Fathers were often at sea or worse lost at sea, and mothers had too many mouths to feed. The poverty to be found in some coastal ports was grinding; he had often thought he needed to help more somehow.

He turned his collar up against the wind which had sprung up and went to see his captain. He looked out to sea hoping the weather was not about to turn. His business with Nathan concluded he headed for The Hope and Anchor buffeted by the strong wind that had become more troublesome over the last half hour.

Dun coloured rain clouds were pushing in, the swell at the harbour wall was heavy, he was glad he was not sailing today for the sea was turning rough and argumentative. Nathan might not be able to get away if this turned nasty; time was money and Gabriel would be sorry for the delay. The quay was always busy and today was no exception. His deck hands were victualling The Alnmouth Boy pushing barrels up the gangplank. Another ship nearby was hoping to catch the same tide and huge bales lurched as they were winched aboard in the howling wind. He headed to the tavern. He pushed his way to the bar and ordered ale from the landlord.

Mr Squires, good day. You know my stable lad, Jax?'

'Aye Mr Reynolds sir, he do come for Abner's porter sometimes.' He put a tankard of ale in front of Gabriel.

'Has he been in the last couple of days do you

remember?' The landlord rubbed his stubbly chin as if the act would help him to access the information he was seeking. 'Not seen him 'bout this week.' The sound of raised voices erupted from further down the bar, Gabriel looked to see what the commotion was. He could see two French sailors face to face, yelling obscenities at each other, their arms flailing in the air like flapping gull wings. Only the strength of two other French seamen kept them apart; arguing over a card game no doubt. The landlord raised his eyes heavenward.

'That Frenchy crew! Allus trouble – they've bin ashore two days now causing bother, all sailors likes to drink and womanise but them lot are a wormy crew sir I can tell yer.'

The voices were getting louder and angrier, red faces looked like ripe plums fit to burst. The sound of a table being upturned and crashing could be heard; a full scale brawl broke out. The landlord moved his considerable bulk quickly for a man of his size and arrived at the scene dragging first one, and then the other, to separate the two men. With the help of the local muscle they were held apart still spitting and cursing. The doors of the taproom were flung open and the two men were unceremoniously ejected. Gabriel paid his money and left the inn no wiser but a little warmer.

Outside, the wind was still hollering and rain plopped heavily upon his head. He looked about the harbour trying to decide what more he could do. He buttoned his coat against the gale and headed back to The Alnmouth Boy. The weather was now going to delay her sailing he felt certain of it, he and Nat discussed whether it was worth the risk to sail. Finally Gabriel decided to delay until the morning, it was frustrating but not worth risking his crew and the ship. Nat walked with Gabriel back to his offices, both men held onto their cocked hats as gusts blew the sea onto the dock giving their boots a rinsing.

His clerk was poring over books as Gabriel and Nat were blown into the warmth of the outer office. Removing his coat and shaking off the rainwater from his hat he greeted Joshua Willard who had worked for his father for twenty two years. Gabriel went through to his office and closing the door behind them poured himself and Nat a brandy. He sat behind his father's old desk and motioned for Nat to take the seat opposite.

The two men had known each other many years, Gabriel liked Nat and knew him to be good at his job. Nat Pearson would not shy away from sailing unless the weather meant risking life and limb; he had been a sailor all his life and had captained one or other of the Reynolds' ships capably and without fault. Gabriel hoped to make him captain of the new ship. Nat would appreciate the gesture he knew.

Gabriel had sailed with him on his first trip when, with his father, they had done the hop to Newcastle. Nat was a typical straight talking Geordie but he fancied himself as a bit of a story teller – like a lot of seafarers he was good at spinning a yarn. When Gabriel had been a boy, Nat had thrilled him with his stories of shipwrecks, smuggling and pirates, mostly apocryphal Gabriel now realised. On that first sailing with him, Gabriel was green with seasickness all the way to Newcastle; it was a story Nat liked to remind him of in jest from time to time.

'I wasn't aware we had many French ships put into Alnmouth at this time of year?' Gabriel said.

'It happens, but less than half a dozen times each year, apart, of course, from the smuggling ships which drop anchor further off. Usual port for the French nowadays is Newcastle; we can't accommodate some of the biggest frigates these days.'

He took a drink of the warming brandy. 'They like a drink for sure, the working girls like it when they arrive they seem to have plenty of dosh to throw about, although some say they won't go with them, says they have strange tastes!'

Gabriel laughed, 'Stranger than the Dutch?'

'For certain aye!' Nat then related a bawdy tale he had heard the night before in The Schooner; which was their chosen inn now they had been thrown out of every other tavern in Alnmouth. The story was about one of the seamen dressing up as a woman and singing in a falsetto voice.

'From far off yer would have thought him a lass!' Nat said shaking his head at the memory. 'The Frenchy took out his pigtail and made a hairstyle like a woman's, he was wearing a shift and had a shawl around his shoulders. He had even fashioned,' and here Nat cupped his upturned hands under his chest, 'bosoms from rags stuffed down his front! We all laughed till he started moving about the tables. At first he were lolling about his own shipmates and singing and cavorting, touching up his own crew. We were enjoying it like but then he meks a bee line for young Harry Trigger and starts crooning in his ear and grabs him, well yer can guess where.'

Gabriel laughed. Harry was sixteen and a new crew member. He always turned bright red if Gabriel spoke to him.

'Poor lad he would feel the shame.'

'Aye well he felt summat! The next minute he shocked us all by landing the "fair maiden" a right punch in his belly, A nearly fell off me chair laughing, never knew he had it in him. Next thing a brawl starts as one of theirs goes for young Harry so one of ours has to get stuck in; it were all over soon enough.'

Gabriel topped up their drinks. 'Seems they have a different way of enjoying themselves?' Gabriel offered.

'That there captain of theirs is a right dandy; more gold braid on his uniform than an admiral. He stands up and shouts, in French mind, and they all starts singing, no idea what the words meant but us could guess by the hand signals what the gist were.' Nat smiled as he remembered. 'There's a wench I know says it's not girls the captain wants, he has different appetites.'

'Different appetites, what sort of thing?' Gabriel, like most men, was curious about such things.

'Well she says he started mekking eyes at her right enough and then asked if she had any brothers, when she said she did he wanted to know how old they were! She told him she only had one an' he be twenty, he soon lost interest. Then he asked her if she could bring him a boy, a young boy like, said he'd pay her to bring him a lad not older 'en fourteen! She told him to fling his hook and left him to it.'

'Did this take place on this trip?'

'Nah, she told me this afore, possibly spring time if A

212

remember right.' The story struck a chord with Gabriel. His mind went on a path he did not like.

'What is the name of the French ship in port now?'

'Bon Chance, that's her there on yon side of the Dutch frigate.'

'You say they've been in port for a couple of days?'

'Aye Sunday night they dropped anchor. Why, what's on yer mind?' Gabriel hurriedly told him about the missing stable lad; the light mood of a few moments ago had gone. 'Yer don't think he's been taken...'

'It could be coincidence.' Gabriel's mind was racing. Before Nat could finish the sentence Gabriel ran out of the office and down the quay not stopping to pick up his coat. The rain was heavy now and the wind whipped at his hair, he ran towards the Bon Chance dodging people and animals and scattering boxes in his wake. He didn't know what he was going to say when he got to the ship; he would think of that when he got there. All he knew was he had a bad feeling about this story of Nat's.

He strode up the Bon Chance gang plank, arriving at the top out of breath and soaked to the skin, 'I need to speak with your captain' he asked the first man he saw. The First Mate understood and led Gabriel below deck until they reached an oak door, the seaman knocked and left.

Gabriel heard a noise from the other side: it took a minute before the door opened to reveal a stocky, heavy bellied man, clean shaven and wearing his grey hair tied in a queue. He wore a blue uniform with gold trimming; he looked a little dapper for a merchant ship but Gabriel thought he recognised him from Nat's description.

Now he was face to face with the captain, who he suspected of having Jax, he still had not thought what he was going to say. He had acted on instinct before he had had time to think. The captain looked surprised to see Gabriel but greeted him well enough.

'Bonjour Monsieur, how can I 'elp you?' The French captain smiled showing the glint of a gold tooth. Gabriel stepped inside the cabin. 'My name is Gabriel Reynolds, good day to you sir.'

In the event Gabriel did not have to invent a story for he got no further into his discourse. Before he could proceed further the sound of wood scraping against wood could be heard behind the Frenchman's desk. Gabriel looked over the captain's shoulder just in time to see a shaven headed boy leap out from behind the bunk and launch himself through the gap between the captain and the door jamb. There was a scuffle as the Frenchman tried to grab the boy by the collar but Jax was too nimble and was behind Gabriel's legs clinging to his coat tails, sobbing.

'I think you'll find that's my stable lad!' Gabriel roared. He felt his temper explode; before the captain knew what had hit him, Gabriel landed a punch square on his jaw sending him reeling backwards onto the floor.

Gabriel somehow managed to drag and carry Jax and headed up towards what little daylight there was left on deck. Nat, who had followed Gabriel to the ship, was waiting and grabbed Jax from the sweating and panting Gabriel. He ran down the gangplank carrying him. Gabriel rubbed his knuckles and bent over trying to get his breath back.

Once ashore Nat righted Jax onto his feet and held the trembling boy by the shoulders; Jax flinched and pulled away.'

'Hey, hey it's okay lad you're safe now it's me, Nat.' The two men exchanged concerned glances.

'Let's get you home,' Gabriel said kindly. The wind still blew and buffeted hard in gusts but the rain had decided not to bother hanging around. The two men towering over the boy walked either side of him back to the offices.

A fire was still burning in the outer chamber; Joshua had gone out, which saved Gabriel from having to explain what was going on. He poured Jax brandy in the hope it would stop the boy from shaking, his teeth chattered from fright and the cold; his pale and petrified face stared blankly at the floor.

'I'm just glad we found him when we did.' The two men had moved away and talked in whispers to each other whilst watching the boy shake as if in a convulsion. Nat brought Copper around. 'Nat, thank you, one of your stories turned out to be true sadly for Jax.'

'Come, let me get you home and warm.' Nat held Copper. 'Looks like being embayed was lucky for Jax if not for us Nat.' Gabriel's voice was whipped away by the gale.

'Come for supper?' he yelled through the storm as he mounted. He held out his hand to grab Jax's slender arm to pull him up to ride pillion, Jax hesitated and avoided looking up into Gabriel's face. Eventually the boy held out his skinny arm and clambered up.

♥

Lisbet almost smothered Jax as she enfolded him in her lardy arms but Jax was sullen and withdrawn and held himself rigid and tense. Gabriel gave instructions for a bed to be made up indoors. Lisbet made it ready once she had put enough food in front of the boy to keep him full for a week.

Jax sat head down, with his hands on his knees, not even looking at the food. Lisbet, who thought food a cure all, looked anxiously at Abner; she had never known the boy to refuse food before. Abner followed Gabriel into his study.

'Where'd yer find him?'

Gabriel shook his head. 'I'm not sure Lisbet needs to know the whole truth for it is possibly a sickening tale. If what I think has happened to Jax he has been ill used, very ill used indeed.'

Gabriel told him what he suspected, that the boy may have suffered abuse of a sexual nature at the hands of the French captain.

'I don't know how long he had been there when I arrived but I would imagine he has been on board for two days perhaps?' He repeated the story Nat had told about the Frenchman and how he came to suspect Jax had been taken. He explained how the subsequent rescue of the terrified boy was brought about.

'The man, if you can call him that, has depraved tastes.'

'Man alive it's not normal,' Abner looked shocked. 'A been at sea and A heard of such things afore but poor Jax, he be only a bairn.'

Gabriel, with Abner's help, removed his riding boots

and wet clothes. 'It is up to you what you tell Lisbet, whatever you tell her, both of you need to tread lightly with him. Of course he will now live in the house as was promised him before. Go and fetch Dr Chaffer will you? Who knows what marks are under his clothes.'

'Yer won't have to tell Lisbet to have a care for she's that relieved to see him back.'

Within the hour the doctor was shown into Gabriel's study. Wilson Chaffer had a small practice in Alnmouth and had a good reputation; he was young and idealistic. Although Gabriel rarely had need of a doctor himself, Chaffer had attended his father in his last weeks, so he and Gabriel had become friendly. Gabriel had heard told Dr Chaffer often helped the poor of Alnmouth even if they couldn't pay; he was an intelligent man and forward thinking in his work.

Gabriel told the story again. Lisbet had taken Jax up to his new room and given him night clothes and tucked him up in bed. The doctor went to see Jax and on his return Gabriel handed Wilson a glass of port.

'The lad is scared to death, it took all my powers of persuasion for him to tell me where he had pain, although we could have guessed if what we think is true. I was just hoping you had rescued him before he'd been assaulted but it seems not. He wouldn't let me examine him; he is embarrassed or ashamed. – I have left him ointment, poor lad. It's what it has done to his mind which is most worrying; he must have been scared for his life if he didn't do as he was bid.'

Both men were silent pondering the horror that had befallen the boy. 'He's safe now and if I know Lisbet he'll not be running errands alone until he is one and twenty. She will look to his needs before mine for the foreseeable future.' He would not mind if she did.

'I'll call again tomorrow and see how he is getting on. He's lucky to have you as his master; I don't know many who would put themselves out for a stable hand.'

'Stay to supper; Nat Pearson one of my captains is coming and Lisbet always cooks enough to feed the navy.' At that moment Nat was shown in and the three men went into supper. Lisbet began to serve them still worried and concerned but silent which was always a bad sign.

'Mrs Cotter, Jax may not want to eat – I know you said he had no appetite earlier, but we need to keep his strength up. If you could make him some bone broth that would nourish, if he would take it,' She loaded the table with dishes.

'It's on the stove now Doctor, me mam allus made us a bone broth when we was poorly and it made us grow an inch while we got better A'm sure.'

'You won't outdo Lisbet with your medical knowledge Wilson, tomorrow she will be collecting herbs for her tonics and potions; when I was a boy I had to be really ill before I admitted to it for fear of the foul tasting mixtures she would concoct.'

'An' look at yer now! Six foot an a yardarm!' Lisbet liked to take all the credit for Gabriel's health and well being. Any malaise she saw as a reflection of something she had omitted to provide for him, it was a testament to her he never ailed. She took it badly and as a sign of her neglect when Mr Reynolds Senior had died at the age of seventy two.

After supper they played a friendly game of cards for low stakes and drank run French brandy. Jax was still on Gabriel's mind.

'Have you ever heard of this sort of thing in these parts before, where young boys are preyed upon? As a boy the only thing I ever feared at the harbour was being press ganged.'

'One wouldn't hear of it if indeed it did go on – it's not discussed in polite society. Any boy, ill used in that way, would probably be poor and so not able to afford a doctor if he needed one, the shame would deter no doubt, even if he could find the means. The boys are probably never rescued so they either have to put up with the treatment or try to escape. My guess is some of them will end up dead by their own hand or by their captors. There is no law to protect them, though clearly an offence has been committed against them.'

'He should hang for his crime but instead he is free to cause harm again.'

Nat added, 'Well at least he'll think twice next time he puts into port here, and like me he will be gone in the morning if this wind drops, The Bon Chance is fully loaded and ready to set sail. Jax has a lot to thank you and the weather for; if the wind had not got up and you not put two and two together from my tale, Jax would probably be half way to France by now.'

Gabriel dealt the cards, he had not won a hand yet and was becoming disgruntled; he hated to lose. The hour was getting late and he was tired, the strain of the day catching up with him when Abner announced a visitor; Colonel Bird the local magistrate.

'Show him in Abner, what is he doing abroad at such a time and on such an ill night? He must be soaked through.' The Colonel came in dripping wet.

'Good evening sir, come by the fire and attempt to dry yourself, what a night to be out. It must be some pressing reason or you would have waited until the morning I am sure,' Gabriel smiled to himself as he handed the magistrate a glass of run brandy. The Colonel was as sharp eyed as his namesake and had a stern reputation where smuggling was concerned. He was introduced to the two men who stood and bowed. Relieved of his wet cloak the magistrate looked at the assembled company.

'Thank you Mr Reynolds, it is indeed a troubling matter that brings me out on such a foul night; it is also a private matter I should think.' The two men sitting rose to leave.

'Please gentleman, let Colonel Bird give me a hint to what he is about before you venture out.' They both sat again.

'Very well Mr Reynolds, it is about an incident aboard a French frigate earlier today, The Bon Chance?'

'Then please keep to your seats for they both know of this matter, in fact Dr Chaffer here has been treating my stable boy for his injuries.'

'We are at cross purposes sir. How is your boy involved?' Bird asked.

'The captain had taken him.'

'Would you explain, I do not follow your meaning sir?' Gabriel told the story again.

'My stable lad went missing two days ago and through Nat here, I thought he had been taken without his consent aboard the Bon Chance. I went aboard to ask the captain if he knew of his whereabouts but as soon as Jax heard me introduce myself he leapt out from where he had been told to hide and fled behind me; he recognised my voice. He was in some distress when I took him above where Nat was waiting and we brought him home.'

'Ah I see. Are you saying there was no violence involved in getting the boy back?'

'Well I did punch him to the ground – I was furious at what I suspected he had done to the boy. Is that what this is about? Has the captain made a complaint about me? If he has I wish to make a counter claim after what he did to Jax, the poor boy is traumatised. The man should be pilloried.'

'How do you know your stable boy did not go of his own volition may I ask? You know what boys are like.' He swallowed some of the brandy and nodded his approval. Gabriel explained what evilness he thought the captain had been about with Jax. The magistrate listened frowning.

'Well what a sordid, sorry tale but I am afraid you have had your revenge Mr Reynolds. The captain is dead.'

'Dead! That is nothing to do with me I hit him but not that hard, maybe someone else had a grievance with him after I left? How did you even know I had been aboard?' Nat and Gabriel exchanged looks.

'General enquires led me to believe it was you, Gabriel. The magistrate looked uncomfortable. 'We had a description from the First Mate and set about the bay asking questions. I called into your offices to see if anything had been heard of the incident and spoke to your clerk. Willard told me he had seen you and your captain coming off the ship with the boy. He said he had seen you earlier and that you had left your offices in some haste. He had business to attend to on the dock and left after you ran out into the storm; as he was returning from his errand he saw you.'

Gabriel's face dropped. 'I still maintain someone else could have boarded after me,' Gabriel knew he was clutching at straws.

'When the captain fell he must have cracked his head on his desk, I suspect that is what killed him. You knocking him to the ground could have done the damage, I am not saying it is murder but a man is dead; manslaughter looks more likely. I can see from the circumstances why you would lose your temper with him but all the same, he is a foreigner in our port. The first mate says he didn't see anyone else after you left – the captain was found later when his supper was taken to him; laid out on the floor in a pool of congealed blood.'

Gabriel ran his hand through his hair and took a deep breath. He detested the captain for what he had done but he hadn't meant to kill him. He could see from the magistrate's face he was going to have to follow up on this even if he was loathe to do so. Bird broke into his thoughts.

'Might I suggest Gabriel that first thing in the morning you engage your man of law, I am sure if you give me your word as a gentleman not to abscond, you can abide her tonight.'

'Am I arrested?'

'As I say let us not be too hasty. With a clever lawyer

we may be looking at death by misadventure or at worst, manslaughter. I have always known your family to be law abiding and you yourself have never been in trouble with the law. It will depend on whether the case goes to the assizes which I expect will be the case.' There was a stunned silence.

'Thank you I will of course give you my word.' Gabriel shook the Colonel's hand.

'Very well I will leave you all to your game. gentlemen.' He bowed and before he left the room said, 'This is a bad business I hope for your sake some way can be found to extricate you from this confounded mess but I will be honest Gabriel, it does not look well. Most men would have acted as you did but it was an ill wind that blew for you today in more ways than one.'

When Bird had gone Gabriel poured everyone more brandy. There was a silence while each of the three gathered their thoughts. Gabriel was the first to speak.

'Man alive! I can scarce believe it! Who would have known he had such a thin skull. I must send word to my lawyer right away; I need to see him as soon as possible.'

Wilson said: 'Hold fast Gabriel, this is some shock to us all but especially to you; I'm sure as Bird says all will be sorted out satisfactorily.'

They drained their glasses and after consoling noises both men left to let Gabriel write to his lawyer.

15

Gabriel leapt without hesitation into the crashing waves, the freezing cold momentarily taking his breath away. He had slept as badly as one would expect when such shocking news had been delivered. For the first time in his life he truly appreciated his liberty as the cold began to diminish and a feeling of exhilaration exploded over him. If Colonel Bird had not had such respect for the family name he could be sitting in gaol now he realised.

Dawn was breaking, a shimmer of rose just brightening on the horizon. Still too early to go and see his lawyer; he hoped soon there would be a reply to the message he had rushed off last night. In the meantime he had to keep active to stop himself from going over and over both the event on the Bon Chance and Colonel Bird's visit. One split second action could have ruined his life; one punch, one loss of control. Thinking over it again and again he had come to realise that despite the dire circumstances he found himself in now, he would most certainly do the same again.

He had been so furious at the conduct of the man he had lashed out; not normally a man prone to violence yet, when faced with injustice his temper, which was usually slow to rise, had led to this state of affairs.

Manslaughter! He had heard the term but was uncertain how it differed from murder in terms of the law. It was a word he would never have expected to be attached to him.

He swam hard before eventually turning to look back at Westshore; his home. His life, such as it was, suddenly became more precious, more essential, more to him than he had ever realised before. Not for the first time since Colonel Bird's visit did he think of Eleanor. Whatever relationship he had started to have with her was surely gone. The thought entered into his head like a worm burying down into the earth; he could feel the darkness descending. He knew he could not face incarceration, he had to be free or his black mood would pull him down below the surface and he would never come up for air again. He began to tread water – the thought dug deeper into his troubled mind. The waves dipped and buffeted, he kicked harder, swam deeper.

Deep breath. Dive down. Let go. It crossed his mind again.

It would be easy to end it, he dived down hard – deep down until his chest strained to bursting; it would be preferable to a half life locked up, or worse, to lose his life on the gallows. He felt his body struggle, self preservation kicked in; he clawed himself to the surface gasping. Cold air slapped him across the face, he shook his head and breathed deeply and knew he had to first try to clear his name, he would not give up so easily. He had too much to lose; his life, his liberty but most of all Eleanor.

He noticed a figure on the beach waving frantically. He began to swim to shore. As he drew closer he could see it was Bendor, his friend passed him a towel a concerned look on his face.

'I thought to get here before you went to a watery grave,' he said attempting a joviality he did not feel. On rising Gabriel had written a hasty note to Bendor giving him the briefest outline of the situation. Bendor had raised the household on his arrival; a grumbling Lisbet was now preparing food for the two men. As Gabriel dressed he gave Bendor all the details which had not been given in the note.

'This is such bad luck. All that happened seems to be the result of chance encounters. Jax's unfortunate chance encounter with the Frenchy, your chance talk with Nat as a result of the change in weather and-'

Gabriel interrupted 'It was not chance that made me go to seek out that devil, it was determination to find Jax. The poor lad still lays abed in a poor state, in my troubles last night I thought to go and see him for I thought he would also be awake, yet I held back for fear of frightening him. Imagine going through what he has endured to see a man appear in the dark in his bedroom, it would have scared him half to death. That man has done this, he has changed us all forever, neither Jax nor myself will ever be the same after this.' Gabriel was pacing nervously about the breakfast room.

'Gabe slow down, think man. Wait to see what the lawyer has to say, I am sure there is reason to hope?'

Lisbet carrying a tray of food was about to begin a tirade about getting knocked up in the middle of the night when she saw the countenance of the two men and thought it wiser to keep her own counsel. Although it was not yet seven in the morning Abner joined them, he handed a letter to Gabriel who tore it open hastily. It was from his lawyer and said he could see him as soon as Gabriel could reach his office on Pease Road.

When the two servants had left the room Gabriel passed the letter to Bendor and poured himself strong black coffee. 'I will come with you for moral support if you would allow me. How is this man; does he practice criminal law?' Both men ignored the food in front of them.

'I have no idea, he has been our family lawyer since father took over from my grandfather and we have used him for all things legal to do with the business. To my knowledge we have never had felons in the family before.'

'There is a black sheep in every family, remind me on another occasion to tell you of my great Uncle Hubert. He was a real bad lad.' They ate sparingly and left for Mr Coate's office.

♥

Saul Coates was a man of late middle age; he was be-wigged, his face was ruddy and whiskery. 'I have only the briefest account of the circumstances which bring you here this morning but I am relieved it is you that is visiting me and not I coming to you at Alnwick gaol. Colonel Bird obviously holds your family name in esteem, as well he should.'

'Yes I am very grateful to him. If you would permit me I will give you a full account of the events that led me

227

here this morning, perhaps then you will be able to tell me just how deep in trouble I am?'

Gabriel succinctly and with a calmness he did not feel, told his story. The lawyer listened and made copious notes.

When he had finished speaking Saul set down his quill and steepled his fingers together thoughtfully.

'Well that all sounds very clear. Let me try to explain what I think will happen.' He sat back in his chair. 'Your case will most likely come up at the next Quarterly Assizes and that is in just over three weeks time.' Gabriel, shocked, looked with dismay at Bendor.

'As like as not you will not be gaoled until then because we will apply for bail. In my opinion you will most likely be charged with Voluntary Manslaughter, which means you acted in this instance under severe provocation. What you did, you did to save your stable hand from further ignominy; you had no Malice Aforethought. How could you have as until shortly before the incident you were unaware of the French captain's existence? Manslaughter gives the court grounds on which to excuse a killer from the death penalty by shifting attention from the state of mind of the accused to the contributory behaviour of the victim. The victim in this case can no longer speak for himself and you have extenuating circumstances which made you act as you did. You could not have foreseen a single punch could result in this man's death, had you set about him with a crow bar and your feet it would be an altogether different matter.

However, the judge and jury I must point out may well take a dim view of the case nevertheless. Voluntary

Manslaughter, I must warn you, may still be a hanging offence. I have no way of knowing what the prosecution have in mind and no way of knowing how a judge and jury will find, they can be notoriously fickle. In your favour you have never had dealings with the law before, you are an upstanding, well respected gentleman and businessman and you acted in the defence of a minor.'

Gabriel had flinched at the words "killer" and "death penalty" but with grim determination had tried to concentrate on the positives, however slender they seemed to be.

'I had not expected the case to come up so soon.'

'But this is a good thing is it not Gabe?' Bendor looked expectantly at his friend. 'A quick hearing means you can move on and put this all behind you much better than having it bearing down on you for months.' Bendor ever the optimist was trying to buoy up Gabriel who he could see was sinking under the enormity of the situation.

Gabriel took a moment to compose himself. 'A good thing if I am found innocent but as Saul has been at pains to point out, I could hang, which means my life could be over in no time at all!' The enormity of the position was not lost on the two friends and before either one could continue, Coates interrupted.

'It is as well not to get beyond ourselves here gentlemen lest we become overwhelmed, let us think positively and get first matters sorted. I shall this morning call upon Colonel Bird with surety that you will continue to reside at Westshore for the time prior to the case coming to court. Some monetary recompense will be needed for this. If he and the prosecution lawyer are agreeable to this then we need to proceed by setting about getting as many references of good character for you as we can, I am sure you will have no problem in this instance. We need people of rank and substance such as Sir Percy here, they will help to sway the judge and jury to see what sort of man you are and show how you acted yesterday was out of character.'

Gabriel suddenly thought: Was this only yesterday? It seemed a life time ago. There was a knock on the door and the clerk announced Colonel Bird. Mr Coates. asked for him to be shown in.

'Ah good morning Colonel I was going to come and see you this morning, you have saved me the trouble,' the lawyer said.

'Good morning to you all, I went to Westshore Mr Reynolds and your manservant told me where you were bound so I thought to kill two birds as it were.'

Bail arrangements were made and it was agreed Gabriel would present himself to Alnwick Gaol the night before the trial.

'Your gaolers will furnish you with a cell, you will need to provide yourself with the necessities for what, I am sure, will be a long night. As a gentleman you can expect, for a price of course, anything you may need that you may have forgotten. They will sell you brandy or rum or any other item you may require.'

'The situation feels unreal as if you are speaking of someone else,' Gabriel sighed. The strain was beginning to show.

The business side concluded Colonel Bird prepared to leave.

'Once again Gabriel I am sorry for the situation you find yourself in. The Bon Chance sailed this morning on the early tide; no doubt the prosecution lawyer will have summonsed the first mate to return to give evidence at the trial, or indeed detained him as the case is not far off.'

After Colonel Bird left the lawyer said, 'I think it would be beneficial if I outlined what will happen at the trial; it can be quite confusing for a lay person or would you prefer to see me at a later date?'

'Yes I am sure it is, please tell me now, I should sooner know.'

'Generally cases are heard in batches so we will know the day before roughly what time you will be brought before the Judge. Some cases may take very little time, perhaps thirty minutes or so, while others may take longer. The jury will deliberate usually in the court room unless it is a difficult case and then they may retire and leave the court. Do not worry over much if in your case they leave; very little can be deduced from the action. It may just be that one juror is keener than the rest on some point.

Gabriel listened grim faced. 'When you are brought in the clerk will read the charge and the prosecutor presents his case against you. Any witnesses he presents take an oath. As we have to second guess the prosecution's case we do not know how many witnesses he will call but it is likely there will be just the first mate, of course he may call your Captain Pearson to ascertain your frame of mind. That is what I would do.'

'Will Nat not be speaking to defend me?'

'So he will, but the prosecution can call him just the

same, he will be under oath remember.' Bendor and Gabriel exchanged worried looks. 'As the defendant you will then be asked to state your case. At this point I suggest you remain silent and I will speak on your behalf.'

'I would want to tell my side of the story to convince the jury that although I punched the man I did not mean to kill him. It was an accident.'

'That is precisely why I think it imperative I speak for you. If you admit to punching him the jury may convict; simple as that. They can be extremely mercurial. Why leave yourself open to this charge, there are no witnesses to see that you hit him, it is the first mate's opinion you were the one who knocked him down but he did not witness it. I will state this in open court. The jury will see the prosecution has no case. The first mate saw you go aboard and a few minutes later you appeared with the boy but he cannot say to anything that happened below deck as he was not there. Captain Pearson will testify he saw the first mate on deck as he waited for you. The only persons present were you and the captain and he is not available to give his opinion. There is some time, as I understand it, before the First Mate went down to the captain's cabin and found him dead. Anyone in the meantime could have come aboard and done for him.'

'I have already told Colonel Bird I hit the captain, I should not want to lie.'

'Lie? Omission of a fact, not a lie! Colonel Bird most likely will not be called by the prosecution in any case. If you admit to knocking him down the jury may get the impression you are headstrong or reckless and take against you. The burden of proof must be passed onto the prosecution; you can remain silent and let me do the talking for you.'

'But what of Jax, he was witness to what happened.'

'I am sure your lad is very grateful to his rescuer and will say what we tell him to say. That is, he had left the room immediately after he heard and recognised your voice. He saw nothing.'

Gabriel looked horrified. 'I cannot in all conscience ask him to lie for me. Surely if I tell the truth and say exactly what happened the jury will see I acted from a moral standpoint; I was protecting Jax.'

'Gabriel think. Were you really? Or as the prosecution will definitely state, did you act in revenge for the hurt he had caused your stable hand? You were angry and you lashed out to pay him back! We would all have done the same no doubt but we cannot give them *motive*, you must see that. I repeat, juries can be very unpredictable, better to err on the side of caution. Your morals do you justice but could get you hung or a prison sentence, be careful to what you admit, that is my advice.'

'I think this is the best course of action Gabriel; do not put your head in the noose. You cannot afford morals when your life is at risk,' Bendor agreed.

'But what if the Judge asks me directly; "Did you punch him?"' Gabriel looked exasperated.

'I shall speak for you,' the lawyer looked challengingly at Gabriel.

Bendor asked. 'Will that not look as though Gabriel is avoiding the question?'

'It will look like he can afford a lawyer to speak on his behalf; one does not keep a dog and bark oneself sir.

Along with your character witnesses the judge will see that the evidence is circumstantial and that you are an upstanding, honest, gentleman who sought only to right a wrong and get back something that belonged to you.'

Gabriel shuffled uncomfortably in his seat. It crossed his mind that in his privileged position he was at an advantage. A poor man without a clever lawyer would have only his wits to defend himself. Mr Coates continued, 'We of course have no way of knowing what proof there is against you but we can speculate there is none, the first mate may lie. He could state he saw you attack his captain; if he does we will produce Captain Pearson to say that when he waited for you on deck he saw the first mate supervising the loading of the ship or some such thing. It will be his word against a Frenchman's and we can guess how that will look.'

'I shall have to think about this sir. I appreciate you know your business better than I but it leaves me with a bad taste in my mouth. I am a straightforward man and would prefer to state my case in clear and simple terms.'

'And take a chance? If you do not want to take my advice Gabriel then you should look to your friend and his viewpoint. Put simply, you cannot afford scruples.'

They left the lawyer's office and returned to Westshore where they met with Dr Chaffer who was about to leave after checking on Jax.

'Join us for dinner and you can tell us how the lad does.'

'Thank you but I am afraid I will have to decline I have other patients awaiting my ministrations. I can spare time to update you about Jax and then I must be off.'

Gabriel took the tray that Abner proffered and poured three glasses. 'Jax is still in shock I am afraid, he tells me he is in a little physical discomfort but nothing that he cannot bear. Again it his mental state that worries me, he is very withdrawn, he will need time, as I said last night. Who knows whether he will ever come to terms with the monstrous thing that happened to him? Lisbet says he has had the beef tea and she has cooked some of the boy's favourites to try to tempt him. Both will help to regain his bodily strength I hope. In his favour he is young; perhaps his mind is still pliable and the memory will begin to shrink in time.'

'We have been to see Coates; he tells me Jax could be called to give evidence against me.'

'I should not want the boy to relive these events in open court and if they tried to compel him I would speak up for him as his doctor and say he is unfit to give evidence, if it would help?'

Bendor looked at Gabriel. They each knew what the other thought. Gabriel explained briefly that the lawyer wanted Jax to lie.

'While it distresses me greatly to hear he does poorly it would be a relief if we could spare him the ordeal of going to court at all and it would also relieve me of having the boy lie to save my neck. I should not like to burden him with the responsibility,'

'Your humility does you proud but if he loses his master then he loses his livelihood. You need to do what you can to save yourself; people depend on you and your friends would mourn you. I am sorry this has happened, you have done nothing the rest of us would not give a second thought to do,' Wilson reached out and touched Gabriel's arm. 'I must be off now; Mr Grange at the tobacconists is not long for this world I fear and I promised I would call today. Get some rest Gabriel and allow me to do anything I can to help. I shall call on Jax tomorrow.'

After he had left and both men had failed to do justice to Lisbet's cooking again, Gabriel sat back in his chair. 'What Wilson said about people depending on me has given me pause for thought. I have a fortune to leave yet no son to inherit, I have a small house staff here at Westshore, crews for my ships and people employed in other businesses I own, I need to make provision, make plans. I have to write a new will in case the worst should happen. I cannot go away to the assizes presuming I shall come back – the facts have to be faced. I have much to think of and much to do before then, the one thing I am short of it seems is time!'

Bendor looked at his friend, 'You are under considerable strain, let me know if there is anything I can do. I can stay as long as you like for moral support or whatever you need, I know it must be hard but you must remain positive – try not to get into one of your black moods though you have much to worry you.'

'There are some priorities I must consider; the people who depend on me for their livelihoods; I need to make sure they are provided for just in case.' The two men sat awhile composing a plan of action then Gabriel convinced Bendor after some difficulty that he must go home to his pregnant wife assuring him he would keep him in touch with the proceedings.

16

Gabriel had been at Reynolds' Shipping all afternoon; it was two days since being charged with manslaughter. Through the windows that looked out over the bay he could see the weather worsening as the sky grew dark. The rain lashed at the windows so nothing could be seen beyond, rivulets of water obscured the view of the men working on the wharf loading his sister ship The Jack and Alice. She was to set sail on the morrow taking iron ore to The Netherlands. He wished he could escape on her; the thought crossed his mind to abscond but he quickly dismissed it.

The morning had been fine and he had walked along the beach to his offices reluctant to be indoors on such a splendid day. He always liked to be outdoors but today especially he had felt the need to feel the wind in his hair and smell the sea air. He had met his other captain Roger Tillerman and they had gone to The Hope and Anchor to drink porter and discuss the Dutch trip, now he was going to get soaked on his journey home having no coat or horse being convinced the day would stay fine; the fickle Northumbrian weather had tricked him again.

He was about to send a boy with a message asking Jax

to bring his overcoat and horse when he realised Jax was still recuperating. He had looked in on him that morning and found him quiet and morose.

Gabriel had one more duty to perform before leaving for the evening; it was not one he was looking forward to performing. He opened the office door and stared at the torrent of water pouring from the sky. Night had fallen and the rain set in.

He debated whether to put off the task for a more clement night, then remembered time was of the essence. He launched himself headlong into the night running out of the warm office into the cool wet before he could change his mind. He reached the house in less than three minutes and knocked at the door; Libby opened it and peered out into the foul night.

'It's me Libby.' He entered the room and went to stand in front of a well built fire that threw light and warmth about the small parlour.

'Let me take your jacket, you're drenched to the skin.' He removed his hat and held it passing it through his fingers along the three sides. 'No, thank you I won't be staying I have to talk to you about our arrangement.'

'Oh I see.' She poured him brandy and they stood with a little distance between them. He took a sip; it warmed but did not cheer. He knew Libby would possibly not have heard about his troubles, she had no friend but him. He had not seen her since the accidental meeting on Northumberland Street. He again noticed the slight gain in weight suited her; he had never admired scrawny women.

'I have decided our arrangement must end.' He

paused and looked to see what effect his statement had made. 'I hope this will not inconvenience you too much financially and I am here to tell you I will help you in that respect until you can arrange your situation to your satisfaction. I can pay the rent for you until you can find other lodgings or employment if that would help but I will no longer visit you. I am sorry if this comes as a shock but I find my circumstances are to change and feel I have not been the best of friends to you. I am ashamed at my behaviour; I have taken unfair advantage of you all the time we have known each other. For that I apologise.' Gabriel saw her face fall.

'This is some surprise though not totally unexpected, I knew once you were married I should probably be set aside.'

Gabriel did not want to get into discussion about why he was ending the agreement, so let the error stand.

She continued. 'It is strange I had planned to tell you some news of my own when next you called, I have thought for some time this cannot go on but you are wrong Gabriel, you have been the only friend I have had or needed, but you know I always wanted to return to Alnwick.'

'I did and a true friend, an unselfish one, would have helped you to realise that dream.'

'You do yourself an injustice; I do not need your apology. I have been looking for employment as a companion which is all I am suited for and I have found work where I can live in at Alnwick.' Her face lit up in a smile. 'I am to be companion to a widow of good repute, the pay, although not overly generous, will be adequate for my needs. You have always been most supportive of me and through being frugal I have been able to save some little money to be able to make the move.'

'That is good news! You at last will have your wish. I will help in any way I can, just say how I may be of assistance; when are you to go?'

'I was hoping to go by the end of the month it will be a fresh start for me and a new chapter to my life. You have been so kind to me and saved me from who knows what depravities, you have always shown me respect and I thank you for it. I will think if I need help but am sure all can be managed by myself thank you.'

'You make me feel very humble Libby, for I have ill used you I have come to realise, no matter what you say. You should never have been allowed to be in this degrading position and I am only glad you have been able to free yourself.'

'It was my wastrel brother who brought me to this, not you. If anything you saved me from a worse fate, I will miss you Gabriel for I have no other friend.'

Still dripping water on the floor Gabriel tossed his hat onto the table, moved towards Libby and took her hands in his. He lightly kissed her forehead. He reached into his pocket and put a bag of coins into her hands.

'Take this to pay for your needs, there should be enough to help you to settle in Alnwick and to feed and clothe yourself in a little style. I shall miss you too. Ours has been an unconventional relationship and ashamed as I am about the circumstances, you have been a good friend to me too; when I have been lonely you have been a comfort to me. I am pleased you shall have a fresh start, you of all people deserve it.'

More warm words were spoken by both of them then Gabriel retrieved his still wet hat and went to the door. 'Goodbye Libby and good luck.' He stepped out into the dark and headed home.

♥

Gabriel Reynolds, businessman and charged felon, went about Alnmouth trying to order his affairs in a calm and methodical way. Anyone seeing him out and about over that three week period would not have suspected the turmoil which raged beneath his composed demeanour. Another of his direst tasks had just been discharged.

When he had summonsed his servants earlier to tell them he had made provision for them, Lisbet was already in high emotion; she had taken his hands in hers. The terrace of chins wobbled as she tried to contain her feelings.

'When you first telled us about that French man being killed A could not believe such a thing could happen. How A wish you had your father here now more than ever. Don't you go worrying about us for A know in ma heart you shall be home for yer supper on trial day.' With that she had rushed from the room managing to keep her composure until she had reached the sanctity of her kitchen. Abner too had been moved.

'Who would have thought such a thing could happen? A man's character, such as yours, must stand for somethin'.

Gabriel was moved 'You had better go to Lisbet for I think I hear her breaking her heart. Perhaps in a day or two we will all be a little more composed? I will just say you will both be well provided for as you deserve and Jax too of course.'

He thought to clear his head and regain his equilibrium; he set off to ride along the beach the northerly wind buffeting and bothering him. The clouds, backlit at the edges with a pale watery light, were scudding across a grey sky. The waves crashed, spume frothing and tossing pebbles amongst shingle as he rode out along the sand. The crashing waves creating a cacophony of discordant sound; the waves as disturbed as he felt.

The waves continued to cause trouble and a crack of thunder made Copper start. He had not noticed the lightning but now he saw it flash out at sea lighting up the sky, the thunder boomed. He gave Copper her head and she took off galloping at full stretch across the sands.

Both spent, Copper at last slowed and Gabriel slid from the saddle and pressed his face to the soft muzzle of his horse. She lifted her head and gently nuzzled his face; he loved this creature. Her huge copper head nodded up and down. He slid to his knees on the damp sand, put his head in his hands and wept loudly. The sound was drowned by the tumultuous sea.

The storm seemed to be passing; no rain fell though he could still hear distant rumbling. He saw a rider coming toward him and recognised Bendor. Gabriel mounted and turned Copper about. They began to ride back to Westshore.

'How do you do, you look like sleep is a stranger to you. Are your affairs in order? I came to see if you needed help.'

'It is surprising how much one can accomplish when pushed,' Gabriel frowned. 'There is still much to do but over the past few days Eleanor has been much on my mind.'

'I expected she might be.'

'I had begun to hope at last I had found someone to make a life with; to share my fortune and future someone to love. Now I may not even have a future.' He could see her face in his mind's eye and wished he could see it once again, here in front of him.

'I am sorry for you my friend but try not to lose hope; Coates seemed to think there is reason to be optimistic.'

'I had hoped Eleanor would be mistress of Westshore and fill the empty rooms with noisy children as my parents had hoped to do. I could picture her married to me and with a houseful of children. Westshore seems doomed to be filled only with air and light. Now the scene before me is bleak and hopeless, I might never see the love of my life again, never laugh and banter with her, never...'

'I knew you would be in this mood, come let us go inside before the rain pours.' They had reached Westshore.

'I can see how your hopes and dreams seem dashed yet you have to try to be positive, it will do you no good to dwell on the negatives.' Gabriel was pacing about the drawing room.

'Even if I am cleared would Eleanor consort with a past felon?

'Why not go and see her?'

'Time my friend is not on my side; by the time I had sailed there and back to Whitby and allowing for time to speak to her on this very sensitive matter, at least four or five days would be lost. I cannot complete my arrangements, meet with bankers, agents and my lawyer and expect to have all completed before the trial – which is now but seven days away. I should dearly love to see her but now I fear I will never see her again.'

'Gabe, I don't know what to say; have you written?'

'I could not compose such a letter. How does one say, 'how are you keeping, the weather is fine and by the by I have killed someone and am to stand trial for my life!'

'Perhaps you might write a letter that could be delivered if the worst happened? Rest assured I would take it to her myself and tell her what was in your heart but wait – you have me a pessimist now! I shall not be needed, you will be able to see her and tell her yourself.' Bendor poured them rum. 'I had not realised you were in so deep – were you not still weighing up the relationship?'

'Nothing had been declared between us as such, but next time I saw her I hoped to declare my hand. Now is it not presumptuous on my part to assume she would care?' That she did care he had no doubt, in his more rational moments, but to what depth her feelings went he was still unsure.

'One thing I do know is if I were to see her and explain myself, she would feel me harshly judged, I know her to have a social conscience and know she would be glad I had rescued Jax.' He sighed. That she may never know his true feelings now locked him in a room where the light could not penetrate. The darkness threatened to smother him.

♥

The next day Gabriel arrived home from a share holder meeting to find Thomas Hodgeson waiting for him this last hour and half. Gabriel breathed deeply and entered his drawing room. Thomas met him half way across the room, grabbed Gabriel by the shoulders and looked into his face.

'Why on earth have you not been to see me? I only found out this morning I have been out of town these last ten days but Caroline is at home. Gabriel am I not like a father to you, did you think I would turn you away?' The look of anguish on the older man's face almost sank Gabriel.

'I was going to come and see you today but events got the better of my time. Of course I did not think you would desert me I have been busy trying to get my affairs in order. I suppose you have heard when the trial is to be?' Thomas took the glass which Gabriel offered.

'I am sure I can take some of the shipping work over for you until after the trial, your father and I know each other's systems for they are virtually the same, let me do anything I can to help you my boy.'

It was arranged Thomas would take over some of the workload at Reynolds' Shipping, the most imminent business that needed urgent attention, leaving Gabriel to concentrate on his not inconsiderable other businesses. Yesterday Bendor had taken on the responsibility for helping with some of his concerns; Gabriel was grateful for any help. Thomas insisted Gabriel went home with him for supper.

Caroline was in the drawing room at Eastshore when Gabriel and her father arrived. 'I am so glad you could come Father was away so long I thought you had missed each other. How are you? You look dreadful,' she said wringing a handkerchief in her fingers. Gabriel took her hands in his. 'I am as you would expect I am afraid, these are worrying times for me, I do not sleep well – I have a mind overrun with thoughts. You on the other hand look well.' He smiled as he kissed her hand.

'I shall not sleep a wink until I know you are safe, I know we had changed our paths Gabriel but you are still like family. Why have you not been to see us? Do you have any good news regarding the trial?'

'I am sorry I should have called but there has been much to do and little time to do it in. The only good news I have is I have enough character witnesses to fill the courtroom and if only the judge will listen to them he will think me the best man that ever lived!' He tried a smile; it felt foreign to his face.

They ate supper and talked of other things to try to distract and lighten the mood. Caroline who was much distressed, retired early to bed with a headache and after a heartfelt leave taking left Thomas and Gabriel discussing the immediate needs of his business affairs.

♥

The next morning before Gabriel had broken his fast, Wilson Chaffer was shown into the morning room having been to check on Jax. Gabriel invited him to share his meal.

'I have been up most of the night delivering a fine boy for the Pritchards so Jax was on my way home to bed. I am famished and will gladly stay to eat. How are you?'

'I have an over active mind as you will imagine and it is particularly busy at night. I want to sleep but my thoughts tell me I have much life to live and so little time to live it if things do not go well for me.'

'I can give you a draught that will help you get some rest. Do not shake your head for you will need your wits about you in the courtroom and you cannot function without rest, will I leave it with you?'

Before Gabriel could argue, Abner brought in a card. It was the prosecutor come to question Jax; this was unexpected. Gabriel told Abner to have him wait in the drawing room. He showed Wilson the calling card. 'It is fortunate then I am here, I can tell him the boy is in no fit state to see anyone let alone appear in court.'

Gabriel was reassured and the two men entered the drawing room; Gabriel introduced himself and Dr Chaffer.

'Sebastian Strange KC at your service gentlemen I am here to speak with the stable hand known as Jax to gather information regarding your case Mr Reynolds, is he about?'

Gabriel frowned. 'I am afraid you have had a wasted journey sir as he is still taken to his bed recovering from his ordeal.'

'Come man you must allow me access to him, it is the law. I need to question him as a witness to the crime.' Strange was a tall spindly man with a powdered wig. His ruddy complexion grew redder as his impatience grew.

'I am treating the boy and it is my opinion he is unfit to see or speak with you and will be unable to do so in the foreseeable future. He has suffered terrible scars both of the body and especially the mind at the hands of that man,' Chaffer said.

'Come come Dr Chaffer, I will need to at least see the boy to determine what might be done.'

He sounded amiable enough but Gabriel was in no doubt the prosecutor was of a determined mind. He glared at Gabriel with a challenging stare.

'As you might imagine for one so young, he is but fourteen, he has now developed a fear of unfamiliar men, for you to appear before him, whilst he is abed, would possibly set his recovery back.' Chaffer reasoned.

'Then bring the boy to this room and I shall talk with him here.'

'He is too ill to be moved sir, I cannot permit him to leave his bed at this time.'

'Cannot or will not Dr Chaffer? You could be held in contempt for withholding the boy.' Gabriel could sense Strange would not be moved.

'If you wish to proceed against me sir then you must do as you see fit but if you insist on speaking to him let me at least talk to him first to let him know who you are and what you are about.'

Strange laughed cynically. 'Sir, I am sure you have had time enough to coach him on what to say so I am not afraid he will need prompting on his answers. However it is my duty to inform him that he must tell the truth or the law will fall about his ears with its full might.' He did not bother to hide his disdain.

Gabriel frowned: 'As a gentleman I give you my word sir I have not discussed the matter with him. Jax is as yet unaware I face any charges or indeed that his kidnapper is dead. I did not want to distress him further by telling him I have been charged with manslaughter.'

'Come sir, we both know telling him the captain is dead would quite possibly be the best tonic he could have, why would you keep it from him?'

Gabriel could feel his temper rising but would not let the man rile him. 'The lad has barely eaten or spoken since the event and Dr Chaffer here advised against mentioning it lest he shows signs of reliving the ordeal.'

'Let us not keep going around in circles,' Strange said irritation in his voice. 'Perhaps a servant could show me the way?'

Gabriel and Wilson looked at each other in frustration. What could they do? Gabriel wanted to throw the damned man out on his ear but he knew it would not help matters. He sighed and raked his knuckles down his cheek.

'Very well, you can see him but I insist his doctor be present and ask you, as one gentleman to another, if he becomes overwrought you shall let him alone.' Strange nodded curtly. Dr Chaffer led the way. Gabriel took a slug of brandy to steady himself and paced the room. Within minutes Dr Chaffer and Mr Strange were back in the room. The prosecutor's face was florid.

'Well by stealth or design you have your way, for the lad acted dumb and even when threatened with the law would not be induced to speak about that or any other matter.'

'You threatened him despite what I asked! You try my patience sir. If there is nothing further I will not detain you – I bid you good day, I trust you can see yourself out.'

249

Gabriel marched onto the terrace for air. Wilson joined him and the two looked out to sea in silence.

When Wilson had left, Gabriel went to the kitchen and asked Lisbet for some refreshment to take to Jax. He tapped lightly on the bedroom door and let himself in.

'I have brought you some lemonade, are you thirsty? I need to speak with you about the trouble two weeks ago.' Gabriel handed him the beaker and paused to see what effect his words had on the boy. 'You have to be brave for what I have to say may well upset you.' Jax sat up in the bed and took a drink.

'When I hit the man, the French captain that is, he fell and banged his head – as a result he died.'

Jax opened his eyes wide. 'Yer mean he's really dead? That man said he were, but A thought it couldn't be right.'

'Yes Jax really dead, he won't be bothering you or any other boys from now on, I did not mean for him to die but that is the upshot. It was an accident and I feel guilty for it.'

Jax took more lemonade. 'Guilty? A think A shall get up sir A believe the 'orses will be missing me as much as A'm missing them and A know Abner could do with a hand.'

'I did not tell you to make you get up, you need rest; take as long as you like.' Gabriel noticed the lad's young face seemed thin and pinched.

'If it's okay with you master, A want to see the old nags. Sleeping above 'em like A normally do meks me miss the noises they mek, especially at night.' With that Jax threw his blankets back and rose from his bed.

17

The next day Jax was in the tack room when Gabriel leaned over the stable door. 'I was wondering Jax, can you ride a horse?'

'A never tried sir.'

'Would you like to? I could teach you the basics, seems odd you are a stable hand yet cannot ride; what if I needed you to take Copper to the blacksmith? Normally you lead her I know, but it would be better to ride her would it not? In future you could take Ned to do your errands. I have a couple of hours to spare, what do you say? Do you feel up to it? – or if you would rather wait until another day then we shall.'

Gabriel thought not only to distract Jax, but himself too; his head had been in documents for days now. 'A say aye, now if yer like sir.' Jax looked excited. It was a relief to see the boy more like his old self.

Ten minutes later Ned was saddled and ready in the stable yard, his father's old horse stood patiently. 'Old Ned could do with a bit of exercise I think; he is looking a little fat.' Gabriel smoothed Ned's flanks affectionately.

After showing Jax how to hold the reins and how to keep his heels down in the stirrups, Gabriel led Ned around the yard. Soon Jax felt confident to go into the large paddock behind the house. 'You are a natural Jax,' Gabriel shouted grinning as he watched the boy ride up and down the long field. Ned was a quiet horse, he had always had a soft mouth and Jax was very gentle with him. Lisbet, who had been watching from the kitchen window, came and leant on the fence giving words of encouragement like a proud mother. Gabriel sat on the gate next to her crunching an apple watching Jax ride.

'That's the first time A've seen the lad smile since it happened,' Lisbet sighed.

'I'm not sure he's had much to smile about of late.'

'Neither have you.' Lisbet touched his sleeve.

The sun appeared from behind a cloud. Jax at the far end of the paddock was mastering turning Ned to right and left; Ned was quietly compliant. He came trotting towards them bumping up and down while Gabriel shouted instructions about his knees, seat and hands.

'Well done! We'll make a rider of you yet, I think that's enough for today we don't want you getting saddle sore.' Gabriel sprang down from the gate and opened it for Jax to ride through. Back in the yard he held Ned's head while Jax slid to the ground.

'Give Ned a few extra oats for not throwing you off,' Gabriel called after Jax as he led the horse back to his stall.

'Yer a good man, yer old man would be proud.' Lisbet looked at her employer with affection.' A reckon that's bucked him up no end.'

'I hope so – he might feel a little less affected if he has other things to think about. I just hope he trusts us to help him. I may not be here, but I know you will take the best care of him in my absence.'

Lisbet's eyes misted. 'You will be here if there is a God in heaven. Abner did try to mek me know what had happened to the mite, it med me that mad; the wickedness of some men.' She rubbed her hands on her apron to cover her discomfiture. 'You'll be cleared A'm sure and we can all get back to normal.' She squeezed his arm.

Gabriel leaned on the paddock gate and thought about Jax. He had taken a gamble telling the boy his seducer was dead but it seemed to have paid off so far. Of course Jax had not had time to think of it long but it seemed to have given him the impetus to get out of bed at least. Probably there was much to do before the boy's mind healed.

Jax came out of the stable bolting the door behind him.

'Well did you enjoy that?' Gabriel asked.

'Yea A did thanks sir.'

'Do you want dinner Jax.' Lisbet appeared in the door way. 'It's yer favourite; rabbit pie.' Jax looked directly at Gabriel.

'A'm glad he's dead, A know it's wrong headed to think like that but A can't help it.' Gabriel watched as Jax walked into the kitchen and took his place at the table.

♥

Gabriel had asked Wilson to dine with him and after supper the two men sat with their port talking of local news. 'Tell me if you want to speak about the trial Gabriel, I am happy to listen.'

'Ah, I wonder my head has not burst with all the contradictory thoughts swilling about in there, just for one night I should like to try and pretend it is a normal evening, spent with a good friend and try not to think of the past or the future.

'Bendor and Thomas have been busy helping me to sort my business affairs; my personal affairs are somewhat harder to fathom; I had a very disquieting meeting with Abner and Lisbet.

Wilson inclined his head. 'I had wanted to tell them simply and in a businesslike manner that they should be looked after if the worst should happen but emotions ran high and Lisbet in particular was overawed. It was with some surprise that when I began to think of providing for my old retainers, I realised they were already in early old age, they have been long with the family, I cannot remember them not being at our family's beck and call. Perhaps they should already be retired and replaced?'

'I remember Lisbet telling me once she had nursed you as a small boy.'

'It is true; I could not imagine coming home without them to greet me. I realise in any event their duties should certainly be reduced now, Abner should not be climbing ladders and digging ditches at his age. I remember recently Lisbet complained of overwork but I had dismissed it as her usual griping, I am angry with myself for not noticing what was in front of my nose.'

'You have had much do especially since your father died; it has been a difficult time for you.'

'Abner now has Jax to help with the horses, or had until his recent trouble. At least two others should be employed, and one of those for the heavy outdoor work; only of course if I am to survive this trial. If, God forbid, I do not then naturally they must retire. I will of course provide them with money enough to do so in comfort for the rest of their lives.' He smiled grimly: 'I cannot imagine either of them taking to a life of idleness; neither are of a disposition to sit twiddling their thumbs.' Gabriel shook his head despondently. 'I am sorry my friend I go against what I said earlier but it is hard to be in the present; if you would allow me I should like to try.'

'The mind is a contrary organ – I just want you to know you can count on me. How's that boy of yours doing? Is his mind preoccupied too?'

'I am glad you brought him up for I wanted to ask you about Jax, how best to help him that is. I think perhaps his physical injuries are better, although none of us can be sure of course, he will not talk of them but what does that sort of thing do to a boy's mind?

'The mind is complex and a young boy's especially so when it has had to process such an ordeal who is to know how things will go. Our own unique character could possibly pre-determine how we react to adverse things that happen to us, yet some say adversity builds character? But what if one's mind is not strong or stable to begin with? How then does the mind react? Fear, such as Jax must have felt, is not easy to forget. The science of the mind is in its infancy but there are men now studying the brain and how it works so in years to come we may be better able to help the afflicted.'

'I was hoping you might be able to suggest some way in which I could help him to come to terms with his situation, I fear he may not want my help, my intrusion.'

'Time, they say, is a great healer but too much time on one's hands when one is feeling low is not such a good thing as you, no doubt, can testify.'

'I thought to teach him to ride so he may help more about the place and also so I would have an excuse to talk to him. We began yesterday with him riding my father's old horse; Ned is very quiet and perfect for a beginner. I have told Jax the Frenchman is dead.'

'Let him speak of the subject if he wants to but try not to force him if he is unwilling. He may want to talk but not have the words to express himself or indeed the maturity to do so. For a young lad's first sexual experience to be a traumatic one can unhinge the mind. As I said, if he is of strong character he may well grow up undamaged mentally. We can only hope.'

'If the worst should happen to me I know you will try to help Jax, he has no one except the three of us here at Westshore.'

'There now, you are letting your mind wander on to the very subject we were trying to avoid.'

Gabriel laughed a hollow laugh. 'Tell me about yourself then Wilson, let us change the subject, how do you fair?' The two men chatted about Wilson's work and about his plans to try to help the poor, especially the widows and orphans which were much in evidence in a seafaring town like Alnmouth.

'Do you have a lady? I have never thought to ask you before, is it impertinent to enquire?' Wilson told about his lost love who had been sent away by her father when he had found out she was seeing a "quack".

'Her name is Charlotte Lambton.'

'I know her a little, she is friendly with Caroline; she is a striking lady.'

'She has been sent to a finishing school in France – it is a ruse to part us. Thankfully she is strong willed and in defiance of her step father we have been corresponding.'

Gabriel thought of the stash of letters he had from Eleanor. 'It seems the world is changing and young ladies have minds of their own.'

'They do indeed. Lottie, as she likes to be called seeks out medical books for me which are not available in this country and sends them to me; they are extremely interesting. I do not know how she understands which ones are relevant but somehow she does, she is extraordinary, I miss her very much.'

'You must be concerned then that you cannot be together – what shall you do when she returns?'

'According to her we will elope!' Wilson raised an eyebrow and smiled.

'You are agreeable to that?'Gabriel was unsure if Wilson were serious.'

'I should not like to act in such an underhand way but as they say, needs must.'

When at last he was ready to leave Wilson raised his glass.

'To life!' Gabriel paused before raising his own. So long as it is not a life of imprisonment he thought.

It was long after midnight when Gabriel saw Wilson to the door.

'Let us hope when we meet next we are able to celebrate as I am sure will be the case.' Gabriel watched Wilson walk into the night. He went to bed hoping sleep would find him.

♥

The next morning arrived with a chill north wind and a sprinkling of showers; autumn was ever changeable. After Gabriel broke his fast he strode out to the stable purposefully. Keeping himself occupied on little sleep was beginning to take its toll, but he would not give himself the space to think anymore; thinking too much was sapping his strength. He leaned over the stable door, an apple in his hand and watched Jax as he put the bridle on Copper' huge head.

'How do you feel about a gallop on the beach? It is about time you left the safety of the paddock.' He twisted the apple in half and gave it to Copper on the palm of his hand; he passed the remainder to Jax.

'Here give this to Ned and remind him not to throw you off; if your first gallop should end in a fall best to land on soft sand rather than hard earth.' He laughed when he saw the excited look on Jax face.

'A'll not fall off A'll hang on for grim death.'

'Then you are certain to be thrown as Ned will sense your fear.'

Side by side they began to saddle the horses. The smell of the fresh straw and hay was sweet and Gabriel stroked Copper's flanks as he saddled her.

There was a well worn path through the dunes Gabriel had taken since he was a boy which led down to the beach. They rode to the water's edge. 'Remember to keep your hands soft, ease him through his paces slowly then let him go and if you do get unseated, cover your head with your arms and try to curl into a ball so that you won't be so easy to kick.'

Jax turned his head and Gabriel saw him throw a sly, sideways grin in his direction. He kicked Ned's sides and was gone, leaving Gabriel standing. Jax flew down the beach like the devil was after him: Gabriel gave chase Copper dancing though the surf, the bracing wind tugging at her mane. He watched as Ned's flanks pulled further away. He kicked Copper on and she responded not wanting to be beaten by the old nag. They tore the beach up making ground and coming within a length of Jax before both riders began to pull up; Jax looked exhilarated, his cheeks were rosy and his smile wide.

'Blimey, A never moved so fast, it were grand!' He puffed hard trying to catch his breath.

'I think you could have waited,' Gabriel said laughing. He came alongside, the two horses were breathing hard. They rode through the surf while the wind blew the soft sand across the beach. Gabriel looked over to Jax who looked so small on the big, bay horse.

'They say you are not a real rider until you have had a fall but watching your seat just then Ned would have had a job to upend you! You are a natural, Ned may be old but he still has spirit and if he chose, he could drop you in the sea easily enough. I think he feels the light touch you give and he respects that; an ill used animal will never give you his trust, remember that Jax.' Gabriel frowned as he thought of the parallel; Jax had been cruelly treated, would his nature change now he had been ill treated?

The sea and sky merged into a gauzy grey, the colour palette moving from off white to slate. Jax suddenly said: 'Afore A came here the only animals A had any dealings with were the pit ponies at the coal mine, now I love these two. They are ma friends. This is the best A've felt for days and it's all because of them.' He patted old Ned's neck. Too late Gabriel saw the cheeky grin on Jax face.

'Race yer back?'

Before Gabriel could answer, Jax let out a roar and raced off. Gabriel caught napping again, soon responded and gave chase but this time old Ned was soon caught and the younger horse reached the turn off to Westshore with lengths to spare. Gabriel turned Copper and saw Jax pulling up. 'That serves you right for cheating.' He grinned.

As they walked back into the yard Gabriel didn't know who had benefited most from today's therapy but for the first time in days, for just a few minutes, he felt something akin to contentment.

18

Gabriel had done all he could do, the trial was almost upon him. He had prepared as much as he could; he had made a new will and with no immediate family of his own to leave his fortune to, he had had a lot of difficult decisions to make.

Bendor and Grace had already told him that he would be Godfather to their as yet, unborn child. They had wanted him to know they held him in high esteem regardless of the outcome of the trial. It was a sobering thought he may never meet the child; even more sobering if he never got to see a child of his own.

He had provided for Lisbet, Abner and Jax. He had left small legacies for Thomas and Caroline, trinkets that he thought they would like as keepsakes. He had left Libby enough to see her comfortable for the rest of her life. He had established scholarships for his old school, hoping to help boys less fortunate than himself.

After spending so much time with Wilson Chaffer he had also decided to give a large donation to a charity Wilson was trying to set up to build a hospital to help the poor. The rest he had instructed Bendor, as executor, to give to charitable causes or to distribute as he saw fit.

They had talked over what these were to be in a broad sense but Gabriel had lost heart and said he would trust Bendor to make the right decisions should it become necessary. He could not contemplate what would happen to Westshore.

As he rode on towards his awaiting gaolers he grew more and more despondent. The leave taking at Westshore had been as bad as could be imagined. Jax had become aware of the consequences Gabriel now faced and felt himself to blame; it had set his recovery back and he had turned inwards and uncommunicative again.

Gabriel had told Bendor not to meet him at the gaol except to send one of his grooms to fetch Copper and take her to Bendor's where he knew for certain she would be cared for. Of course, Bendor and twelve or so others who were to be character witnesses for him, would be in court on the morrow; that was some comfort. Now there was nothing anyone could say or do which would alleviate the utter misery he felt on what could be his last day of freedom. Once again he thought of Eleanor and sighed.

He looked long at the sea; it rolled in and out idly, hardly disturbing the shore. He turned off the coast road and headed through Alnwick, as he drew up in front of the gaol he saw the incongruous sight of a coach and pair waiting outside and immediately recognised it as Bendor's. He dismounted and walked over to the window where Grace could be seen behind the curtain.

'We could not let you endure this alone Gabriel, please forgive us?' Bendor was behind him having just come out of the gaol.

'I have made sure all is as it should be for you, or

as best as can be bought in such a pit, I know you said not to come but if my name can help a little to see you comfortable tonight than I shall feel better for myself and for you.'

The two embraced each other warmly then Ben handed Grace down from the carriage and she hugged him too. Gabriel passed Copper's reins to a groom. Gabriel rubbed her muzzle then gave her an apple he had kept in his pocket as a leave taking. The horse munched and then nuzzled his hand for more. He stroked her neck then with kitbag in hand entered the gaol and reported himself present.

♥

Sleep evaded him until daybreak when he dreamed fitfully of his father, of Eleanor and of mad things that had no significance. His lawyer, who had stayed at a local inn, had been to see him after supper to tell him his case should be heard in the first batch; he thought this to be good news as the jurors might not have had time to get bored, drunk or distracted by then.

It wanted ten minutes to nine when the gaoler unlocked the cell and he was handcuffed before being taken along with eight or nine other prisoners into the courtroom. After the charges had been read for each of the defendants they were taken back to a holding cell, all except the woman whose case was to be heard first.

After two or more hours Gabriel was taken back up to the courtroom where he saw many of his friends and business associates, these included Thomas and unexpectedly Caroline, who gave him an encouraging smile.

He stood beside his lawyer while Mr Strange put forward his case. Mr Coates huffed loudly and shook his head. Gabriel was reminded of being an actor in a play as the crowd jeered and shouted as though they were on a night out at the theatre. The judge looked over his spectacles and asked in a thin, reedy voice if the prosecutor had witnesses to call. He used his gavel in an attempt to quieten the mob to little effect.

The prosecutor called Jacques Blount, the First Mate, which was no surprise to anyone acquainted with the case. After a few minutes when he had not appeared, a clerk was despatched to hurry the witness up; he came back moments later saying that he was nowhere to be found. Mr Strange looked annoyed but not unduly worried. His clerk was despatched in an effort to find the Frenchman.

In the meantime Strange called his second witness – Jax Slipper. Gabriel looked furiously at his lawyer, he could feel his temper rising. Saul Coates put a restraining hand on Gabriel's arm.

'Has Strange no scruples?' He supposed not. How and when had the boy been brought here Gabriel wondered?

'Leave it Gabriel the damage is done, you can only make things worse for yourself if you lose your temper. Now is the time to show contrition; the jury watch your every move.'

Jax, wearing his Sunday best clothes stood in the witness box looking small and scared. He clutched his cap in his hand and kept his eyes downcast; Gabriel's heart went out to the boy. He had thought, naively, he had saved him from this ordeal.

'Now boy remember to tell the truth here today and you shall be free to leave – if you lie it could be bad for you and may result in the loss of your liberty, do you understand?' Jax uttered the single word 'Aye.' He continued to stare at the floor.

'You went aboard the ship of your own choice did you not; perhaps you thought to have an adventure in France? Is that not the truth of the matter?'

'No, the Frenchman grabbed me on the docks, him and the first mate, they locked me in the cabin an' A couldn't get out.'

'We have only your word about this matter have we not?' Strange looked at the jury. 'Boys will be boys and no doubt you were keen for a little jaunt.'

Jax made to answer but Strange carried on. 'Let us move on to the day of the captain's death. Do you recall Mr Reynolds entering the captain's cabin? On the day in question what did you see and hear?'

Jax shuffled on the spot and twisted his cap in his hands. 'A heard Mr Reynolds tell the captain who he was, as soon as A heard the master's voice A leapt out from where A was hiding and went behind the master an' out of the door as quick as A could.' Jax's voice grew in confidence. 'Mr Reynolds' skipper Capt'n Pearson were on the deck; when he saw me he grabbed hold and carried me ashore, like.' Jax voice was surprisingly clear and calm Gabriel noticed.

'You say you leapt out? Did you not wait to see what Mr Reynolds might say or do next? That would be the obvious thing to do would it not, to stay close to your rescuer?'

'No A din't. A wanted to get away from the Frenchy as quick as A could sir.'

'Are you sure you did not see Mr Reynolds strike the captain of the Bon Chance? Remember you have to tell the truth in a court of law.'

The judge added: 'Do not lie in my courtroom young man or you will come to regret it.'

Gabriel tried to catch Jax's eye to tell him to do as the Judge bid, but the lad stared straight at the prosecutor and in a confident voice said, 'A saw nothing; A was not there.'

The mob laughed and jeered and after a time the Judge again used his gavel to try and restore order. Mr Strange shuffled a pile of papers in front of him.

'Very well you may stand down'.

'Strange has banked on the boy being intimidated by the proceedings,' Saul Coates whispered to Gabriel, 'When threatened he hoped he would tell the truth as any God fearing boy should do, he has misjudged the lad'. The lawyer smirked.

The first mate was called again but it was clear from Strange's resigned look he knew the man was not in court.

'I'll bet he has sent the Frenchman's expenses to secure his evidence, it would have been a gamble,' Coates whispered. 'Strange should have kept him here in this country; he might have known the scoundrel would not show up. After all what was in it for him? He was probably as guilty as the captain where young boys were concerned and he would have known the arm of the law did not extend as far as France. He would have thought himself safer in his own country.' Saul Coates made a note on his papers and added: 'The prosecutor's last hope will be Captain Pearson but it will be a waste of time to call him, I imagine the First Mate will have told him Pearson did not go below deck, so he is hardly likely to say otherwise.'

'M' Lord, I will question the defendant Mr Reynolds.'

Judge Haywood looked at the charge sheet before him and then at the list of names who were to be character witnesses for the defendant. 'Very well Mr Strange, perhaps you will have more luck this time for at least we can see that he is here!' The noisy laughter which followed took time to die down.

'Mr Reynolds should you wish to defend yourself?' the judge asked Gabriel directly. Before he could respond Mr Coates said he would speak on behalf of his client. He went on to state what had happened on board ship, carefully omitting any act of violence to the French captain.

When he had finished his succinct speech he added, 'Mr Strange cannot bring forth the burden of proof that Mr Reynolds struck the wretched Frenchman. He cannot produce one witness to say that he did.' He leaned nonchalantly on the desk in front of him. 'We could call Captain Pearson Your Honour, to say he saw nothing untoward that day but we are aware Your Lordship has a long list before him and do not want to waste the court's time any more than we need to.' He smiled indulgently at the jury. 'I state therefore there is no case to answer. It is not proven by Mr Strange any act of violence was perpetrated against the captain by my client Mr Reynolds.'

The Judge adjusted his wig and looked first at Gabriel and then at the jury. He began his summing up. Gabriel could hardly believe the case had taken so little time. Save saying his own name, he had done nothing so far to further his cause; he felt impotent.

'Members of the jury I have in front of me twelve highly esteemed men of the district, a sir and two lords no less. All are willing to testify to the good character of the defendant. It is not my intention to call them as I know that they will no doubt all concur on the defendant's good character otherwise they would not be giving up freely of their time here today when they could be at their leisure. I cannot see how you can convict the defendant without the necessary evidence.' He sounded as if he had better things to do himself, Gabriel thought; his attitude was one of resignation.

'Doubtless if Mr Strange had been able to produce Jacques Blount then the outcome may have been different but we have no way of knowing what the man would have had to say as he could not find it in himself to attend these proceedings.' Here he glared at Mr Strange.

'Why you did not think to detain him in this country for the short period of time required I do not know sir! However, Mr Reynolds here has never had cause to the law before and has witnesses to his good character that any one of you would be proud to own. I make my feelings plain here gentlemen. Do you need time to debate? It is a clear cut case in my opinion and you can save your debating skills for later in the day if that would satisfy you. The evidence such as it is, is all circumstantial. The burden of proof lies with Mr Strange and is not forthcoming. The charge of Involuntary Manslaughter therefore is not proven.'

The foreman huddled together with his fellow jurors for less than a minute before rising and pronouncing Mr Gabriel Reynolds innocent. Gabriel breathed for what seemed the first time in hours.

♥

Sometime later in an upstairs room of The Quiet Woman a short walk from the Assizes, a merry crowd celebrated the victory. Abner, who had been taking care of Jax was away with the boy to tell Lisbet the news of their master's acquittal.

When the bar bill was still mounting, Gabriel too made his excuses to leave; the strain of the previous weeks had caught up with him. Bendor had been so confident Gabriel should be freed he had led Copper in with him that morning and so Gabriel could set off for Westshore without further delay.

Before he left, Gabriel shook hands with Saul Coates and again thanked him. 'I still feel I have been untruthful by not admitting to the violence I committed against the captain.' Coates shook his head in frustration: 'Gabriel you did not say one way or the other what happened that day, it is all a game and the dice was loaded in our favour this time. Do not lose sleep over this matter, forget it and live your life. I know you were upset – despite trying to protect Jax he still had to appear, but he acquitted himself well.'

'He perjured himself for me and for that I shall never forgive myself.'

'You are a good man Gabriel and you did not mean to kill anyone on that fateful day, it was a tragic accident; let it lie is my advice.'

Gabriel rode back with Caroline and Thomas, some of the others had left earlier, some friends and business partners were still making merry and would follow on later. Bendor rode with them as far as Dunstanburgh.

'When you are recovered in a few days come and see us Gabe, Grace will want to see you, as will mother; we shall celebrate in style. I did not think it fitting Grace should be in court in her condition; if someone had spoken ill of you she may have forgot herself and been charged with contempt of court.' He slapped Gabriel on the back laughing.

At Westshore Caroline and Thomas declined the invitation to dine; they could see Gabriel was all in. Lisbet came rushing out to the stable yard crying tears of joy. That night Gabriel had his first decent night's sleep in weeks.

19

Eleanor opened the letter which sat on her dressing table and began to read it whilst Charity dressed her hair. Strangely, it was from William Seamer seeking a meeting with her. She wondered what he could possibly want. He had specified a time and place; tomorrow at eleven of the morning at a private room in The Angel Inn.

She would have to meet with him of course; her curiosity had been aroused. However, she did not look forward to seeing him again, bad enough they should run into each other socially but a meeting alone was not to be relished.

The next morning, dressed in a navy blue riding habit and a tricorn which gave her a jaunty, sailor look and not a little confidence she arrived at the appointed time and was shown to a private room.

'Good morning Eleanor, you look very nautical this morning.' He took her hand and kissed it lightly.

'Good morning William shall you tell me what this is about? I have errands to run.'

'Blunt and to the point as always my dear!' He smirked; how could she have thought him charming?

'I will come straight to the point, as I do not want to take up more of your time than is necessary. I wanted to speak with you regarding the Breach of Promise your father is determined to bring before me. I wondered if you might use your influence with him to drop it; you must see nothing can be gained by dragging both our names through the courts.

'Must I? The way my father and I see this matter is that it is your name which will suffer, not ours. I am not the guilty party, you are the one with secrets to hide, not that your philandering is secret as you hid your mistress in plain sight as I understand it.'

She saw William swallow down his anger.

'Perhaps you too want to seek revenge, a woman wronged and all that? Let's not pretend we were "in love" Eleanor. Your pride, I understand, has been hurt but perhaps by continuing with this in law you are prolonging the agony.'

'Agony? William do not get above yourself; you are right it is a matter of pride to some degree, yet I see I have had a lucky escape. My father will not be moved for I have asked him myself to give it up but he is quite determined to pursue the matter in the courts.'

'Surely you have not tried so very hard as your father can refuse you nothing! He has always given in to you. Come Eleanor let us part without enmity.'

'If that is all William I will take my leave.' Eleanor dropped a curtsy and turned to go.

'What does your new suitor think of the matter, for I see you have not been slow to replace me, or perhaps you too were having an *affaire* of your own, only were a little more discreet than I?' Eleanor felt her cheeks colour. 'Mr Reynolds however, has his own secrets to hide. You cannot afford to act so high and mighty yourself Eleanor, do you think him a monk and that he is 'saving himself' for you? Young ladies have such romantic ideas.'

William stepped nearer: 'I think I can prove he is neither, there is also some other matter he has brushed under the carpet or perhaps your intimacy is such that you know of his violent streak?'

Eleanor felt her temper flare: 'You seem intent on bringing everyone down to your level William, there is no understanding between Mr Reynolds and myself and even if there were, it has nothing whatsoever to do with you. I am aware that up until recently he has been engaged if that is to what you refer; he has made no secret of the fact.'

'Yes he is a busy man! I was aware of his previously being engaged but that is not to what I allude.' She could see he was clearly enjoying himself. 'You always liked to get your own way – this time you will not.'

Eleanor was furious; 'How dare you speak to me like this, you do yourself no favours – you must know how stubborn I can be. Do not rile me further William.'

'Very well, If I agree to keep Reynolds' "indiscretions" away from your dear papa, perhaps you would urge him more vehemently to drop the case. You see my dear I can be discreet when I need to be. There may be no understanding between the two of you – yet, but rumour has it that there soon will be. Your parents should not like to hear of his lack of morals for I think they believe, as do you, he is a suitable replacement for me; they think him a rich business man with influential friends and a good reputation.'

Eleanor flushed with anger but attempted to maintain her dignity. 'Just what do you wish to tell me William? You clearly are no gentleman or we would not be here now. You think to hurt me with your revelation, well just tell me what you came here to say then we can both go on our way.'

Despite everything, William had sown a seed of doubt in her mind; she hoped he could not see through her bravado.

'Not so fast my dear,' she thought he was playing with her now, 'first you must promise to get this matter about the Breach of Promise dislodged from your father's head; without your assurance I am not inclined to tell you anything. Or perhaps you do not wish to know the particulars and will just agree to get your father to change his mind, better to remain in ignorance, what? After all it is nothing to me who he beds or... worse. Who am I to judge others?' He had half let the cat out of the bag – Eleanor wanted to let it escape fully now.

'I can see you are enjoying yourself, watching me squirm, but I will not give you the satisfaction of asking again,' she moved towards the door.

'Then I shall tell you anyway as one good turn deserves another. I am certain once you hear what I have to say you will push my cause, as you will not want your papa to hear the sordid details – or perhaps you will refuse Mr Reynolds; soon you shall realise there are no perfect men left in the world and will remain a lonely spinster?'

He laughed knowing he had scored a point. 'But

I digress. Very well I shall tell you what I know.' She watched as he drank from his glass and watched her face closely.

'Firstly for the last few years your Mr Reynolds has kept a mistress in Alnmouth.' He smirked as he saw he had scored another point. 'He possibly pays for the roof, albeit a very modest roof, over her head and enjoys sole rights to the lady as a result. He keeps her tucked away in a not too salubrious part of town down by the bay where he can visit her when he chooses; she has been his mistress even when he was engaged to Miss Caroline Hodgeson. How's that Eleanor? If you think I lie ask him who Miss Libby Lawson is and watch the colour drain from his face.'

Eleanor felt faint. 'Secondly, and more damaging I should think, is his recent court appearance at the assizes for the manslaughter of a French sea captain! Who would have thought it? No doubt you think him very sober and mild mannered.'

She felt light headed, shaking visibly she replied: 'Earlier I said I had had a lucky escape in finding out what sort of man you were before we married; I reiterate the sentiment again. Mother was right you are cruel; cruel and vile. As you rightly pointed out our relationship was never a love match but I thought there may have been some sort of friendliness there, some little affection; clearly not I see. I shall thank God for the rest of my days I did not marry you Captain Seamer.' She drew a calming breath. 'You must do as you wish with the information, I will not be bribed. Goodbye William.' She turned on her heels and left the room.

♥

Back at Mulgrave House and in her room she flung her hat on the floor and herself on the bed. She was so angry! Angry and confused; angry with William, with Gabriel and even angrier with herself; how could she be so immature to think Gabriel was any different from other men? She should have taken more heed of Gabriel's viewpoint at her cousin's wedding regarding Lester Ives – he had made no apology for his reasoning; it was true, she thought, all men were the same.

Her mind turned to the other matter. How did they not know of the manslaughter charge? Was he guilty? Her mind was in turmoil; the truth it seemed was that she clearly was not a good judge of character. Others seemed respectful of Gabriel, he had a good reputation, so how was she to know the real man? Even her father and uncle respected him she thought.

It was she who was the fool; all men it seemed were rogues. Thoughts, memories, questions with no answers, arguments for and against Gabriel all washed about in her head making her even more bewildered.

She went to her brother's room, she needed to talk. Tomas sat on the bed and pulled on a boot.

'Are you going somewhere?' It was after supper Eleanor realised; she had feigned a headache to avoid leaving her room. She had paced about all day; even sneaking to the beach had not helped. She had wanted to think and now she had thought so much she really did have a headache.

'I am away to Lythe for a meeting.'

'At this hour?'

'Yes at this hour, there could not be a better time for

the type of meeting I have in mind.' He chuckled softly and reached for his waistcoat.

'Is that all men think of? I wonder anything ever gets done in the world with men spending so much time fornicating!'

Tomas laughed loudly then saw the look of anguish on his twin's face. 'Dear God Eleanor why the long face? What's amiss?' She helped him straighten his stock and looked up into eyes that were remarkably like her own.

'Tell me,' she said 'if a case were to come up at the assizes, for a serious case that is, it would be reported in the broadsheets would it not?'

'Oh dear what have you done, is it a hanging offence? If it is then it would certainly be published, who have you murdered...' He noticed she was close to tears.

'Sorry my love, I see you are not in jest, what is it?'

She told him of the meeting with William, but left out the part about Gabriel having a mistress; he was blackened in her eyes yet she would feel strangely disloyal to Gabriel to condemn him without a hearing, besides her brother would possibly admire such behaviour and that would incense her all the more. Uppermost in her mind was the manslaughter charge; she told him the little she knew.

'I have seen nothing in the papers nor have I heard any talk, but then we are a little distant from Northumberland and not entirely in the same social circles. I would think it would depend on where the case was heard. He must have been acquitted otherwise I would think we would know if such a prominent ship owner had been found guilty and charged. He would face gaol, hanging or transportation. Father would have heard regarding the ship we are building for him.' Eleanor sat down heavily. 'You have feelings for him, I never guessed.'

'So much for twins' intuition!' She half smiled. 'Perhaps the case has not yet been brought. Dear God he could still be in danger, I can't believe he could murder someone.'

'Manslaughter is different to murder, I have studied the law a little, but I seem to remember that a case where there is no malice aforethought is manslaughter so that if the accused can prove or have just reason why he killed, then he may get a lesser sentence or be acquitted altogether. I have met him but two or three times yet am shocked to hear of this, how did William hear of it I wonder?'

'He is much in Northumberland as that is where *that* woman lives I think.'

'Well I hear the rich widow has moved on to pastures new and left poor William, well, poorer!' She has gone to London; apparently she has tired of the country.'

'Serves him right but I wonder why he is so keen to be rid of the law suit then, I had thought it was on account of her fine feelings.'

'He is off at the end of the week for Greenland so no doubt he is anxious to settle the matter before sailing.'

'I don't want to believe Gabriel has killed someone, it seems not real to me; out of character but possibly I do not know his real nature after all. He appears so,' she wiped away fresh tears, 'kind and thoughtful, in command of his emotions. It is true we have met him infrequently but I have grown to admire him and his friends are all good,

Uncle Brown had good things to say of him, he seems respected.' She said this hopefully trying to convince them both of the truth of the statement. 'His letters are so sincere.'

Tomas raised an eyebrow. 'Is there some understanding between the two of you?' He put his arm around her as they sat on the edge of his bed.

'I'll never understand men,' She sighed heavily and twisted a lock of her hair between her fingers. 'It is true I do care for him and I thought he felt the same but something else William said makes me think he is not the man I thought he was.' She was so distraught now she decided to unburden her heart fully; tell Tomas about Libby Lawson, a woman who until today she had not known existed.

'Oh dear, the cardinal sin as far as you are concerned! I do not know what to say little sister; you seem to like him well on such small acquaintance.'

'I told you we have been corresponding.' Eleanor bit her lip. 'Do Quaker men stay faithful to their wives do you suppose?' She suddenly blurted out.

'Lord, Eleanor you would not return to The Friends! Imagine being married to the likes of our brother-in-law, better to be a spinster of this parish I should say!

'Do you never think of how ill used the woman is that you lie with Tomas? You are not a bad man in other ways – you are moral, honest and all for equality so why is it that in this matter you behave against your better judgement?' Tomas sighed. 'Eleanor you are a woman and I am a man. It's just...'

'I know, "different for men". I've heard this argument

many times before.'

'Of course I am glad I am a man. Most men I know, when they marry for love that is, are faithful to their wives. I'm sure Reynolds is the same, it is just the way of the world.'

'How can we find out about the manslaughter charge?' she asked.

'I will see what I can find out, although as you say we are unsure how progressed the matter is at this moment;' he led her to the door. 'Try to get some rest you look done in.' Eleanor went back to her room and spent a long, sleepless night.

The waves crashing loudly against the cliffs all night, the pounding not unlike Eleanor's head, made her rise early. The rising sun smeared the sky with ribbons of light in shades from ochre to vermilion. She had reached a decision and needed to speak with her father; it was still too early for him to be up yet so she slipped down to the beach to swim.

Walking back up the cliff she hauled the ozone into her lungs trying to clear her head which still felt muzzy. Back at the house the staff were stirring; blinds were being opened, fires laid and breakfasts cooked. The aromas reminded her she had hardly eaten yesterday and now she was famished but by time the food arrived her appetite had gone. Tomas came and sat across from her. She smiled as he loaded his plate.

'We are both early risers this morning Tomas?'

'You may be dearest, but I am just returning from Stiddy Lane – I thought to go straight to bed for an hour or so before going to the yard, but seeing you at table I thought to tell you what I found out last night.' Eleanor was about to reprimand him about his habits until she registered the last part of the sentence.

'What did you find out, where did you get the information?' She was eager to hear what he had uncovered.

'I went to the library and looked through the last few weeks' worth of newspapers before I found the article; luckily the servants had not used them as fire starters! Come to my room and you shall read for yourself.'

'Is it good news or bad?' Eleanor looked at her twin expectantly.

'Both I should think, but on the whole not as bad as we feared.'

In Tomas' room she read the article which was lengthy and detailed.

'So it appears he is acquitted.' She was mightily relieved.

'It seems so. He should quite possibly never have been prosecuted but on such a charge the law had to run its course; he seems to have come out of the ordeal a hero. The chief witness for the prosecution hopping it back to France and not returning to give evidence was the final nail I would think. The French captain sounds a thoroughly despicable character and Gabriel did everyone a service dispatching him, even if it was accidentally. Gabriel, it says, had so many character witnesses willing to speak for him, including Sir Bendor Percy, who being of the aristocracy would carry some weight, that the jury didn't hesitate to find him innocent.'

Eleanor felt dizzy with relief: 'But it must have been

such an ordeal to be accused of something so awful and have to go through a court case, I expect he has suffered much from the experience.' Despite everything she found she wanted to see him and comfort him she realised. She could see the manslaughter was not to be held against him, she felt sure in his position she would have wanted to rescue the poor stable hand too; but she still could not see her way to forgiving him for the other thing. How could she admire a man who kept a mistress?

'Thank you Tomas for finding this information; your education was not totally wasted it seems. I wonder when father saw it why he did not mention it to one or the other of us?' Eleanor walked about the room feeling restive.

'I thought the same thing then I looked at the date on the paper and realised it was when he was away from home, gone to Thirsk to see about the iron, coincidentally, for Gabriel's collier. He was gone three days and would not read old broadsheets on his return so he must have missed it.'

'Well I for one am glad he missed it, yet no doubt the news will travel or else Gabriel will explain himself when next he sees father,' Eleanor said.

By now Tomas was yawning wanting to sleep before he went to the shipyard, she reached up and kissed him on the cheek and returned to her room to dress properly.

During her wakeful night she had come to the conclusion she would try to persuade her father, but not too enthusiastically, to drop the case against William. She had devised a plan to help her come to terms with the awful news William had taken such pleasure in delivering. She knew her father was determined to go ahead but she also knew she could talk him around if she really wanted to. It would suit her interests in this instance to let her father think he had got his own way.

It wanted twenty minutes to eight o'clock when Eleanor went in search of him. He had broken his fast and was heading to his study to collect the papers he would need for the day's business when she stopped him.

'Can I speak with you Papa before you leave?'

'These light mornings wake me early so I find I have time in hand,' he said grumbling, are you recovered from your headache?'

'Yes, thank you I am well today.' She followed him into his study. He sat behind his large desk which was awash with papers and documents; he had never been a tidy man but refused to let anyone touch his desk maintaining there was order in the chaos that he alone understood.

'Eleanor stop pacing and sit down child.' She continued to pace then pitched herself into the chair opposite her father.

'Yesterday I went to see William – that is he asked to see me and I went being curious to know what he could want.'

'I can guess what he was after no doubt! I'll wager he wanted me to drop the case against him and thought to use you to persuade me, the scoundrel!'

'Yes it is true he was most obnoxious but I wish you would drop it for he is right in thinking it will rekindle something which has died down, the gossips have moved on to some new topic.'

'Eleanor I will have justice; I know I should let it lie yet I cannot. He used you badly and I intend to make him suffer for it, I will not be moved child, so save your breath. I am sorry if you think it will put you in the spotlight again but it will be shining on him, the philanderer, not you my dear.'

'But I shall be talked of again and that will not please me father,' she said using her best wheedling voice.

'Well then you shall have to be deaf for a while.' Eleanor squeezed tears to her eyes; she could wrap her father around her little finger she knew.

'Then perhaps if I went away for a while I could escape from the gossip and the ridicule; Abalone as you know is with child and I would dearly love to see her. If I were to go to Amsterdam I would not hear of the case at all. William upset me greatly yesterday Papa. Might I have your permission to go?' She hated being deceitful but needs must.

'You would not be playing me would you my dear? I have over twenty years of experience of being manipulated by your mother, I recognise the trait, he smiled. 'Nevertheless, being an old fashioned gentleman I will give you the benefit of the doubt; I will spare your blushes if I can.' Eleanor heaved a sigh of relief.

'So long as you agree to go in a legitimate way this time I think it would serve all well if you were abroad, I am sure your mother can spare you but I will talk to her this evening to see what can be done.' Eleanor kissed her father's cheek. She was home and dry.

20

After the trial Gabriel took some time to adjust and reflect on all that had happened. With the help of those nearest to him he had seen the need to give thanks for the result and not, as sometimes was his nature, to dwell on "what might have been".

Through all of the unrest and terrors, for it had been a terrible thing to endure, his love for Eleanor had grown. When he almost reached the sea bed, it was the thought of Eleanor which had brought him back to the surface, the thought of seeing her again had been just enough to keep his head above water.

He decided the time was right to ask to see her. He did not want to write to explain himself, he still thought he could not write about what had happened, but if he met with her he could explain everything. All his immediate business dealings were more up to date than they had ever been as a result of the trial, so he had leisure to spare to go to Whitby. He wrote a short note stating he should like to see her on a matter of some importance.

She of course, was oblivious to all that had been happening in his life since their last meeting; unless of course she had read of the events in the newspapers, which he thought could not have been the case for she had not been in contact since her last letter. She was no doubt waiting for a reply to her last letter, a reply he had not yet sent. He hated the fact she might know the sensational details as described in the papers without his side of the story. He felt certain she was unaware however, for he thought she would have written to him if she had known of his troubles.

He hoped to see her soon and if all went well, if she could accept what had happened to him, he would ask her to marry him; if this terrible thing which had happened to him had taught him anything it had taught him that life was short and precious.

While he waited to hear from her he decided to go to see Bendor and Grace and once again thank them for their support. He intended to celebrate life as Bendor had suggested.

♥

After a rough crossing Eleanor arrived in Amsterdam and soon settled in with Abalone who was big with child. Her husband Bartel, was as excited by the prospect as his wife. Eleanor was swept up in the excitement too, she was pleased for her dear friends, yet she was also slightly envious of all they had together. They were obviously still very much in love, perhaps even more than before.

Abalone explained while they drank a cordial. 'It is like this child completes us, it was conceived in love and it will be so welcome, we have waited so long for this.' Eleanor thought Abalone was even more exuberant than usual.

'You look so well too, have you been well?'

'Yes very well, sick at the beginning but it soon passed – Do I not look like I shall soon burst like a pumpkin? I never imagined I could get so enormous.' She ran her hand over her belly.

'Yet you look even more beautiful to me, what do you think Eleanor?' the big Dutchman asked.

'It is true, some women look as if the child is draining the life blood from them and lose their colour. But Bartel is right; you have grown into a softer version of yourself. I envy the two of you, your excitement is contagious.'

For the next few days Eleanor and Abalone were inseparable and as Bartel had to be away from home on business, all were happy with the arrangement as it meant Abalone had company so near to her time of confinement.

'You have not mentioned Gabriel, except in passing, have you still feelings for him? When you wrote last I had expected to hear good news in that respect; you were full of admiration about his house and its location I remember.'

'It is true it is a beautiful house in a spectacular location.' She remembered being so happy there, the romance and the excitement she had felt getting to know Gabriel. She knew that was when she had begun to fall in love with the sensitive, thoughtful man. At Westshore she had seen what she thought was his true character. Had she been wrong?

'But still you do not speak of him, what has happened?'

Eleanor began with the account from the newspaper about his trial and subsequent acquittal. 'That must have been shocking for all concerned; thank goodness the boy was saved, was he press ganged, is that what you assumed?'

'It is possible, the newspaper was not very clear on the point but that is what I imagined. I am proud of Gabriel for saving the boy, but there is more to tell which makes me feel somewhat different about him.' She told her friend about her meeting with William Seamer and what he had told her about Libby Lawson.

'Ah, I see now why you look gloomy, that is unforgivable to you is it Eleanor? That he has a mistress.'

'Possibly; it depends on the day and the time, I can change my mind often enough it seems.'

'Here in Holland such affairs are commonplace, it seems men want experience before they marry. There are whore houses everywhere in Amsterdam! I know Bartel had a similar dalliance before we wed, no one thinks of it here in the city which is awash with brothels. I have friends, married friends, who have lovers; they tell me it keeps the marriage fresh. They enjoy their husbands more when they are not suffocated by them; they say the bonds are strengthened rather than the opposite.'

Eleanor's face must have shown her disbelief because Abalone said, 'I think we two are alike though Eleanor, we want to be the one and only do we not? Bartel says he does not stray since we married and I have to trust him; what else is there to do? I cannot live my life in fear of him straying, a life lived in fear is a life half lived. Our marriage is a success; we adore each other – most of the time.' Abalone smiled wryly. 'Gabriel may be of the same temperament as Bartel, perhaps he will give up his mistress on marriage. Have you asked him?'

Eleanor shook her head. 'Our British reserve will not allow us to be so open minded as the Dutch. However, I have not seen or heard from him in weeks, we had been writing to each other as you know.'

'He has had a lot on his mind I expect from what you have said. It is certain you need to speak about the matter to him.'

'He perhaps confides in his mistress,' Eleanor said sullenly.

'You are very hard on both yourself and Gabriel. I would not have married Bartel if I could not trust him; we cannot keep men on a leash. We all sometimes see someone who catches our eye, I have had advances and opportunities to stray myself, but I have so much to lose, I just hope my husband thinks the same when he too has chances.'

The tea table was cleared and Abalone said she would take some rest in her room. As she left Eleanor to think over their conversation she said, 'You must wait until you see him of course to hear what he has to say but ask yourself these questions: Could you be happy to live without him? How much do you love him? If it is a little then you could find someone who you could love more, if you love him so much your heart would break without him then perhaps you may have to find a way to compromise my dear.' She left the room leaving Eleanor with much to think about.

By escaping to Holland to be with her dearest friend, Eleanor thought to cure herself of the heart pain she felt. If only she could resolve the one issue that above all others troubled her.

The next day Abalone sat by the fire with Eleanor, they had pulled the chairs up close to take full advantage of the blaze. Abalone knew Eleanor needed to talk, she had explained about the other matter which she could not, it seems forgive or forget.

'When William told me Gabriel kept a mistress I had at first thought he was just paying me back; I still do not know for certain he tells the truth.'

'Yet you are prepared to believe him, he who has lied to you before.'

'What does he have to gain by telling me a lie? He already had enough against Gabriel to blacken his name telling me about the manslaughter charge – if Gabriel does have a mistress then he is not the man I thought he was. Do I want to exchange my life as it is now for a man who falls short of what I deserve?'

Abalone let the rhetorical question hang in the air. 'I realise now if I had married William I would have lived a life of compromise and I will not allow myself to fall into that trap again.' Eleanor wrapped her hands around her hot chocolate.

'Had you expected Gabriel to propose marriage?' Abalone asked.

'I hoped so, I began to think the next time we met he would have asked me and I would have accepted but now I have begun to see my self-worth. His behaviour regarding this matter shows an attitude which is hard to accept; to marry any man I would have to have him be loyal, trustworthy and honest. Honest above all else and I feel Gabriel has not been honest.' She sipped her drink.

'I do not blame you for having high standards, but is there any man alive who can live up to them? I see preserving your heart for a man who is worthy of it is an ideal to be sought after, but in all things there is compromise.'

'You think this makes me an idealist? Is it too much to ask to have a faithful husband? I have lost trust in all men; first William and now Gabriel. My own judgement I think is impaired, perhaps I am naive I cannot change the way men think or act, I have to either accept men as they are or not at all. I have to decide whether to accept the unfairness, the duplicity, or remain a spinster for the rest of my life; remain childless. I do love Gabriel but do not know whether I can trust him. To share him with someone else would be unthinkable; can I content myself with having him for a percentage of the time and try not to dwell on the times when he deceives me with another? I would be jealous I know. I have to make a choice and I accept with reluctance a woman cannot always have all that she wants.'

'You ask such a lot of questions! You have a very black and white view of marriage; I am here to tell you it need not be so very complicated. He may have been going to propose marriage and give this other woman up – who knows until you ask him; all is speculation.'

'Tomas said the same thing, about men changing when they meet the right woman but do men ever change?'

'My dear, you must decide whether your heart rules your head or the other way about, of course without speaking to Gabriel you cannot know the answers to the questions you put to me. Do you want to forget him? Is that why you came to Amsterdam?'

'Each day I break the promise I make to myself to forget him, each day is a battle between remembering and forgetting. I truly love him; I can see we would be happy together if only -'

'We are none of us perfect, if you allow yourself to remember what it is you love about the man, you will surely see he has many more good qualities than bad. It sounds to me he has made errors of judgement; the killing of the Frenchman must have affected him greatly. Was your first instinct to feel compassion for Gabriel as he must regret the taking of a life even if it was an accident? You say you do not blame him, that you would have acted in the same way to save a young boy but does it not show then that your characters are alike? You are a good judge of character Eleanor; if he is the man you think he is he will certainly be suffering as a result. You too have your faults, you admit to your impulsive nature, you told me how you met Gabriel, were you not curious to explore that which is not open to a woman of your rank?'

'I see the double standard; perhaps if Gabriel were to give up this woman we could start with a clean slate at least. I fear he would only have to look at me with those beautiful eyes and I would be powerless to resist. Can I risk my heart being broken?'

'Life, my dear, is a risk. He may want to give all his love to you, he may say he will give her up but if you do not trust him to do the right thing then you will never be happy.' Eleanor frowned. 'Why not write to him and tell him what is in your heart? When you return home perhaps you could meet with him and see what compromises, on both sides, can be made. What is destined for you will not pass you by. You are strong and wise, but still young; use this time here to know yourself a little better, if you love each other enough you will find a way to be together.'

21

It was mid morning when Gabriel set off for Bendor's estate; he was in the sunniest of moods. Since the trial he had been able to reframe his life and see it in a new light. Day to day irritations such as Lisbet's chatter, were now not so annoying to him, he appreciated what he had and believed himself to be fortunate. The condemned man had lived to see another day.

The weather too was in a good mood with only a few fluffy white clouds that would burn off. He thought about Eleanor; on his return he hoped a letter would be waiting for him. It was altogether a pleasant ride and he arrived refreshed.

A footman showed him into the library – no one was about but there was an air of solemnity about the way the footman had said he would fetch his master. Minutes passed, not unusual, the house being large and the grounds sprawling Bendor could have been anywhere on the estate. At last the door opened and an ashen faced Bendor came in.

'Are you ill?' Gabriel asked when he saw his friend.

'Not I, Grace – last night she became unwell and would not take supper; she went to lie down. I have begged her to take more rest, yesterday she had been out and I feared she had over exerted herself. By the early hours she was worse and I sent for the doctor.' Bendor was pacing up and down anxiously. Gabriel poured brandy and handed it to his friend.

'The doctor thinks the baby is trying to come early, he has prescribed something for the pain, she is in a lot of pain Gabriel; she looks gravely ill to my eyes. The doctor stays with her and she is restless and afraid, she is frightened the baby will be lost again.'

'I am sorry to hear this, do not mind me go and be by her side if she is anxious – she has greater need of you than I. Have you spoken privately with the doctor?'

A maid came and said Grace was asking for him. Gabriel was left alone again; he felt of little use. His friend had asked him to wait and told him to send for refreshment, whatever he needed. The time passed slowly until early in the evening Bendor came to tell Gabriel the news.

'She has had a very bad time; the doctor thought earlier one or other of them would be lost! I could not have borne having to make a decision of which one to save but thankfully it has not come to that. Gabriel I have a daughter! Both are frail as yet, the baby was facing the wrong way about and has had such a struggle to come into the world. The doctor said he is more hopeful now than he was earlier that both will pull through, but he tells me there is still danger; at least Grace can now rest. The baby is very big too, especially so as she has come early.'

'I am glad to hear you have a daughter! We should

be celebrating, yet from what you say it is too early to conceive of such a thing. Here take a drink and let us at least make a toast to their safe delivery so far.'

For two more days and nights Gabriel stayed to support Bendor. Gradually mother and baby grew stronger until, on the third day, Grace felt well enough to let Gabriel see her and the baby who was to be called Flora. The household which seemed to have been holding its breath suddenly began to breathe again.

♥

Gabriel returned home but there was still no reply from Eleanor. He did not presume to know her at all well, but was convinced she would have replied if only to reject his advances. Bendor happened to be at a shareholder meeting in Alnmouth, Grace and baby Flora were now well enough for him to leave them overnight without worry. After the business of the day the two friends dined together at Westshore. Gabriel told Bendor of his long wait for a reply to his letter.

'You should have let me write for you, I have had much more experience of flowery prose I think, when Grace and I were engaged and she was in Yorkshire I wrote often and she told me I wrote a good love letter.'

'It was just a note asking to see her!'

Bendor laughed. 'I am of the same mind as you; a well bred young lady such as Eleanor would reply if only to refuse you. Fear not my friend a reply is probably winging its way here as we speak. I see from your face my platitudes do not convince you, here this will buck you up.' He refilled Gabriel's glass with rum; they had drunk much of the port, a little of the brandy and now were keen to finish off what was left of the Jamaican rum.

It was not helping Gabriel's mood, nor were his friend's remarks. Bendor, now happily wetting his new baby's head, seemed to have forgotten the trials of love of his single life. The two friends continued to drink until Gabriel downed his last drink in one, bid goodnight to his friend and staggered up the stairs to bed leaving Bendor to finish the bottle alone; he felt thoroughly dejected. Why had he not heard from her?

Despite the amount he had drunk the night before, Gabriel was up with the lark as usual, he felt a little rough around the edges but nothing good food would not cure.

'Shall I wake young Sir Bendor or will you let him sleep it off a while longer?' Abner asked.

'I shall wake him – I have just the thing for his sore head.'

Bendor was roused: he was dishevelled, his hair ruffled, his eyes bleary his clothes appeared to have been slept in.

'Man alive! You were up all night it seems,' Gabriel said.

'I feel as if I have only just gone to bed I pray I will soon die and be put me out of my misery.' He slumped on a chair and scratched his unshaven chin. Gabriel laughed. 'Come on, I have just the cure.'

He grabbed Bendor by the arm and dragged him to his feet, he knew Ben would know what the cure was and be unwilling to take it.

'Leave me be, I am not long for this world.' Gabriel was not put off.

'Man alive, what drama, come on.' He dragged and pushed Bendor onto the terrace, down the garden and onto the beach. It was wet and windy, the tide just going out leaving the sand soft. Bendor protested loudly all the way to the sea.

In their younger days when they were unable to hold their drink, it had been their custom to swim it off; it always worked despite one or other of them being totally against the scheme. Gabriel gave one last push and launched Bendor into the waves fully clothed. He struggled to his feet the waves knocking him about, he managed to rid himself of some of his clothes.

After a few minutes Bendor had colour back in his cheeks and the horse play began, each tried to drown the other beneath the rough waves. After half an hour they staggered back up the beach where Lisbet stood with towels.

'Yer ready ter break yer fast now? It's bin goin cold this last hour, yer like big kids.'

'Sorry Mrs Cotter,' Bendor said just as if he were a child and not Lord of a very large manor, 'It is the fault of Gabriel for I would have sooner sat down to eat rather than be half drowned upon rising from my bed.'

Bendor fed, watered and dressed looked like he had slept the sleep of the just as he mounted his horse to ride home. 'What will you do if a letter does not arrive soon; do not for God's sake go dashing to Whitby on some pretence for that would surely smack of desperation.'

'I seem to remember you were full of good advice last night too, thank you for your concern.'

Bendor sighed, 'Sorry Gabe but it looks like you've

backed a loser this time, I know you hoped something would come from this liaison but...plenty more fish in the sea eh?'

'Get gone before I'm tempted to throw you in again.'

'I know you are pining for the Whitby wench and I'm sorry to tease you but perhaps it is not meant to be? You said yourself she was unusual, she certainly does not seem biddable. If she cared for you she would surely have written by now. Let Grace find you someone; Cora is still unattached.' He winked at his friend.

Gabriel watched as Bendor rode off. He was not prepared to let the love of his life escape so easily. He had a plan.

♥

The Jack and Alice was set to sail to Amsterdam via Whitby at the end of the week delivering coal and returning from Holland with Geneva for the British market. Gabriel decided to take the trip despite what Bendor had said; he thought about "appearing desperate" and decided to ignore the advice. He would not waste anymore time. He had to see her.

Gabriel landed at Whitby and headed straight for her father's ship yard. Tomas greeted him all smiles. 'Come to take a look at your baby? She is growing daily and is on schedule I am pleased to report.'

Gabriel would have liked to see his ship but was keener to see Eleanor. 'I was hoping to see your sister, I expect you know we have been corresponding but I have not heard from her recently. Is she well?'

'She is but I am afraid you have missed her; she has

gone to Amsterdam to be with her friend who is with child. I would have thought she would have told you.'

'Amsterdam! Perhaps she did not receive my last letter?' Gabriel's heart sank.

'Who knows, I'll never understand women. I recently thought I had met 'the one' but it turns out she was as fickle as all the rest and has agreed to marry someone else; said she was tired of waiting for me. Ah well lucky escape – for me and for her!' He laughed loudly.

Gabriel chewed his lip and was thinking what to do. He had come all this way for nothing it seemed.

'Now you are here you may as well look at your ship.'

Tomas led Gabriel to the dry dock talking all the while about a problem there had been with the iron ore that had now been resolved thanks to an idea his father had had. Walter Kemp stood by the enormous structure; he shook hands with Gabriel. 'I am afraid I will have to leave you in Mr Kemp's capable hands; I am sailing to The Hague today, you almost missed me as well. So long my friend I must dash or miss the tide.' He shouted 'Farewell' as he made his way onto the quay and was gone.

♥

Bartel Visser was well known in Amsterdam so when Gabriel arrived in the port and asked for him at the first agent he came to they were able to tell him where he lived immediately. He strode down the canal until he reached the address he had been given; the door was opened by a maid wearing a traditional Dutch bonnet and wooden clogs. He asked to see the lady of the house; he had been told by the agent that Captain Visser was at sea.

He was shown into a morning room which overlooked the busy canal, as he waited he turned his hat in his hand.

He looked out onto the hustle and bustle of life on the canal belt; it was a pleasant scene. Although he could never imagine living anywhere but besides the sea, he could see this aspect had its charm too.

The door opened and he turned to see a most beautiful woman, in fact he thought possibly the most beautiful woman he had ever seen in his life. Everything about her was light and fair; her white blonde hair, her fair, flawless skin, her eyes the palest periwinkle blue. For a moment he was taken aback. She smiled showing perfect white teeth as she came forward to welcome him.

'Mr Reynolds, how nice to meet you I have heard much about you from my dear friend Eleanor. I expect it is she you are seeking?' Her English was perfect with just a hint of an accent.

He regained his senses and replied. 'Yes I am honoured to meet you Mevrouw Visser I understand Miss Barker is residing here and wished to speak with her on some urgency.'

'Please take a seat, will you take tea or coffee?' She pulled the bell and made the order. Abalone took a seat by the fire, Gabriel joined her. 'You are a frequent visitor to Amsterdam?' she asked not answering his question.

'I used to come more often than I do of late. My business is freight; we often used to bring over grain or coal and return with Geneva but since my father died last year I have had to pass the role to one or other of my skippers.'

The coffee was brought in and poured. 'Eleanor is out

I am afraid, I do not expect her until later today. I have just given birth to a daughter and cannot be away from home for long. Eleanor was keen to see a new exhibition of water colours, she left but an hour ago. As I say, she will not be back until after dinner at the earliest.'

'Congratulations on the birth of your daughter; Miss Barker, told me you were with child, I am possibly keeping you away from the new arrival?'

'Mercifully she has just been fed so you do not disturb me. Can we, as I am sure we both have Eleanor's best interests at heart, speak frankly? Eleanor has told me a little of what has been affecting your life of late.'

'She knows about the trial?'

'She does and understands some, if not all of the circumstances and thinks she would have acted in the same way in your situation.'

'I was not sure if she had heard. Does she know it was a tragic accident? I regret the man's death every day, despite him being the most disreputable man whoever walked the earth!' Gabriel drank his coffee. 'It is some relief to know she is sympathetic to my cause. I did not want to write to her about it as you can imagine; it is not something I could put in a letter. When the trial was over I wrote to her asking if we could meet so I could explain myself but she did not reply. I know not whether she received it and wanted to be rid of me or, as I am hoping, that she had already left for Holland and has not yet received it? I went to see her in Whitby but she had already sailed.'

'She has seen it now; her father forwarded it with some other papers that needed her attention.' Abalone dazzled Gabriel with a smile: 'Why not go to the gallery and meet her there? You both have much to talk about and I am certain the sooner you meet with her, the better it will be for all concerned.'

'I will if you think she will want to speak with me,' he said.

'I cannot speak on her behalf but you will never know unless you go and see for yourself.'

♥

Gabriel entered the gallery and looked about. He found Eleanor in an ante room, she had her back to him looking at a seascape.

'Hello Eleanor.'

She spun round. 'Oh what a surprise!' He looked at her astonished face and thought his heart would explode. He explained how he had found her.

'Are you on business in Amsterdam?'

'I wrote to you but it seems you have only just received my letter. I have come to see you, to explain. Could I meet with you when you have seen the exhibition, perhaps you would accompany me to a coffee house?'

'I have finished here as it happens. I think it would perhaps be better if we went back to the Vissers we should have more privacy there I think.' Gabriel dared to hope. The walk back was tense; they restricted themselves to discussing the weather and the sites they were passing.

Once back at the Vissers they were alone in the conservatory.

'Before I left Whitby I met with William Seamer,' she said.

'I see. Am I to understand your engagement is back on?'

'No!' Eleanor looked shocked. 'He asked to see me, we met and he told me he had two pieces of information to tell me; about you. He said he thought there was an understanding between us and that I should know your true character. This was not a friendly gesture you understand, it was not from any thought for my well being, he was threatening to tell my father in order for me to talk Papa into dropping the Breach of Promise suit he has against him. He thought if we had some feelings for each other that I should want to hide this information from him.'

'Blackmailing you?'

'Exactly; if I cared nothing for him before I care even less now if that were possible.' Gabriel was pleased to hear this. 'Did he tell you about my arrest?'

'He told me you had been charged with manslaughter, he wanted to gloat when he found I was unaware of it.'

'Let me explain why I did not write to you about it.'

'Oh I can imagine why you did not want me to know.'

'It was because at the time I was possibly facing a death sentence or imprisonment, I would not presume but I thought if you knew you would worry for me. What if I had been found guilty, I could not have borne to see you in the courtroom and felt sure you would have come if only as a friend to support me. I had left a letter for you in case the worst should happen but—'

Eleanor moved to stand close by him but at the last moment she turned and looked out of the window.

Gabriel tried again. 'There had been no declaration as

such but I think we both knew the tenderness we spoke of before was -.'

'Please Gabriel, let me finish telling you what William said before you go any further.' He nodded assent. 'Aside from the charge, he told me something else, something I do not know whether to believe or not, forgive me but I have to ask and know the truth.'

'About what? Did he say I have lied to you about something? I cannot think that I have, perhaps he was speaking of Caroline, but you know all there is to know on that front.'

'No not Caroline, I do not know how he would know such a thing but he says for years you have kept a mistress. He told me her name; Libby Lawson?'

'I see he really did mean to separate us,' Gabriel said.

'Well, I think by the look on your face he told the truth?'

'Can we sit down and I will explain?'

'So it is true; should I have continued to live in ignorance? You would have courted me and then what – carried on with this woman behind my back? What of the tenderness you talked of?' He could see she was trying hard to control herself; she looked close to tears.

'Eleanor you must know it is more than that; I love you.' He moved towards her and wanted to hold her but knew he would be rebuked so held off.

'When I thought my world might end I had much to do.' She tried to interrupt him. 'Please Eleanor let me speak now, I will try to explain, 'I had people, upward of two hundred people and their families who depend on me for their livelihoods to consider. My employees needed to be taken care of; I had to make provision for them and try to put my business in good order, I had a little under three weeks in which to do this. It sobers the mind I must tell you to write a Will thinking that what is written in it may be implemented sooner than one would like; it is very trying to say the least.' He thought he saw a look of pity in her eyes.

'During this time I had much to occupy me, including trying to come to terms with perhaps never seeing you again. I went over my life and realised I had regrets, one of which was that if I should die I should have nothing of real value to show for it; not a wife, nor children. It all seemed so, so... such a waste, I would never get to tell you how I felt or hold you in my arms again. I do not expect you to understand but I also reflected on Libby; we met by accident when I was just eighteen and yes, though not by design, she became my... '

'You make it sound—'

'Please let me try to explain, I know this is not easy for you. We have talked of the matter before, about how men behave before they marry.' He told her the story of how he had met Libby and how the relationship had developed.

'Over the years I helped her in small ways and yes she became what I suppose you would call my mistress though I do not think I treated her as such. I never loved her although I did care for her.'

Eleanor had listened patiently but now he saw her anger flare.

'Yet instead of helping her up again you pushed her further down! Not only was she ill treated by her brother you came along to compound her misery. Did you never think with all your wealth to help her out of her poverty?'

Gabriel hung his head. 'Yes I tried but she wanted to help herself and said for the longest time she was going to go back home, she had no money and no way of earning any save for labouring which she was not brought up to do. At the time, I was young when it began, she had no one else to turn to and now she has risen again and is dependent on no man.'

Gabriel stopped while he tried to read the look on Eleanor's face. He continued: 'In the time before the case came to court I realised I loved you with all my heart to the exclusion of all others – I went to speak to her and told her I would not see her again. To my surprise she had found a position so was leaving anyway. We parted amicably; I came to see I had been selfish.'

He looked into Eleanor's stricken face and saw the anguish; he hated himself for hurting her.

'I can see how it looks, I am not proud of the way I have behaved but believe me I would give up everything for you if you will only return my love. I love you with all my heart.'

There was a long silence. 'It pains me to say it Gabriel but perhaps you are not the man I thought you were; I cannot see this matter as you do.' He saw the look of despair on her face, he could see she was wrestling with all he had told her.

'I am sorry but I must ask you to leave, I am so confused; my head tells me one thing and my heart another.'

'Then I beg you listen to your heart! Just tell me you love me, I came to Holland hoping once I had explained about the trial you would take my side and know what I did, I did to save Jax. It was an accident the man died and I know you well enough to know you would have seen the injustice too. Eleanor – I had hoped to ask you to marry me.' The look in her eyes was breaking his heart. She turned her back to him.

'Very well I will do as you ask, I will go now, but I will come again, I will not give up so easily, you mean the world to me.'

Still with her back turned she said: 'I do love you, but I do not know if I can get past this, I know you have not betrayed me as this affair was before we met, or mostly so. I do see you were not meaning deliberately to hurt this woman but you naively and selfishly used her Gabriel. Llike always, women are ill used at the hands of men, how do I know you will be faithful to me? This is not something which can be rushed; I need to think over what you have told me.'

'I am loyal,' he could think of no way to convince her. 'I will give you time my love but I will not give up hope.' Gabriel moved towards her, stood close behind her. 'Please go Gabriel.' He left her looking out of the window.

♥

Gabriel called for the next two mornings and was told Miss Barker was not at home to visitors. On the third morning Gabriel waited by the canal side and watched hoping Eleanor would leave the house; he waited all day but there was no sign of her.

On the afternoon of the fourth day Gabriel saw the

door open and Abalone stepped out. Gabriel's heart sank. He put on a brave face and approached her.

'Good afternoon Mevrouw Visser. I was hoping to see Miss Barker but it seems she does not want sight of me, if only I could speak with her.'

'Good afternoon Mr Reynolds. My friend has a stubborn streak has she not?' Gabriel was unamused. 'Eleanor has a soft heart and a very moral outlook; the two do not always sit well together,' Abalone smiled, 'She may not be a Quaker in name but she has all the sensibilities of the philosophy.'

'I know it and it is my doing which has caused this rift.'

'Eleanor has a very strong will and sense of right and wrong that does her credit but sometimes her wilfulness can be taken to the extreme and she hurts herself by refusing to move on. I hope this does not sound disrespectful to my dear friend; I have her best interests at heart. At present she is going around in circles trying to decide what to do. Given time I am certain she will come to see she loves you and cannot be without you.'

'I wish I could be as certain for the longer she waits the more I think she will never see me again.'

'As I see it, with a little push in the right direction she will accept you – I should not dream of interfering if I were not convinced of the outcome.'

'Each day I call she refuses to see me, what am I to do – knock the door down?'

Abalone smiled: 'I do not think there is need for such a grand gesture Mr Reynolds; she turned and opened the door. 'Eleanor is in the conservatory.'

Eleanor was looking out at the garden. Gabriel coughed to let her know he was there. As she turned he saw a look of pleasure and pain on her beautiful face. 'This cannot go on Eleanor, I will speak with you if I may?' She did not speak but walked toward him.

'Eleanor my love, we will not be happy until we have spoken again, one way or another this matter between us must be resolved, here and now.' Much to Gabriel's relief Eleanor looked at him expectantly.

'All my life I have been prone to dark moods but never so black as now when I fear I will never see you again; the thought of losing my life at the trial was only a burden to me because it would mean I would never hold you in my arms again. If you can believe me then you too will see no man could love or respect you more. I promise you can trust me. Eleanor, will you marry me?'

She half smiled and said: 'In my life I have taken risks; not calculated risks but impetuous, headstrong risks which have not always worked out as I had planned – or hoped. I have always behaved impulsively, gone by my instincts but I have come to realise that in life sometimes we have to take a chance, a *considered* chance – take a calculated risk as it were. I too have made errors of judgement, thinking I would be content to marry without love for example. We are none of us perfect, you have made mistakes, errors which you have sought to rectify. I refer of course to your, your...'

'It is true but I have seen the error of my ways and if you put your trust in me I swear Eleanor all that is behind me. If you could learn to trust me you will not regret it; I love you and need no other but you.' She let him hold her hands.

'I want to believe you, she smiled, ' I think you are about to face another trial.' She squeezed his hand. 'Of all the men in the world you are the only one for me Gabriel, when faced with living without you I know I would rather die, I love you and cannot wait to marry you.'

Gabriel beamed. 'Do you really mean it? He laughed. 'With you as judge and jury how can I go wrong?' He kissed her.

♥

The next few days were the happiest Gabriel had ever known; in the past when he thought he had been happy he realised he had only been content. Now he was truly happy; loved by this most wonderful woman.

It was agreed Gabriel should return to England, he had secured a berth going to Whitby, where he would go to see Eleanor's father and ask for her hand in marriage. They had almost had a tiff about this custom with Eleanor once again complaining she was to be given over from the care of her father to another man as if she were chattel. Gabriel had teased her and made her laugh when he said if it made her happy he would ask her mother instead. From Whitby he would return home to prepare Westshore for its new mistress.

Eleanor was eager to leave with him but baby Beatrice was to be christened at the end of the week and as Godmother, Eleanor was torn as she wanted to be in two places at once.

It was decided she would travel home on a ship which

belonged to a friend of Bartel's; "The Come What May", which was leaving on the first Monday in December. The arrangements were made and Eleanor and Gabriel saw as much of each other as possible; Amsterdam's liberal attitudes and the Vissers' bohemian lifestyle, meant they were unchaperoned, left to their own devices for much of the remainder of Gabriel's visit.

One evening Bartel Visser said, 'Why not stay the night before you sail back to England? You can take supper and get a good night's sleep before your journey; your crossing will not be so pleasant at this time of year.'

He was already liking Eleanor's choice of husband and would have invited him to stay even if Abalone had not prompted him. It was agreed Gabriel would stay at the Vissers on his last night in Amsterdam.

After a pleasant supper Abalone and Bartel again made baby Beatrice their excuse to leave the newly betrothed couple alone, Gabriel and Eleanor sat together until late; they were reluctant to part. Eventually, as Gabriel was to leave before dawn, they said goodnight to each other.

Once in her room Eleanor undressed. She sighed with happiness but it was tinged with sorrow at yet another parting. She thought of her betrothed just down the corridor as she brushed her hair; her heart missed a beat. There was a light knock at the door; she rose to answer it smiling. She hoped he would come to her.

Gabriel stood in his shirt sleeves: he looked so handsome, so sure of himself. His blue-grey eyes shone in the light of the candle he held. He grinned and leaned against the door jamb. With a look of expectancy he murmured. 'Let me have you Eleanor.' She opened the door wider and let him in.

22

John Barker had not been so very surprised when Gabriel asked for permission to marry his daughter. However, he had not known Gabriel had been to Holland to secure her, nor did he know of the troubles that had led eventually to this happy day.

After Gabriel had been congratulated by the rest of the family he was invited to stay the night before sailing back to Alnmouth to prepare for his bride; Gabriel thought he was going to enjoy being part of this gregarious family.

After supper Anne Barker took Gabriel aside. 'You will never know how happy I am Eleanor has finally come to her senses.' Gabriel looked puzzled. 'When she was engaged to Captain Seamer I could see they were ill matched yet Eleanor, being pig headed, was determined to marry him despite our protestations. I am sure she has told you her reasons for this yet she would not be swayed. Now you tell me she is finally in love and loved in return which is all I ever wanted for her; she would have been miserable married to that man.'

'She has taken some convincing but we are both certain we are doing the right thing. I love her dearly, more than my life.'

'I am glad to hear it. I know you will be as happy as her father and I are, I think you will do well together. You are strong enough to let her be herself and clever enough to let her have her own way from time to time.' She smiled. 'Eleanor will be an asset to your business too, I am sure my husband has told you about her not inconsiderable dowry and she also has her own money – money she has made over the last few years from shrewd investments.'

'Mr Barker has informed me, yes. As far as I am concerned any monies will be put to making Eleanor as secure and happy as can be. As I explained to Mr Barker I am in a relatively good position financially since my father's demise. As for her own money – I know it customary that I as her husband would "own" her funds at our marriage but I do not intend to take them; Eleanor has every right to keep what belongs to her.' Anne Barker smiled as she laid her small hand on Gabriel's arm. 'Does she know this?'

'Why do you think she agreed to marry me,' Gabriel said laughing.

'It is a pity you do not have a sister.' Gabriel did not follow her train of thought. 'My wayward son is in need of a strong lady to show him the right path in life – if you had a sister and she was of your disposition I think she would suit him.'

♥

Back in Alnmouth Gabriel lost no time in seeing Bendor to tell him the good news. 'What do you think of your master's news Mrs Cotter; shall you enjoy having a new mistress about the place,' Bendor asked as she served them at table.

'It's about time! We thought him set to be an old bachelor.' She smiled proudly.

'Thank you Lisbet, I am but four and twenty not as old as Methuselah! I hope by the time your new mistress is aboard you shall have grown a little tact – she is not used to such forward servants. From what I have seen of her household her staff are seen and not heard. You shall perhaps learn from Miss Barker's lady's maid who will be joining her here.'

'So long as she doesn't interfere with ma kitchen A'm sure me and the maid shall get on fine.'

She waddled out of the room. 'Do you suppose she means she will get on with Eleanor's maid or Eleanor?'

'Who knows! Eleanor will be a match for her I am sure although I see troubled waters ahead while boundaries are reset. I am sure Eleanor will want to do things her way, Father and I just followed Lisbet's lead, life ran smoother then.' Bendor proposed a toast: 'May you both be as happy in marriage as Grace and I.'

♥

After the Christening Eleanor set sail for home on the morning tide on a freezing December day. She would miss Abalone, but she and Bartel had promised to come to England for the wedding; no date was set but Eleanor hoped it might be late spring or early summer. Her head was full of plans for the future; she was happy to be returning home to be married.

Although early December, the North Sea was unusually calm. Eleanor was a good sailor but kept below deck for most of the journey; it was the only way to stay dry and warm in the bitterly cold winds that blew.

On the evening when she expected to dock, as the sun had set ember red and the evening star had risen, she stood on deck wrapped in a thick velvet cloak, the fur lined hood shielding her from the wildness of the wind. She could just make out the twin piers of Whitby harbour reaching out to her like welcoming arms; the lighthouse, a beacon of light guiding her home. She was excited to see her parents and to share her news with Tomas.

The whaling waters heaved, swelled and rocked. All at once the ship was hauled up and halted. An almighty jolt uprooted her causing a low grumbling groan which seemed to come from deep in the bowels of the frigate. There was a splintering and cracking of wood like a tree being felled in a silent forest: then there was stillness, a calm before the storm.

They could not have run ashore, they were too far off? She heard a deep growling far below her, the ship lurched drunkenly, throwing her off balance. Eleanor stumbled, was thrown forward and back again against a prop, the breath was knocked out of her and a pain shot through her back. She clung to the rigging, the torn skin on her fingers burned with pain. She fought to cling on. Another thrust and she lost grip, sea water was tossed about the deck wetting her through. Sea spray smacked her face as the hood was torn from her head.

'Help me.' Her words were tossed upon the wind. A low rope swung by, dangled tantalisingly close above her head; if only she could grasp it. Her hands flayed the air as it passed by swinging wildly like a hangman's noose.

A sailor reached out to her – she tried to grab him, he fell and slid down ship, washed away. She was slammed backwards, lost her balance again, her hands trying, but failing, to grab hold of something, anything solid. A sudden sharp pain to her head brought darkness and she knew no more.

♥

Many a ship had floundered on the Whitby Rock, the shale reef below the east cliff; the sand bar was notorious. Eleanor's berth proved to be yet another casualty. The Come What May's' captain, though experienced, had been caught out and the ship had been swept around causing it to strike the ridge hard. Fortunately there were but twenty on board; several cobles saw the accident and were quick to pitch in and come to the rescue. Though all hands were saved, by the morning the ship was driftwood and her cargo gone.

Eleanor, along with five others, was injured, but it was Eleanor who came off the worst. She had been rescued unconscious and brought ashore, she was immediately recognised and carried to Mulgrave House and the doctor summoned to meet her there.

On that first night ashore she remained knocked out and insensible. The doctor stayed all through the long, winter night watching and waiting for signs of life but there was little he could do.

Anne Barker sat by her daughter's bed. 'Eleanor my dear come back to us, we need you.' She looked at the doctor.

'Her body needs to rest, she needs time to heal.

Perhaps by morning we will see an improvement. Tomas paced the room. 'Should we not send word to father? He could be here early tomorrow if we sent to Thirsk tonight.'

'I am torn. Why worry him – he will be home tomorrow night anyway, let us spare him a harrowing journey if we can.'

'She is lucky to escape without broken bones,' the doctor said.

'Her poor face is all the colours of the rainbow...' Anne Barker held her daughter's hand.

'Eleanor is strong Mama, she will soon be complaining about being out of action, you know what she is like.'

The freezing December rain lashed against Eleanor's window; lowering clouds advanced upon the shore. Cormorants dived in the urgent tide. Giant waves thundered against the cliffs; a storm raged. Eleanor, unaware slept on until the following morning when from the deep, dark, depths of somewhere below the sea Eleanor swam to the surface and was aware of the waves crashing furiously from below. She gasped for air as she regained consciousness. All became temperate once more. Her mother and brother were immediately by her side; the doctor felt her pulse. She was on the way to recovery.

♥

When Gabriel heard a galloping horse approaching Westshore at break neck speed he knew it could not be good news the rider brought. After reading the letter he flung it on the fire and within minutes was issuing orders for Copper to be saddled and hurrying to make ready to leave Westshore. 'Damn' he said to Abner. 'I'll miss the tide if I don't hurry, I'll ride to the bay.' It would be a fraught journey until he could be by Eleanor's bedside.

John Barker had assured him she was in no immediate danger now but he would not rest until he saw for himself. By the time he arrived, Eleanor was battered and bruised all the shades of green, yellow and blue but was much better. She still had a head that thought it was to split like a coconut but otherwise she was regaining her strength. After four more days she was chomping at the bit and trying, against doctors orders, to get out of bed.

'I am so bored lying abed like an invalid, she complained. 'You are an invalid, you need to rest, give your body time to recover.' Gabriel reluctantly carried her downstairs. He knew she would not be happy until she was fit again.

'You could help me with my business correspondence?' Directed by his future wife he made a start. 'What is this lease renewal?' he asked. She took it from him and read it. 'Ah it needs my signature; you will have to sign it on my behalf.' Her right hand was still swollen; she could not hold a quill. 'It says it is for a milliners shop?'

'It's a long story – Mama likes hats!' She laughed.

'Life will be anything but dull with you my love,' he said. 'I once thought I wanted a compliant wife now I see I would have been bored with a country mouse.'

'Instead you are to marry a slippery fish!'

'I hope not! I cannot wait to marry you.' He stroked her sore hand affectionately. 'Why are we waiting to marry in spring, why not do it sooner, what is there to wait for? We are both clear in our minds and after this accident I want you where I can see you at all times. All these partings are hard are they not, should you like to marry as soon as possible?'

'You are as impulsive as me! I agree – a Christmas wedding would be wonderful but Christmas is only three weeks away could we get the banns read in time I wonder?' Eleanor looked animated.

He said: 'I had not thought quite so soon but if it can be arranged then why not?'

Eleanor's mother came into the room and her opinion was sought. 'I should think there is time enough, a special licence could be got if needs be. Are you to limp down the aisle?' She looked at the raised leg and Eleanor frowned. 'I am sure it will not come to that.'

'What will you wear? You would have to be content with a dress you have already for there will be no time to order a new one. My daughter is always very impatient Mr Reynolds; you will see this for yourself soon enough.'

'It is Gabriel's idea Mama and I agree I would sooner marry than wait for a dress to be made, the gold I had for the Browns' wedding would look good for a winter wedding; Christmas Eve would be perfect?'

Anne Barker laughed. 'Well, you two seem equally matched in temperament I must say, that was a quick decision. I think I shall go and warn cook; she needs to know if that is what you have decided. The cake wants as much time as it can get... or perhaps the Christmas cake could be used instead as it has long been made. Dear me what shall I wear I wonder? There is much to do and organise, shall you marry at St Mary's as you had originally planned?'

They looked at each other and agreed they would. Mrs Barker stood and smoothed her dress with her small hands and looked at the happy couple. 'Well then I had better make a start,' she said leaving the room.

'Is your mother not going to speak with your father first?'

'I would not think so; she will tell him when he needs to know.'

'Oh I see, is that the lines on which our marriage will run?'

'I think so – then hopefully it will last as long as my parents' has.' She took his hand in hers smiled and kissed him softly.

'Man alive! I am lost!' he said grinning back.

23

Eleanor had decided on one addition to her wedding outfit; a large and spectacular hat. She was to wear the gold gown but decided she would like to transform it by having a new hat designed and made especially for the occasion.

On a frosty December morning she set off to Tattishall's Milliners and Haberdashery now owned by her friend Eva Drage. Eleanor had kept an interested eye on the small business since Eva had agreed to take it over; so far it seemed to be doing rather well.

Eleanor heard the familiar tinkle of the bell as she entered the shop and the usual assistant appeared smiling at her potential customer. Eleanor explained the reason for her visit and after she had been shown a book of designs Eleanor was shown into the workroom at the back of the shop.

Eva, looking transformed, stood by a work table strewn with ribbons, fabric swatches, scissors and shears. She wore a simple but elegant black dress edged in cream lace. She looked so pretty. Eva recognised Eleanor immediately.

'Well this is some surprise! I wondered if I should ever

see you again.' They approached each other and Eleanor took both Eva's hands in her own.

'Are you not astonished to see me here for when we knew each other I was a sail maker?'

Eleanor laughed sheepishly. 'And I a governess!' They moved to sit on a small sofa.

Eleanor confessed about who she really was, finishing with how she now wanted Eva to make and design her wedding hat. Not once during the conversation did Eleanor allude to who made the hat venture possible for Eva.

'You will be astounded to know who I am to marry.' She explained to an incredulous Eva. 'Lord! I don't believe it, who would have thought it? You to be married to such a handsome one and I am all set up here doing just what I always dreamed of doing.'

Eva's brow furrowed. 'It could not be you who is my benefactor? I have long thought of who it could be and until now I never suspicioned it might be you?'

Reluctantly, for she did not want to lie to Eva, she confessed but she had not come for praise or thanks,

'Mrs Tattishall was very kind and helped me to learn the basics of the trade, I had help from all the staff who stayed on thank goodness, they are so experienced and skilled and have been generous and patient; they were also keen to keep their jobs. Eva winked cheekily at her old friend.

The two young women spent a happy time chatting and then began to talk about the wedding hat. Eva sketched some designs quickly and expertly.

'You are so clever! You had this hidden talent all

along,' Eleanor said proudly.

Eva beamed. 'I now know if it had not been for you I should never have realised my dream, I'm that grateful.' After further discussions about the hat's size, shape and whether it should have feathers or flowers, Eleanor was ready to leave.

'There is just one other thing Eva; I should like to ask if you will do Gabriel and I the honour of attending our wedding? After all, as I recall, you were our matchmaker were you not?'

'Are you sure? I've never been to a society wedding afore, will I not be out of place?'

'No you shall not; there will be people from all walks of life come to help us celebrate. Please say you will come, some of our tenants will be there and people from the shipyard too.'

'I'll be honoured, I will need to work every minute on the hat, there is some work involved in it. Three weeks is not long from design to completion; I promise you it will be the best hat I have ever made.' Eva took Eleanor's hands in her own: 'Since I took over the shop things have bin different an' not just for me – I've bin able to help my sister and her children so more than one person had benefited from your good deed.'

When Eleanor left the shop she was more pleased than she could say. She was so proud of Eva and so glad she had raised her up; she had just needed a chance. Eleanor could not wait to see how the hat turned out; she knew it was going to be special.

24

St Mary's, high on the East Cliff and standing close by the ruined abbey, candlelit on this frosted Christmas Eve, saw most of Whitby society gathered in their private galleries and box pews to witness the marriage of Eleanor and Gabriel. They had toiled up the one hundred and ninety nine steps to see the happy couple exchange their vows.

The altar was decorated with white hot house roses, rosemary and ivy. Eleanor's golden dress shimmered in the candlelight. Her hat, a triumph, threaded through with green silk and jasmine, matched the fur lined mantle she had worn to keep the bitter cold at bay. The groom in deepest green velvet, his dark curls shorn and for once under control was handsome and happy.

The wedding breakfast was a feast for all the senses; Mulgrave House ablaze with hundreds of candles cast their softening light on the ladies' faces, smoothing out what harsh winter would otherwise expose. The rustling silks of the gowns in deep jewel shades and the sparkle of gems added to the festivities. The gentlemen, not to be outdone, were peacocks in embroidered waistcoats, silver buckles, fine linen and silks.

Fragrance mingled from hot house flowers with rosemary, ivy and holly. Fires blazed, their woody base notes carried on warm air adding cinnamon, leather and tobacco to the heady scent.

Course after course was served with the finest champagne, robust reds and sweet dessert wines from Madeira; and later, music, dancing, supper and entertainments. By then Eleanor and Gabriel had fled by carriage to begin their honeymoon and their first Christmas together. The bridegroom allowed himself a second to remember last Christmas, his first without his father. It had long been his inclination to linger over the past, but not now. A new love of life and a new love in his life had meant he could only see what was in front of him; Eleanor, his wife. With her hand in his and laughing as their guests bid them a fond farewell they set off into a new life together.

♥

They travelled to Alnmouth by carriage stopping off on the way at several places Eleanor had never seen before. They called at Newcastle where a lot of Gabriel's business interests lie, Eleanor, being a shipbuilder's daughter, was keen to see the places he frequented so when he was away she could picture him there.

Gabriel had once been to Morpeth with Bendor and had liked the place so they stayed two days there looking at the town and its sights. Each day they became closer and found new things to admire about each other.

When they finally reached Alnmouth it was a bright clear afternoon and as they came around the bay

Eleanor could once again see the sea. The sun shone magnificently, the tall masts of the ships reminded her of home. They swept past as Gabriel pointed out The Alnmouth Boy to her: 'She will be sailing for Whitby on the morning tide.'

'So if I am grown tired of you I could escape back home in the morning?'

'This is your home now, but you could I suppose; I should charge you passage if you do! Do you want to leave me already?'

'Of course not but now the honeymoon is over it will be a true test for both of us.'

'That is a very serious thought; do you not think we can make our marriage work?'

'If you give in to my every demand I am sure it will be a great success.'

'You would become bored if I let you have your own way all the time I am certain, but at this moment I cannot see me denying you anything.'

The carriage pulled up at Westshore. 'Welcome to your new home,' Gabriel said as he handed her down and turned to see Abner and Lisbet waiting to greet them; Jax was in the rear looking sheepish. Slate came running when she heard her mistress's voice and Scrabble sulked now he was to share his house with another dog. Charity was to arrive in the next day or so.

Once they had settled in and supper had been taken they sat either side of the fire with a glass of port for Gabriel and lemonade for Eleanor.

'What is this? You do not want wine or other spirits?' Gabriel asked.

'I like a cordial sometimes when I am thirsty, it is refreshing,' He looked perplexed.

'Surprised I do not take wine or spirits all the time?'

'Well, yes.' he admitted.

'For many years we had no alcohol in the house – remember; we were Quakers. I find it makes me sleepy sometimes when I would rather be alert.'

'Alert; are you expecting an invasion?'

'Of sorts I had hoped,' she said cheekily.

The events of the last few weeks and the travelling today had made them both tired. 'Are you ready to go up?' Gabriel took the hint.

'Yes if you are.' He led her out into the hall where he lit two candles but headed towards the kitchen, rather than the stairs. Eleanor was confused at the direction they took. 'Where are we going?' He stole a look at her and smiled.

'Am I to sleep in the kitchens?' She had no idea what he was up to but laughed as they passed Lisbet and Abner who were sitting by the stove. They had no time to rise before Gabriel led Eleanor to the scullery door which led to the stable yard. He took both her hands in his and spoke as a parent might speak to a particularly dim child.

'There is the key to the back door.' He pointed to a large heavy key hanging on a hook. 'If you feel the need to get out at full moon, or whenever the fancy takes you, there will be no need to wake the household now. Should I leave a lantern to light your way perhaps?' He laughed as she caught on to his joke.

'Why should I want to leave our bed for a cold windy night abroad?' He still held her hands.

328

'Who knows, but I shall try my best to make it worth your while to stay.' He wrapped her in his arms and they both grinned like adolescents. Gabriel began to lead her back through the kitchen with a pair of servants looking on in bemusement.

It was a foolish thing to do but he had thought to make her laugh and put her at her ease on her first night in her new home. He knew it would be strange for her.

'Goodnight both,' Gabriel said as they passed by. Eleanor was following in his wake trying to stifle a laugh.

When they had left, Lisbet puffed on her pipe and shook her head. 'I hope this tomfoolery is not shades of what is to come. Gentry is very strange sometimes.'

In their room Eleanor said: 'You are so thoughtful Gabriel but that is not the reason I first was attracted to you.'

'Was it my handsome good looks and strong physique?'

'Well possibly! She rolled her eyes at his modesty. 'I think I first thought you could be the one for me when we dined here a Westshore and I saw your house had such wonderful sea views.

'So are you saying that if my house had been inland you would not have thought me marriageable?'

'I suppose you might have won me around eventually,' she giggled. 'Because of its proximity to the beach and the sea you had a head start.' She leaned against him and closed her eyes.

On the bed was a blue velvet bag, Gabriel picked it up.

'I have something for you my love; a wedding present actually.' He placed the bag in her hands. They sat on the bed and she looked up at him excited at the unexpected gift. She untied the cord and a wooden box slipped out. The top was inlaid with an intricate Mother of Pearl design and had a tiny golden lock and key.

'Gabriel it is so beautiful, where ever did you find such a thing?' 'It was my mother's, my father gave it to her for her wedding gift and so I wanted you to have it for yours; look inside.'

She unlocked the box; inside was lined in the same blue velvet as the bag. 'How romantic you are, I feel very honoured to receive this; I shall treasure it always. Thank you, my love.'

'There is something else – can you find the secret drawer?' She was much moved and after looking over the box admitted she could not. 'Does it need the key?'

He took the box from her hands. 'Let me show you.' He slid a finger to one side of the box and a slim drawer opened out from the side.

'How clever, I should never have found it, it lays so flush – unless you know where to push it would remain a secret.' She saw there was something in the drawer; a ring.

'Was this your mother's too? What a stunning stone.' The rose gold band had an oblong pale stone at its centre.

'I had it specially commissioned for you. I asked the jeweller which stone was closest in colour to the sea on a summer's day and he showed me this; it is an aquamarine. You are like the sea, constantly ebbing and flowing. Your temperament is the same, ever changing; sometimes calm, sometimes turbulent but always constant.'

Eleanor laughed. 'I think there is a compliment in

there somewhere! She was about to slip the ring on her finger when he said: 'There is an inscription.'

She looked closely to read it. "For My Constant Lady: 24. 12.1765" Tears threatened to fall as he slipped the ring onto her finger. 'There it fits perfectly, just like us.'

She kissed him softly. 'If I am the sea then you are my moon; your pull commands me,' she said feeling unusually poetic. He smiled. 'I like the sentiment my love but I doubt anything or anyone could command you, especially not a man!

'Would that not be a good name for your new ship Gabriel? "My Constant Lady."'

He thought for a moment then said, 'It would but I was thinking of calling her "The Whitby Wench" which is possibly nearer the mark! ' He took her in his arms and kissed her before she could reply.

This was not their first night together but it was their first night in their new home. Without a maid to do for her, Eleanor let down and brushed her hair. They watched each other through the mirror; he moved close behind her and traced hot kisses down her neck making her shiver. He did not take as much care with her clothes as Charity did. They were soon in a heap on the floor.

25

Over the next few weeks Eleanor began to get to know her new home and its surroundings. They were invited to many social gatherings and had many callers, all wanted to meet the new bride. It was inevitable that sooner or later she would meet Caroline Hodgeson and the hot ticket was the annual Alnmouth Ball. All of the local upper crust would attend and without doubt Caroline would be there. Although the gossip of the broken engagement between Gabriel and Caroline had died down long ago there was renewed interest in the first meeting of the discarded and the successor.

One morning Eleanor was at her correspondence, when Lisbet announced a visitor; Caroline Hodgeson came into the library looking radiantly beautiful in a well cut riding habit of Prussian blue. There was a moment of assessing on both sides.

'Good morning Mrs Reynolds.' Eleanor smiled and wondered if the title seemed strange to her predecessor.

'I was riding by and thought to call and introduce myself, I hope I do not inconvenience you?'

'Not at all Miss Hodgeson I am delighted to make your acquaintance.'

Lisbet brought tea and biscuits. Eleanor saw Lisbet was lingering and summing up the situation.

'Thank you Mrs Cotter we shall manage for ourselves.' Lisbet reluctantly left the room; Eleanor would not have been surprised to find her cook loitered in the hall finding many specks of dirt to wipe off the door; her ear would inevitably be very close to it she suspected.

After pleasantries were exchanged Caroline said: 'I hope you do not mind my coming to see you but I thought it would be preferable for us to become familiar with each other before the ball later this week which I am sure you will be looking forward to. Alnmouth, much like your home town I expect, can be quite insular and the good people will be keen to see you; a fresh face as it were. They no doubt will be striving to draw parallels between the two of us and to see whether we should be friends. I, for one, would like that and father has already made me like you from the things he has told me about you. I was grateful to you both for thinking to invite him to your wedding.'

The speech Eleanor guessed was rehearsed but thought it kind of Caroline to make the effort nonetheless; it cannot have been easy for her she thought.

'We must think alike,' Eleanor said, 'I too had thought to ask you and your father to dinner before the ball in order to get to know each other privately. Alas time has flown by and I have been remiss in making myself known to you.'

Once the ice was broken both ladies began to relax. Caroline was extremely beautiful Eleanor noticed; she wished Gabriel had warned her she thought irrationally.

Her riding habit was elegantly cut and her hat very becoming. Eleanor felt quite dowdy in comparison. When she realised her fingers were ink stained the new bride tried to keep her hands hidden, not easy when serving tea.

'Perhaps I could show you around, help you to make new friends. Alnmouth is such a small place we have to entertain ourselves I am afraid. Do you hunt?'

'I don't but I love to ride.' Caroline looked disappointed.

'How are you getting on with Lisbet,' Caroline whispered, 'I bet she is listening at the door.' she smiled. 'Lisbet can be quite formidable when roused, she used to run rings around Gabriel and his father but she is a good cook and housekeeper and they are hard to find. Keep on her good side is my advice.'

♥

Lisbet was about to return to her kitchen when she became aware of someone behind her.

'Is there something I can help you with Lisbet?' Gabriel stood close by his face expectant. A flustered Lisbet was caught red handed. She had indeed been eavesdropping. She flushed and moved off muttering about dirt, visitors and baking. Gabriel smiled to himself and wondered who or what was of interest behind the door. He watched her back to her domain before entering his drawing room.

His wife, along with his onetime fiancée, were standing side by side in conversation by the French window; they had not seen him come in. He now saw why Lisbet was so interested. He looked at them both and unselfconsciously compared them.

Caroline was the taller and the most beautiful it had to be said; she had regular classical features and her curls were a golden halo. Eleanor was certainly attractive and could hold her own against most women, but despite her ivory skin and her sprinkling of freckles she was second best in this contest. Eleanor's red hair casually dressed was still the thing he noticed most about her; it was her crowning glory.

Then just at that moment Eleanor laughed at something and she became the more striking, the more captivating. Her features had an animation he loved; she seemed to glow with vitality.

Since the first time he met her he had come to see that whatever she was thinking was written for all to see upon her face, which made it all the more beautiful to him. She had no artifice, no pretence.

He noticed Caroline did not possess this quality. She looked demure but aside from that he could not tell, even after all these years, what she was thinking. Perhaps it was to be expected under the circumstances she would appear guarded. Caroline may be beautiful but Eleanor had something more; a special indefinable exquisiteness, a loveliness which came from an inner beauty, he went to join them. There was a moment's awkwardness as the two women saw him approach.

'Good day Caro, you look well,' he said and kissed the proffered hand. He nodded to his wife. He had gotten into the habit of kissing Eleanor at a reunion but saw in this company it would not have been fitting.

'I am thank you, how well married life suits you too I see. I had hoped you would have been to call before now, you and Mrs Reynolds of course, but I expect you have been busy since your marriage?'

Gabriel noted the hesitation before Caroline had said "Mrs Reynolds"; was there just a hint of something underlying the words? Gabriel was unsure what it could mean – it could not have been jealousy for he knew Caroline had not wished to marry him. Perhaps it was simply the awkwardness of the situation.

'Yes indeed and my business always takes much of my time as you no doubt remember.' His reply had been curt and he saw Eleanor shoot him a look. She glanced at him in some surprise and he realised his remark had seemed a little off hand.

'Caroline was good enough to call to see me before the ball on Friday to make my acquaintance, which is thoughtful is it not?'

Gabriel agreed it was; he then sought to make amends by being as charming as he could to try to rectify his error; he complimented Caroline on the colour of her outfit then explained why he had returned home: 'I have come to collect some papers I need to take to Alnwick, I had forgotten them. I must go soon if I am to reach the solicitor before he shuts up shop.'

'Will you not take tea?'Eleanor asked.

'I'm afraid not, as I said I should make tracks.'

'I am riding that way; would you like company for some of the way, I will ride as far as Boulmer.' When her horse was brought they rode off together with Gabriel telling Eleanor he would be home for supper.

She watched them ride off and saw how good they looked together.

26

Gabriel who had taken time and care dressing for the ball, was on his second brandy and still awaiting Eleanor who had been getting ready for what seemed to him like hours. He knew she would want to pay particular attention to her appearance, on this her first introduction into Alnmouth society, so had half expected a wait.

At last she swept into the room with a flourish ready to receive his attention. She wore a gown of deep turquoise watered silk edged with fine Chantilly lace. Her hair looked ravishing tumbling down in loose curls from high on her head. At her throat she wore a single diamond drop on a ribbon. Gabriel rose to look at her closely.

'Man alive Eleanor I am not sure Alnmouth is ready for this!'

She giggled. 'The dress or myself?'

'Both! Is it not very, well, revealing? I am suddenly thinking a night at home is appealing.' He moved closer to her and ran his forefinger from her chin to her décolletage. 'I am not sure I want to share you looking like this.'

'I ordered it in Amsterdam where it is the height of fashion; I did not dare wear it in front of Mama! Yet all

Abalone's friends wear their gowns this low cut, I believe also in London the style is all the rage.'

He smiled to himself as he placed her cloak about her shoulders; she was clearly as excited as a school girl going to her first dance. They set off before he lost control of himself.

The gentry of Alnmouth, most of whom were not at all conscious of the latest fashions, were gathered wearing more conservative dress on this February night. Granted some of the younger set had new gowns, it was after all, one of the most important evenings of Alnmouth's social calendar.

Gabriel and Eleanor made a striking couple as they entered the ballroom and all heads turned in their direction: Several hearts had been broken when Gabriel had married. It was natural therefore that there would be a certain curiosity to see the new bride; newcomers were often viewed as suspicious until they had lived there for forty years. There was the added thrill of how the two young women would tolerate each other. Eleanor's daring gown certainly set tongues wagging and she received admiring glances, especially from the gentlemen.

Gabriel spotted Thomas Hodgeson and led his wife through the throng to his group, which of course contained Caroline; eyes followed them in anticipation of the meeting between new wife and old flame. Of course this was not a first meeting and the two greeted each other if not as old friends but with more feeling than might have been expected by the onlookers.

The band started up and people began to lose interest in the newcomer, all except the men of course; Eleanor's dance card began to fill. 'Do you suppose I will get the chance to dance with my wife this evening?' Gabriel watched as a business partner moved off having secured two dances with her.

'I thought you did not enjoy dancing and would be glad of the excuse?' Gabriel smiled and flicked a discreet look at her breasts.

'That was before I saw every man in the room had designs on you'

When Gabriel had first seen the daring cut of the dress which showed off her charms so obviously, he had been a little perplexed. He knew she would want to wear something to give her confidence as she was after all new to this society but he would have imagined, if he had thought about it at all, she would have erred on the side of conservative for her first entrance.

Then he remembered who he had married; he should have guessed she would do the opposite. She would have known she would draw attention as the new wife of a prominent businessman and as the successor to Caroline Hodgeson, so why not make a spectacular first impression. He kissed her hand and proudly led her to the dance floor knowing that later that night he would enjoy removing the beautiful but revealing gown.

♥

Since coming North, Eleanor had been very disappointed with the weather, it seemed to have rained incessantly for weeks keeping her indoors much more than she would have liked. Eleanor had been married for four months and had settled at Westshore very well, excepting for the weather. A chill wind seemed to blow effortlessly and without concern for the fact it was supposed to be early summer. The sun had seldom made an appearance and on the few days it had, seemed reluctant to spread the warmth that was expected of it.

Each day she looked out to see rain clouds lined up in regimental order, elbowing each other out of the way in their rush to reach land first and drop more water on the wet sand. The waves, as if in competition would rise up taller and crash down like thunder claps that would in no time echo from the troubled sky.

She was reassured by everyone this weather was freakish and soon the sun would be making everything dry and bright again. Being confined indoors was not good for Eleanor's well being; she longed to be outdoors exploring her new surroundings.

She had much to occupy her indoors if truth be told. With Gabriel's blessing she sought to make minor changes to the decorations and furnishings of the house. She liked the large, light, airy rooms with their huge picture windows and French doors. The only alteration she made was to add wedding gifts, such as the beautiful silver candelabra and candlesticks Bendor and Grace had given them. She had also made space for herself in Gabriel's study; they had been to Alnwick and purchased a desk for her sole use.

Lastly they had ordered a new bed; now they had moved into his parents' suite of rooms he thought they should have a new, bigger bed. He did not want himself and his new bride to sleep in the bed his mother had died in; that would surely feel morbid.

Most days when Gabriel was not away on business he tried to come home for dinner. He was so happy to have someone to come home to and enjoyed sharing his meals, which for some time had been solitary affairs. One day he had been at a meeting in Alnwick and so was not home until after supper. Whilst pulling off his riding boots in the hall he saw Charity coming down the stairs. 'Is your mistress in the drawing room?'

'No sir she has retired, I have been dismissed for the evening.'

'Is she unwell? It is early yet to be abed,' he added.

'No, she is well sir.' She curtsied and went through to the kitchen.

Gabriel poured himself a brandy and after storing papers in his desk he carried his drink upstairs; he opened the door quietly in case Eleanor was sleeping. She was not abed and not asleep.

'Am I lost; am I in the right house? I seem to have wandered into a Bordello.'

Eleanor lounging on a blue velvet chair by the window, wearing not so very much in the way of clothing, smiled up at her husband. It was a most unladylike pose she had adopted. The blue velvet choker at her milky white throat and the stockings held up by matching garters were all she wore.

'Are you acquainted with such places sir?'

Gabriel began to undo the buttons of his waistcoat. 'It seems I have no need of such places now even if I were.' He looked at her admiringly. 'I thought to find you sleepy?'

'I'm not tired, I have had very little in the way of

exercise as the weather refuses to allow me to ride without getting soaked.' She looked up at him. 'I hope you are not tired.'

'I was, but I find I am wide awake suddenly! I cannot think why; is it exercise you are in need of Milady?' She walked over to him wrapping her arms about his neck. 'I might be.'

'Had I known what awaited me at home I should have finished my business sooner.'

'Let that be a lesson to you not to leave me waiting, you never know when I might have need of you.' He stroked her hair then pulled her closer breathing in her familiar scent. She began to undo his shirt.

'Now let me see if I can make you breathless,' he whispered in her ear. They enjoyed an early night.

♥

It was early June and the day had dawned sunny at last. Eleanor stood on the terrace and looked down the garden towards the sea. The sun burning bright scorched the sand. She was glad of the fine day as she was expecting a visit from a landscape architect recommended by Bendor.

Eleanor thought more could be made of the garden to the fore of the house; the terrace looked good and was perfect for sitting out but from there the view of the garden was disappointing. She thought to draw the eye down to the sea and make the garden somewhere to linger and look at before reaching the glorious icing sugar sand and the sea beyond.

'I want roses and shrubs and sweet smelling climbers, but I need someone to help me put my ideas into practice.'

She said.

'I remember the evening sitting in the summer house at Mulgrave with you, if we have one here it shall remind me of the occasion.' Gabriel had given her free reign having every confidence in her choices. The one thing he had requested however was a summer house.

'I think one would look good here and would provide shelter as it is always breezy hereabouts.' Eleanor agreed it would indeed be a welcome addition and thought it a romantic gesture that Gabriel had thought of it.

Eleanor had already had one meeting with Richard Greenlaw and today he was to present his plans for her approval. Lisbet showed the architect in and the plans were studied whilst walking about the garden.

'As you can see Mrs Reynolds there is ample space for the summer house you particularly requested.' He pointed to the furthest edge of the garden. 'If it is placed there it will afford wonderful views and being enclosed can be enjoyed in cooler weather.'

'Of which we seem to have had in abundance lately, Mr Greenlaw.'

'Yes, as you say the summer is a disappointment so far this year but it is early days. Last year was exceptionally dry and all complained of that too.' They went about the garden with the architect proposing where a stone seat might be placed or a pergola erected when suddenly Eleanor felt a little queasy.

She begged to be excused and restraining herself from setting off at a sprint, walked purposefully into the morning room. She looked about for a receptacle but finding nothing suitable made a dash for the empty fire grate and was violently sick. She clung to the mantelpiece with one hand and held her heaving stomach with the other waiting for order to be restored.

Lisbet pushing through the door backwards with a large tea tray in her hands, saw what had happened and advanced toward Eleanor.

'I'm fine now Mrs Cotter.' She still could not call her by her first name. 'I have made a mess I am afraid – it must be something I ate which disagreed with me.'

Lisbet flushed. 'Well no one else has been put out with food served in this house ma'am. Shall A go and tell Mr Greenlaw you have been teken bad?'

'No. Thank you. I feel quite well again now; better out than in as my mother used to say, I am sorry to cause you more work. Please put the tray on the terrace, I will serve tea to give you time to clear up in here, I am sure I shall be fine now.'

Eleanor saw Lisbet soften; they had begun to rub along well together. Over the past months Eleanor thought Lisbet's initial resentment of the loss of having free will in the household had subsided. As a new mistress she had made some changes to Lisbet's routines and methods but she had wrought these modifications sensitively she hoped. Lisbet even seemed to get along with Charity, which was a relief to Eleanor. Charity had told her Lisbet had said it was a nice change to have women about the house.

Eleanor rejoined Mr Greenlaw and their meeting concluded. She continued to sit outside as the day got hotter; it was a pleasant change to feel the sun on her skin. It was the second day in a row she had been sick.

She had missed two of her courses and she was beginning to admit to herself it was probable she was with child; she had not expected to fall so quickly.

Her life recently had undergone a lot of changes and now it was to change again. She was pleased to be expecting but they were still making adjustments with one another. Gabriel had lived along with his father in a very masculine way, not taking much notice of the niceties unless guests were present. It was a big change for him to have a woman about the place, even though he maintained he liked it.

She wondered what Gabriel would say. They had talked about children and he had often said he wanted "a house full". Eleanor had laughed and suggested one would be enough to begin with. Perhaps they would be lucky and continue with her family trait of twins; a boy and a girl would suit both of them she thought.

Perhaps she would wait a while to make sure of her condition before telling Gabriel. He was due home for dinner today and she realised she was starving hungry. She walked on the beach and enjoyed the luxury of not getting wet.

When she returned Eleanor had expected Gabriel to be waiting on dinner. As he had not appeared she again sat on the terrace to watch out for him. Sometimes he went straight to the stable yard and then came through the kitchen. On these occasions Lisbet was used to passing on bits of news or took the opportunity to grumble about something which was bothering her. She wondered if this was where he was.

♥

Gabriel had wanted to talk to Jax about getting Copper shod and was then met in the stable yard by Lisbet who was in a flap; she told him about Eleanor's sickness. He rushed through the French windows and saw his wife sitting with her face upturned towards the sun, her eyes closed.

'Lisbet tells me you are unwell my love, you have been ill?'

'I should have guessed Lisbet would have told you, I had forgotten you sometimes come by a different route.' He examined her face closely.

'I am fine now there is nothing to worry about.' She squinted up at him lifting her hand to shield her eyes from the sun.

'Are you sure? You look well enough, in fact you look like you have caught the sun a little – your freckles are coming out.' He stroked a finger down her nose before bending to kiss her.

'Lisbet is at pains to assure me she has not poisoned you and I have just wasted ten minutes reassuring her I am not suffering also, she does fuss.'

'Lisbet's dialect mystifies me sometimes I find her hard to understand on occasions.

'I think the Geordie accent easy on the ear – I am used to her prattle I think. Gabriel smiled his eyes crinkling against the sunlight.

'Jax is also indecipherable. The other evening he brought in the coal and said he had brought the "black diamonds" fortunately I have heard of that colloquialism before.'

Gabriel was reassured now he could see Eleanor

looking radiant in the summer sun and chatting amiably, if somewhat disparagingly, about the staff. He knew how she bloomed when the sun came out and knew she would be pleased it was at last warm and dry.

He sat opposite his wife and poured himself lemonade, a drink he remembered Lisbet making when he was a child. It had been newly resurrected; Eleanor liked it especially in the daytime when the weather was warm as it was today. 'If you feel unwell again and I am from home get Jax to run for Wilson Chaffer to look you over just to be sure all is well.'

Eleanor shrugged, 'We need to think of hiring more staff, I thought to place an advertisement locally?' Gabriel watched as Eleanor topped up her glass. 'Perhaps a maid-of-all-work and an under-cook for Lisbet to train up; she is not getting any younger. When the garden is landscaped we shall need a gardener. Do you not think you should have a valet?' Gabriel took off his jacket and hung it on the chair back.

'Abner suits me well enough, but he too is getting long in the tooth and needs a younger man to help with the heavier work, that will leave Jax to be solely responsible for the horses, I know he is up to the job.'

'I think that will do for now – Lisbet seems to be able to summon up extra help when we entertain.'

Gabriel felt pleasantly relaxed and was enjoying talking of such mundane household matters. 'It will feel odd to have servants about the place – when I come across Charity, it takes me by surprise sometimes, for so long it has been an empty shell save for Abner and Lisbet.' He rubbed his chin thoughtfully. 'It is a large house for them to maintain.'

'Well trained staff will not get in your way; you will hardly notice they are here. Charity does not bother you does she? I thought her quite discreet?' Gabriel smiled. 'No she is very easy on the eye when I do meet her.'

'Oh you think so do you?' Eleanor feigned jealousy. 'Perhaps I need to replace her: I should not want your eye, or any other part of your person, wandering!'

He smiled at the thought. 'I think I have enough to occupy me with you my love, I have no wish to go wandering.' He looked out to sea and noticed a frigate passing by.

'I should hope not but to make it fair I think I shall choose the new staff to make sure they are easy on the eye for the mistress.' Gabriel looked at his wife with desire.

'Perhaps you need reminding of your good fortune in having a handsome, virile husband at your beck and call.' She laughed at his conceit. 'Handsome! Virile! You think well of yourself sir.' He pulled her to her feet and held her in his arms. 'I sound big-headed do I not? Shall we have an early night this evening? All this talk makes me want you.'

She smiled up at him. 'Does it now and you can wait until tonight?' That does not flatter a lady.' He kissed her feeling her body yield to him; he began to explore her body expectantly.

Suddenly she blurted out. 'Gabriel I think I am with child.' Gabriel was stunned; his arousal checked as though he had plunged into the icy waters of the North Sea.

'With child, Man alive, who would have thought it

– so soon? It is some surprise is it not?' She pulled away from his grasp. 'I must admit I am shocked!'Gabriel said.

'Shocked? That is a strong word. It is a word one uses when one has been given bad news.'

'Surprised, shocked what is the difference? The meaning is the same surely?' Eleanor was riled he could see.

'Surely it is not. Rarely have I heard anyone who has had a nice shock or a bad surprise!'

Gabriel silently watched the ship, its sails bright white in the sun. Eleanor said: 'I am not certain of my condition; if Lisbet had not told you about my sickness I would have waited until I was sure. I wish I had kept my own counsel now; I have spoilt our afternoon. I have hardly come to terms with the pregnancy myself yet and now here we are bickering like this!'

Gabriel lost for words, continued to stare out to sea. 'I had not thought how you would react but if I had I would have hoped not in this way, you hardly seem pleased Gabriel.'

He came to his senses noting the anger in her voice: 'I had not expected you to fall so quickly, is this not unusual?'

'Some have honeymoon babies while others, like Abalone, can wait years, it is how nature works. I would have preferred it had happened later, rather than sooner, but it is done and cannot be undone. Are you not a little pleased?'

Before he could answer Charity appeared on the terrace. 'If you please Ma'am, Mrs Cotter has sent me; she says you are unwell. I just got back from town and came straight away.' Gabriel excused himself and strode off towards the beach.

♥

Eleanor wanted to follow him but thought it better to leave him to come to terms with the news. She wondered what the matter was. Perhaps it was just shock?

'Have I come at a bad time?' Charity asked.

'Tell Mrs Cotter to hold dinner I suspect my husband may be some little time.' Eleanor's own hunger had gone.

'Do you need anything, you look a little pale?'

'A housekeeper who minds her own business would be nice.' Eleanor snapped. Charity knew when to make herself scarce.

The next few days proved to be unsettling for Eleanor. Since their marriage they had grown closer in all things: they shared opinions, enjoyed debating, rode together, entertained and found happiness in each other when alone; all this had changed since she had told him she was with child. Meal times were no longer sociable times where they exchanged news and views.

Eleanor missed the tender little gestures. She had been used to him touching her hand or her hair or stroking her back; he had never left her without a kiss, until now. Now there was no physical contact between them at all.

At breakfast like every other day Gabriel asked after her health. Every evening he retired to his study until bedtime leaving Eleanor alone with her brooding thoughts.

At night he lay distant from her in the enormous bed; the big bed made it easy to keep apart. Other than a chaste kiss goodnight there was no bodily contact at all. For three nights he had blown out his candle and turned his back. He had not said how he felt about becoming a father; Eleanor had always thought he wanted a family: "a house full"; had he not said so? She never thought anything could come between them, yet here they were not more than a few months into a lifelong commitment and already there was a rift opening up between them.

27

As if to be contrary the weather continued to im-prove. Eleanor had been waiting for this weather all summer long yet now she was so despondent even the sight of the sun did not lift her spirits. She had eaten an early dinner alone, as Gabriel had work in Craster and said he would not be home until early evening. During the afternoon the air began to become oppressive. It was unusually still; the blazing sun seemed to blister all it fell upon. It was the kind of rare day which made necks and top lips damp, eyes squint and throats parched.

The heat had been mounting all day and she had retired to the shade of an old elm tree and sat reading. Often times she gazed at the sea shimmering in the heat haze. She still missed Mulgrave but she loved this different part of the coast and its glorious sands. She had before her a jug of lemonade which Lisbet had brought for her. It had helped with the nausea earlier and now was a refreshing drink on this scorching afternoon.

As she reached for the glass her eye was caught by something in the sea bobbing up and down. She had brought Abner's spyglass down to the garden with her on the off chance one day she too, might see a pod of dolphins as Abner had told her she might. Whatever this was, possibly a seal, it was solitary and splashing.

She lifted the spyglass to her eye and tried to focus on the moving object. She got it in her view and was surprised to find it was not a seal but her husband. She moved the glass towards the shore and saw a pile of clothes discarded on the beach. Holding the ribbons of her straw sun hat she set off down the beach looking right and left. There was no one except herself; the beach was quite private and secluded. She began to kick off her shoes and unlace her dress. At the edge of the sea she let it slip to the ground; stepping out of it she was now just in her shift. She began to wade into the cool refreshing water trailing her fingers in the blue. Gabriel was far out and she could see he had stopped swimming and was floating on his back like a gleaming marble statue. Once her shoulders were under the water she pulled the soaking shift over her head and flung it sopping to the beach.

With a strong, sure stroke she swam out soundlessly so as not to alert Gabriel to her presence. As she drew near she could see his black hair fanned out like seaweed behind him; he was facing towards the horizon. She reached out and gently laid her hand on his forehead whilst treading water. There was a tremendous splash as he spun round then laughed loudly when he saw her.

'Man alive is it a mermaid come to lure me onto the rocks?'

She laughed too. 'There are no rocks on this stretch of beach.'

He held her by the waist as her hair floated around her and he realised with pleasure she too was naked.

'Well for shame madam, I hope Abner has not his spyglass handy!' He pulled her towards him and she wrapped her legs around his bare, wet body. They kissed salty kisses as she clung to him her arms entwined around his neck. The closeness after the last few days took her breath away.

Suddenly she broke free and dived down under the surface of the water and pulled him by the leg so he lost his balance and fell back with a splash. They larked around like small children until breathlessly they surfaced together and he caught her by the shoulders and spread her hair out behind her like a veil. She lifted her legs to float on her back. The sun was still burning hot despite the breeze. She could feel her body relax and her breathing slow in its heat. His hands held her.

They floated and swam and curled around each other, enjoying each others' bodies neither shy of touching, feeling and responding. They were like playful seal cubs slithering and winding around each other. They came together again her legs clasped around his hips and her hands pushed the dripping hair from his face. They looked into each others' eyes. No words needed to be spoken but each knew what was in the other's mind. They swam slowly around each other diving under the water and watching each other's body move effortlessly.

After a while they swam languidly back to the shore. Eleanor trod water while Gabriel rescued her drying shift from the beach. She pulled it on over her head; he helped to pull it over her hips as it billowed and tried to float to the surface. He stroked her hair and whispered: 'Gone but not forgotten,' as her naked body was once

354

again covered. She watched his taut back and buttocks as he went to gather his clothes. He shook the sand from his linen shirt.

'Never mind Abner and his spyglass what if Lisbet comes looking for us? She will get a sight she was not expecting!'They lay on their backs in the soft sand, feeling the sun dry them.

'She will see nothing she has not seen a thousand times before; she used to bathe me as a boy, she knows my habits and knows on a day such as this I will no doubt swim. I will lay odds there are towels hanging on the terrace waiting for us so we do not drip water over her floors. We know each others' ways so well. They have watched over my father and me for years.'

The glare from the sun drained all colour from the scene. Gabriel propped himself up and looked at Eleanor. 'You are dry I think,' he said his eyes sweeping the length of her body.

They walked back to the terrace and picked up the towels that were not needed on this most beautiful of days.

♥

The swim had restored intimacy to the couple. They woke to another glorious day. After breakfasting alone, Gabriel had said he hoped to return earlier to take advantage of the weather, Eleanor busied herself with a new venture she was planning; a business deal here in Alnmouth had opened up to her.

In the early afternoon Eleanor wearing a straw hat to shield her face from the heat of the sun went to collect flowers from the garden.

She saw Gabriel come out onto the terrace and raised her hand to wave to him as he tripped down the steps to meet her. Her basket was almost full of large ox-eye daisies, which despite the worst of the weather had managed to survive. Without a word and with a boyish grin on his face he took the basket from her hand laid it on the path and led her down the garden.

'Are we to swim again? My flowers will wilt in the heat.' He led her towards the beach.

'Lisbet will rescue them, come slip your shoes off, let us have none of your nakedness of yesterday my girl!' He laughed as he pulled off his riding boots. 'Fancy a boat trip Milady?'

He ran over to the rowing boat; it was soon righted and Eleanor helped him to push it into the gently lapping waves. Grabbing handfuls of her dress she scrambled inelegantly into the boat while Gabriel held the little craft steady. Chest deep in waves he scrambled aboard and secured the oars.

He rowed out with long even strokes that sped them through the sea away from Westshore. On he rowed until the house was a speck in the distance. He slowed and shipped the oars; Eleanor trailed her hand in the cool water the sun burning the back of her neck.

She was thinking about the baby. She was still unsure of his real feelings about the coming child but actions had consequences surely he knew that? He should not have lain with her if he did not want the result. Men were strange creatures she thought. Just when you let your guard down they changed tack. Her anger began to simmer in the heat of the sun, spoiling her mood. Eleanor tried to push the thoughts from her mind; yesterday had been a turning point she had hoped.

Gabriel in just a linen shirt, having once again discarded his clothes on the beach, pulled it over his head where it was sticking to the sweat on his back and chest; the hair on his chest glistened.

'Here let me help you,' he said taking her hands as she tried to stand. He helped her undress the boat rocked frantically from side to side. When they were both undressed they dived in together. Once again they enjoyed each other in the cool waters.

Once back aboard Gabriel laid his shirt on the bottom of the boat then rolled Eleanor's dress to make a pillow and invited Eleanor to lie beside him; they looked up at a cloudless, cerulean sky.

'Were you nauseous again this morning?'

'As a romantic opening line Gabriel that leaves a lot to be desired!' she teased him, 'Just a bit, not as bad as yesterday. Lisbet says to eat the dry biscuits she bakes – I think they help a little.'

'I am sorry Milady is not impressed with my chivalry.' He tickled her and laughed at himself. 'Poor you, I'm told it will pass but in the meantime I am sorry for you.'

There was a silence broken only by a solitary herring gull squawking discordantly above. The heave and swell of the little boat seemed to still. Eleanor squinted into the too bright sun using her hand to shield her eyes to follow the gull's progress.

She broke the silence. She had to know how he felt. 'Are you come to terms with the thought of a baby yet, do you still regret it?'

'Regret it! No not at all.' He sat up. Again there was a silence. Eleanore was confused. She turned her head to try to read the expression on his face but could not fathom the look; he was staring straight ahead. He put his arms around his knees interlacing his fingers together. She could see the muscles flex in his back and his shoulders tense. The boat bobbed up and down gently the sound of the sea lapping against the sides of the boat was the only sound in the world. Eleanor sighed in frustration.

'Please talk to me Gabriel, I have to know what is in your mind. Ever since I told you about the baby, save for yesterday, you have been distant, quiet, not your usual self at all. I too would have liked a little more time to get to know each other's habits and moods, it would have been nice to go about together now we are a married couple, but as a consequence of our love there is to be a child and I for one am glad of it. It is how it is and we cannot change it now. What would you have me do?'

There was what seemed to Eleanor an interminable silence broken at last by two words uttered in a dejected low voice. 'Don't die.' The words were almost whispered. He did not move from where he sat with his back turned towards her.

She put her hand on his shoulder. 'I do not intend to! Eleanor was shocked at his words.'Is that what this is about? Oh Gabriel I shall live and the baby also.'

'You cannot promise me that Eleanor,' he said struggling to keep the emotion from his voice. She stood up, the boat rocked madly as she knelt in front of him. She took his hands in hers.

'You said your mother had always been delicate even before she was with child, Gabe I'm not fragile. Do you not see me swim and dive and ride and clamber into boats? I am young and strong I am never ill – I'm only sick now because it is a sign the baby within me is growing. I'm not ailing. What happened to you and your father was awful, so tragic but history will not repeat itself I am certain. Look at me!'

He lifted his head. 'From the minute you told me you were with child I have feared I would lose you and I could not bear it my love. You are my world and I could not live without you.' Eleanor pressed her forehead to his and placed her hands on his shoulders.

'You won't have to; we shall both live long and happy lives and have children a plenty to fill Westshore. We shall teach them to swim and sail and ride just as you said your father did with you. If only I had realised how you felt I could have helped you, until now it had not occurred to me, I thought you were not pleased I was pregnant so soon.'

'Not at all I cannot wait but... I am reassured by the sense you speak, I have been a gloomy chap. Bendor is always chiding me for what he calls my black moods. I have not been a help to you at all, in fact I am so sorry for causing you worry and strain. I cannot wait to start this next chapter in our lives. I will take care of you better from now on I promise.'

They lay back down in the bottom of the boat and Gabriel kissed her tenderly. 'For so long it was just me and my father and then it was just me now I have you I was overwhelmed thinking you should be stricken in the child bed, I must learn to appreciate what I have here and now.' He kissed her again with more urgency. 'I love you so much.'

'And I you but please Gabriel do not shut me out – these last few days have been hell.'

'I know I am sorry. I did not know how to cope, how to tell you how I felt. Having just gained you I feared I would lose you; I am a fool.'

'Not foolish – all life is a risk; I took one marrying you remember.' She wanted to make him smile, 'We have to learn to overcome the anxiety and look to the future with confidence. We should never get out of bed in the morning if we tried to avoid risk.'

'You are a very wise woman Eleanor Reynolds.'

'I know, you are a very lucky man.' she grinned

By the time the boat was dragged back onto shore the moon was rising. They walked hand in hand back To the house. From behind a balustrade Lisbet watched the lovers and smiled.

28

Eleanor had taken to riding out with Jax sometimes as a way of helping him to recover from his ordeal. Now she knew the full facts about what had happened to him she wanted to help him. She had used the excuse that she needed a companion when riding due to her condition. Jax was happy to accompany her and was glad of the practise.

One warm afternoon Eleanor and Jax had returned from a hack and were sharing a joke as they entered the stable yard as he helped her dismount she winced. 'Are you alright – sorry mistress did A hurt you?'

'Not at all my back feels a little sore. Perhaps I have been positioned a little differently on the side saddle, I am used to riding astride but you know I must heed my husband for once and take to the side saddle for my rides now.'

'Master has warned me only to put the side saddle on Jet now you are in the...' Jax flushed and left the stable yard quickly to hide his embarrassment – he did not have experience of talking of such things.

For the rest of the day Eleanor felt the odd twinge then later she felt the pain again but stronger this time.

Gabriel was not expected home until after supper. 'I will have an early night I think,' Eleanor said to Charity. 'My back might feel better lying down, the pain seems to come and go.'

It being close to midnight when Gabriel got home he went straight to their bedroom; he crept in quietly. Eleanor was sitting up in bed.

'You are still awake; I had thought you would be sleeping.'

'I had a back ache but was not really tired so went to the library and found this book about a whaling ship that was lost in the Pacific and the crew ended up lost for ninety days and had to resort to cannibalism!'

'It must be one of my father's books it will give you nightmares – what a book to choose!'

'It is a strange tale – despite being surrounded by water they were dying of thirst. Of course they could not drink the salt water. You would think they would have been able to catch fish but it seems not.' Gabriel sat on the side of the bed and began to undress. He yawned then leaned over to kiss her cheek.

'You smell of brandy.' she wrinkled her nose.

'And you, my love, smell of roses.' He gently took the book from her hands. 'You should perhaps read something a little less stimulating late at night, this is hardly relaxing reading.' He climbed into bed and kissed her goodnight. He blew out his candles.

'Perhaps you are right but I shall finish it tomorrow to see if they survive; it is a true story not a work of fiction.' She looked over to him when he did not reply and realised he was sound asleep.

Just before dawn Eleanor woke with a gasp; 'Dear Lord!' The pain in her back was worse. It felt as though she was being attacked with a pickaxe. Careful to not wake Gabriel she slid her legs from the bed and immediately felt wet trickle down her leg; she was gripped by fear.

'Gabriel!' He was slow to rouse. 'Gabriel.' This time she almost screamed. 'What is it – I said you would have a nightmare?'

Gabriel lit the candles saw the situation and ran to rouse Jax to fetch Wilson Chaffer.

Dr Chaffer examined Eleanor: 'The baby is lost, I am so sorry for you both.' Gabriel, who had refused to leave Eleanor's side throughout the examination, squeezed his wife's hand as the tears slipped down her cheeks. Wilson took Gabriel by the arm and led him over to the window. Eleanor sat up. 'Please do not talk about me as if I weren't here Dr Chaffer.' Both men turned.

'I am sorry but there was nothing to be done it is a sad thing to happen but it is nature's way sometimes, You will be well in a few days, the pregnancy was not very advanced – perhaps just a couple of months. You seem in good health otherwise so in time there is no reason you should not have successful pregnancies.'

Gabriel said; 'How has this happened, I could not...'

'I have just left a woman in Amble who has delivered her sixth child but before the first she suffered three miscarriages. Nothing in this life is certain Gabriel but I know Mrs Reynolds is not in immediate danger.' Gabriel reached for his wife's hand.

'Birthing is always precarious but medical knowledge is growing steadily, sometimes this happens for a reason perhaps the baby was not developing as it should, who knows. Make sure you rest Mrs Reynolds and all shall be well.'

After a few days of bed rest and being cajoled into eating plenty of nourishing food by Lisbet, Eleanor was able to get up and sit on the terrace. Gabriel had been very attentive. He was fussing over her. Lisbet was making her comfortable and Gabriel continued to hover. He was ready to leave for the bay but Eleanor knew he was looking for signs she wanted him to stay by her side.

'Can you get me the book I was reading please Mrs Cotter it is beside my bed, Gabriel is going to his office today and I shall be fine here in the sun.'

'I do not think a book about cannibalism is suitable reading for convalescing, I could get you a book of poetry instead.' Gabriel moved to go to the library.

'Gabriel stop fussing I am well. You said the book was too stimulating, I need stimulation now it might distract my mind.' Gabriel knelt by his wife's chair. 'I believe you agreed to rest. Did you not agree to obey your husband when we married?' Eleanor kissed the top of his head.

'I believe at that point in the ceremony I crossed my fingers.'

'Are you sure you will be alright? I can postpone my meeting.'

'Go, it will do you good to think of something else – I can send for you if I need to but I will not need you.' Lisbet arrived back with the book. 'Make sure my wife does not exert herself Lisbet, she is to rest.'

Lisbet huffed. 'A'll try, but mistress do have a mind of her own sir.' Eleanor sighed. 'I am not a child, you talk as

364

if I am not here!' Lisbet shuffled off looking chastened.

'It is only because we care about you, my love.'

'I know, I am sorry to snap but I feel like an invalid.' They had talked at length about their loss. 'Gabriel do you think we lost the child because it was ill-wished in the beginning, perhaps it did not feel wanted?' He had tried to console her although she suspected he too felt the same guilt.

'Try not to torment yourself my love, we cannot give in – I am sure Wilson is right when he says it is nature's way and there is no reason we cannot have another child in the future.'

'Another! But I wanted this one! It was part of me; of us. It is as though the baby left and forgot to tell my heart.' she sobbed into his shoulder.

On one occasion she had been even more distraught and cried, 'I could walk out of the door and keep on walking out into the sea until the waves swallow me.' The tears coursed down her cheeks.

'And I could come with you.' He put his head into his hands.

'Oh no, do not say so Gabriel! We need to be each other's life raft – we need to help each other to keep our heads above the water.'

Gabriel looked at her. 'I should be strong for you my love, I should be able to take the weight but…'

'You are. You do. Without you I would have drowned days ago, this has happened to many before us and if others can come through it so shall we.' He had held her close, she had felt protected.

She sighed, 'I need to be active to stop myself from

365

thinking. My mind is tired but not my body; if my body was tired it might stop me from feeling so much.'

'What would you like to do, we could walk on the beach?'

She shook her head. 'A ride – that is what I need.'

'But Wilson says you are to rest. Is it not foolish to put your health at risk?'

'My body is not the problem, come with me? You know it is pointless to argue when I have made up my mind.'

'Very well I trust your instincts.'

They rode north for some miles both enjoying the sea air. After a gallop they came to a halt watching the waves gently rolling in. Gabriel broke the silence. 'Why is it we let the one thing we do not have affect how we feel about all the things we do have? What if today we were grateful for each other and forgot about the past and the future?' Eleanor saw the sorrow in his eyes and tears spilled down her cheeks. 'I think it is a good plan my love.' She smiled trying hard to unfasten the sadness which had tied itself to her heart.

'When I thought there was a chance I might hang for manslaughter I promised myself I would live each day as if it were to be my last; it is easier said than done I find.'

'We have each other and that is all that matters.'

'You are right,' Gabriel sighed, 'Of all the hearts in the world yours is the one that makes mine smile, tomorrow the sun will rise and we will try again.'

Eleanor remembered the summer's day in the rowing boat where she had promised him she would not die. She had kept her promise but the baby was lost to them; she felt she had let her husband down. Then she remembered

Abalone had suffered a miscarriage before Beatrice was born successfully and it gave her hope.

'I try to count my blessings and not my problems; soon we shall have a house full of children just as you always wanted.' Eleanor thought to try to be optimistic. They rode back a little restored and with a new hope in their hearts.

29

The days turned to weeks and Eleanor began to be her old self again. She had not told her parents about the miscarriage for fear of worrying them but now as she felt better she thought to write. She went to her desk for paper but there was none to be found. She suspected Gabriel had used her supply. She went to his desk and shuffled through the messy drawers; Gabriel really was as untidy as her father. She tried the next drawer and lifted out the top few documents to check beneath.

She noticed a letter, it stood out as it looked pristine amongst the other dog-eared papers. It had a lock of fine, black hair curling out of the side. She hesitated before carefully lifting it out. She stood for some time with it in her hand trying to decide what do; had she not seen the lock of hair she would not have looked twice but she had seen it. It was clearly addressed to her husband and she thought the handwriting looked feminine or was it her imagination?

Her curiosity was roused but it was beneath her to open it, it would be underhand to even think of reading it. The hair looked baby fine and dark; it couldn't have been an old love letter from Caroline as her hair was blonde and thick.

Before she could stop herself she began to open the letter handling it as though it was some precious historical document, the lock of hair fell onto the blotter. She looked for a date – it was dated three weeks ago. She unfolded the letter and took a deep breath; guilt and curiosity were pulling with equal force within her. She hated herself for reading his private correspondence yet she had to know who it was from. Was it a lack of trust which made her want to read it – why? Surely he had proved his love for her.

In a second she flipped it open and looked straight to the bottom of the letter. It was signed *"yours Libby"*. She felt her lack of trust justified. She scanned back to the top. *"Dearest Gabriel."* Eleanor's heart pounded, her stomach turned.

She read the letter. She read it twice.

She picked up the lock of hair and carefully placed it back within the letter. With shaking hands she folded it back down the same lines Libby had creased before posting it. Eleanor gagged. She heard voices outside the window; it was Gabriel. Was he home already? She checked the clock. It wanted thirty minutes to three, he was early for dinner. She heard another man's voice but it was a gentleman's, not Abner.

Eleanor placed the letter back and replaced the detritus on top just as she had found it. She went to the dining room her hands trembling and her mind full of what she had just read. Two gentlemen stood and smiled as she entered.

'Good afternoon Mrs Reynolds.' She recognised

Thomas Hodgeson. 'Gabriel has gone to warn Lisbet we are gate crashing your dinner – we hope it won't put you out.' He laughed. 'She didn't answer the bell so Gabriel has gone to seek her out. In his absence may I introduce you to Walter Craig of Berwick? We concluded our business sooner than expected so Gabriel offered us dinner – Mrs Cotter's cooking is always to be preferred to The Hope and Anchor's offerings.'

She felt on edge and wished herself anywhere but here; she needed to think. She sat in her usual place trying to smile but her mouth felt dry as sand. Gabriel breezed in.

'Eleanor, I know you won't mind guests joining us. I have found Lisbet – she was in the hen house, now she's in the dog house for not being where she should be!' They all laughed politely.

The dinner seemed endless. She excused herself as soon as she possibly could and went to lie on the bed. Soon she heard hooves in the stable yard. The three men were riding back to the bay.

She walked on the beach mulling over the letter and trying to come to terms with what she now knew. She vacillated between rage and sorrow. She railed against herself for reading the letter in the first place; she could have been in blissful ignorance. Now her heart was broken, her trust in Gabriel shattered.

'Charity I have a slight headache, tell Mr Reynolds I have retired early and not to disturb me should I be asleep when he returns.' She knew Gabriel would not be back until supper.

She wanted to confront him about the letter but she

felt betrayed; the hurt she felt was raw, a flesh wound. Her heart was torn apart and bleeding and she did not know how to staunch the flow. She needed time to think. For once she would sleep on it and decide what to do in the morning.

♥

Eleanor had lain awake for what seemed like hours when she heard her husband come quietly into the bedroom. She heard him undress as she feigned sleep. The bed sagged, he climbed in beside her. She felt him kiss the back of her neck gently before turning away, she hardly dared breath. A lump in her throat threatened to choke her.

Presently Gabriel's breathing slowed and she thought him asleep; she still did not dare move in case she roused him back to wakefulness. At last she eased onto her back – her body tight and tense. She stared up at the ceiling wide awake and exhausted. She turned her head to see the man who, until today, she had loved with all her heart. She still loved him – but she hated him too.

Soundlessly she slid out of bed and out of the room. She padded down the dark stairs and headed to the kitchen where the stove might still provide some warmth. Slate and Scrabble ventured out from their beds wagging their tails wondering why she was there. She stroked them absentmindedly; shivering she lit a candle. From the pantry she took down an unopened bottle of brandy and poured a generous glass, she hoped it would help calm the rage that once again was gaining ground on the sorrow she felt.

She shuddered at the first gulp; it warmed as it slid down her throat. Great sobs racked her body and frightened her. She refilled the glass, the brandy was fuelling the fire inside her now not quenching it. She drank more pacing around the table with the empty glass. Her mind, now fully alert and teeming with thoughts, words and accusations was in turmoil. She retrieved the letter from the study racing back to the kitchen where the candle was guttering, she read it again:

Dearest Gabriel,

I have thought long and hard before writing to you. Having come to the decision you have a right to know what I have to tell you I am at pains to say I ask nothing of you. I expect nothing from you. I write only because I am certain you would want to know. Please believe me when I tell you I do not give you this information to hurt you.

When I left for Alnwick I hoped to start a new life. To this end I decided to reinvent myself as an impoverished widow of a sea captain; I thought to give myself some respectability. My role was as companion to Mrs H an older lady of some class and I was therefore at pains to be accepted, she was kind and provided all she had said when she offered me the post. The work was light and the accommodation comfortable. At first all was well and I was making a new life for myself and if not happy, I was content and secure.

I shall now come to the point my dear and tell you I found myself to be with child. I expected Mrs H to want to be rid of me but she is a kindly woman and a Quaker and thought only of my welfare. She, of course, believed the child was my late husband's. To disabuse her of the fact would have placed myself and my unborn child at risk from becoming homeless though it troubled me to lie to her I could not risk being without support.

It is your child Gabriel. You have a son. He was born safely and does well. Mrs H has continued to support me by allowing me to keep him with me so that I can maintain him and myself.

I am aware this news will come as a great shock to you as it did to me in the beginning. Although I am sorry for the circumstances I would not be without my darling boy he has brought me nothing but joy.

I do not know whether you would want to see your son? If you would like to meet him then I have no reason to stop you. It is your choice and I will respect whatever decision you make. Just know Gabriel whatever you choose I understand. I do not seek support from you my dear, thanks to Mrs H we do well enough. It would have felt deceitful and wrong of me not to inform you of your son's birth. I am sorry for any distress this may cause.

Yours Libby

Eleanor did not know whether to cry or scream. The brandy, which she was unused to drinking in such quantities, was impairing her judgement. Suddenly she flung the empty glass at the stove where it crashed and broke sending shards of glass in all directions; Scrabble and Slate cowered and whimpered. With the letter still in her hand she ran back to the bedroom, flung the door open wide and stumbled into the room. Gabriel sat bolt upright as she arrived at the bottom of the bed.

'So were you ever going to tell me about this?' She waved the letter at him. Gabriel trying to focus in the

373

dawn light at once realised what she had in her hand.

'I was going to show you but you have been ill and I did not want you to relapse as you were doing so well. I knew you would be upset -'

'Upset. Upset! How dare you. You have ruined everything. When you came to Amsterdam I allowed myself to be convinced you were not like other men – I was a fool, you are worse than other men. Well now you have your son and heir so I hope you are happy.' Her words were slurring as she sank to her knees on the turkey rug. She was aware of Gabriel kneeling on the floor before her.

'I am so sorry, I would never hurt you intentionally. I do not know what to say. It was some shock to me too – I do not know how to make this right. I love you, I am so very sorry.' She looked at him drying her eyes on the sleeve of her nightgown.

'Sorry! You should have told me – we are married and should have no secrets.'

'How could I tell you this when we had just lost our own precious baby, it is a cruel trick of fate. I am paying for my past and you are being forced to pay too. I cannot stand to see you this way, you do not deserve this – please Eleanor can you ever forgive me?'

Eleanor all at once felt sober. The storm which had been raging within her had blown itself out and she felt becalmed and exhausted; she tried to stand but staggered a little. He caught her and pulled her towards him but she pulled away and walked to the window where the sun was just rising in a milky white sky.

'Will you tell me the truth if I ask you a question?

Think carefully before you reply Gabriel, our marriage may depend on the answer.'

'I may be many things Eleanor but I am not a liar.' She saw his temper suddenly flare. 'I have never lied to you so I can promise you I shall not start now!' She gulped back tears that tried to fall again.

'Have you seen your son?' she searched his face.

'I have not. It has been killing me I could not tell you of this. It felt like I was lying by omission – I hoped that sometime, when you were stronger perhaps and the pain of our loss was gone a little from our minds I would show you the letter and we could decide what to do together. That is why I didn't destroy it. Even though I know I risk losing you I could not keep this from you and carry on as if nothing had happened. I would have told you, I am not deceitful; if you really think that of me then you do not know me at all!'

She felt him close behind her. 'I have written to Libby telling her of our misfortune and saying I had to find the right time to discuss it with my new wife. She, of course, still thought I was engaged to Caroline as we have not been in contact since she left for Alnwick.'

Eleanor was silent staring through the window at the new dawn. 'This is all your fault! I cannot say how I feel about this Gabriel I am so confused, angry – hurt. I cannot say how I am going to feel tomorrow or next week or next year. Whether I shall stay or leave I cannot decide. I wish I had never met you, I was a fool to trust you.'

'I am sorry for all the hurt I am causing you,' he said reaching for her but she shied away. 'We are both

375

overwrought; I cannot say more to you other than to say I will be guided by you and what you need. If I had known about this before we married I would never have asked you to throw your lot in with me. How was I to know?'

'I cannot bear to look at you but...' The tears began to flow again but this time they were tears full of sorrow, not of anger. She was sorry for herself and sorry for Gabriel. She was sorry for the baby they had lost and she was sorry for his son. She was even a little sorry for Libby Lawson. If only the woman had kept this to herself – yet in her shoes would she have done the same? Eleanor could not imagine ever being happy again.

'What do you want to do?' she asked.

'Do? I have had more time than you to think of this but I am still hard pressed for an answer; it is what you want us to do. Whatever you want will be done.'

There was a knock on the door; it was later than she had thought. Gabriel told Abner he would be down shortly. 'Tell Charity her mistress has not slept well and wants to be left until later in the morning.' He went away no doubt to inform Lisbet they were arguing.

'Try to get some rest -I will leave you to think.' He went to the door 'I do not want this mess I have made to make you ill again, go back to bed my love.'

♥

Eleanor lay wide eyed and staring at the ceiling. She heard a knock at the bedroom door.

'Morning, how are you feeling?' Charity put tea by the bed. Eleanor tried to speak, her mouth was dry, her lips cracked. 'I do not need you. I can manage for myself this morning.' She looked at her maid through sore eyes; they felt swollen like a hundred bees had stung her lids. Her head was pounding and the brandy was making her stomach churn. The thought of all that had been said and done earlier lay heavy on her heart.

'Lisbet says she heard shouting last night.' Eleanor knew Charity was not malicious but sometimes her curiosity got the better of her.

'The shouting was me – I stubbed my toe on the end of the bed in the dark and cried out in pain.' Eleanor doubted Charity was taken in.

'Lisbet thought something was amiss 'cause she says there was a glass smashed in the hearth and most part of half a bottle of best French brandy drunk. She thinks Mr Reynolds is fretting over the loss still and has been drowning his sorrows in the night. She says he feels things deep sometimes but she's never known him to drink over much when he's in what she calls his "black moods".'

'Inform Mrs Cotter she is not paid to think but to run the house. Please leave me, I can fend for myself!' She turned over and pulled the covers over her head instantly regretting her abruptness. She knew the staff would tittle-tattle even more now. She didn't care; not about anything anymore.

♥

Gabriel with the weight of the world on his shoulders threw himself into the sea. As he swam he thought how he still missed his father's guidance. For so long it had been just the two of them; they had been used to talking together on any topic. Since his marriage he had started to talk to Eleanor in the same way and she had begun to fill the void his father had left. She was a good listener and offered opinions sometimes which Gabriel knew to be useful.

He needed to talk over the events of last night but as yet he did not think they had anything more to say to each other. He needed counsel himself. when Libby's letter had arrived telling him he was the father of her child it had floored him. He knew he could not tell his wife, and until he did he knew he could not seek direction from Bendor as that would have felt disloyal. Anytime would have been the wrong time to impart such news to Eleanor but under the circumstances with his wife's pain being so raw he had been forced to keep the news to himself.

Just when he thought his life was heading in the right direction this had to happen. After bathing he readied himself and without breaking his fast rode at a gallop to Bendor's.

'Have you been up all night, you are early abroad?' Gabriel slumped in a chair. 'Eleanor continues well I hope?'

Gabriel poured himself coffee and told Bendor the story beginning with the letter he had received from Libby and ending with the confrontation last night. Bendor listened in silence throughout.

'This news, unwelcome as it is, could not have come at a worse time – no time obviously would be ideal but Eleanor must feel it most grievously having just lost a baby, you too of course. I know from experience what a terrible thing it is to lose a child. I know both of you have been devastated by the loss.' Bendor pushed the coffee pot towards his friend.

'A son you say? Man alive, I should not be in your shoes for anything. I am sorry for you, truly I am. Any advice I can give you I am sure you have thought of already, some men would brazen it out, but you are not that man.'

'I know her to be shocked and angry and know I need to be patient and give her time to come to terms with the news if our marriage is to survive but what if she leaves me? She has every right to do so.'

Gabriel scrapped his fingers down his unshaven chin. 'Libby did not say how old the boy is and she asks for nothing but how can I pretend he does not exist? I had to get away this morning yet I feel I have abandoned Eleanor, left her alone... If I have to choose between Eleanor and my son –'

'I think you are going to have to be patient as you say, she needs time to ponder all aspects of this situation. You say you told Eleanor you would be guided by her in what to do next. How shall you feel if she does not want you to see the boy?'

'I cannot answer that. I am more concerned Eleanor will leave me at this moment. She has strong opinions – she will not be easy to placate. I could not bear it if she goes back to Whitby but at the same time I know Eleanor has a kind heart and she will no doubt see the child is the innocent in all this but –' He put his elbows on the table with his head in his hands.

'Let us cross that bridge when, or indeed if, we come to it. Gabriel you look terrible my friend, have you eaten?

Come help yourself it might make you feel better. I suppose you have already jumped in the brink!' He slapped him on the back then squeezed his friend's shoulder 'Things look bad Gabriel, but Eleanor is an extraordinary woman, you know that; she is strong willed but sensible. You once told me she learned to debate at the Friends' Meeting house – she will be able to see both sides of the story. She will see that you could not have foreseen this. It will hurt you both but if you can get through this your marriage will be all the stronger.'

'*If* we can get through this – that is the crux of the matter.'

Gabriel ate the food in front of him; he was hungrier than he had imagined yet tasted nothing.

He had met no one else on the ride back until he saw a lone rider in the distance. As horse and rider came nearer Copper began to snicker and became frisky. He realised the reason; she had recognised her stable mate.

'Have you come to meet me?' Gabriel tried a light tone as they drew level with each other.

'I did not know which way you had gone so I cannot say truthfully that I have.' Eleanor turned Jet around and began to walk back the way she had come, the two horses side by side.

'Have you been this far before unattended? You should not be so far from home alone.'

'I never have – the beach is so long I never imagined it to be so big.' He noticed she looked resolutely ahead.

'You should have a care, perhaps bring Jax with you if you intend to come this distance. You would most likely be safe but you should not take the risk.'

'Thank you for your concern I shall bear it in mind.'
Unsurprisingly there was a stiffness in her reply. They
rode on in silence. It was not the companionable silence
they had become used to of late; there was tension in the
air and words unspoken between them.

Gabriel knew Eleanor would know where he had
been. He was unsure how she would feel about Bendor
knowing their travails.

'Did you find Bendor well?'

'Yes he is.'

'Disturbed to hear of our trouble no doubt?'

'I did not go to break the news from gladness or to
break any confidence but because I needed -'

'To unburden yourself?'

'Yes I suppose so.'

'I wish I had a friend close by in whom to confide.'

'None of us can be everything to each other all the
time Eleanor. I am not enough for you in this instance, I
see that and you are not enough for me either under the
circumstances,' Gabriel looked at his wife's profile. 'My
dearest wish is in time we can return once again to be
everything to each other.

'When we married I was not blinkered I did not think
we would lie on a bed of roses every day but I had not
thought we would meet with so many thorns so quickly. It
is very unsettling for me. I am afraid to trust my instincts.'

'May I enquire what those instincts are telling you?'
he asked.

'They tell me this matter of your son is a result of
your previous entanglement; it was an affair for which
I forgave you – it was before we married. You explained

your side of it in Amsterdam and whilst I did not condone it, I accepted it as a fact I could not change. I wanted to marry you despite this. It was my choice – my risk. I could have turned you down but I did not. Now we find there were consequences to this liaison which neither of us could have foreseen. My instincts tell me I forgave you once and so should do so again – you did not know what had happened; but that is my head talking and not my heart and it is my heart that needs convincing – again.'

'If you give me the chance I will try my best to persuade you. In Amsterdam I asked you to trust me – I feel that trust has been broken but it was never my intention to hide this matter, it was something I never expected. I love you more than anything in the world.'

'I do not doubt that love Gabriel, but I do not see where we are heading with regards to you now being a father and yet,' she swallowed hard, 'I am not a mother.' They rode on. 'Life is not so simple. I love you and you love me but there is a problem which has to be resolved to the satisfaction of all involved. I cannot in all conscience stop you from seeing your son yet it breaks my heart to know you have something I have not. You share a child with another woman. I am not part of that, I am on the outside and always will be. He is not my son. He is yours – and hers. I sound bitter even to my own ears but this is the reality of the predicament we find ourselves in. He exists in the world and you must rejoice in this, how could you not but I cannot join you in celebrating, he will always be between us.'

'I know all you say is true, we have reached an impasse, I understand how hurt and shocked you are.' They rode on each deep in their own thoughts.

For the rest of the day no more was said on the subject. They were polite and cordial with each other through dinner and supper. At bedtime Gabriel began to put out the candles. In the hall he handed Eleanor a candle to light her way to bed and lit one for himself. 'I shall sleep in my old room to give you time to consider.' He longed to hold her but knew she needed to be alone. She looked so forlorn in the half light.

He bent and kissed her cheek. 'If you say the word I will write to Libby and say I will not see the boy.'

'I am so tired Gabriel, do not ask this of me now. Goodnight.'

♥

Lisbet sat opposite Abner at the kitchen table. 'That's three nights they've slept apart, must have been some argument!'

'It's nothing to do wi' us old woman.'

'No but A don't like to see them apart this early in the scheme of things, it don't bode well for the marriage you must admit.' Before he could agree or disagree Jax hurtled into the kitchen, for the last few months he had seemed more like his old self.

'Is there some of that rabbit pie left?' He threw his legs over the bench.

'Say please!' Lisbet admonished. She cut him a slice; he gobbled it down. Lisbet was glad to see his appetite had returned as she cut him a second, smaller slice.

'The lad'll be as big as a house soon!' Abner reached for the knife and cut himself a slice before it all went.

'Lisbet, when the babby is born shall they call it after Mr Gabriel do yer think?'

'Jax, there is not to be a baby I told you that the mistress has lost it.' Jax looked puzzled.

'A know – not that babby, the new one, the boy babby.'

Lisbet caught Abner's eye. 'What baby boy Jax, you aren't making sense.'

'When they both went out riding separate the other day an' come back together A was in the hay loft. A never heard em come in but then A looked down an' saw em putting Copper and Jet in their stalls.' He ate more pie and chewed thoughtfully. 'A heard mistress say there would have ter be decisions made 'bout the babby's future as befits, is that the right word? Yea befits a son and heir.' Jax was pleased with himself for remembering the word even though he did not know what it meant. 'Any road A came down the ladder an' said A'd see ter the horses. Mistress jumped, surprised to see me like. They din't know A were there.'

Lisbet shot a look at Abner. 'Yer should not be earwigging young man.'

'A couldn't help it, they din't know A was there.' Jax wiped his mouth on the back of his hand and was off at a run.

'Well! What you make of that old man?'

'Not much, Jax has had a sleep since then, he's possibly mis-remembering what he heard.'

'What can it mean them in separate rooms, talk of sons? A have no idea what's going on!'

Gabriel appeared in the kitchen. His chin was unshaven and his hair uncombed; he looked in need of sleep. The household had been walking on eggshells for days.

'Is there to be food served this morning do you think or are you just taking care of yourselves?' He didn't wait for an answer but glowered and headed for the breakfast room. Lisbet bustled about making tea and filling trays seeking to appease her master with her quiet efficiency.

♥

Eleanor and Gabriel sat in stony silence whilst Lisbet unloaded the tray placing food on the table. When she left Eleanor said, 'I have thought about what you said and I have come to the conclusion you should meet your son as soon as possible.' Gabriel watched as his wife twisted her napkin between her fingers nervously.

'Babies change so quickly and you will miss something if you defer too long.' Gabriel saw his wife's eyes were red rimmed and he felt guilty knowing he was the cause. 'However,' she took a deep breath, 'I should not like you to meet his mother.' She sighed. 'If it could be arranged perhaps a third party could bring the child to a specified location, I should come to support you if that would be agreeable?' Gabriel saw the effort the speech had taken. Eleanor looked pale and drawn and it was all his fault; the guilt he felt was unbearable.

'That could be arranged, but are you sure you would want to see the boy; would it not pain you?'

'It would, but I think I need to see him -' Lisbet came in carrying kippers which she placed on the table before making a hasty exit.

Eleanor said, 'Do you think she heard?'

'What if she did? It is no business of hers! Very well if you are certain Eleanor I will write and make the arrangements.' The meal continued in silence.

♥

Lisbet went in search of Abner to tell him what she had overheard; she found him in the hen house. 'A heard her say "I think I need to see him". If you put that together with what Jax earwigged, well what do you think?'

'That you both have big lug 'oles!' Abner carried on collecting eggs.

'Yer can be very thick headed Abner Boatwright and vexing an' all!'

'She needs to see who? Mistress could mean anybody, you are letting your imagination run ahead of you old woman.' Lisbet smelled burning, she raced across the yard still thinking over what it all meant.

Charity returning a tray to the kitchen was interrogated: 'You've bin with your mistress a while you said, has she bin married afore, is she a widow mebbe?' The look on the maid's face told Lisbet she was barking up the wrong tree.

'Course she's not a widow; she was engaged to a sea captain, but he played her false. I never liked him; he was a shifty sort – eyes too close together. Caught him watching me sidelong more than once, never could see what the mistress saw in him.' Charity stole a biscuit from the cooling tray. 'He went off with a widow now I come to think on.'

'Did he...' Lisbet tried to make the pieces of the puzzle fit, but could not.

'Why do you ask?'Charity stole another biscuit seeing that Lisbet was distracted. Lisbet barely heard the question she was deep in thought.'

'A'm more confused than ever now.' She took the singed cake from the oven and uttered an oath. She poured tea and sat by the stove to think.

30

The letter was despatched and in due course a date and time was arranged for Gabriel to meet his son. In the intervening period a thaw had begun to take place between the couple and Gabriel had moved back into the marital bed. It was not thawed so much there had been physical contact, saving a light kiss, but it was a start.

Later the following week the couple arrived at an inn on the outskirts of Alnwick where a private room had been booked. A woman had been hired to bring the baby at midday. Gabriel and Eleanor arrived almost on time and were shown upstairs to a room where a dour looking matron was waiting with a bassinet placed on a table. Both husband and wife were tense.

'Good day Mrs West thank you for your trouble, this is my wife Mrs Reynolds.' The woman nodded, barely acknowledging either of them. Gabriel thought he sounded calm and in control though he felt none of these emotions.

'I think it is arranged you will wait downstairs until we have finished here, I will send to you when we are ready to leave.' Without a word the woman left the room.

Alone now with the silent crib, both stole a look at the other. The blankets around the child meant from where they were standing the baby could not be seen.

'Well go and look at your son Gabriel.' His wife's voice was almost a whisper. He looked at her trying to read how she felt as he moved to the crib. There was a silence. At last Gabriel spoke.

'You know how some babies look like old men? He half smiled. 'Well he looks just like my father, come and look and you shall see what my father looked like.' The tide of emotion threatened to sink him; he watched Eleanor as she looked at the son that was not hers.

'Such a lot of hair, thick hair likes yours.' The boy lay contentedly wrapped in his blanket. Gabriel reached out and stroked the chubby cheek gently with the back of his forefinger; the boy's eyes flew open as though he had received a charge. Gabriel withdrew his hand quickly and for a second father and son regarded one another. The baby clearly not impressed with what he saw let out a loud cry which continued into a wail of deafening proportions. Eleanor and Gabriel exchanged looks. 'What now!' Gabriel looked at his wife.

'Perhaps you should pick him up; he needs comforting we are strangers to him, he is used to waking to familiar faces.'

Gabriel nodded and reached into the basket and carefully lifted his son into his arms talking softly to him. He saw the look on Eleanor's stricken face. Joy and guilt were in his heart. He saw Eleanor move away.

'It should be my son you comfort and cradle,' she blurted out bitterly.'

'Eleanor I am sorry, perhaps you should not have come; I would have spared you the pain...'

'I thought I could cope – perhaps this was a mistake.' Gabriel saw her swallow a sob. 'Yet I see the look of love in your eyes, the look which up until now has been reserved solely for me. How can I feel jealous of a baby? Yet in some strange twisted way I am.' He saw a tear roll down her cheek.

'I am so sorry my love. Would you prefer to wait downstairs – we could leave?'

The baby screamed louder. Gabriel began to jiggle the infant up and down; the volume continued to rise. He walked around the room rocking him and saying soft words, nothing was working. Gabriel looked to Eleanor. Above the noise she said. 'Shall I try?' Gabriel hesitated then placed his son carefully into her arms. Gabriel watched the baby's face crinkle like a walnut as she held his son on her lap; the crying continued.

'Perhaps he is hungry? I thought the time was chosen so he would have been fed?'

'It was but perhaps he misses his –'

At that moment the crying stopped and the child began to kick his legs and gurgle contentedly. Gabriel noticed there was not a trace of a tear on the boy's face. Eleanor handed him back to Gabriel who had sat beside her.

'There now my man, what was all that about?' Father and son once again looked into each other's eyes. 'His eyes are blue.'

'All babies' eyes are blue silly! Gabriel stole a look at his wife and saw she was smiling radiantly at his son.

At the appointed time Gabriel sent for Mrs West, a groom carried the sleeping child to the hired carriage. The couple sat in silence sipping canary wine before sending for their horses so they could return home; childless.

♥

A week later Eleanor said 'It has been a trying time for both of us, but gradually I think we are coming to terms with the situation, learning to accept that which cannot be changed.' She was trying to be optimistic as she lay in the crook of his arm. It was bedtime and Gabriel had been almost asleep

'Thanks to you my love, I cannot imagine how difficult this has been for you.' The strained atmosphere had begun to lighten over the past day or two. After further discussion it had been decided Gabriel should visit the child along with Eleanor on a regular basis from now on.

'I can see no other course that is agreeable; I cannot pretend I like it but what else is there to do? She remembered the look on Gabriel's face as he held his son; she knew she could not deny him access.

They had agreed, even though Libby had not asked for support in raising the child, that it was fitting Gabriel's son should receive money to maintain his upkeep so the boy would be raised and educated as the son of a gentleman; Eleanor held no malice towards the child for this decision.

'These 'visits' will now be part of our lives. I see that and I will learn to live with it in time, you will have to be patient with me.'

'You should not have to learn the lesson – it is I who is at fault, my past actions.'

Eleanor knew the visits that would be a joy to Gabriel, though she knew he tried not to show it out of concern for her, would nevertheless be a continuing trial for her. The strain was hard to take sometimes but then he would look at her and she knew he was hurting too, knew he was doing his best for all concerned.

'I have to be honest – it is sometimes hard not to blame you for this situation, yet I love you still and most of the time I forgive you. I am not perfect. I cannot help feeling resentful not all the time just...'

'I hate to see you struggle with this. I cannot keep apologising but I am so grateful that you even try to come to terms with it, I do not deserve it.'

'No you do not,' Eleanor stroked his chest and smiled grimly, you had better think of a good way to make it up to me.' She didn't feel light hearted; she just wanted things to be as they were before. She knew they never would be, not now. If only they had a child of their own, perhaps then the burden would not seem so great.

31

When Eleanor had moved to Westshore she was amazed to find only a rusted old tin bath hanging in the scullery. Gabriel had admitted he always sea bathed or used the outside pump. He had never thought to replace his mother's old tub so she had immediately ordered a copper bath of the largest size.

After the trials of the last few weeks she sought to ease her tensions with a soak. The rose perfumed bath steamed in front of the bedroom fireplace. Eleanor with her hair wrapped in a swathe of green silk sank down in the deep water and sighed. She closed her eyes and began to drift off.

She heard the click of the latch as the door opened and saw Gabriel creep to peer at her dozing figure. Through half open eyes she watched as Gabriel rolled up his shirt sleeves, after dipping the scented soap in the rosy water he turned it around in his hand until it lathered and foamed He dabbed his forefinger on her nose leaving a blob of soap. She smiled up at him lazily as he knelt by the tub.

'Better?' he asked.

'Yes, I think so.'

'The green silk reminds me of the first time I saw you at The Fleece.' He smiled.

'That seems such a long time ago.'

'It is a pity you fibbed about being able to read palms, had you seen me in your future you would probably have run a mile.'

'I doubt that, with hindsight I think it was love at first sight for me.'

'And I; after you ran out on me I could not get you out of my thoughts, I never expected to see you again.'

There had been little physical contact between them of late and the sight of Gabriel looking so handsome melted her heart

'I do not regret marrying you my love, I could not live without you, surely you know that?' Gabriel kissed the top of her head.

'Shall I leave you, or bathe you Milady?' He adopted a servile pose.

'What do you think? Have I not been waiting for your touch?' He filled her with desire.

'I hoped you would say that – I have missed you so much my love.' That night Gabriel and Eleanor returned to each other.

♥

After the first meeting between father and son, Eleanor and Gabriel tried to carry on with their normal lives. Gabriel went about his daily work and Eleanor sought to implement some of the household changes including the hiring of new staff.

One evening as they waited for Grace and Bendor

to arrive to sup, Eleanor said: 'A problem will arise of course when the boy is of an age to understand what is happening, when he is three or four how is he to greet us? What will he be told of your relationship with his mother? Shall we be Uncle and Aunt?'

Gabriel frowned. 'My love, you are wont to suddenly spring these questions upon me without preamble, it grieves me the boy is so often at the forefront of your mind.' Gabriel looked concerned. 'I cherish you all the more for the way you have behaved throughout these last weeks. You are a remarkable, unselfish woman.' Eleanor batted away the compliment.

'Uncle and Aunt could be one solution,' he said. 'I had thought about the same thing myself and would prefer to be thought of as Godparents, that way we can seem to have some influence over him and perhaps we could be passed off as friends of his fictitious sea captain father?'

'That would be a good plan, has he not been baptised yet?'

'His mother asked, in her last letter, which came this morning, if we had any preferences – she favours a name but said if I wanted to name him after myself she would not be unreasonable. She is keen to get him baptised I think,' He went over to his desk and passed her the letter which was businesslike and contained just what Gabriel had said and no more.

'He is your son, what would you like to do?'

'Give her the choice I think she has been fair so far and it is little to ask. As you see the proposed name is Steven which is not unacceptable to me. If we are to be blessed with a son he should have our fathers' names perhaps?' She tried the name out. 'Yes I think you are right, let him be Steven then at least we can stop calling him "The Boy".

Bendor And Grace had brought several bottles of canary wine Bendor was keen for Gabriel to try; it seemed the men intended on making a night of it. When they came to sup usually the ladies did not leave the men to their port but on this night both husbands were in high spirits and were getting noisy. Grace and Eleanor sauntered out onto the terrace. They needed their shawls but it was not too cold in the evening air. Eleanor knew Grace was aware of Gabriel's son; they had not discussed it but Bendor and Grace had no secrets from each other.

'You are looking better each time I see you. The bloom is back in your cheeks. Do you feel well? The miscarriage must have taken its toll I am sure.'

'Yes fully recovered in body thank you. Some days the mind dwells unbidden on the past but I am determined to look forward and not back.'

'It is an attitude that does you proud but it is easier said than done is it not? Often I think back to the baby we lost...and how I nearly died giving birth to Flora.' The two women exchanged looks of recognition. 'I almost take a turn when I think of the birth – what if I had left her motherless? It is irrational, I have so much to be thankful for but in the depth of the night sometimes these thoughts arrive from nowhere do they not?'

'Yes but my thoughts divert to the living and what will happen if the son Gabriel has is the only one he will ever know?'

'I thought the doctor said he could see no reason why

you should not have as many children as you wanted?'

'He did – it is as you say – irrational. Why do I torture myself when I could be happy?'

'Because you love Gabriel and you want to bear him a child that will belong to the both of you. You would not be human if you did not feel bitter about the situation you find yourself in, I think you are remarkable.'

'I do not know about that, if you could only read my mind sometimes. Until the day I am with child again I do not think either of us will be happy.'

The air grew chilly and the two women returned to their husbands who were becoming over familiar with the port bottle. They seemed determined to get drunk. There was a light knock at the door and Abner entered, nodded to the assembled company and handed Gabriel a letter. Gabriel took it from the tray and tossed it upon the table

'A drinking game is called for.' They banged their glasses on the table laughing. They became even more exuberant and Grace cautioned them shaking her head. 'Are you not married gentlemen? You act like silly young ruffians.' Ben knocked over a glass spilling claret down his breeches. Gabriel roared with laughter.

'Hey wastrel! Have a care.'

Eleanor laughed at their behaviour which encouraged them to carry on. Gabriel was very merry, she thought him in need of light relief.

'You will be unable to ride home,' Grace said to Bendor, 'you can barely sit on a chair let alone your horse, see how you sway!

'Better stay the night or there will be an accident,'

Eleanor said. Gabriel held onto the table as he staggered to his feet. Eleanor rang for Abner and together they helped her drunken husband to bed.

♥

The next morning two husbands with very sore heads and two bright eyed and clear headed wives sat down to break their fast. 'You look terrible the pair of you!' Grace laughed at them as she tucked into the food before her with relish.

'I don't think I can bear to eat anything – where's Abner? We need something to settle our insides.' Gabriel rang the bell. Abner arrived carrying a concoction of his own devising which was a hangover cure he had from his seafaring days. After eyeing the drinks suspiciously both men downed them in one.

'Gabe how can you eat!' Bendor still looked green about the gills. Gabriel threatened Bendor with sea bathing as a further cure but Bendor said he had business to do and needed to be off. Gabriel spared him this time laughing at his weak will.

Grace and Bendor left soon after and Gabriel, who was feeling decidedly better, also spared himself a swim in favour of more coffee. He was content to linger with his wife but then noticed the letter propped up on the mantelpiece where Lisbet had no doubt put it. He had a vague memory of a letter arriving last night. He read it.

'You look bad again Gabriel.' Eleanor had seen the look on his face.

Without speaking he handed her the letter. It read:

Dearest Gabriel,

I know what I have to say in this letter will cause you great distress and I am truly sorry for it. Please believe I have not done this to hurt you or your wife. You have always been so good to me but I have to consider what is best for Steven and myself. I will try to explain as succinctly as I can and hope in time you will both forgive me.

By the time you read this I will be on my way to a new life as a married woman in America.

My employer Mrs H has a son, who from my arrival in Alnwick, has proved to be a good friend to me. Of course in the beginning I was calling myself a widow and when I found out I was with child he was sorry for me. I knew he had feelings for me and before he went to sea [he is a sea captain, how ironical!] he asked me to marry him. He said he would take on the role of father to my, as then, unborn child if I would agree to the marriage. I had never thought to be so lucky to receive such an offer but after some thought I decided I must tell him the truth about my marital status and the circumstances which led me to my predicament. I did not mention your name in this discourse. I knew it was a great risk to confess all but could not begin a marriage with a lie. After I told him, he said he could not after all consider marrying me and he left for Greenland on a whaling mission.

Last week he returned and met Steven for the first time. He said while he was away he had reconsidered and if I would agree to one or two conditions that we could be married. One of the conditions was I had to agree to remove to America where he had secured a Captaincy of a whaling ship out of Nantucket Island; he wanted us to have a fresh start. The other condition was he should in time, when we were settled, *be allowed to adopt Steven and raise him as his own son.*

This I know Gabriel, will be most hurtful to you but I agreed as it is a great opportunity both for myself and for Steven. I know you who have so much would not begrudge me who has so little, a chance of happiness. He loves me and Steven and I will learn to love him too in time as I admire and respect him. He is a Quaker and a good man. I am sure he will take good care of us both.

The loss of your son will be a grave sorrow to you I am certain as you have only just started to know him, I am deeply sorry for this. Perhaps with hindsight I should not have told you about him in the first place yet I am glad you have met Steven and hope the memory will sustain you until you are fortunate enough to have children with your new wife. I know you to be an honourable man and although I have caused you great distress by removing Steven abroad I know you will understand I have his best interests at heart. He will now have a father and I a husband.

Please forgive me and wish me well my dear. By the time you read this we shall have sailed to our new life.

Yours Libby

When she had read it Eleanor moved to his side.

Gabriel murmured to Eleanor. 'Another shock. Will it never end! If only she had not told me of Steven's existence in the first place.' Eleanor put her arm through his.

'Would you really not want to have met your son, even if it was just once?'

'No but -'

'The most important thing to remember in all this

is Steven's welfare. He will have a new life with new opportunities. He will be loved by two parents; the man must be good to take on someone else's child, not all men would do that. It seems Steven will be raised a Quaker if his step-father is a Friend. It will be a good life for him.'

Gabriel realised he had begun to make plans for his son, now he would play no part in his upbringing or his future; he would not see Steven grow up.'

As if she read his thoughts she took his hands in hers and turned him to face her. 'It is too cruel for you my love but I agree with Libby she had no choice but to take your son to America, what is there here for any woman with an illegitimate child? Yes she had you as some support but it would not be the same as Steven having a father living with him and guiding him, you could never outwardly acknowledge him as your own. She had to take the chance which was offered to her and sadly, you are the loser in the bargain she has made. I know Steven is also the loser as he will never know you as his real father.'

All she said, Gabriel knew she felt. Yet he could not help but think this decision, made by Libby, would ease the load on his wife – set Eleanor free. Without his son to consider they were essentially as they were before they knew of his existence; except they were not.

'Let us walk on the beach my love, this has been some shock for us both,' she said. They donned cloaks and set off.

Eleanor said, 'Is it not sad that Libby does not love the man? She is emigrating half way round the world with him yet says she "hopes to grow to love him." I should think it a great adventure to travel but only if I was going with the man I loved. We have much to be thankful for as we have each other. The start of our marriage has been far from easy yet I know the trials we have faced already will serve us well in the years to come.

'Everything has changed,' he said 'The compromises we have been forced to make have made our marriage all the stronger I hope.'

'I hope so too- our understanding of each other is all the greater do you think?' He put his arm around her shoulder.

Eleanor half smiled: 'I suppose so. While I cannot ever promise to be dutiful I *have* learnt to give and take, learnt to see a situation has many points of view. I love you "till death do us part" Gabriel Reynolds.'

'I love you too "excluding all others" Eleanor Barker. '

Gabriel realised he was not concerned with the future, only with the here and now. Though his heart ached for the loss of his son he had everything he needed, had every reason to feel happy; he smiled as he squeezed Eleanor's shoulder and drew her closer. It would do no good to look back and think of what might have been as he would have done before his marriage – dark thoughts were a thing of the past for him now.

'Whatever the future has in store I know we will weather it – with you by my side how could we not. The black moods are banished for good. In time we will have our own children I hope – a house full of them.' He laughed and stroked her hair away from her face.

'Westshore will hear ringing laughter as our family grows and fills the empty rooms.'

The day was turning bright. A golden sun lit up

Eleanor's hair as it blew about her shoulders; he had always loved her hair. He loved her and always would. The tide was high, waves rolled in and out as regular as ever, barely bothering to make a ripple upon the shore. With his constant lady by his side he knew the future was set fair.

The End

Before you Go.

The next installment in the Reynolds saga, **The Turning Tides**, will be published in Summer 2020